D0097489

LATTER-DAY CIPHER

LATAYNE C. SCOTT

LATTER-DAY CIPHER

Moody Publishers

Chicago

© 2009 by
LATAYNE C. SCOTT

Published in association with the Books & Such Literary Agency, 52 Mission Circle, Suite 122, PMB 170, Santa Rosa, CA 95409-5370, www.booksandsuch. biz.

Editor: Diane Eble
Interior Design: Ragont Design
Cover Design: Gearbox
Cover Image: Neil Guegan/zefa/Corbis
Author Photo: Frank Frost Photography

Library of Congress Cataloging-in-Publication Data

Scott, Latayne Colvett, 1952-
    Latter-day cipher / Latayne C. Scott.
        p. cm.
    ISBN 978-0-8024-5679-3
    1. Murder—Investigation—Fiction. 2. Mormons—Fiction. 3. Utah—Fiction. 4. Code and cipher stories. I. Title.

PS3569.C646L38 2009
813'.54—dc22

                                                            2008048543

We hope you enjoy this book from Moody Publishers. Our goal is to provide high-quality, thought-provoking books and products that connect truth to your real needs and challenges. For more information on other books and products written and produced from a biblical perspective, go to www.moodypublishers.com or write to:

Moody Publishers
820 N. LaSalle Boulevard
Chicago, IL 60610

1 3 5 7 9 10 8 6 4 2

Printed in the United States of America

For my Lord
Dedicated to my children, Noel and Kimber

PART ONE

CHAPTER 1

THERE ON THE DAMP pine needles, Kirsten Young lay on her back, a serene Ophelia in her dusky pond of blood. The dark irises of her bloodshot eyes stared unseeing into the branches above her. The sun had burst through the clouds after the sudden downpour and now blazed above the canopy of conifers and aspens in Provo Canyon. Deep in its recesses, the light filtered down in vertical sheets of champagne dust that played across the body.

Her skin, once the faintest of olive, now was pale as churned cream, mottled in the dark pooling of what everyone called her hot Italian blood. An angry oval bruise, dark as a plum, marked the side of her forehead.

The slit in her throat cut deep. Her left arm lay loosely at her side, still bearing at the wrist the friction marks from the plastic rope that had bound her. Her right arm crossed her chest, with the elbow supported by a rock underneath the triceps so the arm stayed in place. Her fingers curled slightly around her own shoulder, as if she gave herself a final hug in death. The tip of her thumb touched, delicately, the edge of the open wound under her left ear.

The scene on the forest floor was meant to set things aright.

No, no, she wasn't Ophelia at all, he thought. She was Eve, temptress and sinner cast from the garden of Utah, wearing a hasty apron of cottonwood leaves heaped around and across her plump belly, from just below the navel to mid-thigh. Tiny rivulets of blood snaked down through the leaves.

The other four wounds, the little ones, were postmortem, made after she'd already bled out.

On the right side of her chest, incised with surgical precision, the first cut penetrated deep, a backward L. It depicted a carpenter's square: the straightedge, true-maker, indispensable for right angles. The desired angularity could not, alas, be achieved on the soft roundness of this still-warm flesh.

Nor could the second, the compass. On the left side, a chevron gaped open with edges that wanted to lose their definition, a tiny V on this day of defeats and victories.

A third inch-long slit carefully cut into the muscle just above the knee that would never again bow.

A final slit traversed her stomach just above the navel, a sign of nourishment for a body that would never again eat; of health for one who would only decay.

They were all symbols only the initiated would understand.

But below her navel mark, Kirsten harbored her own tiny secret, one that held the seed of her killer's downfall, her own unwitting fleshly vengeance.

In the sheeting light, her murderer stood above her like the angel guarding Eden, the knife-sword flashing this way and that in his gloved hand. He had brought along a plain white sheet he'd bought at a garage sale and kept stored in a plastic bag. But he changed his mind about putting it over her. She was beyond the veil now.

His shoulders sagged beneath the once-white jumpsuit. The leaves embroidered on the green cloth apron he wore were speckled as a measles plant. The X-Acto knife lay at his feet and he picked it up and threw it and the sheet into the stream. Then he laid the note carefully on the ground, its edge secured by a rock.

The white cap still contained his close-cropped hair but it had lost its starched definition. It, too, sagged as he backed away from Kirsten, brushing over with a fallen pine branch the near-invisible footprints they both had made when they came to this, his sacred grove.

His breathing was heavy as he recited. They'd said it was "the pure Adamic language" he'd learned that first time, at age nineteen, scared half to death by all the temple vows and disembodied voices behind the veils:

"Pay lay ale. Pay lay ale. Pay lay ale."

He swallowed hard.

"Oh Lord, hear the words of my mouth."

CHAPTER 2

THE MAN WHO discovered Kirsten Young, the one everyone thought was the first murder victim, found her quite by chance: He nearly tripped over the body after stumbling through the underbrush seeking a secluded place to relieve himself.

Terrance Jensen, Dr. Jensen to his students but Terry to his family, jogged every day now, after his doctor told him that the stress of holding too much inside was going to kill him. Jensen had squelched a retort—how would you like the faith of 12.8 million followers on your shoulders, he'd wanted to ask—and thanked the doctor meekly for the free pedometer.

Always one to take such a warning from an authority figure most literally, Jensen dutifully took up running to reduce his thickening waist and his stress level, and found that as his stamina increased, so did his enjoyment. But reticent by nature, he would drive miles from his off-campus home to the new trails in the mountains northeast of Provo to run in solitude, this place where he could jog and talk to himself without anyone commenting.

Later, he wondered if his secret sin of drinking a cola drink—forbidden on the Brigham Young University campus—had been what had made his bladder so urgent that he'd had to veer off the rain-slicked path. On other runs he'd occasionally encountered other hikers and runners, so he had to be careful. When he caught sight of what could have been a police car on the distant winding road, he hid even from that.

His mind tangled into the greatest dilemma of his life. With what elegance of speech and imagination, he wondered, can you extract fifteen words out of one Egyptian hieroglyphic, fifteen words that have nothing to do with the hieroglyphic itself. Mnemonics? He snorted. Even he couldn't believe that. And how do you sell such a translation technique for scripture to an increasingly literate group, with access to the Internet? Everyone was depending on him, the Church's foremost Egyptologist, to hold the line, to keep saying that these ancient Egyptian hieroglyphics could be finessed into saying what they did not say.

He was still panting as he found a good spot, his sinuses aching and his blood chanting in his ears.

Then he saw her.

He didn't dare come near—the woman was obviously dead. But the folded piece of paper under the rock—surely, he thought, he could look at that and put it back before anyone could get here. No harm would be done. He hesitated and dialed 911, only mildly surprised when the dispatcher recognized his name and took down the facts as he dispassionately related them: female, certainly dead, trail location; and yes, he'd wait.

Jensen looked around for a stick but thought better of leaving fingerprints, so he took his water bottle out of his fanny pack and used it to push the rock off the piece of paper. On the outside was written in a small, neat hand the words "THE SECOND PROOF." Using his car keys, he coaxed the edges apart and unfolded it. It was written in a code that any student of Mormon history would have recognized at once, but few could read immediately.

But Jensen could grasp it. He read it over twice, the color draining from his pinched face. Then he stepped closer and looked at the dead woman. Anyone who lived in Salt Lake City and watched the news or read a local paper knew Kirsten

Young. Any one of the millions of Mormons who wore temple garments under their clothes would know what the cuts on her meant.

And anyone who could read the Deseret Alphabet, taught to schoolchildren in Utah during the 1860s when Brigham Young's word was law, would know the connection between Kirsten Young's pitiful body and the note he held in his hand.

One thing the Church of Jesus Christ of Latter-day Saints didn't need right now was bad publicity, and Jensen knew that the media would alight soon after the police. Whom to tell about the note? He first resolved to look for the raised ridges of the peculiar neckline of temple garments beneath the uniforms of policemen identifying which were brother Mormons.

But he changed his mind. No. He wouldn't tell anyone. He'd keep the note, at least for a while. He'd be protecting it. He'd be protecting everyone. He put the note into his fanny pack, having squeezed it into the little wallet full of gas receipts and gum wrappers, and walked back to the trail to meet them all.

CHAPTER 3

TOO EARLY FOR lightning bugs but not yet cooled down, the west Tennessee evening held in its breath a promise of more moist, stifling air. A sullen breeze pestered the drooping tomato vines, bringing with it the green smell of their leaves, but no relief to the shaded porch on the east side of the old house with the white siding.

Brushing her dark blonde hair back from her damp forehead, Selonnah Zee stared into her lap at the blue-granite dishpan whose chipped interior held the purple-hull peas that had so stained her fingers. It would be days until she could get the stain out; and no use trying to explain the subtle (and defended-to-the-death) differences between them and field peas and black-eyed peas and such to city folks—why one would stain and another would not when they all looked pretty much the same once cooked. She would scrub and scrub and still need to invent a story about an accident with a printer ink cartridge. Anyone could relate to that.

"Enough snap beans here for a mess too." Her mother's voice startled Selonnah. The bent woman carried another old pan on her hip, this one grey granite, full of green beans. She sat down into the old metal chair with a sudden dismissal of her muscles and began snapping the beans. Each rubbery green tube made soft sounds like young boys popping their knuckles before a brawl.

Selonnah stood and stretched. "I need to go." She'd told her mother, Mary, the same thing several times in the last hour, and she'd said she understood. *May-ree.* That's how her mother said her first name. She'd told *May-ree* she had to go. But here they were, beginning the same farewell conversation again as if she'd never spoken the first one.

Selonnah looked at her mother's weathered mudslide of a face, with its rising pout of protest, and wondered if her mother really was so lonely she would so shamelessly, repeatedly ask Selonnah to stay longer. Then Selonnah's best friend, Guilt Everpresent, like a shawl of weight on her shoulders, stopped her.

Her mother murmured. "Darlin', I know, but you fixin' to leave . . . don't hardly never see you no more . . . just let me get a bag, put these beans and peas in, just hold your horses and I'll be right back. . . ."

Selonnah's cell phone buzzed her side like a wasp in her waistband. "Selonnah here."

It was Selonnah's boss and editor, Deborah Wiley, on the phone, her voice another insistent buzzing. Deborah had little patience with Selonnah, and it showed each time they talked. Selonnah knew she wondered why her reporter had gone all the way through a criminal justice degree—and then just walked away from it to get another degree in journalism so as to then start at the bottom at a struggling metropolitan newspaper. A girl cop who became a reporter didn't make sense to anyone, even to Selonnah.

"Hey, Selonnah. When do you actually fly out to Utah?"

Deborah's voice and words revealed her resentment of the fact that Selonnah was taking the two-week vacation she'd earned after working more than a year at the newspaper, the *Memphis Telegraph*. No doubt she'd earned her stripes, and Selonnah could dress well and knew which fork was for salad. Yet despite her background in law enforcement, she was assigned pretty-girl stories. Writing for the lifestyles section of a Southern newspaper could mean covering anything from the Junior League to women farmers, now that they'd gotten rid of anything that smelled like a society column. Today it meant architecture.

"Look, they're building a new Mormon temple out in Germantown," Deborah began, referring to the east Memphis area exploding with growth.

"I'm on vacation. Can we talk about this when I get back—what am I saying? I haven't even left. I'm here in Alamo checking on my mom before I fly out tomorrow."

Deborah upped her curtness. "We'll pay you extra. For a big feature you can research while you're in Utah. This new temple is raising a lot of hackles. Very futuristic. . . ."

Nearby, her mother's murmuring became part of the conversation, no matter how hard Selonnah tried to exclude its familiar rhythms. "Inside out and ringside rumpus and holes in the bottom to boot. Plastic bags worthless in the grocery store, worthless here at home, worthless as a paper shirt in a fight. Hellacious."

". . . and we want you to do a big piece on the history and architecture of these temples. Kind of give people some background. And people are curious after all the fallout about Mitt Romney and the raid on the polygamists' compound in Texas. Let readers see that the temples in places like D.C. are modernistic too, but see what they all have in common. And why they're so secretive."

Selonnah hesitated.

"We'll reimburse your airfare."

Selonnah stayed silent.

"And any meals when interviewing."

That settled it. Deborah got the details out of the way—word count, areas of emphasis for the features. Selonnah hung up and returned her attention to her mother.

"Mom, anything you want me to tell Roger?"

Roger Zee was Selonnah's cousin, the white sheep of a black sheep family, small-town boy unfleeced by the big city. With good looks and lucky breaks, he had smiled his way from weekend weatherman in Jackson, Tennessee, to high-profile features reporter for CBS, shedding everything extraneous from his drawl to his wife as he went along. When he'd been assigned to cover the Salt Lake City Olympics, all of Crockett County, Tennessee—and especially his hometown, Alamo—claimed him as native son and scion of success. But he'd inexplicably given up his national television career to stay in Utah after the Olympics, marrying a standoffish Native American woman whom nobody in Tennessee could see much in. Then he started teaching at a university.

"Roger." Her mother sighed. "Some folks ain't likely to forget that stunt he pulled last time he come home, going back to the Primitive Baptist Church and offerin' to preach when Brother Hensley was sick."

"Stunt? How was that a stunt?"

"He got up there big as daylight with what ever'body thought was a Bible and said, 'The scriptures say this,' and 'the good book says that,' and 'it reads right here,' and folks sayin' to him, 'ain't nobody could ever preach like you did, wisht you was comin' back here all the time,' and pleased as punch till they found out he's turned Mormon and was teachin' out of that Mormon bible the whole time and ain't nobody knowin' diddlysquat difference, a-tall." Her mother smoothed her hands over her apron and continued on. "Served 'em all right anyways. Footwashers."

"I don't know about all that. That must have happened when I was away at school. And why would it matter anyway, what book he preached out of?" Selonnah lost touch with the Tennessee mind-set when she attended the University of New Mexico in Albuquerque, living there with her father before he had died. Besides, her branch of the family had been more religious observers than practitioners, and theological niceties were a foreign language to her.

"I'm just looking forward to seeing Roger and Eliza and little Maria, and having some downtime," Selonnah said, returning to the subject at hand. "That phone call I just got—" Selonnah stopped at the same puzzled look from her mother she'd seen so often lately. Could Mary have missed what just happened?

Taking a deep breath, Selonnah repeated, "That phone call means that I'll actually get paid for doing a little extra research on the Mormons while I'm at Roger's. He can help me out with things."

Her brother, Frank, lived close by and hovered over their mom. Selonnah knew he would check in daily. Nothing more she could volunteer, really. "And if you need me, you can get me on my cell."

Resigned, her mother handed her a brown market sack filled with triple-tied plastic bags of green beans, greens, butterbeans, and the purple-hulls. Selonnah knew better than to remind her mother she was leaving in the morning. She'd eat all she could before she left for the airport at noon and freeze the rest.

As she drove away in her sturdy, paid-for Toyota pickup, she felt a sense of an intruding new atmosphere in the familiar landscape of her hometown, one that carried a sense of inevitability, a prescience of things coming to an end. It wasn't the new grocery store/video rental that perched on the edge of the century-old town square, built there while she was away at college. What was changing most was the architecture of her past, the disintegrating buttresses that comprised her mother, the scaffolding of beliefs and blood; and Selonnah knew she was powerless to do anything about those emerging transitions.

That helpless feeling was nearly as familiar as the guilt, and knit together into it, an old, old maiden aunt of a feeling, always there, always untouched.

She'd stood in an emergency room when her dad was dying, telling everyone, "My dad is really sick, you gotta find out what it is, you gotta help him." The feeling was there as the doctor told her it was just the flu and sent her and her father packing. The feeling was there after the worthless emergency surgery, as he died, his infection-blistered pancreas within him necrotizing, dying weeks before he did.

She feared that her life had become about what she could not save.

From: [mailto:adam1830@hivenet.net]
Sent: Thursday, May 30
To: liahona@hivenet.net
Subject: [none]

I dreamed of you last night.

My most beloved one. The day you left, I took the tuliped page for the month of April (it was indeed, my love, the cruelest month) from the calendar on our yellow bedroom wall, and in my grief ripped that day out with my teeth and spat it on the ground. I would chew and ingest time itself, shorten my own mortal days, to persuade you to return.

You believe that my doubts make me less worthy—is there no room for questions? Why do our Sunday schools have classes for "investigators"? Are only the Gentiles able to voice the contradictions?

You will see. I can show you that I believe, I can champion the old truths, the ones of our fathers. I can believe, I can enforce them. Just as we spoke the words together, in the pure Adamic language, I call you to come with me, back to the purity of the gospel. Instead, you have made me walk backward in shame, from the Celestial Room regressing to the Lone and Dreary World.

I cannot live without you. I hold your sacred name, your temple name, in my heart. After Joseph Smith resurrects me, I must call that name so that you can come forth, on that glorious morning of the first resurrection. I hold your name secret, treasured in my memory. When I die, I want to be buried above you—or you above me—so that we will melt into each other until that day.

I cannot live without you.

I have three proofs for you. Look for them in the newspaper headlines. When you read them, you will know.

CHAPTER 4

SHE HAD PROCRASTINATED too long. Selonnah packed for the trip like a madwoman, frenzied, wadding up underwear into projectiles she lobbed across the room into the big travel bags, grabbing stacks of jeans and shirts like a bargain-basement stocker transferring merchandise. Actually, most of what she owned, clothes-wise, fit into the two bags if coaxed. She could lay her two good outfits—blazers and pants and a broomstick skirt—on top and gamble they would arrive relatively unwrinkled.

She surveyed her living quarters: the carefully framed art prints (a Navajo dye chart, Maxfield Parrish, the intense ocher face of an ancient Egyptian scribe); the kitchen countertops populated only by a small microwave, a coffee grinder and pot, and a food processor; the garage-sale tables and bed she had painted all the same color. She remembered how she'd settled on just the right earthy red after searching for spray paint to use. Her favorite color, she discovered to her dismay, was paint primer.

No phone, no pool, no pets. Her ex-boyfriend-now-buddy would come over and water the aloe vera plant; everything else in the efficiency apartment was indeed efficient enough for a two-week solitary confinement.

One small suitcase was stuffed full of materials she'd downloaded the night before from the Internet. (She had no idea there was so much mystery—and controversy—about Mormon temples.) Her backpack carried her laptop and the dim-screened BlackBerry she hated and always forgot to use, her suite of communications thus on her shoulders like those of a WWII radio operator.

Once she'd checked her big bags, she sped through the security checkpoint at the Memphis airport oblivious to the normal irritations of removing her shoes and jewelry, onto the airplane that meant freedom for two weeks. To her relief, her seat partner was a bony woman who kept her elbows to herself, gobbled a few pills, and promptly fell asleep. Selonnah, wordless too, stared out the window and watched the landscape change from hazy green to large square fields to irrigated circles to mountain ranges and dun, sealike desert.

As she walked down the corridor of the Salt Lake airport with the other deplaning passengers, she knew from long experience she would be able to forecast her cousin's arrival by the buzz of humanity that would surround him. Her two lumpy rolling bags tumbled off the baggage return and she stood considering the logistics of pulling them behind her, one in each hand, through her milling fellow passengers. Then the familiar dynamic erupted: the low buzz of intensifying conversation, the "isn't that the guy on TV," the parting of people like the Red Sea before the staff of Moses; then the stinging-clean scent of him.

26

Roger reached around and hugged her, firm and wall-like, feeling more like a brother than her own brother, even though she hadn't seen Roger for five years.

His dark blond hair seemed lighter, and then Selonnah realized that it was greying; but the Cary Grant cleft in his chin, the trademark deep blue eyes, the newscaster voice hadn't changed.

She'd never met his daughter, Maria, before. At first glance, the seven-year-old girl seemed oddly monochromatic, a sepia tone to her entire being. Her black hair was straight as a hank of ironed linen, gathered behind the nape of her neck and neatly braided into a rope nearly as big around as Selonnah's wrist. Her bangs were a flat corrugated board of texture on her forehead, over grave eyes, so dark they seemed to have no pupils. She didn't speak, but offered a sturdy brown hand in greeting, and a polite smile when Selonnah hauled the carefully chosen icebreaker, a goofy-eyed stuffed dog, out of the backpack and presented it to her.

As the adults fussed over the luggage, Selonnah saw that Maria was holding the toy out at arm's length, scrutinizing it unblinkingly. Seemingly satisfied, she clutched the dog with both hands, close to the side of her waist, in a way that looked as if she had chosen to protect it.

National Guardsmen, heavily armed, walked in twos through the baggage claim area and Selonnah saw more jumping out of the backs of trucks outside the large glass doors that led to the street and parking area beyond. She turned a questioning face to Roger.

"Maria and I had wanted to meet you as soon as you got past the checkpoints, but we couldn't because of all the extra security," he explained, nodding toward a group of soldiers whose eyes roamed the crowd, palms resting uneasily on butts of weapons. "We've had quite a morning here. First a bomb threat at a Masonic temple in the downtown area—"

Selonnah interrupted, breathless with their quickening pace, the weight of the luggage she pulled, and the lack of Utah oxygen in her Tennessee lungs. "Don't you mean a Mormon temple?"

"No, it was a Masonic temple. I know that some Masonic temples in other parts of the world have been attacked. For instance, suicide attackers stormed a Masonic lodge not long ago in Istanbul. A couple of other Masonic temples have had small bombs explode, with no injuries, in Alabama and in Georgia. But this is a first for us."

His speech was precise and in full sentences, even in conversation. Selonnah wondered if he ever let down, or if reporting had become second nature for him.

"Huh," she breathed and swallowed. "Anybody taken responsibility?"

"A militant Islamic group says they are responsible for the Alabama and Georgia bombings. And al-Qaeda claimed the Istanbul attack. But there has been no word on this one, and frankly, everyone's nerves are on edge here. Add to that the murder out in Provo Canyon, and you can see why the governor called out the Guard."

Selonnah stopped walking. "Did I walk into a war zone? What murder?"

"You must not have seen the news in the last twenty-four hours," he said. She nodded assent, remembering how she'd spent her last night at home watching a recording of *Ladyhawke* and downloading Mormon temple information. He continued on, "We've had a very high-profile murder here yesterday. Kirsten Young, the daughter of our former governor Nephi Young, was killed night before last, apparently in a particularly gruesome way." He glanced back over his shoulder at Maria, choosing his words. She was absorbed in a book held at eye level, the dog in the crook of her other arm, walking unerringly behind her father.

"Nephi Young? I thought he died in a plane crash a couple of years ago."

"Yes, he did. His wife died in the same crash. You may remember that they were extremely wealthy; and upon their death their only daughter, Kirsten, inherited all their family fortune. She'd been busy spending it in some very controversial ways."

Selonnah was breathing hard now as they sped across the street, but Roger briskly wheeled a bag on a careening, up-on-one-wheel course around curbs and other obstacles while scooping Maria with his other forearm. The luggage wheels rasping on the asphalt overlaid her fading voice in the echoing parking garage.

"How?"

Roger was matter-of-fact as he helped Maria into the backseat of the small SUV and began piling Selonnah's luggage into the small back compartment. "Well, she was spending it in ways that would make her parents turn over in their graves, as we used to say back in Tennessee. She was a model teenager, a beautiful girl, even got a spot as a singer in the Mormon Tabernacle Choir while she was a BYU student. She was briefly married to a kind of a milquetoast guy and they divorced under some mysterious circumstances; after which, she took back her maiden name." Roger cleared his throat delicately, unwilling, Selonnah thought, to speculate or slander.

"But—something snapped when her parents died, and she abandoned any pretenses of being a good Mormon," he continued. "She cut off at the knees every charity her parents supported, and she's pouring those millions into abortion rights and backing a couple of our state's smaller Indian tribes' efforts to build casinos."

29

Still full sentences, Selonnah thought.

"Okay, that kind of behavior would rub a conservative society the wrong way," she said. "But are you saying that you think her death may be related to the way she was spending the money?"

They were out of the parking structure now, onto the freeway, and Roger's body relaxed. "Well, that ties into something I was wanting to talk to you about anyway when you got here. Eliza is on one of her tours, so Maria and I are baching it. I was looking forward to some extended time with you to discuss an area that has me thinking."

Roger's intelligence and voracious curiosity were dessert to Selonnah's blue-plate existence: Every email, every phone conversation with him included a new, stimulating thought—art, literature, astronomy, quantum mechanics. "I've been doing some reading in an area called representational research," Roger said. "Eliza and I talk about it a lot. It's kind of related to semiotics, the foundation of linguistics—something that Umberto Eco, in *The Name of the Rose*, and others have explored."

Selonnah struggled to see the connection between Eco and a rich dead woman. She remembered the headache that semiotics gave her in college, the first time she'd wrangled her mind around its perimeters.

Roger continued. "It concerns the relationship between facts—things and people and events, for instance—and the representations of those facts. For instance, your apartment back in Memphis is a fact. You have in your head right now an image, a visual icon that lets you access it—even though the apartment itself isn't in your head. The fact of it isn't in your head, but the representation of it is."

Selonnah was remembering the linguistics class she took at UNM. "And words—they're linguistic representations of facts. And gestures, like handshakes—they're a type of representation too."

Roger beamed. "There are three types of representations of facts. I knew you would be clued in."

Selonnah's mind vaulted. She had a sense that this understanding of facts and relationships was going to reformat her mind, that she would never think the same way again. "Are you saying that Kirsten Young's murder is a representation of something else, a fact that's behind it?"

Roger stiffened, and Selonnah saw a different wall-ness in him.

"Um, no, no," he struggled. "Not that. Not those symbols. The way she was spending her money."

Sentence fragments, she thought. *Interesting.*

He paused, then gripped the steering wheel a little more loosely. "I was thinking that she was trying to use the spending of her money as a representation of something that had changed in her. The facts of her life had changed. Whereas her parents had been big supporters of the Church, when they died Kirsten began backing causes that her parents, and the Church, would oppose. Take the casino issue, for instance. We Latter-day Saints see Native Americans as cousins in a quite literal way, and would want to help them be self-supporting but not with gambling. None of us wants those kinds of things here."

The wall of separation again. The "us" in his words reminded Selonnah that there was a "them," of which she was a part. The them-ness made complete strangers of his real cousins, like her. Though she was his blood, she was an outsider to Roger's faith, family yet foreigner. He must have felt the gulf his words had created too.

"I guess I better get you to that newspaper office."

Selonnah's head jerked around. "Why? We're not going to your house?"

Roger chuckled. "You'd better check your voice mail on your cell phone, little cousin. Somebody named Deborah—and she's a pushy gal, isn't she?—said you gave her my phone number as a backup. She wants you to go straight to the *Salt Lake City Journal* and find someone named Lugosi."

Selonnah groaned. Lugosi Humphrey's parents, inveterate and devoted fans of old horror movies, named their firstborn after a dark and brooding screen "vampire"; and must have been sobered with the irretrievability of the situation when their son manifested a recessive gene of looping auburn hair and cherubic facial features along with a peculiarly grating asthmatic voice. When Lugosi left the Memphis newspaper to "head west" late last year, Selonnah purged him from her mind and now he seemed resurrected, perennially renascent as his namesake.

When Roger dropped Selonnah off at the newspaper office, she kept only her backpack. She made no attempt to call Deborah; it was an hour later at home and besides, she didn't want to talk to both Deborah and Lugosi in the same exhausting first day of a vacation that, less and less, resembled a holiday.

CHAPTER 5

AS HER MOTHER, Mary, would say, *Lugosi had done gone and turned Mormon hisself.* Selonnah knew it the moment he walked around the corner. He'd gone from tie-dye to GQ and was wearing a lapel pin that was a tiny version of the gold Angel Moroni, his long trumpet aimed at the sky, that she'd seen atop the Mormon temple downtown as she and Roger drove past.

Lugosi wheezed a welcome explanation for why she'd been summoned. "You always wanted to use your criminology background with your reporting, Miss Society Page." His breathing sounded like leaking fireplace bellows pumped painfully through a bunch of hollow cocktail stirrers. "So Deborah wants you to cover the turmoil here with the bomb threats and the murder. You do know about the bomb threats and the murder, don't you?"

She nodded. Always one-upping people. She looked around the steel and glass lobby with its tasteless fake tropical plants in urns. Did Lugosi spell aesthetics with an *a*? Probably not.

"Plus Deborah is promising you a bonus to cover all this on location, and an extra week vacation when it's all over."

His voice made little heh-heh sounds after long sentences. How did he have a right to details about her pay? Selonnah dragged her tired mind back to the new assignment. Maybe this was a way out, a permanent escape from reporting on poultry-flesh charity dinners. And eating them.

Her stomach, empty save for airline peanuts, growled at the thought. She wondered how her hair looked to others in the office, and palm-ironed the front of her jeans and the sleeves of her muslin shirt as she walked along.

Her khaki photojournalist vest covered the worst of the wrinkles, but she fretted about it. She knew she wasn't a photographer, and wearing the vest always made her feel a bit fraudulent. Her cell phone buzzed in one of the multiple pockets of the vest. She ignored it.

In front of her, Lugosi yawed through endless hallways as he piloted her, glad-handing, pointing, whistling. Some people seemed startled, some rolled their eyes, a few grinned haplessly. Ah, same old Lugosi, she thought, and heard through their ears his still-rank Tennessee accent with tasteless humor and pneumatic efforts. *Not 'nough sense to come in out of the rain.*

When they arrived at what looked like an upgraded outer office, he pointed out a chair.

"I thought you'd like the lay of the land, so to speak." He paused for breath and she waited, marveling at his expansive self-importance. When he spoke, it was as if he had bulleted what he wanted to convey, pausing after each point.

"You probably already know that this paper is owned by the same conglomerate as yours.

"The other big paper here in Salt Lake City is the *Deseret News*. It's owned by the LDS Church.

"Deseret is a Mormon word, from the Book of Mormon. It means honeybee."

Selonnah half rose from her chair. He was footnoting his bullet points! She was too weary for proselytizing and his superiority about local color. Lugosi waved his hands and continued so she would sit down.

"The editor's name here is Roberta Carlson."

As if on cue, a woman entered the room. She was prickly-haired and angular and brown at all her edges: hair, nails, elbows, lips. Lugosi was already on his feet, introducing her to Carlson.

Their meeting was short and to the point. Selonnah would have access to an unused cubicle if she wanted it and press credentials and key card—okay, they didn't have hers ready, she could use a key card borrowed from a woman named Annabel who was on maternity leave. Lugosi snickered, said she and Annabel were a lot alike; he'd help Selonnah get up to speed on procedures around here. *Gee, thanks*.

Carlson revved on. Selonnah was to continue with the temple architecture story and would have a photographer available whenever she wanted, but the paper had plenty of photos on file. The newspaper chain's fifteen papers across the country would carry the story as a syndicated feature, sort of like a movie-on-demand whenever a new temple was built. Selonnah nodded. If, as her Internet research had revealed, Lubbock, Texas, had a Mormon temple, then they were likely to pop up anywhere. So there'd be an ongoing market for her articles in syndication. And she had the additional bulletproof impartiality advantage, since she wasn't LDS.

"The other story, the murder," Carlson began. Her words

had a caution to them that her wrinkled brow and pursed lips seemed to ratify.

"Apparently none of us in this state realized the 'entertainment value' that Kirsten Young's murder would have. Guess even out in Tennessee somebody smells a real story and your editor wants you to cover it. Don't worry about police access. We have friends inside the SLCPD. In fact, I've arranged a ride-along for you with the police in the morning. Actually, it sounds like it may turn out to be more of a walk-along, but we'll take what we can get. Can't say they're enthusiastic but at least they're willing to let you come."

Carlson paused, her eyes snagging on Lugosi's lapel pin as she handed Selonnah the lumpy Tyvex packet containing her press credentials and other materials. She continued on, "I'm hearing some appalling rumors about this murder, and a lot of people are uncomfortable about it. Not just shocked or grieved. Something else. I'll put the paper's resources behind you, but getting to the bottom of it may be hard for an outsider."

"I think I know what you mean," Selonnah responded. All three of them knew what she was saying and nothing more need be said in a conference in Mormon country. The meeting was over.

When Roger picked her up in front of the *Journal*'s office, two heads popped up from behind the front seat of the car. His daughter, Maria, had brought a friend who would be spending the night, and the two girls sang *intsywinsyspider* and *iamachildofgod* and *sunbeamsunbeam* over and over in the edgy voices of young children, as if they were singing in italics.

The presence of armed men, National Guardsmen they saw as they drove, seemed out of place in this city of genteel architecture and century-old parks. Roger's voice soothed her as he pointed out landmarks and tourist sites and shopping centers. There would be time for other talk tomorrow.

They would scramble eggs for the girls and Roger (she opted for the soy noodle bowl out of her suitcase) and steer her central-time-zone body to the MDT bed as soon as possible. The house was rambling and overstuffed all at once; there were dolls to meet and light switches and bathroom routes to memorize. She stayed awake as long as politeness required and her stinging eyes would allow.

Her cell phone was deep in her vest pocket as she slid it off. She didn't even notice the blinking message light.

Selonnah shuddered into sleep, escaping from herself, that part of her that had to have the right word for everything.

Roger awakened her the next morning, long before dawn, to tell her that a policeman was outside the door ready to take her downtown.

Selonnah's vest on the floor was the last thing on her mind.

CHAPTER 6

POLICE LT. LUKE TAYLOR took the call about the corpse that was discovered downtown.

Technically, his job as assistant to Salt Lake City's chief of police, Helaman M. Petersen, kept him close to his boss most of the time; Luke's affability was the perfect antidote to Helaman's moody personality. Everybody knew that Helaman wasn't any good with the public. No matter—that's why he hired a Luke, who could be dispatched as Helaman's representative, the department's public face.

Today Luke wore two hats of proxy. First was guide and babysitter to this big-boned blonde woman, Selonnah Zee. Ride-alongs were the police department's way of keeping good relations with the media. Somebody somewhere had some pull and had jerked on it to get her permission to tag along with Luke and ask questions about the Kirsten Young murder.

When they arrived at the cramped, airless so-called

substation that was located on the side of a convenience store, two on-duty officers brushed crumbs off the desk and stood to meet Selonnah.

Luke felt terrible about it; but there were actually donut boxes piled in the metal trash can, something that hadn't escaped Selonnah's attention either, he was sure. Now he wished he'd called ahead.

All three officers seemed acutely aware that Selonnah's notebook was out and she was writing. Luke was so relieved for a break in the tension of the room that he welcomed the ringing of the phone.

The voice on the other end was breathless, someone obviously crying, perhaps scared. The speakerphone was tinny against the enameled plaster walls.

"Now look, I ain't givin' my name or nothin' and this a pay phone so you ain't gonna trace me. You get somebody down to the alley behind the old ZCMI Center, where all the Dumpsters are. Berna—" here the voice hesitated, "one of the ladies is dead."

Luke and Selonnah walked the two short blocks from the police substation. The water and sewer line construction that spanned twenty acres of downtown's facelift allowed access to the construction site from the east only. The demolitions blocked off all vehicle traffic, with present foot traffic limited to cavernous tunnel-like passageways.

Luke strode through the undulating plastic-sheet corridors, oblivious to the shadowy figures of construction workers outside just inches away from him. He was trying to call in a report on his stubborn, sputtering shoulder mike. "Ten-One, Ten-One: *transmitting poorly*. Ten-Nine, Ten-Nine: *repeat, repeat.*"

The uneven footsteps of someone behind him seemed to be only part of the ambient construction noise until he realized with a start that it was Selonnah. He turned and cast an over-bleached smile at her by way of apologizing for forgetting her presence, apologizing for yelling into the mike. She didn't seem to notice, too busy scribbling down something in a notebook.

They emerged out of the tunnel to sudden sunlight that blared into their blinking eyes. As if summoned from the realm of shadows into life, a group of construction workers in their hard hats and yellow and orange vests stood in front of a clutch of backhoes. A young African-American woman in pink shorts sat on the edge of a giant spool of electrical wire, sobbing hysterically. She wiped her nose on a fringed paisley scarf and wailed. All eyes but hers looked up as Luke and Selonnah approached.

One of the workers with foreman's shoulders walked toward them. He pointed in the general direction of the Dumpsters. The backhoes beside them all faced outward like defensive insects, fanned out from a recessed corner of what would become an underground parking garage in phase two of the downtown transformation.

A wide-eyed young Hispanic man stumbled out from between two of the backhoes. His left hand clutched his hard hat to his stomach.

With his other hand he crossed himself. Was he genuflecting too? No, he was stumbling, near to passing out. With a shudder and a cough, he vomited onto his forearm.

Luke saw that there were six-foot-high bales of flattened and bundled cardboard boxes behind the backhoes. Hooray for recycling. Another man, pale and also crossing himself, emerged from between two of the stacks.

The smell met Luke a few paces in.

The foreman was in Luke's ear as they walked: "Yeah, we smelled it too, but we thought it was the Dumpsters . . . we haven't used the backhoes for about ten days . . . we'd

41

hemmed in their recycling but they didn't mind 'cause it kept people from stealing the boxes while the trucks couldn't get in . . . that prostitute you saw outside found the body when she crawled in amongst the boxes to shoot up . . . hey, brace yourself for what's in there."

Suddenly the foreman stopped, stepped deferentially aside; and so it was that only the two of them who entered the buzzing, shaded corner with its nearly visible waves of odor. Luke started to warn Selonnah, but her unflinching look ahead reminded him of what she'd said about her own law-enforcement background. *Well, we'll see how tough she is,* he thought; but kept her behind him, felt her peering over his shoulder. He noted with some admiration that Selonnah wasn't gagging.

The face of the dead woman—swollen, turned slightly to the side—looked familiar to Luke. But his attention was snatched away to the rest of her body.

If Luke had been a swearing man, he would have cursed. He put a hand to his nose and returned to the outside.

"Anybody touched anything in there?" he asked, looking toward the silent group of workers and the still-heaving woman in shorts who glared reproachfully at him.

"If you mean me, no," she choked out. "I turned around and, and, got outta there."

The young man who had vomited raised his hand. "I covered her with my vest. It—" he gagged again but recovered with a swallow, "it didn't seem right to have everyone looking at her."

Luke nodded, compassion filling him. Decency. A rare quality. Not so great for crime scene integrity, but it made sense.

He returned to the small, roomlike clearing between the boxes. "Don't you dare take a photo," he warned Selonnah;

and he saw from her face that she either didn't have a camera or was otherwise unable to use it. She looked disappointed.

"Crime scene guys are on the way." He tried to memorize what he saw, snapped a few pictures with his slim camera, took notes of his own.

Before them, the victim lay on her back, her hands clasped in front of her as if in prayer. Something gleamed at her wrists —clear, shiny—fishing leader? Above them, hanging from her shoulders, lay brown fabric straps, almost like suspenders, that met below her collarbone with a small brown-framed picture. He didn't want to get close enough to see what it might be; time enough for that later.

Her just-beginning decomposition and her nakedness shocked, but they were not what was remarkable about the scene. And it was a scene, intended to be a scene.

The tiny woman lay framed in a blue blanket that was spread beneath her. Its edges had been turned up and over to rest on her shoulders, and up over the top of her head. In the single spike of sunlight, Luke could see the gleam of a hair-pin holding the blanket's yellow border onto her hair. He wondered how the edges stayed on her shoulders, but they seemed quite fixed as well.

Another frame, so to speak, surrounded the blanket. There on the concrete, someone had spray painted yellow lines, all radiating away from the body. The woman's bare feet rested on top of a crescent-shaped piece of paper, poster paper perhaps. Someone had cut this to this shape, brought it with them, he thought.

Prepared. Premeditated.

Just below the crescent lay the torso and head of a life-sized plastic baby doll, its arms extended to the crescent. Nothing looked random, nothing at all.

Something seemed sacred, religious about the tableau.

Was it the crescent? Isn't that the symbol of Islam? Could this be tied to the bomb threats to the Masonic temples? A radical Muslim group had owned up to the foreign bombings and two in Alabama. But a ranting, videotaped message denied any connection to Salt Lake City, and Luke knew the National Guard was even at this moment packing up to leave the state.

Luke's mind whiplashed back to the woman on the ground, and suddenly he realized why the Hispanic workman had vomited, why he'd gone back in to cover her with a vest when no one else would enter the room.

The poor man had sheltered, with his vest, the Virgin of Guadalupe.

Luke had grown up in Mexico, in a Mormon *colonia*. He didn't talk about it much, but like a sizeable number of Mormons, he had been born into a polygamous colony who had settled in Mexico so as to be able to live without fear of the U.S. government's increasing intolerance of what he and others regarded as a sacred commandment.

Growing up in the heavily Catholic state of Sonora, he had seen everywhere the image of the Virgin of Guadalupe, Patroness of the Americas. Even the poorest homes had a framed picture. Men tattooed her onto their backs and chests. Her image flickered from votive candles in hovels, glinted on solid gold pendants on the rich. And now he saw a naked version of her displayed before him. He felt queasy. He backed out of the enclosure this time.

His shoulder-mounted police radio sputtered and cut out and he could barely make himself understood. *Ten-One, Ten One. Ten-Nine, Ten-Nine!* While shouting numbers that must have fractionated into the radio, he nearly bumped into a woman from the crime scene team, which had somehow managed to navigate their van into the lot.

If ever a group of people seemed to fit the job of assessing death, Luke had often thought to himself, it was this grim-faced team of two men and a woman who might as well have been cut from the same humorless bolt of dun cloth. He knew enough from past experience to get out of their way and not ask any questions, nor—worst of all—offer any help.

Somebody would tell them about the vest, and he'd confirm it in his written report of what he'd seen when he arrived. Nobody was going to figure this all out today, he was sure of that.

He stayed just long enough to watch through the opening as they photographed the scene and removed the vest. On the woman's stomach, something was written in black marker. He couldn't make out the words. And he noticed for the first time that to the right of the body, outside the yellow lines, lay a black leather-bound book. Luke couldn't see the spine of it. It had a piece of paper sticking out of it, and on it written in large letters, "THE FIRST PROOF."

He began walking back to the substation. Once again he was startled to find Selonnah behind him, having trouble keeping up with Luke's long-legged pace. He'd forgotten all about her again, so silently had she dogged him. She was saying something.

"Back at the substation, didn't the caller start to say her name? Didn't she say 'Bertie' or something like that?"

Something clicked in Luke's mind. Not Bertie. Bern. Bernadette.

His memory raced to supply the rest. He'd arrested her himself a couple of times for plying her trade, but she had a smart pimp who always posted bail and kept things hopping via his crooked lawyer friends. She was Bernadette Rodriguez. Like many prostitutes in the downtown area, at first she'd found the pedestrian tunnels the ideal place for a quick tryst after hours. When workmen had begun finding mats and cushions secreted in the tunnels, they'd alerted the police. Extra patrols at night—even Luke and Helaman Petersen himself had taken a shift, to show solidarity with the troops, so to speak—and this had pretty much brought the nighttime commerce there to an end.

Luke stopped in his tracks. Selonnah slammed into his back. "Excuse me, I'm sorry, didn't know you were going to stop."

Luke hadn't known either. His body had stopped walking when another thought had arrested his mind in midflight.

Bernadette Rodriguez had been dead for a month. He remembered how sorry he was to read the report about the savage beating she'd endured from her pimp. She was so young, and had a sweetness about her mouth that even the drugs and her profession hadn't yet hardened.

But the body he'd just seen in the May heat hadn't been decomposing for a month. He was sure of that.

How did poor Bernadette come to be transformed into the holiest icon of Mexico? And what was the message on her stomach? What about the book and paper? And where had her body been for a month?

He knew newspapers and reporters too well to even hope that Selonnah wouldn't be pursuing the story ten minutes after he dropped her off. Such a spicy story would put the Kirsten Young case on the back burner, for a while at least.

He was glad the title of the book he had seen by the body was not legible, and was certain Selonnah hadn't read the writing on Bernadette's stomach. He'd get Selonnah back to wherever she was staying, and get on with this mess.

Some details had to be kept undisclosed, out of the papers, so that they could identify the perp. If they ever found the perp. He must be really sick, but really organized. He was making a statement with the killing of this young woman.

One thing was for sure, this was no spontaneous deed, no crime of passion.

From: [mailto:adam1830@hivenet.net]
Sent: Friday, May 31
To: liahona@hivenet.net
Subject: [none]

My Sarah, my only one. I am your only one. How can you even imagine our lives apart? Worse, how could you ever want to be the wife of another man? You have never been a sister to anyone—how could you be a sister wife?

I love you and only you. But if you believe in the eternal ordinances, the everlasting covenant of plural marriage, and that it must be practiced here on earth, I'll take another wife. You may choose her, put her hand into mine. But I swear to you she will in all things be second to you. I'll do whatever you want.

Have you seen the newspapers? Have you seen any of the proofs? What other man do you know who has the courage, today, to enforce the ancient ordinances? Have you seen how I have displayed the covenant breaker, the pig who has returned to her vomit, the great church of the devil who is the mother of all abominations?

I have loved you and only you. I will ever love you, and only you.

CHAPTER 7

AFTER LUKE DELIVERED her back to Roger's in his squad car, Selonnah walked straight upstairs, stepped out of her rumpled clothes, and fell into a deep, jet-lag sleep.

It was the conspiratorial whispers of the little girls that awakened her from her nap later that morning, that, and another much more annoying sound. Maria and tangle-hair friend Billie Rose squatted, arms full of stuffed animals, looking intently at the soft glow of a blinking red message light diffused through the mesh of Selonnah's forgotten vest pocket. The noise was the humming of the cell phone again, moving along the hardwood floor, and dragging the vest millimeters at a time along with it in rhythmic spurts.

"It's alive?" asked Maria. Billie Rose looked exasperated.

Roger's voice coming up the hallway boomed against knotty-pine walls.

"I have an announcement," he said grandly. "Downstairs for cereal--one healthy kind and three that actually taste good—and" (trumpeting through one fist) "one of the great wonders of the world. In honor of Aunt Selonnah, I mine own self have milked a bean for her breakfast. I have not milked a cow but a bean. You ought to try that sometime."

Welcome yelps of laughter from the girls, grateful looks from Selonnah. She'd been promoted to aunt, and Roger must have hunted down some soy milk. The tumble of feet down the stairs, mommy's-gone-it's-junk-food-hooray; the perfect Saturday was back on track.

Almost. No coffee, a scenario for which Selonnah had prepared. She held up a packet of instant. She saw Roger's momentary hesitation and wasn't convinced it would be a good idea to bring it into his kitchen every day, despite his assurances.

"So why is coffee forbidden to Mormons?" she asked as she stirred her steaming cup.

He was careful in his answer. "It's not just coffee but tea and alcohol and tobacco as well."

She nodded. She knew that, but it was fair warning about the future, she thought.

"I'm interested, honestly, Roger. I've heard, no colas either? Tell me about the rationale."

He reached toward an old-fashioned built-in kitchen desk, hefting back a bulky book, thicker for its proportions than any modern leather-bound book she'd ever seen. "Well, actually it has to do with caffeine."

"Joseph Smith knew about caffeine?"

He laughed, breaking the tension. "No, that's just a modern interpretation. The revelation," here he thumbed through the thick book, "says no hot drinks. But lots of Mormons drink coffee substitutes like Postum or even decaf coffee."

He hesitated again, tapping the book. "I've been reading about the actual commandment. It also forbids eating much meat. I have to confess, I don't hear much at church about that part."

Sunlight reflected off the polished knotty-pine cabinets in the kitchen, making it a place almost without shadows, full of gingham and raffia and blue fruit jars of spices and seeds. Through the open door of the room-sized pantry that adjoined the kitchen, Selonnah could see cases of canned foods in tall stacked columns, and toilet paper and large barrels labeled "winter wheat."

"What's that all about?" Selonnah asked. "You expecting a siege?"

"In a way," answered Roger. "Our Church leaders have asked all faithful members to keep a two-years' worth of food and supplies. One of the challenges is keeping things rotated."

Selonnah's attention would not be deflected by the mechanics of food storage. "What kind of disaster are you predicting—a natural one, or a man-made one?"

He thought carefully before answering. "I don't know. Our leaders say that there will come a time when food supplies will be scarce and there will be great political upheaval. As a people, we are preparing ourselves for all eventualities. And when you think about just what a hurricane or an ice storm can do when truck shipments of groceries are delayed, it makes good sense."

As if by way of diversion, he handed her a soft drink whose old-fashioned label read, "Iron Port." She tasted it—not bad—and thought about the fact that he'd only been a Mormon for a few years. She decided to appeal to safer subjects. Architecture was always safe.

"How about helping me do a little research on the way that architecture of the Mormon temples has evolved?"

"Super! When you mentioned it on the phone, I couldn't wait. You know that since I teach classes at BYU, I have access to their libraries. We should be able to find whatever you would need."

Roger had been a real feather in the cap of the Mormon Church when he'd joined years ago; and the Mormon-owned university, an hour south of Salt Lake City, had gathered its venerable bones to action and speed usually reserved only for punitive causes. With remarkable dispatch, BYU hired him as an adjunct professor in the communications department. His charm landed him another good part-time job as a consultant and trainer; and this, combined with his wife, Eliza's, salary as a travel agent, meant they could live comfortably, raise a child, live the American dream in the Zion of the West.

Selonnah pulled a printout from the soft-sided briefcase she'd left downstairs last night on the table. "I've been looking at these photographs I downloaded from the Internet." She spread one out, gesturing toward a five-pointed stone star, one knifelike radius pointing down. "Isn't this a pentagram, like a satanic symbol?"

He looked carefully at it. "Where's it from?"

"It just says, 'Mormon Temple.' Thought you'd know which one."

"I doubt that. You can Photoshop anything." He settled back in his chair, but straightened up again as she showed him photo after photo of constellations, planets, suns, and moons. All were from the outside walls of LDS temples. He soon pushed them gently aside.

"Has anyone told you that what everyone used to call the Mormon Church now refers to itself as 'The Church of Jesus Christ of Latter-day Saints'—or LDS for short?"

"Hmm," Selonnah mused, "something I need to know as a journalist here, huh?"

"Just an FYI," he teased. "An LDS FYI." They both laughed,

the tension breaking. "And I never asked you about the ride-along," Roger probed.

"It was the most incredible thing. I was going to interview somebody, the assistant to the chief of police, actually, about Kirsten Young. But we walked right into another crime scene, a really weird one."

Roger seemed genuinely interested—almost relieved?—when she told him about the downtown murder and what Selonnah saw as a deliberately staged tableau to make the murdered woman look like the Virgin of Guadalupe. His own journalistic nose wanted to smell a connection to the threats against the Masonic temples, but there was no actual proof. He listened attentively to her descriptions of the crime scene and professed no knowledge of Catholicism or Hispanic culture —again he seemed almost relieved to say so. After a short while, he stretched in his chair. Selonnah wondered how much a career of on-air segments had affected his attention span.

"How about we take the girls downtown later this afternoon?" he asked. "There is a great ice cream shop near Temple Square and we can just walk around it. We'll combine a field trip and research with a sugar high."

But Selonnah wasn't quite through with the subject of temples. She decided to press a limit she knew she shouldn't. If there was any word other than "beauty" associated with Mormon temples, it was "secrecy."

"Any chance I could get a tour of the inside of a temple?"

His answer surprised her. "Actually, yes. Before a temple is dedicated, or if one is being renovated, they're open for tours, for anybody. I'll see what's available around here. You might have to get the newspaper to fly you to one just constructed, though, because I don't know any nearby."

She regretted trying to bait him. "I'm sorry. You know as a journalist I can't just be all sweetness and light in writing an article. If there's a dark side, I need to find it. To be fair."

He laughed. "There are no dark sides to Mormonism, I assure you! Now, you get dressed and I'll get my rat killing done so we can leave. And we'll take those photos with us."

Rat killing—the Tennessee term for chores and errands. He bent over the garbage basket to throw her disposable coffee cup away and his lightweight robe exposed just a glimpse of white cloth at his knee. She hadn't figured him for the pajama type, but these didn't look like nightclothes. Too plain. Too limp. Ah, she thought with sudden understanding and embarrassment, a temple garment.

"Wait, I need to ask you a few more things," she said, making no move. "When will Eliza be back? Didn't you tell me she'd won a trip to the Holy Lands?"

"To Israel and Egypt. She's always been interested in ancient art, and this just seemed perfect. I have been so nervous about her traveling with all the unrest in the Middle East, but she'll be getting back tonight," he said, glancing at his watch. "After you're in bed, I'm sure; but she'll see you in the morning before church." He hesitated. "You're invited."

"Might just do that." Selonnah yawned deliberately when she could not think of anything to change the subject.

"So, how are you dealing with Uncle Joe's death?" Roger asked.

Selonnah remarked to herself, as if seeing herself from a distance, how strange it was to hear her father's name spoken aloud. She remembered . . .

She remembered picking up her father, there at the end. Her muscular body served her well as she helped him to his feet, from the chair to the hospital bed. He hefted so light, like feathers and bones. . . .

"Okay, I guess." Even after a year, she wasn't ready to talk about it.

She began to clear the table but he shooed her away, disarming her of the utensils. She offered a polite guest's protest, yielded, took the morning's *Journal* upstairs with her. She spent the next hour scanning the headlines, catching typos, looking for a flavor of the editorial stance in the layout, the emphases, looking for what was significantly not there.

She was about to put it aside when she spotted an article about Kirsten Young. No funeral services announced (that meant autopsy and questions). No real information beyond the background details Selonnah had already heard from Roger.

She looked closely at the photo. It had been cropped far too severely. It showed Kirsten's dark hair splayed into the wind as she turned toward the lens, laughing. An arm lay across her shoulder, and even against Kirsten's dusky skin and coffee hair, it was dark, more *scuro* than *chiaro*. The arm belonged to an African American, Selonnah thought, or possibly someone from India. She'd look into that. Maybe Roger could tell her.

She jumped in the silence of her room as her vest on the floor moved again. Scrambling through the tangle of sheets and newspapers on the floor, she ripped open the Velcro flap and found the phone that quivered with impatience, too many messages stored up.

She decided as she flipped it open that she would have to quit anthropomorphizing everything. You can't feel sorry for neglecting electronics.

The voice on the phone was impatient too: her brother, Frank, just below a simmer.

"Where have you been? Why haven't you been answering your cell?"

Selonnah was sorry, sorry, what was the matter, but her dread told her. She knew.

"It's Mom. She fell out last night at the house . . ."

"Is she hurt? Oh . . ."

"No broken hip, which is what we was afraid of. But Mrs. Lena next door heard her crying and got that big galoot of a son of hers to break in the door. What had happened was, Mom tripped, fell against the floor furnace."

Selonnah remembered the grated yawning hole in the carpeted floor of her childhood house, a place of shadows below the grid that belched heat and the faint smell of burning hairs when it started up. "Thank goodness it wasn't turned on."

"That's just it," Frank said. "She had it turned up full blast. She's burnt right smart on her legs, even though she rolled away pretty fast. They'll let her out of the hospital later today, maybe around suppertime."

"It's May! Why would she have it on? The heater, I mean."

"According to Mrs. Lena, she's been doing a lot of strange things. Telling stories about trips she's been on, when she ain't been anywhere. Carrying around funny things in her pockets, like sweet-gum balls from the tree and pressure cooker rings and old hairnets. Just stuff like that. Even leaving the grocery store with her groceries and then raisin' Cain with the checker for not giving them to her."

Nutty as a fruitcake, as her mother would say. Selonnah remembered her mother's odd behavior and repeated questions during her visit. Selonnah hadn't wanted to know.

"Anyways, a social worker lady came in. They're talking that Old-Timer's disease. They're doing some tests to make sure it's not medications, but the long and short of it is she just can't live alone, not hardly. Not for a while. Probably not never again."

Selonnah wondered about the green beans and purple-hulled pods wilting in the hot afternoon sun. Nobody else's crops were ready to pick. Mary had planted them according to the almanac, above-ground crops planted in the full of the moon, *moon favorable* she called it.

When Selonnah went downstairs to tell Roger, he did not seem surprised.

"I'd heard some things from back home," he said.

"I just don't know how to handle this. I mean, I don't know anything about Alzheimer's."

"Support groups."

She looked at him: questions, questions.

His eyes were lowered. "Well, my best-kept secret has been my drinking habit, before I joined the Church, that is."

He paused until Selonnah's blinking ended.

"I've been clean and sober for ten years, but I go to an AA meeting at least twice a week. I couldn't make it without it—and without the Church, of course. You need a support group. You need people who can help you understand, and know how you feel."

The phone book showed that the Alzheimer's Organization's office was just off Temple Square. They were there in twenty minutes: a field trip/research/adventure exploration for them all. Nobody mentioned the temple photographs. Once Maria and Billie Rose had been placated with bubble gum ice cream and toy store promises, Roger gave Selonnah directions to the Alzheimer's office.

She walked the short block over to the building, fretting over the fact that she couldn't spell the disease, that everyone knew it was supposed to be i before e except after c and this was going to be a problem, *for the rest of my natural born days.*

When she found it, the brown brick building looked a hundred years old. Or at least the stairs were. She panted again from the altitude.

The moment she opened the door, she knew something was changing, slowing down . . . a precognition of some looming event or circumstance, a herald of something important. It was as if time were knitting a caesura.

She saw the back of the man's neck, solid and tanned and a white-rimmed day past a haircut under his Stetson. His hips were slim in the Western-cut jeans, but he was not a young man. Worn brown boots, ropers. Was that sagebrush? Piñon?

It seemed as if he paused too, hearing her before turning ever so slightly to catch her with peripheral noticing.

Ozone. That was it. Scent of storm.

She felt something as visceral as fear, but it was not fear. Suddenly every molecule in her body was feather-edged metal filings, scraped and sifted and heaped into her hollowness; and he was magnet; and everything in her lifted, poised in the air, then oriented toward him, cried for union as her immobile body settled back into place.

She had to lean away, consciously. She had to look down or be pulled into a vortex. She had never felt such a peculiar ambivalence in her life toward a complete stranger: the lightning-flash of immediate attraction, and inexplicable caution.

Without acknowledging her presence, the man nudged a brochure toward a pile on the counter, gathered them all up, tapping them on the glass. No one else was in the office.

Without ever facing her, he turned and walked out the door she still held open. She leaned against it as he left.

CHAPTER 8

SELONNAH WAS ASLEEP when Roger and the children left for church. Midmorning she walked the two miles, straight shot, to the health food store Roger told her about (*catty-corner to the bank and anniegogglin from the big Wal-Mart*, as her mom would say). The air off the Great Salt Lake smelled sulfurous, decaying, the famous local "lake-stink" she'd been warned about. She thought about the man in the Alzheimer's office, the bodies of Kirsten Young and Bernadette Rodriguez, and could hardly bear the last five minutes of the walk; found herself craving fluorescent lights and the sparkling wet-vegetable smell of the store.

The store seemed nearly empty of customers. It was a business in the middle of an identity crisis, seemingly paralyzed with indecision about whether to be an ultramodern urban stainless-steel automat with reflecting-pool polished floors, or a bohemian ethnic market. Incense and disinfectant smells warred with each other.

Selonnah stood passively alongside another woman holding a murmuring baby, waiting for someone to emerge from the swinging door behind the counter. An enormous white-aproned young woman rocked—more than walked—out and surveyed Selonnah over the prodigious pantry-shelf of her bosom from which she idly brushed a few crumbs. After taking Selonnah's order for a field-roast sandwich on sprouted bread and mineral water, she pulled a large cardboard dish out of the blipping microwave, wrapped it carefully in waxed paper, and handed it and a fork to the other woman at the counter.

"There ya go, Annabel," she said, almost tenderly.

Annabel? Selonnah remembered a name like that, from when Lugosi was briefing her. The name on her new key card. How many people had that name, even in a city as large as Salt Lake City? Selonnah turned to the young woman beside her. Her tousled dark hair had a tinge of purple in it. She was muscular under her shirt, stocky, had solid legs under her jeans skirt. She was trying to hold the heated dish out of the way of the brightly colored sling in which the more insistently murmuring baby rested out of sight.

Selonnah reached out to her. "Give you a hand?"

The woman smiled and nodded. She looked grateful—and tired. A canvas bag dangled from one elbow, two plastic grocery bags from the other. Selonnah threaded them onto her own arm and pulled a chair out for the woman, who slid into it.

"Now, you couldn't be the Annabel who's on maternity leave from the *Journal*, could you?" Selonnah asked.

"My notoriety precedes me," the woman said with clipped, precise words. "Tell me, what did I write that made *you* mad?"

Selonnah couldn't hide her surprise. "Actually, I've never read anything you wrote. At least I don't think I have."

The woman laughed. "Ah, I have once again overestimated my own importance." She motioned for Selonnah to join her and began quite unabashedly to wolf down the steaming bow tie pasta and vegetables before her. Selonnah considered how to begin.

"I'm working for the *Journal* too, at least for a while."

Only the woman's eyes indicated she'd heard as the shoveling of food continued. She nodded, chewed laboriously, swallowed, and sighed.

"Breast-feeding. Makes me ravenous. I'm sorry—how did you know me?"

Selonnah produced her key card to the newspaper office's underground parking and front door. It had "ANNABEL" written on it with a marker. She saw an *aha* on the woman's face.

"I'm Selonnah Zee. I'm out here from Memphis—I'm on staff for the *Memphis Telegraph,* supposedly on vacation—you know how that goes—and doing a little research. But I'm getting pulled into following this Kirsten Young murder for the other papers in the syndicate."

Again, a nod of recognition. "You can call me Anne, by the way. Pleased to meet you."

"Anne it is. I guess Carlson—you know her, of course—didn't have any extra key cards," said Selonnah, "and gave me yours while you're on leave." She put the key back in her backpack, then looked at the baby sling, a coat of many colors for its hidden but increasingly louder inhabitant.

The cardboard bowl was empty now. Anne fished around inside the sling, lifted the bottom of her shirt, and hefted the now-adamantly grunting baby to her breast. And all this done without ever seeing the child. Or the breast. Selonnah was impressed. She could hear the child gulping.

"So, are you a vegetarian?" Selonnah asked, looking at the empty bowl.

"Actually, I was vegan, before the pregnancy. I eat fish and chicken now, just to up the protein in order to breast-feed."

"Ah. So that's why Lugosi said we had something in common. I've been a vegan since I was in middle school." Suddenly Selonnah felt the sandpaper of guilt across her raw conscience. Thinking of Lugosi reminded her of Tennessee, and she hadn't checked on her mom today. It took real effort to focus on the intense grey eyes of the woman who spoke to her from across the table.

"I guess it started for me when my parents were teaching me about Adam naming all the animals," said Anne. "I just imagined him saying to Eve, 'Hey, I need some new shoes. Shall we wear Fluffy or Ralph today? And who shall we have for dinner tomorrow night?'"

A nod from Selonnah: vegan empathy. She wondered at the quaintness of using the word "shall." Then Anne continued. "So you've met Lugosi."

"Met him? I grew up in the same little town with him, in Tennessee. I never dreamed I'd see him again."

"Surprise!"

They both laughed.

"I tell you," said Anne, her tone conspiratorial. "Even labor and delivery seemed worthwhile if it meant I didn't have to sit in another meeting with him. At least for a while. Gosh—all those horrible puns. And the corny jokes and knowing looks—wink wink, nudge nudge. I called him a weapon of mass discussion. The red-headed death of ideas."

"That's Lugosi, all right," Selonnah said, grinning. "I'll be gracing them with my presence at one of those meetings Monday morning. Anything else I should expect?"

"Gosh, with all these murders, you'll all be hopping."

"All? All what murders? There's Kirsten Young, and I guess you must have heard about the woman, the prostitute, I mean."

There was a bit of a pause before Anne responded, her question posed with her eyes averted. "So, um, are you LDS?"

It took Selonnah a moment to process the acronym, dredging it up from the cache of her short-term memory. And what did being Mormon have to do with anything?

"No—no, not at all."

"Whew," said Anne. "Me either. And I grew up here. You talk about being a stranger in a strange land. . . ."

Like a black man at a Ku Klux Klan rally, her mother would say.

"So I understand how disoriented you must be feeling here," Anne continued. "This is a whole 'nuther country, Utah is. Didn't you ever read *Riders of the Purple Sage*?"

Selonnah looked vacantly at her.

"A Zane Grey novel. About Utah. It's overblown a bit, but it points out a truth: You better know right now that there are a lot of things people won't share with you because you're a Gentile."

"A Gentile?"

"That's what Mormons call anyone who's not LDS." She chuckled. "Imagine Bernie Weinstein, my lawyer friend here in town who goes to synagogue every week, being called a Gentile by his Mormon partners."

"What's the reasoning behind that?"

"The way it was explained to me is that when you're baptized into the LDS Church, your blood actually changes into the blood of an Israelite. And since Mormons believe they're the real Israelites, everyone else is, well, a Gentile."

Selonnah considered this for a moment, a bit disoriented. She wondered what Roger would say about that representation of a fact. "Guess I have a lot to learn."

"You have no idea," said Anne, laughing. "Your education is about to start."

"So, educate me. Tell me about this Kirsten Young murder."

Anne looked down for a moment as she switched the baby to her other side. "What I'm about to tell you isn't confirmed. That's why the paper's not printing stories about it, at least not yet. But they will. I stay in touch with a friend at the newspaper office, and she tells me that they're going to break the story about the marks on Kirsten's body."

"Marks? Was she tortured or what?"

"No. At least, I don't think so. They've done an autopsy, but I heard the results are being suppressed for some reason. Maybe they're waiting for results of tox screens, I don't know."

"So, the marks, what?"

"There were little slits cut into her flesh. One was on her knee, one on her stomach, and two on her chest. Tiny little marks. They're in the same place on the body where the same things would be on a Mormon temple garment."

"I didn't know the garments had marks on them. In fact, I don't know much about the garments at all." Selonnah remembered the flash of white under her cousin's bathrobe. She spread her hands out, beseeching information, and then sat back in her chair, her arms folded meekly as a novitiate.

"Well, they're underwear. So don't be surprised if people don't want to talk about them. But it goes far beyond just old-fashioned modesty. Not all Mormons wear them, just the ones who've been through a temple, either before going on a mission, or before getting married. My sister became a Mormon, you know, and when she got married in the temple, there I was, my little gentile self sitting on the steps of the temple waiting for her because I wasn't LDS and couldn't go in." She swallowed bitterness so tangible Selonnah could nearly taste it too. But Anne recovered, and continued.

"There's a kind of ceremony they do in a temple, called

'taking out your endowments.' First they go through a ceremony of being washed and anointed with oil. Then they go from room to room—starting with one called 'The Lone and Dreary World,' learning special handshakes and taking vows. That's where the garments are explained to them. I don't know a whole lot about it—they're sworn to secrecy about it.

"Sorry. They insist—'not secret but sacred.' But I know that after you've taken out your endowments you're supposed to wear a temple garment all the time. Under your regular underwear, even under your bra, against the skin." She looked around carefully before she continued. "Growing up here in Utah, you hear stories all the time about garments. Some Mormons believe they have some sort of magical protective powers. Every family has some legend about an uncle who was in a fire and was burned all over his body except where the garments covered him, or somebody's cousin who was shot at in a war and found a bullet in his uniform pocket at the end of the day. All cultures have their legends, and Mormonism, even in its relatively short history, has developed an incredible mythology that goes far beyond their public doctrines.

"My sister, for instance, will take a bath and hang one foot out of the tub with her garment dangling from it so as not to take it off completely. She'll get out of the tub, dry off, step into a garment with the clean foot, and then shake the old garment off and wash that foot."

Selonnah tried to visualize Roger doing that. She began to wonder if Anne had been given a leave from her job for reasons beyond a new baby. *Crazy as a betsy bug?* Anne raised her eyebrows at Selonnah's visible incredulity.

"You think I'm kidding? They are symbols of vows."

So they are representations, thought Selonnah. All symbols are representations of something beyond themselves.

65

"You better take garments seriously—somebody did," continued Anne. "That's why they cut those symbols into Kirsten Young's skin."

"Why do that? What do the marks represent?" Selonnah asked.

"They're meant to be daily reminders of that temple experience. Again, this isn't firsthand knowledge, but I've talked to enough people who've left the LDS Church. Years ago, people were told in graphic detail what would happen to them if they betrayed Mormonism. It's different now, more subtle. People tell me that up until just a few years ago, several times during the temple ceremony, people pantomimed having their throats slit or their stomachs cut open, or their tongues cut out, if they revealed the secrets. But even now, they still make oaths, and commit to very serious penalties—though, I've heard, less specific and graphic."

"Throats slit? Tongues cut out? And, like, disemboweled? You're kidding!"

"I'm not. And I'm telling you, even if people leave the Mormon Church, even if they say they think it's all baloney, many are still afraid—or at least, upset and cautious—when they talk about those vows. Especially the ones who made those vows, say, twenty years ago when they were still pantomiming getting their throats slit."

Selonnah's jaw released. She couldn't imagine Roger and Eliza participating in secret vows, or acting out any death threats. She'd clear that up with him; he'd set her straight when she got home.

Anne peeked inside the baby sling.

"She's done. But I have to change her diaper. Do you mind watching my stuff?"

Selonnah realized that this was the first time she even knew the gender of the invisible baby. She waved Anne on and cleared the table of the trash from their meal. The corner of a leather-bound book peeked from Anne's canvas bag as it lay on one of the empty chairs. Somehow, she'd expected a paperback, or at least a magazine. When Anne returned a few minutes later with a placid, yawning child in one arm, Selonnah was prepared with a new set of questions.

"Look, I feel terrible. We got so involved with the meal and then with all this secret temple stuff that I never even asked you about your baby."

"This is K.C.," said Anne proudly. "Kimber Celeste. One week old. This is our first trip out to the store." She sat down and balanced the child on her knees. She caught Selonnah's furtive glance at her left hand, which had a small gold wedding ring, and began inexplicably—at least to Selonnah, explicably—to cry.

Selonnah didn't know what to do. "I'm sorry . . . I didn't mean . . . oh, man . . ."

"Not your fault," said Anne, sniffing and rubbing at her nose with a paper napkin. "Blame—how to assign blame—"

Selonnah waited quietly.

"My husband, Ryan, he and I . . ." she began, but was unable to continue. After a while she began again. "Let me start over. You've got a few minutes . . . yes? Let me describe what happened. Imagine a relationship that is more a communion than a marriage. Not just something two-way but triadic, connected in a spiritual way to God. Something that is a perfection of union."

She spread her hands out in front of her, palms up, exhausted by the explaining. Selonnah thought of the hairdresser syndrome, where people will often tell their deepest thoughts to someone "safe," who will just listen.

Anne collected herself with small shrugs.

"I'm supposed to be so good with words. All this training,

rich in vocabulary. But when it comes to trying to boil down seven perfect years into words, I feel linguistically bankrupt. Words, even the best ones, are dulled tools. Blunted blades. They're not equal to the task. Do you understand what I'm saying?"

Selonnah nodded mutely.

"I met Ryan MacAlister when I was covering a story about robots in the military. True-blue, a true believer, red-white-and-blue true. He was training with those remote-controlled units that can look under cars and behind rocks to detect bombs. He said he had Nintendo thumbs, was perfect for the job. And he was perfect for me. I was born with a Ryan-sized hole in my heart and he fit; and we married three months after we met.

"We used to say that we were married in spurts, because he was gone so often. I lived for the times when he would come home. And you know how it is when you have only a finite number of days together. At first, you luxuriate in the hours and days. Time is infinite. You squander time with the extravagance of the hour-rich. The joy won't ever end. And as the last days, hours, minutes of time together approach, you begin to panic. You realize that time has drained through your spendthrift fingers. And when the deadline for leaving arrives, you're bereft, absolutely inconsolable.

"But he'd always say, 'Don't cry, we'll see each other again.' And we always did, until nine months ago."

She began to cry again, but silently, tears splattering onto the tabletop, glistening on the wine-colored stained concrete floor.

"He never even knew I was pregnant." She looked up at Selonnah. "But you know what? He was a Christian. I'm a Christian."

She pulled K.C. a little closer to her and stood to leave.

"And you know what that means? I'll see him again."

CHAPTER 9

ROGER CRINGED and shifted position in the pew.

The hapless, strawberry blond boy who stood before his "ward" or congregation, Jared Porter, had stumbled over the wording of the standardized prayer for the communion bread. This was the third time he'd gotten it wrong, in spite of the printed cheat sheet taped to the back of the table where he and five other twelve-year-old deacons stood.

The whole ward held its breath. Jared opened one freckled, scrunched-shut eyelid just a slit, peering sideways toward the lay leaders of the ward. The bishop and his two counselors sat on an elevated platform, they too facing the people. Regretfully, painfully, the bishop—a small beagle of a man—shook his head imperceptibly. His name was Filbert Rasmussen, and Roger wondered idly why anyone would name a son after an innocuous little nut that nobody especially liked. Selonnah would ask that kind of question.

Young Jared ducked his head and swallowed hard. His

freckles were merging with his blush. He looked like he was going to cry. Picking up the platter of tiny torn pieces of Wonder Bread, he began again, pausing after every word, an unprinted question mark making every word a sentence. The sixty-nine-word prayer seemed to last hours.

This time, the obviously relieved Bishop Filbert Rasmussen nodded; and the exhalations of hundreds of lungs whooshed through the room.

Another deacon led the prayer for the tiny cups of communion water. He intoned each word as if he were pronouncing them for a spelling bee. But he got every one right.

This morning, Selonnah had begged off coming to church with Roger, but even though she was still in bed asleep, Roger was seeing everything in his church service through her gentile eyes. He remembered the first time he'd attended an LDS church service. He was full of questions—why regular bread and water for the Sacrament, why no paid preacher but just amateurish speakers, why did people put their checks into labeled envelopes and handed them to a "clerk," why all the handshakes.

And why no nursery. Even though he didn't have children at the time, he noticed right away that the usual noise level ranged from a buzzing hum of tiny people's murmurs and complaints to actual moments of cacophony. After all, every family there seemed to have at least five children each. He'd looked to one side with a questioning look to Eliza, but she seemed oblivious; and besides, the bishop was regarding him curiously, looking down at him from the elevated platform, recognizing Roger probably from the Olympics newscasts.

Roger knew he'd been dragged in almost as a trophy by the two earnest young men still in their teens—the "mission mormonaries," he'd called them, teasing gently—Elder

Packer and Elder Tuttle. "Mormon youngers," he'd tried again. They'd smiled politely.

They presented the missionary lessons to him over the succeeding weeks, and challenged him to read the Book of Mormon. He tried. He remembered reading somewhere that the venerable Mark Twain had called the Book of Mormon "chloroform in print." It was tedious and confusing, despite efforts by the earnest missionaries and Eliza to explain so many things.

But other issues were answered along the way. Okay, so the water for communion was because Joseph Smith said enemies would try to poison wine. Paid ministry should be viewed with suspicion. You put your offering into envelopes so the ward clerk could keep records and make sure you were giving a true tithe when you had your annual "tithing settlement" meeting with him. The handshakes he'd learn about later, he was assured, they were sacred. Just shake hands the regular way until then.

The best way to describe what happened in the end was that he'd been loved into membership, baptized in the curious below-ground font (as much into a lifestyle as a set of doctrines). The Book of Mormon promised a believer a physical reaction after reading its words. Did his bosom ever burn? He couldn't say.

Then he was "confirmed" by the laying on of hands; was granted the Aaronic priesthood to be a deacon, then a teacher, then a priest. He knew now he was being groomed to be a bishop: the leader of a local congregation.

He loved these people. He loved the seemingly ad hoc Sunday gatherings where sermons were on food storage and Nephites and some dead living prophet or another, and what they'd said. Despite the noise, despite the awkward "testimony meetings" where each spontaneous speaker began by saying, "I would be very ungrateful if I didn't bear my testimony of . . ." and ended by saying, "I know this is the true Church and that Joseph Smith was a prophet."

"Bear your testimony." Despite having to explain away for the benefit of Gentiles such touchy things as polygamy and temple garments and not-so-ancient racist policies.

But today he felt incomplete. He missed Eliza, missed her with the kind of ash-covered postponed yearning of a banked fire that you don't stir till the cold dawn when you can add the kindling of presence onto it. His wife was still in New York City—her flight from Cairo had been delayed and she'd missed her connections. He imagined her harried and worn, dozing in a cracked straight-back airport chair, morning-stiff, thigh-wrinkled, rousing, hunting for breakfast.

Nevertheless he wished Selonnah had come with him this morning. But she'd been different when she'd come back from the Alzheimer's Organization office yesterday. She was taciturn and turned inward somehow. He asked her if she'd talked to anyone and she guarded her eyes, said no, showed him some brochures, spoke of inconsequentials. Through the afternoon, they'd spoken about facts and representations and quantum physics and middle knowledge but she never really engaged, mentally.

Nor had he himself engaged, he would honestly now admit, when she pressed him for details about the Kirsten Young case; for background, she said. He'd hedged, parried, deflected, begged off. After a while they both found themselves staring off into space.

In the meeting, little children, old men, college students, housewives, and executives faced the congregation, one by one, each to bear his or her testimony. Sometimes they were memorized phrases like, "I know this is the only true Church," or, "I know that we have a prophet at the head of our Church today," or, "I know the Book of Mormon is true."

Bearing their testimonies. Why do we *bear* it? Roger wondered. Such an odd word.

A rapturous-faced young woman had just finished bearing her testimony about her return from a two-year mission in New Zealand. She was wearing a silver charm of the Salt Lake City Temple around her pudgy neck, and talking about the Glories of the Restored Gospel and the Eternal Priesthood. At the end of each sentence, she clasped her hands in front of her chest.

Part of that extrafertile MacBee clan, Roger thought, all of them with pale eyes and bad teeth, the boys with muddy-colored buzz haircuts and the women with earthenware dish faces and childbearing hips.

She paused and turned almost a full circle from her spot in front of her pew. She pointed a chewed-nail finger, stabbing it in the direction of a group of wide-eyed young girls, caught in the act of passing notes and whispering; about her, no doubt.

"You keep yourselves worthy to enter the temple," she warned, wagging the finger. "You be faithful so you can go to the temple someday. We sisters have a special place in the gospel. Women," she paused for dramatic effect, "we sisters are the doormats on which men wipe their feet, before they go in to God."

Roger sagged. Thank goodness Selonnah wasn't here. He understood the sentiment of the young woman's statement—he'd heard it more than once from Mormon women, no less—but he knew what Selonnah would say, that she'd known some rough men in her life and she didn't like what they'd stepped in and would like to wipe off.

And no way José, Smith, or otherwise, Selonnah would say.

How would he ever interest her in Mormonism, he wondered. Even its best people could be bad publicity to outsiders. And now, the marks on Kirsten Young would bring up everything about the temple. The facts that Kirsten's ravaged body would represent.

Roger felt fear seeping into him like cold air through the crack of a familiar door. Selonnah hadn't yet learned the details of the Kirsten Young murder, the wounds that like tiny mouths would tell secrets he had sworn to keep. Before his priesthood meeting this morning, Bishop Rasmussen had whispered to him that the business about the marks on her body and their meaning would come out sooner rather than later; and anyone in leadership should be prepared to answer some questions.

"And there's another thing," his bishop, he of the long earlobes and mournful eyes, had said, almost shamefaced. He paused to gather other men to himself in the hallway, shepherding them with outstretched arced arms into a room. "You all know that Heber J. Bruce has been stirring up problems with the pamphlets he's been publishing."

The men in the meeting had groaned, almost with one belly-vibration voice: *Why did Mormons who left always want to tell why? You never heard about a disgruntled Episcopalian passing out leaflets to his relatives and friends.*

"And you might know that he's gone missing; at least, that's what his wife has been saying for days. Well, I just heard that there's been a hunting accident," the bishop continued. "He's dead, and there's something about it that's gonna cause us all trouble, you mark my words."

No more details, just ominous looks. Like the pet that won't perform for guests, the bishop wouldn't roll over, wouldn't speak; only at last would he shake hands.

What did the bishop know that he wasn't telling? What

a mess this situation was, Roger thought. What incredibly bad timing that his cousin was here, now, in Salt Lake City. He knew Selonnah's insatiable curiosity, her reporter's nose. When she learned, as she surely would, about the marks on Kirsten's body, she'd not stop until she got at the truth.

But what was the truth? How would he ever explain Kirsten's wounds to Selonnah and still keep his temple vows? It wouldn't be long before she learned that he'd been contacted by the Mormon Church's headquarters, feeling him out about how he could as spokesman put the right spin on this story; to deflect, perhaps, with his shining teeth the questions about the gruesome marks and their troublesome meanings.

And what in the world had happened to Heber J. Bruce that would merit such a "circle the wagons" announcement, as if everyone were to expect a siege?

From: [mailto:adam1830@hivenet.net]
Sent: Sunday, June 2
To: liahona@hivenet.net
Subject: [none]

My Sarah St. George,

I am your Orrin Porter Rockwell, your Danite, your avenging angel.

I have administered the mercy of the atonement of blood. The price has been paid.

I do what no one else has the courage to do.

I am earning you back.

CHAPTER 10

A SIGN OUTSIDE the padlocked chain-link gate to this section of the old ranch in northern Utah announced the presence of the coveted and feared black bear population with an imposing dark ursine silhouette. It said simply, "Never underestimate something that can be taught to drive a motorcycle."

It was as much a boast as a warning. There hadn't been black bear sighted there for years—until the recent decade of drought had brought them ravenous down from the hills.

Heber J. Bruce's murderer reflected on the symmetry, the kind of crude poetry to the names of the hunt regions of Utah: Cache and Book Cliffs, Boulder Mountain and Fish Lake, Green River and Zion.

These, the forests primeval.

Here in the Chalk Creek region, near the notch in Utah's northern border, both public and private lands opened from mid-April to the end of May each year for permit holders wanting to train their dogs to hunt black bear. The art of bear pursuit exercises, like any other time-hallowed hunt, has its own etiquettes and cautions, some regulated by law, some by a type of unspoken chivalry.

The killer violated all those laws with what he'd done to the mother bear and the cubs earlier in the day. The body of the sow, who'd chased her little ones up the tree to protect them from the hunter Heber J. Bruce's baying dogs, remained wrapped around the trunk and cradled in intersecting sturdy branches that threatened to crack beneath her lifeless weight. One thick fringed arm lay outstretched, reaching in death in an eternally mute appeal toward the cub farther up the tree. The other cub, a runt small enough to be hidden completely by a garish red vest the killer threw over it, had fallen to the ground below. They'd all "been left to waste," as the conservation officer would later observe.

He killed both Heber J. Bruce and the animals alike with precision and efficiency, but he had shot the dogs and bears with profound regret. They had never been his prey, and were as much innocent victims as children in a drive-by shooting, collateral damage in this war of beliefs.

The dogs he dismissed quickly and buried them, out of respect for the good hunters they were, the loyalty and years of training in them.

With the bears, he had to shoot the mother before the cubs. Was she wearied of the chase or such a savvy veteran of these "pursuit exercises" that she knew its secret—if she outwaited the frenzied snarling dogs and their owners until dusk, they would go away? In the dying light, she'd have been proved right, mostly right, on that account. All across the state of Utah, all the other hunters with their itching forefingers and empty gun racks and whimpering hounds had gone home on this, May 31, the last day of the season of practice hunting. Only Heber J. Bruce, who'd first treed this sow and cubs on this remote ranch in Chalk Creek, stayed. In fact, he'd never go home again.

After he sacrificed Heber J. Bruce and the dogs, the killer found the mother bear still in the tree.

She viewed him from far above with wary eyes that opened with a brief moment's surprise when he killed her with a single shot to the heart. She moaned like a dissatisfied woman and then went limp, still suspended upright in the latticework of limbs.

He jumped back, fully expecting her to fall, but she didn't. Her babies had scrambled frantically farther aloft, raining bits of clawed bark into his hair and eyes; hard targets. It took a couple of popping shots each from his silenced gun. One cub fell, the other caught in the branches, wedged in one of the tree's many elbows and armpits. He hated hearing those screams. He knew that he'd hear them for months, in silent moments.

He pulled a fallen branch over his tracks, sweeping in the conscientious—and now familiar—domesticities of a crime scene. He was pretty sure they were the only bears on the ranch, and once he found them, he'd had to kill them so they wouldn't be the first to discover and disturb the tableau he'd previously created back in the stand of pines near the escarpment.

He walked back slowly to the coven of pines to retrieve the block and tackle he'd left there after he used it to hoist Heber J. Bruce into the air, a long-haired rebel Absalom, he thought at first. It was the last of the housekeeping details to be attended to on his mental list.

Bruce's body hung suspended between heaven and earth. It spanned two of the sturdiest trees, some fifteen feet in the air. It was now barely visible in the dying light. He'd intended for the body to lie faceup with some sort of dignity befitting the seriousness of the message, but the hammock holding it bowed the back, pigeon-toed the feet, rolled the shoulders forward, and made the elbows and palms of the hands point out. That made it difficult to position the letter, the third proof, in one of the hands.

The punishment—which had included removal of the apostate's tongue—was just. Heber J. Bruce had made a wasteland of truth. His apostasy was public—nay, overt. His only redemption was this death. His blood atoned.

With a sigh, the waving of a white handkerchief, and the threefold Hosanna Shout, his killer declared justice satisfied, this part of the world dedicated like a temple, set aright, according to the message.

Later, it was the circling of the vultures that brought attention to this place of the shedding of so many bloods. But, paradoxically, that very attention drew everyone's notice away at first from the body of Heber J. Bruce. When the vultures attracted them and the smell snagged them, what the investigators would notice first—by design, of course—was the orange hunter's vest at the foot of a rangy Ponderosa pine tree. The shameless color naturally captured the eye, lured it to the tree and up its trunk, seduced the sight into the branches far above.

But the body of the apostate—with all its messages—was what they would remember.

CHAPTER 11

THE NEXT PHONE CALL Selonnah took from her brother, Frank, had been brief and to the point. They'd done a psych exam. Although there was no need for Selonnah to return right away, her mother was worse than anyone had thought. How she'd functioned this long there in the house by herself was anybody's guess. Behind the yellow checkered curtains, May-ree's little pantry was full of ancient long-sprouted potatoes, slow-bubbling opened cans of mushrooms and mandarin oranges, and mounds of spilled-out cereal with scoop marks—actually you could see the finger marks, Frank said bitterly—in the Grape-Nuts.

Selonnah remembered with a pang how voraciously her mother had eaten the takeout fried chicken she'd brought her, remembered the faint odd sweetness in the cool air-conditioned kitchen where they ate that single meal on the red and blue oilcloth-covered table. Selonnah was too busy defending her roasted-red-pepper hummus and pita bread (*hoo-ey; taste like kyarn*) to notice what was wrong in that house with the white siding and the orange patterned and pilled kitchen carpet; too hurried with this shoehorned-in Visit by the Solicitous Dutiful Daughter before her Great Trip West.

Is this what happens to single women? Selonnah thought. Is this the end for them? Only twenty minutes after meeting Anne, the young widow, the proximity of this cell phone call with news about her mother seemed beyond ironic.

She paused as she walked along the street back to Roger's. It was too hot to have even considered walking, this time of year. Why didn't she wait until her rental car was delivered this afternoon? Pendulous bags of tofu and seitan and broccoli were swaying from her elbows, like a lurching Chinese household junk with all its pots hanging from the gunwales.

Selonnah considered all her own single-gal tactics of protection, the strategies that women use to prevent contact, conflict, exposure: the peephole and chain guards on her apartment door, the gun rack in her pickup with the old cowboy hat hanging there, the generic computerized greeting on all her phones. She'd even thought about a recorded dog's barking. She simply couldn't imagine what it would be like to be that alone, and with a newborn child like poor Anne. Perhaps Selonnah would even consider what she'd always haughtily despised: the Inflatable Man to ride in the passenger side of her car when she drove on the freeway at night.

As she neared Roger's house, people were spilling out of the car in the driveway: pogo-bouncing Maria, rumpled stumbling Eliza, and Roger who valiantly loaded himself up and attempted to carry the many-strapped luggage while pulling others, at risk of his balance. The scene made her ache.

Selonnah regretted arriving right at this moment, wished she could have given them a parenthesis of time together without the insertion of her presence.

If only she could stop proofreading herself. If only she had the rental car so she could drive around the block. She stood awkwardly, two driveways away, the plastic bags twisted around her reddening wrists, her shoulders quietly protesting, a tiny snail of sweat running down the side of her face.

"Busted!" Maria was shouting, laughing at her discovery of Selonnah. She was clutching some indeterminate wad of fabric that seemed important to her. She ran toward Selonnah, paused, and rethought with a glance toward Eliza, who waved her on to help yet another beast of burden.

In the jumble of wheeled bags in the entryway, Selonnah embraced Eliza, comforted as always that this woman's large bones never judged hers. Maria's arms encircled their knees. For the first time in many, many months, Selonnah felt the sway of belonging.

There's an art of avoiding overstepping, and single adults become educated in it, whether willingly or not. After the proper greetings and questions, Selonnah excused herself to her upstairs bedroom where she faced her wireless laptop and its seemingly bottomless disgorging of unread mail.

One of the great satisfactions of life for any e-warrior was won: to see that brightly lit icon at the top left-hand corner of the AOL screen transformed from a rage of colors and rampant banner, to a tight-lipped, muted grey box with its subdued flag tucked primly under its armpit. It took two hours to achieve the triumph, however.

Deborah had sent one email, with five others with a "P.S." subject line. She simply must find out what was going on in Utah.

Subject: Re: Bomb threats? Re: Women murdered?
Expense account. Conference call? Re: Rental car.

Selonnah sighed and wondered why the rental car hadn't come yet. She remembered with a pang her once-again silenced and forgotten cell phone. She'd have to become more responsible. She retrieved the messages, made her apologies, promised to wait. After a while she heard the murmur of conversations downstairs, not too intimate, she judged; and started down the stairs.

"Come on down!" called Eliza, who'd heard the squeaks of the cupped old hardwood stairs. "Let me share with you something that happened. This is something you will appreciate." She patted a vacant place on the overstuffed couch.

"I had the oddest experience on the plane," Eliza said. She stroked Maria, who sprawled across her lap, exhausted by the homecoming. Eliza's face was a story that the late-afternoon light deciphered: deep-set eyes, high cheekbones, the soft adobe of her skin, both earth and document.

"I was so tired, on that last flight, but I couldn't help noticing the man who was sitting next to me. He seemed so agitated. I didn't know what to do—I needed to sleep some more but I could tell he needed something too."

That's just like her, thought Selonnah. This was a woman who always looked after others. She remembered Mary's grudging appraisal, the first time she saw Eliza. *If she does as good as she looks, she'll be all right.*

Eliza, unconscious of her own simple beauty, continued with her story. Her voice had that almost-imperceptible tripping of itself, the soft glottal stops of the Navajo language woven into the woman's husky tones. Selonnah thought of the dye chart on the wall of her apartment: the sources of all the richness of colors, the simplest of desert plants.

"So I asked him, 'Is, ah, your trip business or pleasure?'" Eliza continued. "He just looked down into his hands, open in his lap, for so long I thought he hadn't heard me. He had folded into himself, like a human origami. And his voice was so soft when he answered. 'Loss, just loss,' is all he said. He didn't say another single word the whole trip. And I just can't stop thinking about him.'"

"I can identify with that," Selonnah responded after a pocket of silence. "When I flew back to Tennessee after Daddy died," her voice caught a bit, "I was sobbing so much that people moved away from me on the plane. But nobody asked me a single question. I found myself sitting in a ring of unoccupied seats. Even the flight attendants wouldn't meet my eyes. It was like they were afraid the grief was contagious."

Roger and Eliza nodded soberly. His arm lay across his wife's shoulder, the wordless familiarity of possession. Selonnah felt the belonging, again. They all looked at the sleep rising and falling under Maria's shoulder blades.

"Did I tell you what Maria said in Sunday school today?" Roger asked. Eliza stroked the child's elbow. Maria read the comics section of the paper just like her dad, practically on top of it on the table, and the ink transferred. "Her teacher told me that when she was teaching she held up a photograph of a rainbow and asked the children what it was. They all said, 'rainbow, rainbow,' except Maria. She stood with her arms folded until the teacher asked her what she said it was. 'A representation of a rainbow,' she said."

Selonnah gasped with surprise and pleasure. Even a child could understand the difference between a fact and a representation of it. Roger and Eliza continued to buttress their daughter; then Eliza stirred to add her own story.

"Selonnah, one day I asked her, 'Maria, what do you want to be when you grow up?'

"And you know what this little button said? She said, just as proper as you please, 'I want to grow up to be a stranger.'"

Selonnah's burst of laughter was involuntary. She

shushed herself. "What in the world? Why did she say that?"

Roger's look had a hiding bit of hurt in it. "I guess we've warned her so much not to talk to strangers that she's curious. Maybe she wants to be one, to find out why."

"Guess I can understand that, kind of," Selonnah responded.

Eliza nodded in agreement. "And we're so glad you're here. We want you to feel welcome here, as part of our family. And Roger said that you've got a lot of questions about Mormonism—maybe we can figure some things out together."

Eliza had an odd look on her face, but Roger seemed distracted and didn't appear to notice. He stiffened and withdrew his hand from Maria.

"Look, Selonnah. We need to talk about the Kirsten Young case. I, uh, I've been called in as a consultant by the Church. There are a lot of things about that case that directly impact the Church, or its reputation at least. I may function at least for a while as a spokesman too."

He looked to Eliza, as if for some sort of support, but she just stared down at Maria. They had obviously talked about this earlier, perhaps on the ride home from the airport. Roger was showing their united front, but wanted it to be porous, to bring her through it to them by osmosis. Selonnah felt gratitude so profound that it was hard to swallow.

"I know as a journalist you'll be thinking, 'spin,'" Roger continued. "But it goes far beyond that. And the fact that you're here, and you'll be covering it for a more, ah, national audience" (here his face looked pained) "means that maybe I can help keep it from being so, so," he searched for words, "so sensationalistic."

"The death of a governor's daughter!" Selonnah exclaimed. "I guess that's enough of a scandal. But before, you said that there was something . . . 'gruesome,' wasn't that the word you used?"

"Gruesome and symbolic," he answered after a pause. "What happened to her was intended to say something, a symbol that was meant to point to something that had very little to do with most of what that poor kid Kirsten Young did, or thought. Somebody wanted to make a lesson out of her very body. . . ." He ran out of words, looking down at his rousing daughter.

The doorbell was ringing, the rental car was here. Selonnah stood, holding her backpack.

"Look, I really, really want to talk about this. I have to take whomever it is that delivered the rental car back to the agency. It's all the way downtown—my editor's idea, of course. There'll be paperwork, you know. Then I might go to that Alzheimer's support group—so don't worry about dinner for me. I'll be back probably about nine, but don't feel like you have to wait up."

Eliza's expression asked too many questions for the time available, her hands lifting slightly in request. Selonnah kissed her on the top of the head and referred her to Roger.

She was quite certain that she had more questions for them than they would ever have of her.

CHAPTER 12

WHEN PEOPLE FIND themselves in places where they don't believe they belong, they do strange things, think strange thoughts. Selonnah remembered the first time she came to that realization.

She had been in the waiting area at the emergency room of the University of New Mexico Hospital when her dad was ill. Some children lurked under chairs, giggling and hiding from each other while an infant cried piteously, draped over a desperate-eyed woman's arm, limp as a headwaiter's cloth.

Three red-eyed women stood in opposite corners of the room, each with silent angry looks, each wearing two watches. Selonnah learned later of the multicar accident near the Pueblo Indian Cultural Center. Road rage, the newspapers had said.

Everyone in that room had a kind of homogeneity, Selonnah thought at the time. These are all hospital people. *I don't belong here, something just happened to my dad but I'm not a hospital person; I'm not part of these plastic chairs, I don't drink daily from this long-empty coffee carafe sitting amongst the scattered stirrers, I'm different, I have a real tragedy playing out in my life here.*

She had spent her life seeing clerks as department store people, law officers as police people, the people who served her food as restaurant people who wore aprons all their lives. They were all like Athena who sprang forth fully clothed in her armor at birth; these people who must have been born, she assumed, wearing uniforms and hairnets.

She remembered the shock that she'd felt when she was in the third grade and saw her teacher being accused by a store manager of taking a tube of lipstick. It was not the crime so much that shocked Selonnah, it was seeing the woman wearing sweats, out of place, exiled away from her mountainous desk and green chalkboard. Selonnah wondered if the woman would write herself an excuse. Would it be printed, or in cursive?

She now felt the same feelings. The moment Selonnah entered the door for the downtown Salt Lake City's Alzheimer's support group meeting, she had the same sensation she'd had years before in the emergency room. The people milling around were all Alzheimer's people; *she* didn't belong, *she* was coming to find out how to cope with something that had come up in her life, *she* would never be one of them. Everyone seemed older than she, much older, these Alzheimerites. She suddenly felt tired; she'd just drive back to Roger and Eliza's. There'd be another time. She turned to go.

"Give it a chance." The voice startled her.

It was the man she'd seen in the office on Saturday. He was looking directly into her eyes and she felt again all the cells in her body lengthening and then orienting toward him. Time elongated again: eternity in an hour, an hour as a thousand days. His hand nudged her elbow toward the clot of Alzheimerite humanity that had suddenly dissolved into people sitting down in the chairs, scattered randomly, ones and twos.

More ones than twos. Perhaps she was something like some of them. . . .

She dumped herself into the first brown folding chair she came to, and watched the man walk to the front.

A woman was introducing herself, reminding about name tags, "Welcome all you who've come out tonight."

Some of the murmuring persisted: a pointed stare, straggling compliance. Selonnah shifted restlessly in the chair—no wonder, her shirttail was twisted under her, *cattywompus*, her feet still pointed to the right as if they'd intended to just keep walking down the uneven row of same-brown seats.

The room in the community center was cavernous, far too large for the thirty or so strangers in this clutch of jagged-row chairs in one corner. She inventoried the rest of the room: a tumbler for bingo, jigsaw puzzles in progress, neatly stacked yoga mats, blanched paperback books with white creases in their spines, rows of old, donated computers on desks made from sawhorses and doors.

In contrast to this orderly scene, a stack of magazines (mail-order catalogs?) threatened to avalanche down the side of a coffee table in front of a rigid bench that invited you to sit for only a while.

And then the lady in front was introducing Chief Helaman M. Petersen, the finest of Salt Lake City's finest, known for his forensic skills and unwavering ethics: a man of his word, trainer of his peers, elusive of publicity. Women in the audience tittered. Everyone loves a mystery.

Selonnah was astonished to see the man who'd spoken to her rise stiffly to his feet. Add to his resume, she thought, "instructor of Alzheimerites."

The faces of the women in the room, Selonnah noticed with amazement, like flowers to sunshine, addressed him. With visible movement of craning necks, they moved in concerted array when he moved.

"I'd like to welcome visitors and first-timers," he began when he reached the podium. Nothing extraordinary in that voice. Selonnah drew her breath in, trying to analyze why he had an effect on her, searching inside herself like a tongue seeking the sore tooth. He continued on, never looking directly at her. Never looking directly at anyone, she realized. He was reading.

"I've been invited here for several reasons. The most significant reason is that I am the grandson of two people with Alzheimer's. My grandmother recently made the transition to the secure section of a very nice nursing home here in town, a nursing home where her husband, my grandfather, has lived for the past three years. Unfortunately, the situation of having spouses both develop Alzheimer's is becoming more common, and thereby a generation loses its memories. But to me they're both still the great people of their pasts. I'd like to tell you a story about exactly what kind of woman my grandmother once was."

Was. His voice caught as he paused on the past tense.

"When my grandmother Ruby Lee Watt was just a teenager, one of the worst snowstorms in Utah's history trapped their whole family for months. They butchered their cow, and soon all the other food was gone. When their horses wandered off and froze to death, her parents were desperate. They took the two older brothers and left Ruby Lee with the five little ones as they went on snowshoes to drag the horses' carcasses back to cook and eat.

"Well, they never made it back—they were caught in another sudden storm. When Ruby Lee and one of the young

94

boys went to look for her parents and older brothers, she found that wolves had begun to eat the bodies. So, one at a time, with a torch in one hand, she pulled the frozen bodies on sleds back to the house. It took her the better part of two days."

He stopped again. The listening group had melded into one being holding its breath. He let it exhale before he went on. Perhaps he wasn't reading every word right now.

"She washed her parents' and brothers' frozen bodies, then slid them down into a root cellar near the barn, and left the door open. When the wolves came that night, as she knew they would, she pulled up the stairs and shut them in there.

"She would shoot the wolves, one at a time, and haul them up from the root cellar with a meat hook attached to a rope. And for the rest of that long winter, she and the little ones ate wolf, until the roads thawed and help came.

"That's the kind of woman my grandmother Ruby Lee Watt Petersen was. She was someone who would always do whatever it took to get a job done."

Selonnah heard those words echo in her mind. *Someone who would always do whatever it took to get a job done.*

"She and my grandfather Porter Pratt Petersen were two people who homesteaded and together tamed a corner of this state when it was wild. The first thing they built, before the children were born, was a chicken coop, and they lived in it with the chickens until they could finish their first two-room dugout house.

"They were two people who spent the cream of their youth with hardscrabble work. And then, when they'd come to expect to enjoy the fruit of their labors, an enemy came and took all they'd worked for.

"For us, in a way, having such a disease as Alzheimer's

invade your life is like having your country invaded. Everything changes, even your language. You yourselves know that, you have now learned new medical terms, memorized the names of doctors who have become as much factors of your genealogy as your own blood, know all about words that would have been meaningless to you before, the rhetoric of plaques and tangles."

Selonnah looked sharply at the chief and wondered at the disparateness of his language and his demeanor. He was wearing ropers and a plain white shirt, and the crease in the sides of his hair showed where his hat had been, perhaps all day. This was a man of great contradictions.

"They live in a homeland that is certainly no longer home, where objects and even people, once known like the back of one's hand, look strange. And then even the back of the hand itself loses meaning."

Lost as an Easter egg.

Selonnah saw, suddenly saw, how her father's lingering death from necrotizing pancreatitis had not been the worst of all deaths.

"Why am I telling you all these painful things? Certainly I've told you nothing you haven't seen with your own eyes. I was asked to come here to address you" (here a nod to the introducer lady) "because you're organizing the upcoming Memory Walk. As you gather pledges, I want you to think about something.

"Alzheimer's, and its evil twin, dementia, have a course with no markers, no cheering crowds at a finish line. For those who run it, there is no apparent reason for the running at all. So, because often we can't do anything else at all, or it feels as if nothing we're doing makes any difference at all, we come together to run, and walk for people who cannot."

Selonnah saw before her that course, one that would take

96

place for her not here in the Salt Lake Valley but in the hazy damp evenings of Tennessee. She felt more weary than she'd ever felt in her life. She knew, with a slamming finality, the verdict of her fight to save her father's life. She'd lost him. And she would surely lose her mother too. She would become an orphan to two relentless natural processes of disease against which she, and all the twenty-first-century technologies, were helpless.

She saw from the tapping of pages on the podium that Petersen had finished his comments.

At some unspoken yet unanimous moment, all had been said. The formality of the forward-facing meeting collapsed into skewed chairs and individuals gathering purses and keys and making their farewells.

Selonnah was trying to escape the literal clutches of a self-avowed membership chairman when suddenly Helaman Petersen was steering her away.

"You must be Selonnah Zee." It was a statement, not a question.

"How . . ."

He grunted and let his gentle grip on her elbow go. "Crime scene photos—I asked Lt. Taylor. For sure you weren't one of the ladies of the evening, and I know all the CSIs. So— how does this Selonnah Zee find herself at this meeting where I am speaking? Do you have a relative with Alzheimer's, or are you just stalking me?"

Selonnah blushed at the prospect. "My, my mother just . . ."

"That's why you were at the headquarters. Well, I guess you didn't get in on the support group thing tonight. They'll start up again next week, and then you can bare your soul." He was looking at her sharply, looking for a reaction. She blanched this time.

"Oh no . . ." she began. "I'm just at the beginning of this

process. I'm not ready for group therapy." She weighed his literate speech against her feeling of helplessness and decided to deflect his questions with one of her own, a test that would put them on equal footing. She quoted, "'Great is the art of beginning, but greater is the art of ending.'"

He looked at her narrowly, again. "Longfellow, right?"

She nodded, unwilling to entrust any more to this stranger. She remembered the man Eliza had met on the plane—*Loss, just loss*—and couldn't think of any way to end their conversation. "I guess I'll learn to live with loss."

A tightening of the muscles around his eyes. He began steering her again, this time toward the door. She felt him release her elbow and she knew he'd stopped in the hallway. His voice was soft again, almost as if he were speaking only to himself.

"Some losses are worse than others."

She turned quizzically back toward him, but he was slapping his hip, retrieving a cell phone. He turned his head from her but she heard part of the conversation. It was impossible not to—he was having to repeat himself, shouting at times.

"Chief Petersen. Hey Luke. Ten-One, buddy. Ten-One. Got it at the morgue? MORGUE? NO! No, I want to be there when his wife gets there. Yes, wait. Get her to WAIT. Hold her off till I get there. There's no way we can release the body yet. Right. Right. Coming right now. I'M COMING! WAIT! And get your radio fixed, will you?"

The Tennessee part of her was ashamed of eavesdropping. But the reporter part of her couldn't help it. As he finished, she walked quickly outside to the parking lot. She scrambled for the keys, the ignition, gearshifts, all in the wrong places. The windshield wipers squirted wildly, jumped up, precipitous as skeets. Driving the rented SUV felt something like unfaithfulness, and she was ashamed, again, this time of her awkwardness. She steered out of the parking lot feeling the comforting snobbishness of all high-riding drivers who looked down through moonroofs of others, who knew that they sat while others squatted.

An aberrant fog on the freeway surprised her as she headed toward Roger and Eliza's house. She wondered how her mother was doing, tried to remember where her cell phone charger was, couldn't think.

But even the fatigue couldn't stop her curiosity from a kind of resurrection from her muddied thoughts. Obviously Chief Petersen had been talking about a death and identifying a body. That meant news. Actually, new news, because he was talking about a man—not Kirsten Young, not that poor Bernadette somebody. She regretted for a moment not following the chief's car but knew she was too weary.

Still, she wondered.

And then a very conscious conviction. The "worse" loss, the one that Chief of Police Helaman M. Petersen had spoken of, was not the loss of grandparents. Of that—and very little else at this point—she was certain.

PART TWO

CHAPTER 13

IT WASN'T IN Lt. Luke Taylor's nature to be suspicious. True, that wasn't generally an advantage for a policeman, but the cowlicked, sandy-haired cheerful openness that got him the job as the department's spokesman was the same quality that allowed him to gain the trust of coworkers and the public alike. But today, Lt. Taylor was uneasy.

All Monday mornings at Salt Lake City's police headquarters were hectic. Office staff had of course been off all weekend so surfeited fax machines with their endless cascades of papers squealed for attention, phones rang shrilly and constantly. Even though it was only 8 a.m., disgruntled civilians leaned against walls in a grape-green waiting room and stared morosely at anything other than each other. It was a place of urgent misery and distrust, of foreigners awaiting entrance. Only sighs, and the shifting of body weight in chairs where metal rubbed against wood, relieved the silence in a room where cell phone use was forbidden.

Luke walked through familiar territory as he navigated past the place where women of the support staff held court with telephone headgear and computers, then into the inner sanctum of colleagues and their haphazard workstations.

His nose crinkled as he turned the last corner. He'd never get used to it: Officer Donnell's body odor was hovering near resplendent today. Luke thought he must have had a lot of Italian food over the weekend.

Such intangibles don't show up on a resume or a gravestone, but they mark their owners in a way that even actions and words cannot. Luke had hired Donnell sight unseen (of course) on the basis of his exemplary record and hadn't thought much of the guarded language of the recommendations that accompanied it. He imagined this had begun first as a family secret kept at bay with colognes and strong but ultimately ineffective underarm sprays. With the hire, it had become Luke's problem, like the beloved family dog that bites strangers and has to be managed, mastered, and chained up and hidden away when company comes. Thus poor Donnell and his own biosphere was at the back of the labyrinth of offices, where he was, to his credit, the very best Internet hacker/researcher in any police department in the United States.

Donnell waved at Luke but his eyes never left the computer screen in front of him. Luke was glad—most days he'd be happy to chat a minute or two but today he needed to talk to Chief Petersen. He needed to probe the *fondo*, the depth, of what was going on. He found that the English word just didn't cut it—there was more of the profound in the Spanish word.

Luke was surprised to see Helaman was not in his office, this nearly inaccessible terminus of authority and power. The lights were on and the door unlocked and a bottle of water, uncapped, stood by the telephone. Luke entered the office and eased himself into a chair to wait.

Behind Helaman's desk were floor-to-ceiling bookshelves, ruddy alderwood creations reinforced with steel that Luke seemed to recall the chief himself had made. Diplomas, certificates, photos of the chief with various dignitaries and quite a few unknowns, and engraved award plaques broke up the rows of books. Prominently displayed were several incongruous certificates proclaiming Helaman M. Petersen thoroughly vetted in marksmanship, sensitivity training, and bomb disposal. A resolutely staring ten-point buck's head mounted above the shelves curled its neck and disdainfully averted its glassy eyes from all people, forever.

On the shelves, at eye level and above, the books were all business—forensic, procedural, manuals, and equipment catalogs. On a whim, Luke walked around the desk and pushed the massive leather desk chair to one side. There at desk level and below, hidden in daily life by the bulky wheeled armchair, was what seemed to be an odd assortment of objects: several volumes of nineteenth-century Mormon sermons called The *Journal of Discourses*, some accordioned topographical maps, a hefty book with *Palgrave's Golden Treasury* on its faded spine, and a rumpled silken envelope embroidered in spidery letters that read, "Patriarchal Blessing."

And, Luke realized, every family picture in the whole room was down there like a crowded reunion. The smiling elderly couple Luke recognized as Helaman's beloved grandparents Ruby Lee and Porter Pratt Petersen. Luke knew Helaman loved them fiercely and loyally. The story of the wolves and the years of work on the hard-won ranch were local lore.

But he knew the other stories that Helaman never told in public. How Ruby Lee was named after her own father, John D. Lee, the man ordered by Brigham Young to execute the

Mountain Meadows Massacre—the heritage of doing, as Helaman often said, whatever it took. How the last years that mentally failing Ruby Lee lived at home she refused to wash dishes but instead put them into the refrigerator and its freezer compartment and the two cavernous chest freezers in the garage. When Helaman had finally, tearfully, taken her to the Alzheimer's care facility where she now resided, he spent nearly a week just loading and reloading the dishwasher and hand-washing the silverware and crusted cooking implements and putting them back into the long-emptied cabinets. Luke came in the evenings and helped him, wordlessly sharing the task that was beyond grieving. During that time, Helaman had said only one thing of any substance to Luke.

He'd looked his assistant square in the eye, and stated it. "She always did whatever it took. Our family always has. I'm doing whatever it takes."

On the shelf in Helaman's office was the picture of the sad-eyed woman surrounded by five small children Luke knew to be Helaman with his mother, Rose, and his siblings. It was a photo taken before his mother had passed away from cancer. She'd been what Helaman once called, with a catch in his voice, part of "the tribe of one-breasted women," having grown up downwind from the government's nuclear tests in Utah decades before, tests that eventually killed every woman in her family of that generation, one mammary at a time.

Luke's father had actually known Helaman's father, Orson Pratt Petersen. He described Orson as a slant-smiling man who left his wife and five children when Helaman was just a baby, a furtive drifter who would return to his former home only under the cover of darkness when his ex-wife and the children were visiting relatives out of town. He would cut the toes off all her stockings, putting them neatly folded back into the bureau drawers, then take all the pots and pans and load them into the trunk of his car and drive away.

When the family would return—in those days when rural towns in Utah had no fast food and few conveniences in the grocery store—the poor woman would find herself with no way to cook for her hungry brood. It was a reverse emasculation, the forced conversion of a woman from homemaker to scavenger. But Helaman's mother learned to pack sandwiches for every homeward trip, peanut butter and honey for that first cold breakfast, pimiento cheese for lunch. By suppertime the local Mormon Church's women's auxiliary, the Relief Society, would have rounded up enough cookware to see her through.

Rose bought her own stockings, though, too ashamed to tell anyone about that; or stitched those that were salvageable with buttonhole thread and lengthened her garters to make do.

From his vantage point, Luke could see what looked like a light frost on the glare of the glass covering one of the other photographs. With innocent curiosity he leaned closer, trying to see the faces in the photograph through what he finally ascertained to be a cloud of dusty fingerprints. Only when he changed the angle of his vision by moving around the desk could he see that the photograph was that of Helaman's wife, Janine, and their nine-year-old daughter, Gracie.

Janine Romney Petersen was a beautiful woman, no doubt about it. Unlike many a Mormon woman who succumbed to decades of childbearing that transformed her body from Madonna to the Venus of Willendorf—the rotund prehistoric figurine unearthed in Austria—Janine was sapling-thin as she entered her thirties. Their daughter, Gracie's, birth punctuated a long and frustrating first epoch of their childless marriage, but left Janine svelte as before.

Janine's facial features were arresting and prominent without a hint of caricature. Her hooded eyes had hard edges to them, like holes cut in a mask, Luke had always thought. Her lips had a kind of precision, curves without softness. She wore her red hair in stiff waves—marcelled, older people would call it.

When people met Janine, the initial visual impression soon became steel-riveted to the way she talked. Her intelligence was almost predatory—ferreting out information in conversation, getting what she wanted to know, then going on to the next subject on her internal schedule. She had little patience with small talk but in groups would gravitate to whoever wanted to talk about art or politics. Lacking such a verbal sparring partner, she would fall silent—pretending with arched eyebrows and eye contact to be listening, but years of observation taught Luke that she wasn't engaging there at all. Janine Romney Petersen stripped people down to their core of thoughts and if she found them wanting, she gave no second chances. People often compared such a mind to a steel trap, but after witnessing several of her verbal flailings, Luke thought of her more like a cross-cut shredder.

Ah, but then there was Gracie. The child was her name incarnate, a true-eyed illumination of any space she occupied, as soft-edged as her mother was crisp, wise but nonetheless trusting. Only a child could be so near perfect, Luke thought.

Luke returned to his straight-back chair opposite the chief's desk and wondered, wondered. It was really too bad, he thought, such a shame. . . .

He heard Helaman's boots coming down the hall, and Luke roused from his thoughts and rose to meet him.

"Morning, Chief," said Luke. Helaman stopped a moment and looked at him as if trying to insert him into the mental picture of the unoccupied office he'd left short minutes before. He nodded a greeting. He slipped off latex gloves and folded them neatly, squarely before tossing them into a wastebasket. He rubbed the residual cornstarch absentmindedly into his knuckles. With all the biological scares these days, nobody in the department handled anything from outside that building without gloves anymore.

"I've been out, like the balloon man, whistling far and wee," said Helaman. Luke searched his memory for the phrase and shrugged with defeat.

"Something somebody once said about springtime," said Helaman, by way of a not-so-helpful explanation. "So, what's up?"

"I need to run some things past you about the Bernadette Rodriguez case."

"Who? Oh, the prostitute. Go ahead." Helaman whirled his chair to allow himself access and sat down. Was it coincidence that he seemed to push the chair back up against the shelf of pictures?

Luke produced his own pair of gloves from a hip pocket and put them on. He removed a piece of paper from a large plastic evidence folder, unfolded it, and spread it out on the top of the desk.

"Here's the note that was found with her body. The lab guys say it doesn't have any prints, paper and ink are common, and there's no handwriting to compare it to. See, it says, 'The First Proof.' I'm wondering, why 'first'? Don't you think that implies there will be more?" He waited for a grunt of assent from Helaman, then continued. "Does this mean we should wait for a string of other crimes? It's spooky that it should be so much like, hmm, feel so much like, the Kirsten Young case. But that one happened first, and I don't recall any signs at that crime scene—that is, nothing that said something like, 'the second proof,' or anything."

"Me neither. But that was out in the canyon. I guess something could have blown away," said Helaman.

That was a new thought for Luke. He mentally did a save and close on that file of info, then went on. "And then there's what was written on her stomach, on Rodriguez, I mean."

Helaman nodded again as Luke produced a crime scene photo, enlarged to show the writing.

"It's written in the Deseret Alphabet." He waited for Helaman to acknowledge something, but the chief's face seemed impassive, though interested.

Developed as a pet project of Mormon leader Brigham Young in the mid-nineteenth century, the Deseret Alphabet at first held out great hope for helping the polyglot influx of European converts who flooded into Utah at that time. Its simplicity and phonetic quality promised to make reading and writing English easier, and to provide a visible symbol of the set-apart nature of Mormonism itself. Scripture, various articles, children's primers, and other short works were enthusiastically "translated" into this script of curlicues and heavy vertical lines. There was even talk of making a whole library of works written in the Deseret Alphabet.

Like the territory of Utah itself proved to be, the cipher

was of the world but not in it; and after twenty-five years of lukewarm use by the average Mormon, it was abandoned by Church leaders starting with Young's successor, John Taylor —one of Luke's own ancestors. It was that heritage of connection with this oddity of Mormon history that led Luke to the ability to transliterate what was found written on Bernadette Rodriguez's *dulce de leche*–colored belly.

"I worked on translating it," said Luke. He ran one palm back and forth across his close-cut hair, oblivious to the glove he still wore. "But I just couldn't make sense of it. I even emailed the picture to Donnell over the weekend, and he was able to turn up an online cipher, showing the letters of the Deseret Alphabet and their equivalents. He checked it too."

Luke's thoughts were momentarily derailed by an image of Donnell hunched over the cipher, snacking on pickled garlic cloves.

"Okay," said Helaman. "So what does it say?"

"That's the problem. It's just gibberish. I can't make head or tail of it."

"I remember you as being the best linguist in the El Uruguay North Mission," said Helaman. "Isn't that what code-breaking is, really—discovering the grammar and syntax of signs?"

It was true that when Luke had served his two-year LDS mission service in that South American country starting when he was nineteen years of age, Spanish was as native to him as English. But he amazed all his companions with his speed at acquiring French and Portuguese and other tongues spoken there. While others were nearly paralyzed with homesickness and the *zh-zh* affectations of the Spanish dialect of that wannabe-European country, Luke was soon reading the country's classics—José Enrique Rodó and others—and learning lists of Quechua words in his free time. It was a game to him, and an easy one at that.

Helaman put his head to one side, thinking. "So who can we get to find out what it says, if you and Donnell can't, *hermanito*?"

Luke softened at being called "little brother." But he wasn't willing to throw in the towel and turn the challenge over to anyone else. "I doubt even professional code-breakers will figure it out—it's just not long enough to set up any linguistic patterns. I just keep trying to figure it out. . . ."

Perhaps it was the talk about Uruguay and all the memories. Perhaps it was an email he just received from a friend in Peru—one that wrote *ji ji* to denote laughter; hee-hee. Perhaps it was the embedded rhythms of Spanish that become part of the interstices of both memory and consciousness that sparked what happened next.

"Let me read it aloud to you," said Luke, his voice excited. "I think I hear something in it. You listen, and . . ." He twisted his mouth as he began to read.

"Eh—yah. No. Bole—ber-ah. Pore. Tee. El. Sah-vah-thoh."

Helaman leaned forward, showing for the first time in the conversation an animation of both his working lips and eyes.

"What if it's not English—I mean, she's Mexican. . . ." Luke stumbled with his words, fumbled with the paper. He read one word at a time, looking to the ceiling and giving each a twist of his tongue as to somehow make it Spanish.

"*Ella. No. Bolbera? Volvera. Volverá. Por. Ti. El. Sav . . . Sabado.*" He stretched his mind and tongue. "*She doesn't come, won't come back? For you . . . on Saturday. She will not come back for you on Saturday. What could that mean?*"

Helaman stretched back in his chair. "What day was Bernadette's body found—it was a Saturday, wasn't it?"

It seemed a year ago, but it was not even forty-eight hours before, Luke reflected. Yes, it was just Saturday. But part of his mind was mired up with something like a tire in clay— why would someone write such a thing on a poor prostitute?

She almost certainly didn't write it herself. Was it a warning to someone, someone who expected Bernadette to be somewhere else on Saturday?

Then his epaulette-mounted radio summoned him. Luke was embarrassed by it, knew that he hadn't yet gotten it fixed and that Helaman would be irritated. But the chief waved his permission and appeared not to notice as he shouted into the speaker, repeating himself, asking the hapless caller to repeat himself, straining and misunderstanding and in the end terminating the unsatisfying call without really knowing what he was supposed to hear, nor if he had been heard. He'd seen Helaman seem to smile tensely—and just for an instant—at someone over his shoulder; but the chief had pulled the door nearly shut and motioned him to sit down and continue the conversation about Bernadette.

Luke, a bit unnerved, didn't register the fact that the door was ajar. He launched back into the subject.

"First of all, it's pretty obvious that the Rodriguez woman was posed to look like the Virgin of Guadalupe."

Helaman looked mildly blank, professional, practically placid.

Luke added by way of explanation, "You know, the patron saint of Mexico. Supposedly the Virgin Mary appeared to a poor peasant and actually gave him an image of herself on his workman's apron. And this pitiful Rodriguez woman was posed as exactly that image, right down to the crescent moon beneath her feet, and the cherub adoring her."

Helaman nodded, so Luke continued. "Well, I've been thinking about all the things that were found around her body." He took a plastic bag containing a book from a small leather folder, and removed a sheet of paper from it and consulted a list he'd written on it. "You know, the Book of Mormon, with the passage marked in red."

When he'd first seen the leather-bound book at the crime scene, Luke had suspected that it was a copy of the Mormon scripture. He was pretty sure that this fact had escaped the notice of the reporter, Selonnah, since the spine of the book had been facing the wall of boxes. Finding the passage inside, marked in red ink, had caused a bit of a stir from the crime scene team later. He couldn't imagine what a gentile reporter would have done with it.

"What passage?"

"Actually, most of chapter 14 of First Nephi." Helaman motioned him to explain, but Luke was already thumbing through the copy of the Book of Mormon he'd removed from the folder. He began to read aloud, hurriedly running the words together as if racing toward the end of the passage he impaled with his finger on the page.

"And it came to pass that he said unto me: Look, and behold that great and abominable church, which is the mother of abominations, whose founder is the devil."

Luke was aware that Helaman was fidgeting, moving his water bottle across the same watery trail on the glass top of his desk, back and forth between the overstacked wire in-box and a plastic bottle of ibuprofen. Luke looked at the chief, determined to continue. "Look, there might be some clues in this. I think we ought to be on the same page, don't you?"

Helaman settled back into the sighing leather chair, stretching his neck side to side. Luke continued, skipping down past repetitive verses.

"And when the day cometh that the wrath of God is poured out upon the mother of harlots, which is the great and abominable church of all the earth, whose founder is the devil, then, at that day, the work of the Father shall commence, in preparing the way for the fulfilling of his covenants, which he hath made to his people who are of the house of Israel."

Luke closed the book carefully.

"Oh yes, the great and abominable whore chapter," said Helaman. "When I was a kid in Sunday school, we all knew that was the Catholic Church, everybody did." He caught Luke with a direct look in the eye, one of the first ones of the conversation, Luke noted to himself.

"Well," Luke said cautiously, "if not stated, then implied. So I think that passage was deliberately linked to the posing, the scenario."

Helaman leaned back again, just a bit, in his chair before answering. "Ah. So tell me what you're saying."

"The Catholic thing is not accidental. It's the key, I think. And she was wearing a scapular too."

"What's that?"

"Two little picture things, kind of religious jewelry, but made of what looks like brown wool." Luke emptied another small clear plastic bag that held pictures of a woman handing something to a kneeling man. The pictures—more like flaps really, Luke thought—were connected by two brown straps. Luke demonstrated how the two flaps rested on his own chest and back, held on by the straps. He felt uncomfortable, idolatrous, even wearing the thing. But all his life he'd seen Hispanic young men wearing them. He tried once to take a scapular from a gang member he'd arrested. The young man had explained that they came in different colors, with different meanings; how they were really symbols of a protective garment that monks wore long ago—"sorta shrank down," the young man had said, from a robe to their present incarnation as just straps that held the front and back on the wearer. Luke had examined the plastic-covered pictures, saw that they couldn't contain drugs or weapons, and gave them back. Now, explaining all that to Helaman, he wondered why a symbol of protection was on a desecrated corpse. And this scapular was a brown one. Did that mean anything?

"But even knowing what the Deseret script on her abdomen said doesn't make things any clearer," Luke concluded. "In fact, it's more confusing."

"What do we know about this Bernadette Rodriguez?" Helaman asked.

"A prostitute, had a record for solicitation, been through here a couple of times, never went to trial. I saw her several times, talked to a public defender about her. Just a victim, I thought, of her circumstances. But here's the weirdest thing, the thing that can't get out to the media yet."

Luke saw Helaman stiffen, but he went on. "Rodriguez has been dead for weeks. You may not remember this, but she was the one who was beaten up by her pimp and spent several days in County General on life support. I just assumed that when she finally died somebody claimed her body and she was buried. But this body had never even been embalmed. Obviously frozen, but not embalmed."

"So what are you thinking?" Helaman's voice was quiet but insistent.

"I—I don't know. Somebody is trying to send a message. It has something to do with the Catholic Church, and with what the Book of Mormon says about it—it's a whore, Bernadette was a, well, whore. But why her? Why do that to a body dead for days? And what does the scapular mean, if anything? And what in the world does the Saturday business mean?" Luke rose to his feet, practically talking to himself, running down a list of puzzles, turning toward the door. "And why written in the Deseret Alphabet? I bet not one person in a hundred, even in the Church, has ever even heard of it."

Luke felt, as much as heard, the tiniest motion of someone behind the door. He looked past its partial opening to see an odd-looking, fidgeting red-haired man standing by Selonnah,

116

who sat forward in a chair, just outside. How long had they been there? What had they heard? And hadn't Helaman surely seen them before him?

Luke had remarked to himself on Helaman's interest in Selonnah when the chief had first spotted her in the crime scene photos from the Rodriguez crime. He'd wanted to know her name and how long she'd been covering stories in Salt Lake. The press, of course, was always your enemy because they wanted details that you had to keep secret, pried and wheedled for your aces in the hole, those you'd need in order to discern the real criminals from the professional crime confessors and loonies.

Luke gathered the objects he'd brought with him and replaced them in the folder. He knew his conversation was over. Helaman was already looking past him at Selonnah.

"Uh—just wanted to run some theories past you," Luke said, letting his voice rest a beat on the word "theories." "Oh, and don't forget to look at that folder of autopsy reports," he said awkwardly, pointing to a corner of the chief's desk. "We'll have to have a press conference in the next few days about some of them. One of them, at least." He felt an urgency about the autopsy report that even now Helaman was shoving under one of the precisely squared piles of papers on his desk. But Luke didn't want to say Kirsten Young's name aloud, not with Selonnah standing there.

The reporter wasn't a demon, he reminded himself. Her aquiline nose and strong jaw, her short, no-nonsense dark blonde hair, her photographer's vest, all spelled business. She was just doing her job. He shouldn't fault her for that.

As he exited, Luke waved at the peculiar redhead who self-consciously dangled a camera from his neck, finger at the ready on the shutter button; smiled graciously at Selonnah, reached to shake her hand, wished her a good day. At the last minute, he remembered something important. He stepped back inside, pulled the door securely shut for a moment.

"Ah, Chief, one more thing. You've got an interview at 11 this morning with Dr. Terrance Jensen from BYU—you know, the guy who found Kirsten Young. He says he has some important information, and he won't talk to anyone but you. Said it was a priesthood matter."

But though Helaman nodded, Luke wasn't sure the information registered. Luke pressed below the flotsam of his thoughts the discomfort that kept bobbing to the surface. They'd have to squeeze in a few minutes today or tomorrow to look at the autopsy report. Maybe he'd feel better later when they discussed the final secrets that Kirsten Young's body had harbored.

From: [mailto:adam1830@hivenet.net]
Sent: Monday, June 3
To: liahona@hivenet.net
Subject: [none]

My Sarah St. George,

You know why I address you thus? Only I know this name. Do you
not remember that?

Wait, my princess, wait. Of course you could not have understood
the significance of the proofs. I expected that you would read about
them in the newspaper. But nothing has appeared—yet. Soon you
will understand. Do not despise, my beloved, the medium of the
newspaper. It is a Rameumptom, a tower of proclamation, from
which you will hear a message about my devotion to you, and to the
ancient ways of our faith.

Be patient, my goddess. You will see.

And—you are mine and mine alone.

Adam, your Adam

CHAPTER 14

THERE ARE SOME SOUNDS, each innocuous and perhaps even pleasing if disassociated from its source, that can breed fear and heartsickness: the opening of a refrigerator door and the rolling forward of an aluminum can, the sign-on chime of a computer late at night, the furtive click of a car door being shut.

Roger had his own fear-sound; actually, as much a sensation as a sound, the inferred timbre that accompanied the feeling of a seam ripping. On one of the most important newscasts of his career, he had leaned forward in his wheeled anchorman's chair during the quick moments of a commercial break, and put his head between his knees to retrieve the cap to his pen that had fallen between his feet. The sensation of tiny popping sounds as the seam of his trousers gave way reminded him that he'd noticed—and dismissed—that very morning the fact that the inner seam was frayed.

Now the last bastion of his Tennessee boy's modesty was

gone. And he would have to get up in ten more minutes, make his backward retreat, and hope no one noticed as he walked, fruitlessly searching his memory for what color briefs he'd put on in the prehistory of the morning. With those tiny popping sounds, he saw cascading scenarios unfolding: the walk to his dressing room; the confirmation of his fears that he had only spare shirts and ties but no trousers there; strategies for getting to his car; an inventory of resources—who might help him? Who had some gym shorts? How about a towel? Shame and lack. Who might have needle and thread?

That incident happened fifteen years ago, but the heat on his face still arose when he thought of it. He wondered if phrases he'd heard before—about one's life falling apart, about ripping open at the seams—really could convey the sick-stomach feeling he felt growing within him. As he looked around his knotty-pine paneled kitchen, he pondered how very small things could create an entire mental world of domino effects, each worse than the last.

At that very moment, sitting in the cottonwood-filtered light, his palm flat against the security of a red-checkered tablecloth, he felt the sound of the tiny seams of his life stretching, giving way, exposing, threatening a retreat in uncontrolled, raveled disarray.

Before him on the table were papers he had gathered and scattered and then gathered again like the ten lost tribes. He was no closer to coherence with the papers than with that which they chronicled, the top-secret meeting he had attended at LDS Church Headquarters early that morning.

He winced at the memory of the atmosphere of forced fraternalism mixed with what he'd finally characterized in his own mind as a kind of desperation of dispatch.

"Brethren, we have a situation here that has been designed, engineered, to make the Church look bad." This flat statement came from a grim-lipped Alma Fielding Cronin, a grey man who was the secretary and assistant to the triumvirate of upper leadership known as the First Presidency: the Mormon prophet-slash-president and his two counselors.

Roger tried to visualize the meeting called by the three men Cronin served. One man was in such poor health that he couldn't walk alone nor even feed himself, the second nearing his nineties with diminishing vigor, and the third bedfast and (it was whispered) his mind failing more rapidly than his body.

No, Roger decided, Cronin's information had been vetted by a larger committee, probably some or most of the next tier of leadership known as the Council of the Twelve Apostles. There, Roger knew, younger—if you could call the average age of the group at eighty "younger"—and more media-savvy heads would have prevailed to put the proper spin on something that was beginning to counterspin out of control. They must have jumped on this, he thought grimly to himself, faster than you could say "apostolic interregnum."

Roger's mind began to reel. Early this morning, he had no idea why he'd been called out of his office at BYU where he was preparing notes for an upcoming class lecture. Last week's emails from Church Headquarters about Kirsten Young were a high alert, he knew; but he'd thought that no matter how gruesome and symbol-laden her murder, this was something finite, containable.

His suspicions of course heightened with the warnings of Bishop Filbert Rasmussen at church on Sunday. But Salt Lake City Police Lt. Luke Taylor confided in what he'd assumed would be complete secrecy (how little he knew that the chain of revelation went backward too!) to his own bishop about both the death of Heber J. Bruce and the desecration of the body of a pitiful prostitute named Bernadette Rodriguez.

Then the gears of the church began to grind against each other hours before this morning's meeting. One of the Church's primary functions—out of self-protection, Roger thought ruefully—was public image-making. And that image was now threatened by its connection with three very public and gruesome murders.

What all three crimes had in common were their references to peculiarities of Mormon doctrine—in fact, as Cronin put it, "elements that could be considered insider information."

Roger knew that you could walk into any Mormon bookstore in the country, look at every book on their shelves, and never know the meaning of the marks on Kirsten Young's body, the marks that mimic the buttonhole-like embroideries worn next to the skin of every Mormon bishop and his wife, every priesthood leader and his wife, every missionary on the field. Hundreds of thousands—maybe even millions—of people today, in leadership positions from the local ward upward, wore those marks on garments next to their most tender skin every single day. Each embroidery-thickened mark represented a vow to be kept, passwords to be remembered, handshakes and embraces and power-drenched secret names that meant the difference between eternal royalty and eternal servitude. And yet nobody talked about these things—except perhaps husband to wife in a locked bedroom, or maybe slack-handed father to distracted soon-to-be missionary son. Only within the fortified walls of a temple did anyone really discuss them, invite and address questions, speak of them aloud and boldly.

Now a violent someone—the "insidious person," Cronin had described—had made them public. As he spoke Cronin's tone was acrid and restrained, as if he were only by an act of the will keeping himself from irretrievable profanity. Now for Mormons everywhere, everything previously kept under the wraps of polite conversations would have to be explained around. The "faint line between the sacred and the secret" didn't exist in the minds of nonbelievers, everyone knew that; that's why for over 175 years such things could never be even hinted at.

Cronin's clenched-teeth briefing presented Roger with the LDS Church's upcoming "official statement" that Roger would deliver at a press conference tomorrow. Two personalities well known in the Salt Lake City community had been murdered, Kirsten Young and Heber J. Bruce. Reports were leaking like a jelly sack about possible ties to the LDS Church because of the marks on Kirsten Young and the wildfire rumors about something similar on Bruce's body. And then there was the note on Bruce, written in the Deseret Alphabet. Suddenly an obscure cipher had become the subject of whispers and speculations.

Roger's responsibilities were spelled out and Teflon-bulleted: Deflect attention from the LDS Church, implore—even woo—reporters to not press for information about sacred matters, express shock and outrage at the very concept of murder, point at BYU's Law School as proof that the LDS Church supports the U.S. Constitution and all things lawful.

It was unspoken but palpable: *Distance the Church from anything strange. Disavow the quaint anomalies of the past. Spotlight its freckles, demur modestly about its surgical scars.*

Smile. Ingratiate. Be saddened and wounded by anything that looks like criticism. Shake your head as if ignorant of Bernadette Rodriguez—be indeed ignorant of her, surely she had nothing to do with any of the rest of this.

For more than two hours Cronin and two spike-haired media advisors, Oliver and Martin, verbally groomed Roger, even sparred with him in rehearsals for the press conference. Roger began to feel that the grooming wasn't just of his words, it was of his attitudes; powdering any shine of his own personality, probing and proving and trimming his loyalties to size.

They'd done their homework, creatively, and he must do his.

"If anyone asks about the Deseret Alphabet, emphasize its similarity to the Cherokee Syllabary developed by Sequoia in the early 1800s," Cronin coached. "Tell them, just because something is written in an obscure Cherokee text from two hundred years ago, that doesn't prove any connection to the Cherokee people of today, does it?" He stopped, thinking for a moment. "The press won't go after a Native American nation—why should they go after us?"

Roger nodded, saw the reason in this, took notes reminding himself to do a Web search on Sequoia and a score of other matters that pointed to anything else but the Church. He loved the Church. Like Cronin and the other men, he would do all he could, offer the best of his talents, to make sure that people didn't associate it with something as ghastly as those murders. The Church was heritage, home, community, blood, earth, heaven. It was above price, and to be protected at all costs.

The meeting—or was it a commission?—ended when Cronin stood with his fingertips spread on the black marble conference tabletop. "Do not go beyond what is in the official statement," he said. "Field questions but don't be afraid to say to a pushy reporter that you don't know some answers and will have to get back to them on something."

The press was adversary. Roger did not tell them that he was harboring the enemy in his own home. He didn't know how to begin. Then he was dismissed from the meeting as abruptly as he'd been summoned.

He needed time to digest all this. He ached with the

absence of Eliza. He craved her company, but she was volunteering today, chaperoning Maria's day school trip to a goat farm outside the city. She would be out of cell phone reach for hours; while admidst kids and kids, she wouldn't be able to discuss freely what was troubling him, even if she had a clear connection.

Even worse, on Friday Eliza and Maria were going to fly out to the East Coast to begin a ten-day bus tour of LDS historical sites that would meander from Upper New York State back to Salt Lake City.

Months ago, the three of them listed and pored over the itinerary's exotic names, and Maria had chanted them in joy like a litany: *Palmyra, Palmyra, Palmyra, Palmyra.* Maria sang, swayed, swept her arms in front of her. Roger explained. In the Sacred Grove there in New York, Joseph Smith said God and Jesus had spoken to him. Face-to-face. See this painting? Glorious light, light all around. All the other churches were wrong, said Eliza, young Joseph must set things aright.

Sacred Grove. Maria whispered it.

Hill Cumorah, Hill Cumorah! Maria chanted the words and awaited their decipherment: In New York State, the site of the final great battle where the last of the white-skinned Native Americans died. Sixteen centuries ago, here in America. Mounding hill, see here? where the gold plates of the Book of Mormon now lie hidden once again. Legends of hidden rooms, treasure in wagons, gold everywhere deep within its depths. Now, the site of a great drama attended by thousands each summer; the pageant they would attend. *Hill Cumorah Pageant*, Maria breathed.

Nauvoo, Nauvoo, the beautiful plantation. Maria danced. A commandeered table scarf whirled around her, her braids maypoling. The master-planned city of plats and promises, of so many hopes, abandoned in the middle of the night.

Adam-ondi-Adam. Ah, ah. Maria shook her head, fists to her cheeks, couldn't say so many syllables, could never sing them. She clasped her hands in front to listen. The place in Missouri, where Adam, the father of mankind, called his posterity together. Just outside the locked gates of the biblical garden of Eden. All of the rest of the world was mistaken, said Eliza, the garden of Eden had been here, in this God-blessed nation, in Jackson County, Missouri.

Far West, the massacre site at Haun's Mill, Winter's Quarters. . . . The scarf stopped its twirl and settled to the floor as Maria paused, ingested the sorrow in her father's voice. Pain, such pain. But we survived, we went westward, until Brigham Young said, "This is the place."

This is the place, this is the place. Maria posed solemnly, leaning forward with one arm outstretched, finger pointed, a Pioneer Day picture.

Gentiles would never understand these things, the meaning of these places. They were a secret treasure, a sequestered heritage hidden in plain sight among the Gentiles who walked their streets but didn't, couldn't understand.

Eliza's words were brief, tender. These are holy places.

Holy places.

Thus the summer trip promised treasures of discovery, memories for lifetimes. For months, Maria daily checked her little purple backpack, whose straining zippers imprisoned granola bars, lime lip balm, a compass, a collapsing umbrella, the discarded cell phone that would still, she'd been told, dial 911 if they could, alas, only find the charger. Eliza, for her part, was glad to just be a participant in a tour, with no responsibilities. She hadn't even unpacked completely yet from the trip to the Middle East.

Neither she nor Roger had factored in the effect of the

proximity of this trip with Eliza's previous trip. Only five days separated the two.

The counting of the days cleaved Roger. Not enough time, there was never enough, never a satiety of Eliza. What he drank of her presence never satisfied. She was like seawater to him.

Though he thought sometimes that he knew her intimately, he hadn't known her first. An area of her past was impenetrable shale with eroding inscriptions, walls that he had no hope of ever breaching. These were the stories once-mentioned and sworn to shun: a previous marriage, long-entombed secrets about kidnappings and betrayals too deep for even Eliza's vast vocabulary, or her will to speak aloud. These were cauterized memories for her.

He didn't care. The Eliza of now was all that mattered to him. He tried to distract himself from the borrowed future loneliness of her upcoming trip by busying himself with Internet research, answering emails, tweaking of the class he'd give at BYU tomorrow afternoon.

Only after that could he face the pile of notes and instructions about the news conference. He began repeating key phrases aloud, trying them on like an older brother's hand-me-down clothes.

This was a matter of honor, he reminded himself. He had been called into service for something noble and good, the protection of things noble and good.

But when he spoke, his voice in the kitchen startled him. He tried to identify the source of the sound behind the sound, the lack of resonance in the room. It was as if his words were slapping the pine cabinets, careening randomly off the varnished surfaces, settling in mica-thin sheets at his feet.

"We are as shocked as the rest of the world by this meaningless violence."

"Of course, the Church is deeply troubled by the deaths of these members of the community."

"The president of the Church of Jesus Christ of Latter-day Saints joins its twelve million members worldwide—your friends and neighbors—in expressing sincere sympathy to the family members who have lost their loved ones."

"Although police say some aspects of these crimes were staged to try to draw attention to events of the nineteenth century, during the time before Utah was even a state, the Church categorically denies any knowledge or involvement in these heinous crimes."

"We offer our resources and the watchful eyes of our law-abiding members to aid the local, state, and national law enforcement authorities as they track down the criminals responsible for these acts."

Roger sat quietly for a moment. He was pretty sure that there were resources the Church would never give to a gentile world. He had heard of secret vaults of documents, chocolate-colored seerstones, round as eggs in the hand. Peepstones with holes. Charms and Jupiter talismans. Disavowed alphabets and grammars, demoted lectures on faith. Runes and ruses. Forged documents of a father's blessing. And bottomless amounts of money paid out, perennial rumors of the high cost of protecting the reputation of men— and doctrines—long dead.

The phone sounded tinny in the kitchen. Selonnah was coming home, had to talk to him alone for a while, would explain when she got there.

He gathered up all the residual papers from the press conference meeting. Selonnah shouldn't be allowed to see these things. Even Eliza shouldn't. He noticed on his notes from the meeting that he had underlined the word "must," over and over again.

He felt nerves tighten in his stomach, as if hemp cords were being pulled through his dry insides. He tamped the papers into his briefcase and rearranged the chairs of the wooden dinette, one chair here, two there, one here; then began pacing.

He had the time; he would rehearse now what he would tell Selonnah. Surely she would see the Mormon Church as something separate from these horrible events, if he told her using their common language.

"Selonnah." Again he heard his words strike the knotty-pine cabinets. He softened, modulated his voice.

"Selonnah. I know you want to know about these murders, and what they have to do with Mormon doctrine. Yes, I know. I know it's frustrating, seen from the outside. I would be happy to explain.

"I promised you yesterday that we would talk about Kirsten Young, and about the marks on her body. I want to help you understand this with semiotics. Remember how we said that facts and representations are not the same things? How the picture of the apartment in your head, your recollection of what it looks like, is a representation. . . . But we know it's not the same as the apartment itself, the fact of that apartment."

Roger drew a breath, collected himself.

"It's true that the marks on Kirsten Young's body are of the same configuration, and the same location on her body, as embroidered marks on the temple garments that many Latter-day Saints wear. I myself wear these garments."

He brushed his hand across his chest, swept it toward his knee.

"For us, for faithful LDS, those are representations of information, promises. . . . " He stopped. How to explain to Selonnah that the *facts*, the essence of the promises in a temple, couldn't be articulated, couldn't be discussed outside a temple? He began again.

"The garments, and their markings, are representations of facts. Those facts are precious to us, too precious to even talk about aloud."

He stopped again. How to explain it?

"Some things are too sacred to share. For instance, the marital relationship, the physical relationship that Eliza and I have, is sacred. It's not shameful, but on the other hand, I don't discuss it with anyone. Like the garments, and the promises that they represent, they're too precious to discuss."

He stopped, satisfied with how rotundly that explained something that was itself beyond language.

"Those are facts, those promises are facts, that we cache in our memories and we treasure them daily with the representations of them, sewn into garments that we wear, right next to our skin, almost as if those promises are skin to us.

"Now, someone has taken the symbols of those promises that faithful Mormons make, while inside a temple—the representational marks. And those representations have been harnessed to say something that neither Mormons, nor our Church, would ever say. In essence, someone, for some reason I don't know, has re-represented the representations."

Perhaps if he could make her understand that.

"The same is true," he began again, the sound ricocheting around the angles of the room, "of another recent murder. The victim's name is Heber J. Bruce. He had marks on his body too. . . ."

How could he explain to Selonnah that those marks on the poor man's corpse were symbols, representations, of promises that were, themselves, made only symbolically? His head began to ache. How could he explain the oaths—and their penalties?

Years ago in temple ceremonies, people promised not to reveal the secrets they learned there. They took oaths, and promised to have their throats cut, to be disemboweled, to have their tongues cut out. That was all true, all historical. Thank goodness the Mormon Church had seen the wisdom of toning that down a bit so that for the following fifty years in a Mormon temple you just agreed to have your life taken, and stood at attention while pulling your thumb across your jugular, or across your stomach. And how responsive the Church had been to sensibilities: In 1990 they had done away even with those pantomimes. A kinder and gentler set of vows and penalties.

But somebody had actually reified those penalties on the body of an apostate. A revealer of secrets. Heber J. Bruce knew the oaths, would have made the old vows years ago in the temple. Heber J. Bruce paid the penalties. Roger tried not to let his sense of justice, both offended and now satisfied, get in the way of his immediate problem. Selonnah would never understand this. And as for other reporters—that would never work.

"Don't you see, Selonnah?" His hands were outstretched, appealing to the best in his absent cousin. "The facts that these murders represent are not the facts of Mormonism."

The scrambling sound of keys in the front door shook him out of his rehearsal. He tripped over a dining chair in the rush to make sure all his papers were off the table, then stood back to survey the room.

He realized with dismay that he had arranged the chairs around the table just as you would before a camera, with one side of the table unoccupied. He wondered what it meant that he'd unconsciously set a stage, a scene for an audience, but a scene that no one in real life actually would live in.

He turned to see Selonnah walking into the kitchen

carrying a bulging satchel and keys. He took a breath, and looked for her smile.

It was not there. Selonnah looked frustrated. She made several false starts in her attempts to put her belongings down, looked narrowly at the table arrangement, and finally dumped it all onto the floor. Her voice had a tinge of irritation as she sank into a chair.

"Okay, Roger. They announced at the paper that you'll be the spokesman at the press conference tomorrow." She looked at him for his nodded confirmation, then continued. "It's time for us to talk about some things, off the record if you wish, but I have to know. I need to understand. What is the Deseret Alphabet? And I want to know about Kirsten Young, those marks on her body. I want to know about Heber J. Bruce. Why he was cut up that way."

Her voice was flat as suede. He noticed that it didn't clamor against the walls the way his had. He wondered about that.

"And I *really* want to know what the Book of Mormon has to do with the disfiguring of the corpse of a poor Catholic prostitute."

There it was, Roger thought. She couldn't hear the sound he dreaded. Seams straining, tiny threads breaking.

He felt, perhaps for the first time in his life, the palpable difference between salvation and salvage, and wondered if either was possible.

CHAPTER 15

THE PUNK KID wouldn't give his name, and since he didn't carry ID, no one could prove that he was anyone other than "Jet Johanssen," the name he whispered. That ancestral name seemed apocryphal at best—the rangy-boned kid was handsome but hardly Nordic. In fact, he looked perhaps Oriental and mostly Hispanic, even carried a residual accent that lengthened and mellowed all his vowels and made his consonants slippery on his tongue.

Jet called what he pulled out of his pocket "roofies." He repeated it, then tried another tack.

"You know, man, Roche, la rocha. Helps you with the ladies." His stubby fingers had long, straight black hairs on all the joints, even near the fingernails. He had a pocketful of the little white pills, separated into baggie portions for sale, looking for all the world like packets of extra collar buttons for businessmen's dress shirts.

Jet's lip trembled as he handed the fistful of the little bags over. His mouth was moving, ah—he seemed to be adding up his profits. His long wispy beardlet—more of the sparse straight hairs—made him look like a 64th note in the gusting wind. Then with a flapping of his leather vest and a jingling of its chains, he hurried away.

Roofies. Rohypnol. Sometimes called a "date rape drug," the colorless, odorless little tablets slow down the central nervous system of anyone who takes them.

"Well, we'll have to see about that."

The man who now held Jet Johanssen's pills stood in his own home, the vestibule reflecting back at him his spoken words, the shutting of the door, the snap of the deadbolt in the lock. His cell phone was turned off, the television on a twenty-four-hour news station.

The man piled blankets and pillows into the upstairs bathtub and sat on the edge of it as he drank the glass of water and took what he'd identified on the Internet to be an "effective dose" of the drug he got from Johanssen. Then he locked the door and waited.

He would later remember the sensation that he was watching a DVD of himself, and that he could pause himself, or slow himself down, or speed himself up, at least at first. Then he could zoom in. But mainly it was the increasing sensation of frame-by-frame deceleration. When he knew he would soon pass out, he settled himself into the tub with two books and began to read from the first one.

"Then say, what is truth? 'Tis the last and the first,
For the limits of time it steps o'er.
Though the heavens depart and the earth's fountains burst,
Truth, the sum of existence, will weather the worst,
Eternal, unchanged, evermore."

He felt nauseated. He threw the book across the room,

and a stainless steel toothbrush holder clattered into the sink. He reached for the other book.

"Could I revive within me
Her symphony and song . . ."

His eyes were burdened, beyond weariness. The light fixture was twirling. He continued on, from memory, the book open on his chest.

"To such a deep delight 'twould win me,
That with music loud and long,
I
would build
that
dome
in air . . ."

When he awakened he felt like what had been described to him as a hangover. The headache was gargantuan. He slowly, slowly pulled himself up and toward the edge of the bathtub and found to his dismay that he had vomited.

He filled the water glass and drank it, then looked at his watch. Eight hours had passed. And he remembered nothing of them, not the vomiting, not the scattering of magazines from a rack; had no explanation for why the pillows were all against the door. But the door was still locked. He was stiff and queasy. But he felt very, very satisfied. He had tested the drug and knew its effects.

He retrieved the book that was still in the tub with him, and was grateful it had no stain. He opened it again and read, rubbing his eyes as he spoke the words to jump-start his voice:

"That sunny dome! those caves of ice!
And all who heard should see them there,
And all should cry, Beware! Beware!
His flashing eyes, his floating hair!

Weave a circle round him thrice,
And close your eyes with holy dread,
For he on honey-dew hath fed,
And drunk the milk of Paradise."

Cleanup of the bathroom was relatively easy, given the small amount of floor space. He put the soiled linens into the washing machine and noted with relief that when he turned his cell phone back on, there had been no missed calls. He then went back upstairs and showered. He had a date this morning.

As he had done nearly every morning of the last six months, he entered the downtown Honeybee Cafe just as it opened. The slot of a business peeked out from between offices on one side and a dollar store on the other, and maximized its space and waitstaff by its crowded seating and self-serve beverage dispensers before a trompe l'oeil painting of an archway in the back.

The whole place seemed a bit drunken because of the way the lines of the grey floor tiles listed noticeably to the right. Obviously installed by somebody's nephew. If you started walking in the middle and continued along the lines, you would never make it to the beverages.

He waved at the waitress who blew a lock of hair away from her nose in greeting. Words were superfluous for such a regular customer who tipped decently. She clipped his order for huevos rancheros into the string across the open window where two cooks hunkered down over the grills, furiously tapping the sides of stout metal spatulas across the hash browns and scrambled eggs.

He filled up three juice glasses with orange juice and without spilling a drop set one on the table near the window, then carried the two others to the table in the corner where Alma and Mary Ann Angell Woodruff sat. They smiled at him timidly.

"Thank you," said Alma. "Top of the morning, as usual!"

The man nodded with a faint smile at the elderly couple. "This orange juice will make hair grow on your chest," he said, just as he had said to them every weekday morning for the past five months.

The Woodruff woman had an impassive, naturally expressionless face that only became briefly animated in little outbreaks of understanding or emotion. Her mental engagement with her surroundings, the man had often thought, was like a revolving searchlight inside her skull that just for moments would traverse the eye sockets to glint out.

The light passed, and the woman tittered nervously. Then she and Alma looked down at their daily bran muffins, pushing pieces around with their forks and chewing deliberately, as actors do, with mostly empty mouths. Their daughter owned the restaurant, so they'd be coming there until they died.

Everybody knew the wiry, jolly white-haired man and his clingy, tiptoeing wife. They'd opened the restaurant forty years ago as cook and waitress, and when they'd passed it into the capable hands of their only child, they found they couldn't break many of their hardscrabble habits. (In fact they'd even gained some new ones, the man thought wryly.) But nonetheless their lives were still run on an internal calendar, that had them shopping on Saturday, church on Sunday, and doing temple work Tuesday, Wednesday, Friday.

Like many retired couples in the area, the Woodruffs volunteered at the Salt Lake City LDS Temple. Of course, while outside the temple they'd be the last to even hint at their roles there. But the last time the man took out vicarious endowments for the dead in that temple, he'd heard Alma Woodruff's Lord-voice booming behind the holy veil there in the temple, right after the obsequious "veil worker" had tapped with a mallet three times.

It's not every day, the man thought, that you can have the Lord out among us and serve him some orange juice.

And have him be afraid of you.

The man rattled coins into a newspaper dispenser and sat drinking his own orange juice and pretending to read the paper. How like the Brownings this couple were, he thought. Their decades together had melded their personalities. You could not tell where one began or the other ended. He recited in his head, *You will wake, and remember, and understand.*

He saw them out of the corner of his eye. Alma was counting out the tip with flat-tipped fingers, from an oval plastic change holder that opened its slit mouth and spat out pennies and nickels as it did every morning. They both drained the orange juice glasses, tipping them back and licking the rim. *Penny-wise, pound-foolish,* the man thought; *getting and spending, we lay waste our powers.*

He knew their secret.

He was fairly certain that even the Woodruffs' daughter who owned the restaurant didn't know about her parents' drinking. That's why people like them bought vodka instead of scotch, after all. Couldn't be smelled on the breath, just made Alma more jovial and Mary Ann Angell more, well, angel. But one hint of that known publicly, and the sweet old couple would never be able to be temple workers again. Alma had driven drunk more than once; their inevitable public exposure was just a matter of time anyhow.

They waved at him, at the waitress, at the cooks, indeed at everyone in the crowded restaurant as they left, Alma glad-handing to the right and to the left. His empty-headed wife self-consciously swayed her chiffon skirt as she walked, but she was hipless as a boy.

The man winked at them, which he knew made them unsure of themselves. Then—he couldn't help himself from the sacrilege—he rapped the table three times, softly, with his knuckles.

Alma's face reddened. He hurried his gasping wife through the door.

This couple was about to go from being secretly well known to being famous. They'd never connect him to it, would think only of their shame of being exposed.

He thought of Browning again:

"There, that is our secret: go to sleep!"

CHAPTER 16

DEALING WITH LUGOSI—having to spend time with him, one-on-one—*would make a preacher cuss*, as Mary used to say. Selonnah blamed herself, should have seen it coming. Lugosi so adroitly finessed the situation that by the time he sprang the suggestion that he should spend the day "shadowing" Selonnah, Roberta Carlson had actually thought it was her own idea.

During all of that interminable Monday, he was right at Selonnah's side. She had the whole day to try to figure out why he irritated her so much.

It was his manner of communicating. He didn't just speak, he erupted. When something was on his mind, his body would shudder almost imperceptibly before his words spilled out, as if on the end of a whip being snapped. And such words—even at his best, Lugosi's words always came in a torrent of desperate authority, pleading, insisting even over the most trivial matters.

What he overheard with her outside the door of Chief Helaman had shaken him visibly. What's more, in it he heard a private reveille that urged him to try to defend Mormonism.

(First the shudder.) "I'm a faithful Mormon, and I never heard that about the Catholic Church being the whore of Babylon. That's ridiculous. Crazy. I don't know why they said that."

Silence, only a moment of silence, then the shudder again.

"And a Book of Mormon at that crime scene—so what? I mean, this is Salt Lake City. You see them everywhere! Look in the thrift stores—there are shelves of them. Couldn't that just be a coincidence?"

The shudder. "Deseret Alphabet. I looked that up online. Nobody uses that. I promise you the Prophet doesn't use it. Anyone could write a note in that code. It's just intended to make us, um, the LDS Church look bad. Not that the Church is ashamed of the Deseret Alphabet, of course! Nothing to be ashamed of there. They wrote primers for little kids in that script."

The shudder. "A prostitute. Bernadette, who? She's no Mormon. Didn't that Lt. Taylor say that? Right? She wasn't a Mormon. No siree, not LDS."

The shudder. The eruption. The shudder, the eruption. Shudder-eruptions, all day long. His mind was a scrolling marquee.

She dropped him off at the newspaper office to get his car, and even after he left her, she couldn't shake off the Lugosi-ness of him. She rolled down the window.

Git holt of yourself. The phrase reminded her to call and check on her mother. In the post-five traffic she juggled her cell phone and her frustrations, poorly in both regards. It was an hour later in Tennessee and her mother, a snippy aide told her, was at supper. Selonnah remembered the inviolate sacredness of mealtime to her mother and felt relieved that her mother's personality hadn't relinquished its only religion.

At least not yet. Selonnah felt again the desperation of being too far away to help her mother and too unable to do anything even if she were there.

And then there was the anxiety she felt whenever she thought of Police Chief Helaman M. Petersen. She hoped—desperately hoped—he had no idea of how his physical presence affected her—and apparently, other women as well. She herself had no explanation for it. He wore a ring on his left hand, and his conversations with her had been brief and hardly warm. But why did he leave his office door open when he saw her and Lugosi outside? It was almost as if he wanted her to hear what went on inside. (Because she was a reporter? Because she was a gentile reporter?) What she heard had not given her any insights—it had, like Hydra, grown more heads each time she tried to cut one off for examination.

And would her cousin Roger be any help in understanding these things?

She knew that one of the things she disliked most about herself was her tendency to enjoy proving people wrong. When she was a teenager, she'd overheard her mother telling a friend on the phone that Selonnah couldn't tell the difference between a Volkswagen and a Lincoln Continental. A bit of an exaggeration, Selonnah now knew, but not a great overstatement about the daughter who simply didn't care about anything that ran on wheels or could be propelled across a field to put points on a scoreboard. Selonnah, who was in fact oblivious to automobiles (and irritated by sports), saw in her mother's comment both a deficiency in her teenage persona and a challenge.

Like sayin' sic 'em to a dog. The teenage Selonnah had spent the next three months at the library looking at car magazines and *Consumer Reports*. The first available opportunity that anyone said anything about the new car models while she was in her mother's presence, Selonnah pounced. RPMs and pistons, bucket seats and cargo space. She reeled it all out with a dry, bitter sideways look at her mother who stood with her mouth open. And who never criticized her daughter's deficiencies again.

But the habit had stuck, unfortunately, and Selonnah hated the way she prepared herself for *gotcha* with everyone she knew. It had cost her friends, boyfriends, even grades when she couldn't resist doing it to professors.

And she didn't want to ambush Roger, but the conversation between the two police officers disturbed her nearly as much as it apparently had Lugosi. It seemed to her that Roger had not been entirely open with her, and she found that, in her heart, she was laying for him. She wanted to spring on him this "found" information from what she overheard outside the police chief's office.

With the press release that came to the newspaper office announcing the upcoming press conference, Selonnah felt that she had perhaps only this one shot tonight to extract from Roger what she wanted to know. After tomorrow, when Roger became the official LDS spokesperson about the strange events and murders in the Salt Lake area, she felt that a door would close, lines would be drawn, loyalties revealed. She was not so certain that family loyalty would trump her cousin's allegiance to the LDS Church.

How we cover for one another, she thought. Does loyalty redeem a situation?

Selonnah remembered an incident that happened when she was young. She was born with a congenital defect in her bladder, one for which her maturing body compensated by the time she reached her teens. But up until that time, normal activities—sleepovers, recess, even field trips in elementary school—were always strategized: when to drink liquids and how much, packing a change of underwear and slacks.

She lived in the irrational fear of discovery that only a child can understand. But her mother signed her up for a four-day summer camp in the Blue Canyon in northern New Mexico between the fifth and sixth grades, assuring her that her "accidents" were becoming so much less frequent that she shouldn't be afraid. Selonnah for her part was elated that she awakened each morning to a dry sleeping bag, and the last day went out on a hike without preparation.

As she rounded the last bend in the path near the precipitous Red Flag Hill, her capricious bladder released. She let herself lag to the back of the gaggle of girls. When her camp counselor Cari Ann, who alone looked back to check on her, saw her distress and the stain on her khaki slacks, she seemed to know just what to do. Cari Ann uncapped her water bottle, trotted back toward Selonnah, and then shrieked in feigned distress as she pretended to stumble and spill the water all over Selonnah's midsection.

"Look at me, how clumsy I am! Oh, Selonnah, I'm so sorry! Look, I spilled my water all over you! Good thing it's a hot day—it'll dry soon!"

All the wet clothing dried. Nobody ever knew. For the rest of her life, Selonnah lived on the desire to believe that even the most hopeless situation could have a Red Flag Hill redemption.

She felt the weight of an unexpurgated life. Could there be a redemption now? As she drove into the driveway of Roger and Eliza's house, Selonnah wondered: Would they be cousins, or spokesman and reporter?

From: [mailto:adam1830@hivenet.net]
Sent: Monday, June 3
To: liahona@hivenet.net
Subject: [none]

Your email this morning broke my heart. Do you not know the price I have paid to prove to you that I have believed—and instantiated—the teachings of Joseph and Brigham? I have enfleshed the ancient order of Sampson Avard, fought as a Danite, become an Avenging Angel, all for you. You've been bought with blood, or better said, your straying loyalty has been purchased with proofs.

Listen to what Avard said! "I would swear to a lie to clear any of you; and if this would not do, I would put them or him under the sand as Moses did the Egyptian." Like Avard, I would do anything for you. I *have done* everything for you.

But now you tell me that you still choose to go through with such a marriage.

For the first time in my life, I begin to doubt that God ever authorized that kind of marriage. And if He didn't authorize it, why did Joseph and Brigham and all the early Church leaders practice it? What does that say about all the foundations of the church? How much of all that we have held dear, that I have reified with my own blood-soaked hands, how much of that was *ever true*?

What about the Book of Mormon? What about the other teachings?

Did Joseph truly do more for mankind than anyone else, save . . .

Can it be that all we have treasured, the preciousness of continuing revelation and eternal progression, can it be that these must be questioned?

My heart is in turmoil.

CHAPTER 17

THERE AREN'T ANY truly effective ways to describe sciatic pain, Roger thought. Everyone in his father's side of the family mutely succumbed to it eventually, generations of articulate people who came to the ends of their lives paupered of words for this sensation. Before he injured his back three years ago, he had nodded with absent sympathy at other people's depictions of pain shooting down the leg, seen their rolling gait that seemed to convert flat ground into nearly impassable undulating slopes, pondered the silent grimaces.

But there was nothing like the real deal in one's own body when the offended nerve filed suit.

Ibuprofen was like water drops into a hot skillet. Codeine was equally ineffective and made him crazy. Cortisone and epidurals: who could bear them long-term? The pain would appear without warning, ambushing his sensorium, as it had just minutes ago.

Such exquisite, abiding pain could only be fought fire to

fire, with another more dominant pain. He had read that Dr. Paul Brand, the great doctor who first cured leprosy, battled back problems; and Roger months ago turned to the same single relief the doctor had employed. Tonight, walking barefoot on the crushed gravel walk of his backyard, the searing in his back first muffled, then lost its pain-voice altogether. His fists clenched, and when he could trust his dominance of the sciatic, he went indoors.

A third pain, however, made his back and his feet as distant as if they belonged to someone else. The pain of his just-finished conversation with Selonnah, the sting more acrid than if she'd slapped him, called all his thoughts to order.

In the end, Selonnah stalked dissatisfied out the door after his best efforts to answer her questions. What seemed in Mormonism to Roger to be so simple and so logical—and so reasonable and kind—her mind chewed up and her mouth spat back at him. And no wonder—he had always depicted Mormonism as all-American; as something that fanned away the must of worldliness and breathed life-giving air; as sparkling water.

But his encounter with Selonnah, his defense of the Mormonism he loved, turned out to be a great mud puddle of a conversation: soupy, misunderstood phrases, murky undertones, distasteful flotsam, and a sense of unknown depths beneath the scum that floated on the surface. It clung to his ankles as drying spatters of uncertainty and regret, even after he walked—hobbled—away.

He had first tried to calm her, engage her mind, with a history of the Deseret Alphabet, thinking she would see the quaintness of it, the bittersweet obsolescence of the failed project and all its dashed hopes, the charm of the antique children's primer he held toward her as he invited—beseeched—her to see the curlicues on the letters, *look, here,* the pictures of the little ones at play.

Selonnah wasn't buying it. She wanted to know what was written in that *stumbling script* and left on the *tongue-less, gutted body* of Heber J. Bruce and the *fermenting belly* of Bernadette Rodriguez. Roger flinched at her bitten-off adjectives. He realized at the time that she must not yet know that another note—the "first proof" left near the incised corpse of Kirsten Young—had just today been surrendered by Terrance Jensen who found it and kept it until his conscience and curiosity overcame him. And this was in the Deseret Alphabet too, conclusively tying the three crimes together.

Selonnah had smelled the connection, even without the note. And she'd been relentless about the marks on Kirsten's body. Why was her throat slit? The way Heber J. Bruce was left, it had meaning too, *didn't it? Didn't it?*

She pulled from her briefcase two books. Roger's stomach unsettled itself when he saw the photographs in the first one. It depicted LDS temple robes: puffy white hats for the men, demure kerchiefs tied under the chin for the women, shapeless white robes, fig-leaf aprons. The photographs looked frumpy and inglorious. Some photos were staged depictions of handshakes and postures. Like Noah's backward-walking sons, Roger reached with averted eyes to cover the photographs as if they showed naked kin.

Selonnah looked at him with a long, hard look. She closed the book and put it on the carefully posed table. She looked long and hard at that too.

A stanza of silence.

She waited until Roger composed himself—he realized he'd been near to tears. Then she told Roger of what she'd heard Luke and Helaman discussing, about the Rodriguez woman—a prostitute—and the rambling passage Luke read about the whore of all the earth. And how Helaman said it was the Catholic Church.

Roger sprang to life at this, so gratified to be able to tell her that he'd never heard anything like that in his ten years of Mormonism, that the church officials had assured him it wasn't so. . . .

She held up another book. Roger read from photo reprints of documents. Two Mormon apostles and a Book of Mormon commentary widely used even in Eliza's time at BYU confirmed it. The older LDS documents identified the devil as the origin of the Catholic Church, while the more contemporary LDS sources just identified Catholicism as "the great and abominable church" of the Book of Mormon.

He didn't know what to say, felt an old, old feeling of being an outsider. An image commandeered his mind, of how in movies when groups of people were singing, the sound would emphasize the voice of each person the camera rested on. Now he had the unsettling sensation that there were intoning voices he didn't recognize, emerging unbidden and unwelcome in the chorus of what he thought he knew.

"I'll get my answers somewhere, Roger," she said in leaving. He tried to tell her there were many things she didn't know, many sources she couldn't trust. She stood at the open door, turned three-quarters toward him, and held her palms out to him.

There was nothing either could say. She prevented the door from slamming with her heel, but she didn't look back again.

Roger began to move the books Selonnah left but hesitated and decided to cover them with a newspaper. He sat with head in his hands and began calculating hours. Eliza's outing with Maria's school group was over, but his girls had gone for a fast-food dinner and then on to a church activity.

If only Eliza would come home so he could talk to her, he thought. Since the first hours he knew her, he began seeing the world with four eyes, a lover's double vision, a synopsis of souls.

He did not know exactly how much to share with her, yet not sharing all his fears with her felt like perjury. He craved her support for the ordeal he would face tomorrow as he stood in his anchorman best to defend the best Church in the world against the best reporters. Yet he could not share everything with her because he had to protect her.

She had seemed blissfully unaware, for instance, of the atmosphere he entered when he became a professor at Brigham Young University. Nearly two decades ago, the academic community there had been rocked by—and subsequently purged of—one of its best historians and five other scholars. Dubbed "the September Six," all but one had been excommunicated by the LDS Church; and a pall—he thought of it as an emotional muzak—hummed omnipresently over any kind of thinking outside the Mormon box on campus, especially in areas that involved feminism or critical looks at Mormon history. None of these had been "issues" for Roger. His friends and the few colleagues at the university with whom he had much contact were all straight-arrow Mormons like him.

Eliza always seemed untouched by such controversies. Her Church job as a Relief Society teacher and her chosen profession as a travel agent put her neither into the position of controversy nor, as far as he could see, questioning. His mind pictured her iconographically with strong brown hands and steady eyes surveying what many Mormons sarcastically called Happy Valley. There she was protected from the Babylon of the outside world, deaf to any criticisms of the Zion she loved.

Unlike most women he knew, Eliza preferred listening to speaking. Roger yearned for her help in sorting out things. He began to list mentally the press conference issues that Cronin and others had briefed him on. He wasn't nervous about the searching eyes of cameras; he got over stage fright. Tomorrow would be a show like many other shows he'd done. Twenty minutes of representations. He thought of his semiotics background, hoping it would anchor, arrange, create a welcome taxonomy of his thinking. Twenty minutes of representations.

First there were the events and the objects associated with them: the facts. He thought back to how a semiotician would explain a fact as an event, a circumstance, a person, an object. Facts, thus, are morally neutral. They are what they are.

But all facts are once removed from us by representations, he thought, only accessible by representations. You don't have a mountain in your head, you have an iconic representation by which you remember what it looks like.

His job would be to wrangle representations. He couldn't do anything about facts.

The marks on Kirsten Young's body were facts. The Church's practice of blood atonement in the past was a fact. Polygamy was a fact. *Polygamy is* a fact, he thought ruefully. In his meeting Cronin had ground out between his teeth the statistics. Local newspapers estimated the number of polygamists in Utah alone as ranging between three and ten thousand persons. And on any given day, one of them was giving an interview on a national talk show, or was portrayed in a television drama. *Big Love* was big news, a revelation to all of America except Utah.

Worst of all, polygamy was headlined when a practitioner was featured as one of the top ten fugitives wanted by the

FBI, and when a fundamentalist Mormon enclave was raided by the state of Texas.

Roger drew himself up, posing. "Such plural marriages are not sanctioned nor approved by the Church of Jesus Christ of Latter-day Saints, which declared such marriages illegal in 1890," he intoned to the knotty-pine cabinets. He imagined a reporter nodding with satisfaction that this had been all cleared up. And then another reporter bringing up all the communities in the Southwestern states where plural marriage was the tacit elephant in everyone's neighbor's parlor. And bedroom.

Roger's front door opened and he let out a gasp of relief. The girls were home.

"Goat farms are not clean places," Eliza announced wearily. She left their hay-spiked shoes at the threshold and went upstairs to shower. Little Maria stumbled with fatigue on the stairs and nodded between sentences as Roger bobby-pinned her braids to the top of her head. In the bathtub he tenderly washed and anointed her with potions that smelled like bubble gum and lilacs. When Eliza emerged with her own familiar waft of spearmint and almond, he remembered that he hadn't eaten. They laid Maria's limpness into her bed and went downstairs.

"I'm anxious about tomorrow and want to run some things past you," Roger began as he pulled a bubbling cheese sandwich from under the broiler. "There are so many land mines that I have to steer people away from. I wondered if you're too tired to let me talk through them with you."

Eliza's face clouded as she sipped a glass of water. "Go ahead. I've gotten my second wind, as your Tennessee folks would say. I'll listen. I'll—" Here she hesitated. "I'll listen."

The melted cheese dripping onto his hand took Roger's

attention away from the reticence in her voice. He fanned the sandwich and began.

"Tomorrow I have to be authoritative. I have to steer questions, wrangle them, corral them." Here Eliza smiled at his verbal images and dipped her head to acknowledge his fellowship with where she had spent her day.

"There are so many hypersensitivities to things about Mormonism's past, you know," he said, and Eliza nodded alertly, seemed about to speak, but didn't. "But what I have to get across is that these things are just that—part of the past—but not the character of Mormonism's present nor future."

"So the press conference is about the Church's image?" Eliza asked. "When you called me on my cell phone today, it seemed that the press conference was about these murders—the prostitute, that poor man who was killed along with the bears, Kirsten Young." She counted them off on weary fingers. "I thought you were just the Church's 'presence,' so to speak, maybe to answer questions that law enforcement might not want to—because of what the newspapers were saying about a note in the Deseret Alphabet that was found with that man."

The cell phone conversation after their goat farm experience had been rushed, Roger remembered.

"No, this press conference was called by the Church, not any law enforcement entities. In fact,"—here he didn't know whether to be modest or defensive—"I am the press conference."

His job would be to keep on topic, to massage questions to produce the answers he wanted—no, yearned—to give. But what he saw in Eliza's face mirrored all his fears.

A thread popped. There would be no sidebar featurettes, no sound-bite experts, no commercial breaks to check his hair.

He was the whole show. His task would be as much deflection as enlightenment, and more rode on his performance than a job or a raise or a career. Surely Eliza saw what that meant.

He hastened to reassure her. "But don't worry—the Church has people—many of them—who are full-time researchers, who spend every day working on explanations that Gentiles would understand. And of course money is no object. BYU has a Web site, and scores of individuals do too, that make it their ministry to defend the Church." He saw her eyebrows rise. "And they provide explanations for us too! There are so many books out right now that dredge up old history, and try to make the Church look bad. And the Internet—it's opened up all kinds of issues."

Again the odd look on Eliza's face. She seemed to struggle with something, began to speak, stopped herself, and then began again.

"What kinds of issues—I mean, what explanations are you talking about?"

He spread his arms out as if scooping up papers being blown away by a sudden wind. "Oh, my goodness. You know, sweet Eliza, so many things are being published right now. You don't really need to worry about them."

"I want to worry about them." Her voice was uncharacteristically flat. He eyed her with a nascent uncertainty. Surely, surely she meant that she would worry on his behalf, about the press conference.

"Well, for instance, one of the aims of the press conference is to show that, although the Church certainly invented the Deseret Alphabet, that doesn't mean that all uses of it are authorized by the Church. One of the things I was told to mention is that just because somebody wrote something in the Cherokee alphabet, that doesn't reflect negatively on Sequoia. That will make sense, don't you think?"

Eliza nodded. "What other issues will you be addressing?"

"Well, there's the delicate matter of blood atonement—you know that whenever anybody is killed and Mormonism is involved, critics and old-timers alike bring up that issue too. I have to be ready to respond there too."

"What will you say about blood atonement?"

"The Apostle Bruce R. McConkie said there's not a single historical instance of what people call blood atonement in the Church's history."

Eliza folded her arms and sighed. "Roger, you've not been a Mormon your whole life, like I have. Everybody knows—we were all taught—that there are certain sins you can commit that aren't covered by the sacrifice of Christ. That you have to have your own blood shed in order to atone. Like if you murder an innocent person. Why do you think we had capital punishment by firing squad for so long in Utah? Haven't you read Norman Mailer's book *The Executioner's Song*?"

Roger did not know which astonished him more: what she was saying, or the fact that his Eliza of such few words was so passionately articulate. He felt like a heavy sack of grain that she was ripping open with her words. Part of him was rushing out the gap. . . .

Eliza continued. "Don't you know about the Danite 'avenging angels' that Brigham Young would dispatch to people who left the Church? Why, there are even people you know—and know well—who are descendants of the very people who carried out blood atonements!"

She was swallowing, hard, but went on. "And what do you do with the findings of legitimate historians inside and outside the Church who would say that the Church's denials of blood atonement in the 1800s is just bunk? Like Juanita Brooks, who wrote on the Mountain Meadows Massacre? She called blood atonement 'a literal and terrible reality.'"

"You've been reading these books? Why?"

"Not just them. On the plane on the way to Egypt, I met a woman who was doing research for a theology degree. I had known about the old books, the Zane Grey and Arthur Conan Doyle books, and others that caricatured Mormonism and blood atonement. Those were books by outsiders. But I was up to the challenge, I thought. I knew I could defend the Church. So I wasn't afraid to borrow some books she had, and I read them every evening. Some nights I didn't sleep at all."

She wrung her hands, distraught and spent. Her elbow knocked over her glass of water. They both jumped to sop the spill with kitchen towels. For the first time, Eliza seemed to notice the pile of newspapers that covered the books Selonnah had left.

"Where did these come from?"

Roger stared at them as if they had been deposited by aliens, then watched with horror as Eliza picked one up and held it toward him.

"Selonnah left them . . ." he began.

"I've read this one," Eliza said matter-of-factly. "There are issues here that have to be addressed, and not with 'dodges' and self-protective hot oil over the battlements to quiet those who have questions.

"For Pete's sake, Roger. I just came back from Israel and Egypt. I visited all kinds of sites—Jericho, Jerusalem, Bethlehem—that are described in the Bible. They're still there. But there is not one single site mentioned in the Book of Mormon that can be identified. Even by hopeful Mormon so-called archaeologists! Probably because they never existed in the first place!"

Roger was speechless. Eliza's eyes softened.

"Roger, I brought you into all of this Mormonism mess. I asked you to be part of a world I thought was good, and healthy, and sane, and whole." She sighed and leaned back into her chair.

"I guess it had to come out. I was just too tired to deal with it when I first got home. I came back to my refuge and I found that it's become overgrown with thorns and burrs. You're here, and Maria is here, and I'm sure about you two—but not about anything else."

Roger felt chivalry rising within himself. "Let me help you. I'll get some explanations"—here her face seemed to harden, and he changed the words—"I'll get you some information. I'll make sure it's the real stuff, original documents. I have access to all the areas of BYU's library, even the sections where only professors and researchers can go. I'll make copies. You won't have to take anyone's word for anything."

"Some things you won't find there, Roger. And those are the things that are breaking my heart."

"What do you mean?"

"For instance, a geneticist, faithful Mormon bishop, released a book recently that demonstrated beyond doubt that Native Americans aren't descended from people in the Book of Mormon. You do realize the implications of that for me, don't you?

"That means that I'm not a Lamanite. I'm not descended from Jews. I have no Jewish DNA. All the heritage that I treasured, the teachings from the Book of Mormon that I believed that I and other Native Americans had, all of it is a lie."

He tried to process not only her words but the fact that those words were coming from the lips of his wife. The words wounded Roger. But as he looked at the pain in her face, he saw that she was not only wounded but bereft. She began to cry, and he put his arms around her.

"There's more, Roger. You think you've been shielding me from all the intrigue at BYU, the stories about the September Six, about how the Church deals with honest re-searchers and feminists and professors who question things."

She paused in deference to his astonished look, his mental disorientation. "It's me who's been shielding you," she continued. "I've just kept putting aside any questions about why the Church deals so harshly with its own people who do the research, who bring things to light. I've put aside my questions about the way they cover things over and ask you to just trust their versions of things.

"I shut my ears to anything that would hurt my testimony of the Church. I didn't want to hear it, never even noticed when I was being fooled. I mean, years ago I read the most famous LDS book about *The Pearl of Great Price* scrolls—pages and pages of stories about how the scrolls were rediscovered and about how Joseph Smith had translated them and they became Scripture for us—and never, ever noticed that the author left out the most important thing: that the Egyptian writing on the scrolls doesn't say what Joseph said it said!"

Words were spilling out of her, a stream that was emptying her soul as well. Her sobs sounded as if they were coming from drowning lungs.

They both knew what happens to Mormon couples when one spouse leaves the Church and the other won't.

Roger and Eliza went upstairs and undressed in complete silence. With deliberate movements she removed her temple garment and folded it. She put it on the floor, behind the straight-backed rocking chair, the sciatic chair, Roger always called it. She put on a long flannel nightshirt even though the night was warm and began to cry again.

She was far across her island from him. Roger lay on his side next to her in bed and waited for her crying to subside.

She moaned and choked as she slept.

161

Then she breathed a single long breath and settled into a sleep so deep he kept checking her pulse.

How could they raise Maria without the Church? And how could he stay away from the bottle—the Church was what gave him reasons. The Church gave him the architecture of security that he and Eliza and Maria had built a house upon.

In the silence of his home, where he lay beside a person who felt like a stranger, his own battle with back pain engaged again.

This time when it waylaid him, he could almost hear it.

CHAPTER 18

THE MAN HAD once read the final writings of a criminal facing execution, in which the condemned man spoke of the great clarity of mind he had during his last hours. Some understandings, regardless of the horror of their substance, bring with them a sort of settled knowledge, almost a peace.

He himself had felt such a peace even in the midst of enacting what he had characterized as the mercy of blood atonement on the covenant-breakers Kirsten Young and Heber J. Bruce. There was logic and justice in the outflowing of their blood, the substance that would buy their forgiveness when nothing else could. He wondered if in the last moments of her life, Kirsten had understood that he had not meant her harm but good, for she had ceased to struggle at the end. When the light went out of her eyes, they were still looking at him, he remembered, eyes that seemed to forgive him as he expedited her absolution.

Heber J. Bruce had been a different matter. He'd fought

like the adversary he was, and in his final struggles he had screamed out his anguish and rage, holding onto his life as if there were no eternity.

Those two deaths and the displaying of the body of Bernadette Rodriguez had felt like triumphs to him. They were sentences with exclamation points, declarations of truth.

Now he turned to other statements, the questions that cried out for answers, that challenged even those declarations he had made with such confidence.

The time had now arrived to begin creating new symbols about Mormonism, symbols that would not buttress it but expose it. Could a symbol be sarcastic? He would try. And he would begin with the Woodruff couple.

Thank goodness Alma and Mary Ann Angell weren't overweight, the man thought. He tried to carry them out the back door of their home with the dignity that their age commanded, tenderly, as if offering propitiation for his coming sin against them.

At first he was tempted to protect them, to put away the shot glasses they left on their countertop and hide the vodka at the back of the pantry. He hadn't taken them for morning drinkers and felt remorse that he'd given them such a large dose of the rohypnol in the orange juice. But he left the glasses and bottle as they were on the table. Later, police investigators would focus on the liquor, and probably no one would think to test them for any drugs.

Surprisingly, tough old Alma was easier to carry than his oil-jointed wife who kept slipping one deep-winged arm loose where it brushed his side as he walked. He wondered if she was completely unconscious.

In the afternoon sun, the alley behind their house was deserted today as it was most days. This stale-smelling neighborhood itself was a neglected old man whose children had all moved out of state. Its Dumpsters were never full, and contained mostly disposable tableware, empty pill bottles, ice cream cartons, and innumerable little oval black plastic containers from frozen microwave meals.

The man placed the couple faceup in the back of the unremarkable minivan he had secreted between two Dumpsters. He placed a sheet lightly over them, covering their faces. They would not speak to him through this veil. He checked to see if he could see anything through the tinted windows, took a look at himself—stringy wig beneath a baseball cap, unsavory moustache glued on securely—and began the drive to the new Masonic temple. Timing for this venture with the Woodruffs had been tricky—he had to wait until the National Guard had been called from Salt Lake City to the site of the terrorists' more active threats in other states.

This Masonic temple, which nobody was guarding anymore, was wedged up against the city's mountain to the northeast. Its name was Ballut Abydos or something like that, he recalled. It was no accident that the parking lot was sheltered from view from the street. Being a Mason in Salt Lake City was a statement that even those who'd moved in from other places didn't always want to make publicly. So you could drive behind this temple and park as securely as at any of the adult video stores that peppered the metro area.

Within the pages of the books on Masonry he bought on eBay, the man had found what he suspected and dreaded: the Five Points of Fellowship were pictured there. The Five Points of Fellowship in which he himself had participated in, grasping a stranger through a rippling curtain-veil in the LDS temple years ago. The identical symbols that Mormons denied had any connection with Masonry. The Five Points that he would, therefore, illustrate in this tableau that he would create near the back door of the Masonic temple. He would put in the face of Mormon and Gentile alike the truth that Mormon temple rituals and those of Masonry were in places identical. Therefore the Mormon "restoration" of temple rites was either unnecessary, or even better, pagan.

The man lay the thrift-store comforter onto the ground near the service entrance of the lodge and placed Alma on it. Then he placed Alma's wife next to him and knelt beside them.

It took a bit of maneuvering. With gloved hands, he moved them toward each other, almost facing, each on his side. The woman moaned a bit.

With a roll of duct tape, the man taped their right ankles together. He moved respectfully up the woman's right leg, moving aside the frayed wisp of the leg of her temple garment to tape their right knees together as well, inside to inside. He tugged on her skirt and arranged it demurely.

Under the heat of the wig, sweat began to collect and roll down his sideburns. His moustache felt loose and he stabbed at it with one finger: center, edge, edge. The hardest part was yet to come. With a strap-ripping sound, he pulled off long strips of the tape and began to tape the couple together around their shoulders. Then he placed the left hand of each onto the other's right shoulder blade and secured it with the tape.

They began, he observed, to look a bit like Mr. Chandler's mummies.

"I want you to look at the little runt of a fellow over there," the man quoted Joseph Smith under his breath as he worked. "Why, that was Pharaoh Necho, King of Egypt. . . ."

He regretted having to do the next part. He looked closely at the woman's face. In her eyebrows and temples were the evidences of her vanity, faint scars from cosmetic surgery. The skin of her eyelids was crumpled, like old tissue paper someone had used and then carefully ironed and folded for the next use: the faint memory of creases.

But screw your courage to the sticking place, And we'll not fail, he told himself. He glued the man's lips and cheek to his wife's ear. Squatting in the lengthening shadows, he pressed their heads together tenderly until the glue set. He thought about it a moment and then wrapped their heads together in a giant grey headband of duct tape so they wouldn't unknowingly rip their skin before becoming completely conscious. Then he secured their right hands together with a large aluminum plumbing clamp that he tightened with his pocketknife. Anyone could open it—except them, of course. And they would still be unconscious, he was sure, when they would be discovered in a couple of hours.

He stood over them for the briefest of moments, taking the measure of his own misery, listening to the rhythms of their breaths and regretting what he would cause them. The damage to their skin would be the least of it. Perhaps it would take attention away from the other things. Or maybe it would be like the mark of Cain, from which people would shrink in horror. But there would be questions, and that was the whole point of all of this. These questions, about the temple's divine-human embrace, must be exposed, must be addressed.

The last of the details. He took a note out of his pocket and read the cipher to himself, sounding it out like a primer's mysteries.

Yes, he thought, that would do.

He placed the note under Alma's hip so that the words "The Fourth Proof" on the outer sheet showed. He taped a bottle of glue solvent to the bottom of the note, where there was no writing.

Then, with urgency, he practiced in his mind another set of words he'd memorized in the Mormon temple the first time he went as a green missionary: Peter's pronouncement before the veil, Peter's precious words that were no longer part of the LDS temple ceremony, ripped out of it nearly two decades ago.

He cleared his still-rasping throat and spoke the words softly before leaving, the words he had written in the code note.

"The Five Points of Fellowship are: inside of right foot by the side of right foot, knee to knee, breast to breast, hand to back, and mouth to ear."

He turned to walk away, but something in him called him back to the tableau. There was more to be said that would finalize what he was trying to do. It was Yeats, percolating up from within him, from within the warp and woof of all he knew.

Oh body swayed to music
Oh brightening glance
How can we tell the dancer from the dance. . . .

CHAPTER 19

THE TUESDAY MORNING press conference was over. Everyone at the newspaper office was talking about it. Selonnah made a pretext about why she couldn't attend—conflict of interest, it was after all her cousin who gave the Church's prepared statement and fielded the questions. A transcript of the press conference would be as good as being there and besides, she would take no pleasure from watching her cousin squirm under the questions she knew her colleagues were preparing. She wanted the answers, not the show.

Selonnah spent her morning locating and downloading from the Internet a list of the phonetic syllables of the Deseret Alphabet. She pored over it, memorizing the most common symbols—the one for "th," the "s," the "t," the "r," and some of the vowels. She realized with a start that she'd chosen them as pragmatically as a contestant preparing for a game show. Probably would have to buy a vowel or two.

Ᏸ ᏗᏝᏆᏗᎢᏝᏆ ᏝᏝᎠᏋᏰᏝᎠ.

Long Sounds.				Letter.	Name.	Sound.
Letter.	Name.		Sound.	⅂	....	p
Ә	....e...as in....		eat.	੪	....	b
Ɛ	....a	"	ate.	੧	....	t
Ѳ	....ah	"	art.	੫	....	d
Ѳ	....aw	"	aught.	Ϲ	....che as in *cheese*.	
Ο	....o	"	oat.	Ϛ	....	g
Փ	....oo	"	ooze.	Ѡ	....	k

Short Sounds of the above.

				Ѳ	....ga...as in...*gate*.	
ᵻ	......as in......		it.	ρ	....	f
⌐	"		et.	ϐ	....	v
⅃	"		at.	⌐	....eth..as in *thigh*.	
ᶐ	"		ot.	Ɣ	....the " *thy*	
ᒥ	"		ut.	8	....	s
ᒑ	"		book.	ϐ	....	z

Double Sounds.

				Ɒ	....esh..as in..*flesh*.	
Ꮧ	....i....as in...*ice*.			S	....zhe " vision.	
Ѳ	....ow	"	owl.	Ψ	....ur " burn.	
Ɣ	....ye			ᒷ	....	l
Ѡ	....woo			Ϲ	....	m
ᒥ	....h			ᒹ	....	n
				Ͷ	....eng.as in.*length*.	

But other questions raised by the press conference nagged at her. She needed someone with some distance from the situation to help her understand. She rubbed the black cover of her cell phone with a ragged thumbnail before dialing.

"Anne, this is Selonnah—we met at the health food store . . . ?"

"Sure, girl. I remember you." Anne's voice on her cell phone was solid and reassuring. "What's up?"

"I guess you heard the press conference on TV."

"Very interesting." Anne stretched out the words, waiting for Selonnah.

"Let me cut to the chase. I'm not above a bribe. If I bring you lunch from that store where we met, can I come over and talk to you this afternoon?"

Anne laughed. "For tofu spinach lasagna and raspberry ice tea, I can definitely be bought. I've got someone coming in the morning, and K.C. should go down for a nap about noon—is that good for you?"

Selonnah was grateful for the fact that at least the older streets in Salt Lake City were laid out on number grids. So if you began, as she did, from the center of the city, finding the address was simple. Go six blocks toward the mountains, then turn south and go twenty-five blocks.

A car with a logo on it that Selonnah couldn't read was pulling away from Anne's home when Selonnah arrived. The home was a tiny white brick house with ersatz dormer windows, probably built in the 1940s, Selonnah guessed. Solid, like the girl herself, Selonnah thought as she balanced the still-steaming plastic containers and shut the car door with her foot. An enormous weeping willow draped itself all over the gate to the front porch and Anne appeared from inside, holding aside the branches with one hand and the front door

171

with the other. She was dressed in cargo pants and a voluminous knit shirt.

"Welcome to my obstacle course," she said with a laugh. "Another one of those jobs I will get to tomorrow." She motioned toward pruning scissors and a saw resting against the door frame.

The house was silent. Its hardwood floors and tiny-tiled kitchen had probably made it suddenly fashionable again, retro chic. Selonnah rather thought that Anne had worked around its intractable color scheme—those tiles were all pale pink and visible, apparently, from every room in the house—by artfully placing around the house every shiny black and lime green décor item she could find. The house had the resigned air of a shy grandmother of the bride submitting to a makeover at a tony salon.

Anne devoured the food Selonnah brought with the same unselfconscious relish as in the store two days before. Finished, she eyed Selonnah's sandwich with undisguised covetousness and then took without protest what Selonnah's lack of appetite had left untouched on the plate. Not until it, too, was gone did she sit back in the oak pressed-back chair and motion Selonnah to change the subject from the weather and the baby's well-being to what Selonnah really wanted to discuss.

"Now, about the press conference," Selonnah began. "I don't think I told you that I'm staying with my cousin while I'm here, and that—my cousin is Roger Zee."

Anne's eyes said *aha*. She nodded slowly.

"And I tried to talk to him about some of these things last night, before the press conference, but it didn't go very well."

"He got mad at you . . . ? Wouldn't answer . . . ? Threw you out and now you want to live with me?" Anne probed slowly as if she were giving a grade school multiple choice test.

172

"Oh, nothing like that," Selonnah laughed. "No, the spare bedroom and soy milk in the refrigerator seem secure for the moment. And what happened last night, I know that it was my fault, at least most of it."

Selonnah paused. "When I was a little girl, my parents took me to the first buffet restaurant I'd ever been to. I ran from steam table to steam table, amazed at all that food. I couldn't decide. But I didn't want anyone to get in front of me, between me and anything I wanted to look at, and I didn't want anyone to help me. So I grabbed a knife and went from the macaroni and cheese, to the chicken wings, to the fried okra, to the chocolate cake, and dared anyone to stop me. So from that time on, my dad talked about me in terms of 'a knife, a need, and an attitude.'"

Anne nodded and laughed, but with no words so that Selonnah would continue.

"So I went to the house, to Roger's house, with a knife, a need, and an attitude, I guess. I didn't get many answers, and I feel so sorry for him because I know he must have some answers but he's torn."

"So let me try to field the questions you have."

Selonnah relaxed in her chair. "Thank you. I can't tell you how upsetting this is to me. But be aware that I'm just giving you what I remember and what I think was said. So much of what's said about Mormonism, I found, is incomprehensible to me."

Anne nodded soberly. "That's because they define words differently than you or I."

Selonnah cocked her head to one side.

"Like, well, God for instance," said Anne. "I get the idea that you're not a churchgoer" (an assenting nod from Selonnah), "but when I say 'God,' and you hear that in your head, you're thinking of a spirit being pretty much above—and qualitatively and substantively different from—you and me."

Selonnah nodded.

"But our Mormon friends, when they say 'God,' are referring to a supreme being, but who is a former man. Somebody who grew up on another world."

Selonnah's eyes widened. "Like an alien home world, that kind of thing?"

"Sort of. I doubt they'd state it that way, but yes. He grew up, they say, on a world like this one. What's more, their god is somebody you can become like. . . . You can be a god like him someday. Oops, I mean all Mormons will be gods like him someday."

Selonnah felt disoriented. "So—what does that have to do with the press conference? Or with talking to Roger?"

Anne considered her fingernails.

"Nothing. And everything. It's an example of how hard it is to communicate with Mormons sometimes. You can be using the same words but not mean the same things."

Ah, thought Selonnah. Using the same representations—words—but referring to different facts. She looked at Anne with understanding. "As if somebody said they know Selonnah Zee and she's a ninety-year-old Yahtzee champion from China. I'd say, same name, different person. For Mormons, same name, different god."

Selonnah paused as Anne processed what she was saying and then assented with a dip of her chin.

"Well, if I hadn't done a little studying of Islam, I guess I wouldn't have a handle on that," Selonnah said. "I don't claim to be an expert—" She waved her hands in front of her, brushing away any potential misunderstandings. "—But I did come to see that the one they call Allah has some 'history' in common with the God of the Western world. Muslims say he's the supreme being in the Bible, but on top of that he has another whole identity that subsumes and actually redefines him—the Qur'an, Muhammad, jihad."

Anne's expression said she hadn't thought of that. She shrugged and smiled.

"Guess it's a global problem. I can see how representations can muddy up communication," said Selonnah. "So much of the time I feel like I'm saying something and Roger is agreeing with my words—but I'm not so sure he's agreeing with what I *mean*. And that was earlier, when everything was reasonable and calm between us. After our blowup, things are different. From the beginning, when I ask questions, I don't think he's answering what I'm asking."

"Do you trust him?" Anne asked the question almost in a whisper.

Selonnah rushed to his defense, automatically throwing water on his wet clothes. "Yes, of course. I've known him—and loved him—my whole life. He's a good man. He's honest."

Anne looked off in the distance, past the obviously homemade insulated shades in deep pleats atop the cloudy old single-pane windows. "What I'm about to say I want you to take in the right way. I've lived among Mormons my whole life. In the main, as a group, they are honest, moral, conscientious people. Good neighbors, trustworthy business associates. But one thing is a reality above their character, in many cases." She looked peripherally at Selonnah, as if for permission to continue. She drew a breath that seemed to come from her backbone. Selonnah put her head to one side, then nodded.

Anne said this next slowly. "Don't ever underestimate the will, nor the ability, nor the financial resources that the LDS Church has, and will expend, in defending itself."

At least a minute passed before either of them said anything at all.

But Selonnah's mind was far from silent. For the first time, she wondered if what Anne was saying could be taken at face value. What were her motives in making such a statement? Anne had been a reporter—could she document such a thing?

She remembered what Roger had said last night. Selonnah spat out at him that she had other sources, she'd met another reporter who was on maternity leave, someone who had lived in Salt Lake all her life and who would either have—or find out—the information she wanted. He wearily waved away the notion as seemingly inconsequential until Selonnah mentioned her name.

"Are you talking about Annabel MacAlister, the widow of Ryan MacAlister?"

Selonnah looked up at him. "Yes. Do you know her?"

"I don't know her personally. But everybody in Salt Lake City knows her—not just because she was a columnist but because of her husband, Ryan, how he died. . . ." His voice trailed off and she could see he was searching for words.

"She told me that he was killed disposing of a bomb somewhere. I don't remember where. Iraq? Afghanistan?"

"Did she say that?"

"No. I just assumed that it was overseas somewhere."

"Actually, he was on training maneuvers out in the Test and Training Range," said Roger, referring to a remote area in western Utah. "And if anybody has a reason for a grudge against the Mormon Church, she'd be at the top of my list."

Thus, Selonnah decided that this was the time to directly address with Anne this issue of Ryan's death, before she went any further with questions about Mormonism. As Selonnah began to speak, a wail came from behind a closed door, and her cell phone rang.

"Selonnah, are you where you can talk privately?" asked

Roberta Carlson, a crackling insistence in her ear. Selonnah tried turning down the volume, but saw that she'd need to go outside.

"Okay." Selonnah was sitting now in a flaking swing on the front porch, where the traffic noises from the street provided cover.

"I thought about why you didn't go to the press conference, and, I, uh, respect that," said Roberta. No delicacy, what Selonnah's mother, Mary, would describe as *faunchin'*. "But it leads to an additional problem, one that I've discussed this afternoon with Deborah Wiley."

Selonnah felt a surge of resentment that a call had been made to her editor back in Tennessee. But there was no time to protest, as Roberta pressed on.

"She told me that if push came to shove, I could count on your integrity, even if your cousin is a source on a controversial story."

"Thanks, both of you." Selonnah didn't trust herself to say more. Her sarcasm was lost on Roberta.

"So. Push has come to shove, as she said. There's been another incident—maybe two incidents, in fact—that I think could be tied to all the crazy killings around here. I have proof that the LDS Church—" She paused and corrected herself. "—that local officials of the LDS Church have tried to cover up aspects of at least one more crime."

"My cousin? He tried to cover something up?" Selonnah asked.

"Oh no, not him. At least, not that I know of. A bishop and some temple officials, that's what they called themselves, something like that. But that's not the issue here. I have to know where your loyalties lie."

"My loyalties are with the truth." Selonnah's voice was quiet, and if Roberta only knew her better, dangerous.

"Okay. Then you'll want to be here in an hour when we have a briefing about this situation. And I'll need to know you're not discussing this with your cousin."

"I understand very well what you're telling me," said Selonnah. "And I'm not too far from the office. I'm leaving now. I will be there for the briefing."

CHAPTER 20

COULD A PERSON become addicted to rohypnol tablets by ingesting only one dose and never again taking one of the little white pills? Or more accurately, could one become addicted not to taking them but to administering them?

The man had murdered Kirsten Young and Heber J. Bruce, had posed Bernadette Rodriguez, had displayed Alma and Mary Ann Angell in the temple's fellowship embrace.

Now he was contemplative as he fingered the packets of the pills. They had certainly been effective with the Woodruffs. If he continued in his life of crime, he thought bitterly, he might become dependent upon them as indispensable tools of his trade.

Tonight he ate his favorite dinner—roasted chicken with artichokes in a cream sauce on linguine. His stomach was still a bit queasy as he turned down the waiter's suggestion of dessert. He was worried about the Woodruffs.

Could he pray? Not anymore. He felt rubbed-raw weary

with the asking, the requests made over and over. A great gulf was fixing itself between him and what he'd once called faith. Perhaps between him and what he'd called reality.

Sitting quietly in the downtown restaurant, looking out the window, he waited for sunset. He listened to voice mails, but none was urgent. A young couple in a booth across the restaurant cooed at each other and he found that he looked askance at them.

Askance. What an odd word, this little adverb, he thought, that didn't look adverbial but it did retain its archaic meaning of looking out of the side of the eye. He realized it was not only his looking that was askance, it was his being, himself.

His life had become one that was lived askance. Only the proofs that were ahead of him could he look straight in the eye.

He paid cash for the bill and walked out into the night. No one seemed to notice him slouched in his car seat in the shadows of the parking lot. He waited, again, for nightfall.

There is an hour where time seems to suspend itself, these peculiar few moments when dusk disintegrates into night.

He recited, under his breath:
The dusk grows dense,
The silence tense;
And lo . . .

Right on schedule. Around the corner of the Hyrum Building appeared Clarissa Clarissa Nightwalker, pushing a shopping cart. She walked upon painful feet—if the gingerly way she held her toes in her filthy tennis shoes, just off the ground, told the truth of her gait. As she swayed from heel to heel in truncated steps, she looked like a stiff-legged doll forced-marched across a table.

She approached the Dumpster that sheltered her home of

currently collapsed cardboard boxes and slammed the cart into the brick of the building with the clattering finality of a metal gavel. With a moan, she bent arthritically over and pulled the flattened television carton from behind the Dumpster and spread it out to form a five-sided enclosure into which she slung a rancid-looking sleeping bag from the shopping cart.

Clarissa Clarissa was a fixture of downtown Salt Lake City. Some people were afraid of her, but not because she was dangerous. Just creepy, some said, the Native American version of bad *ju ju*. All gave her wide berth, even policemen and social workers. She was harmless, nonconfrontational, rarely begged, stayed sober and to herself. To the horror of health care workers who sought out the homeless, she ate and drank only what she found on her own, never what was offered to her. Like a carrion-eating bird, Clarissa Clarissa seemed to want to make sure it was dead before she ate it.

As the man sitting hunched in his car watched her prepare her nest under the pale security light at the back of the building, he saw her pick up what he'd left at the corner of the Dumpster: a partial package of hoagie buns and a bottle of water.

She held the bottle up to the light and peered through it suspiciously as she slowly chewed a bun, using the teeth on the right side of her mouth only. She tested the tightly closed lid on the water bottle, then opened it and sniffed and sipped. Satisfied, she threw her head back and poured the water down the back of her throat, aiming like someone would at a height for the hole at the bottom of a kitchen sink, gulping and gasping at the end. She tossed the bottle into the Dumpster and then stood a long moment holding her left cheek.

A cracked or abscessed tooth, diagnosed the man with sympathy. He watched Clarissa Clarissa as she rooted through the Dumpster for breakfast, using two lengthened-out wire coat hangers as fishing hooks and tongs. She seemed methodical in her search of the accessible areas of it, as if she had a mental grid over it that must be mined. It yielded several crumpled fast-food bags and soda cans that she hooked with the coat hangers. The cans she put into a yellow plastic bag that dangled from the shopping cart. The man made a mental note to stay away from the coat hangers. She must have sharpened them.

After about fifteen minutes, Clarissa Clarissa held on to the side of the Dumpster and put her head against the rim of it. That was when the man knew that the rohypnol in the water bottle was beginning to take effect.

He waited until she pulled the cardboard enclosure around her and saw it tremble as she lurched against it from inside. Looking around to assure himself that no one was near the practically empty parking lot, the man walked toward the Dumpster and pushed aside the cardboard to enter her home.

She sat spraddle-legged with her back against the brick wall and looked up at him coyly. Her voice was slurred.

"I was a fancy shawl dancer."

He nodded with understanding, murmured soothing sounds, and tried to control his gag reflex in the odor of the enclosure. He pulled his offering, a bottle of hand lotion, from his pocket. She shrugged and took it from him, tucking it under her hip. He squatted next to her and took one of her hands in his plastic-gloved ones. It was surprisingly clean, considering the places where it had been. He began to rub the back of her hands with food-grade 35 percent hydrogen peroxide poured on a cotton pad.

Clarissa Clarissa, apparently thinking this was a foreplay of sorts, turned her head to the side and fell asleep.

"Nothing new there," said the man grimly to himself. "Feels like home."

As he rubbed the other hand with the chemical, he remembered what he'd heard about this woman who was practically an urban legend. Born a fourth-generation Mormon to parents of the Cheyenne tribe, Clarissa Clarissa's name reflected perhaps the beginning of some of her parents' disillusionment, at least with Brigham Young. The man who continued to rub her hand with the potent peroxide had heard that Clarissa Clarissa had four sisters named Margaret Margaret, Sarah Sarah Sarah, Mary Mary Mary, and Harriet Harriet Harriet, all reflecting Brigham's wives who shared the same names: two Clarissas, two Margarets, and three Sarahs, Marys, and Harriets each. He didn't know if all that about Clarissa Clarissa's genealogy was true, but now, he rather believed it.

At any rate, by the time Clarissa Clarissa left the fancy shawl dancing at tribal powwows to come to Utah, her mental illness and the early onset of arthritis colluded to exclude her from ecclesiastical niceties and put her on the streets where she had survived for the last ten years.

Perhaps it was her name, he thought. She never stood a chance.

He put a thick layer of Vaseline on each of her hands. Then he pulled a sealed package of new white men's work gloves from a pocket and opened them carefully and placed them—with dragging difficulty—onto her hands. Something this new, and this white, in this place would surely attract attention. They'd wash the grease—and the peroxide—off in the ambulance before it could permanently damage her skin.

She stirred. "I was . . . a fancy shawl . . . dancer. . . ."

"I know, I know," he said tenderly. "A good one, too, I bet."

He had the note in an envelope, and pulled it out carefully with the tip of his pen. He read it out loud to himself, stumbling a bit over the code.

He placed the note on her rhythmically rising chest. Then he remembered how he had retched under the drug's influence. He wedged the note between a couple of bricks in the building's wall.

"Nobody kept their promises to you, did they?" he whispered as he left. "So they just changed the promises."

At the pay phone around the corner, he called 911 and reported a drug overdose—maybe that homeless Clarissa lady was dead or maybe dying? He ducked back into the restaurant parking lot and then drove quickly away.

Two blocks right, three left, four straight ahead. He began to relax, and to recite.

Through shadowy rifts
Of woodland lifts
The low, slow moon, and upward drifts,
While left and right
The fireflies' light
Swirls eddying in the skirts of Night.

He yawned, shaking with fatigue, and turned a final time toward his house.

From: [mailto:adam1830@hivenet.net]
Sent: Wednesday, June 5
To: liahona@hivenet.net
Subject: [none]

I once saw you, you know, as the Prophet Spencer W. Kimball saw our Heavenly Mother: your "restrained and queenly elegance."

Now you are desire, run amok.

I must have you, must be with you. I am losing something valuable and irreplaceable and it is not only you; it is us. We cannot lose us—not for the church, not for anything.

Let me keep vigil over you, let me protect you. From him. From you. Perhaps, even, from me.

CHAPTER 21

LUKE TAYLOR STOOD respectfully at the foot of the casket. Any time he'd been called into service as a pallbearer, he took his responsibilities seriously, but really, he was having a hard time on this one.

The dearly beloved deceased, Warren Howe, was a distant cousin from what his mother had always called "the loopy side of the family." Luke thought privately it was from all the intermarrying and hiding out that his great-grandparents did after the LDS Church leadership's "Manifesto" declared polygamy illegal and immoral. Around the turn of the twentieth century, many people balked at the Manifesto: those who'd been taught that plural marriage was not only an eternal commandment, but that you couldn't get to the highest degree of heaven without practicing it like Brother Joseph and Brother Brigham had done. Some had moved to remote places in Utah and Arizona.

Luke had hundreds of distant cousins scattered all over Mexico. One family of Taylors in a colonia near Guadalajara prayed for many children and optimistically began naming their children as Spanish numerals: Uno, Dos, Tres, and so on. Fortunately, Luke thought, they only made it to fourteen children and the last one was named Catorce. Thus some forever-unborn siblings were spared the ignominy of being named Dieciséis or Veintiuno or worse. Another branch of cousins had two sets of triplets that they let a Mexican midwife with a Spanish-English dictionary give names to. Exhausted by the first three, the parents didn't even protest when the tiny members of their second set were named Verve, Wrangle, and Aplomb.

Stateside, the fundamentalist Saints who had gone underground, so to speak, in order to practice plural marriage, were understandably mistrustful of outsiders. And you usually don't marry someone you mistrust. So it wasn't a stretch to consider that almost everyone at this funeral was related, by marriage and/or by blood, sometimes in multiple ways. Warren's second cousin—and first plural wife, Maddie—draped herself over the coffin, knocking poor Warren's black-rimmed eyeglasses askew. Weeping, she replaced them, but at an angle on his nose with the earpieces high on his temples.

"That's the way he slept," Maddie moaned. "Every night of our life he fell asleep in the recliner in front of the television, just like that. See, now he looks," she crumbled into sobs, "now he looks natural."

No one offered to readjust them. Warren's other two polygamous wives stood like statues surrounded by their children. The funeral director just raised his eyebrows and nodded sympathetically.

There was another matter Luke had to know about before

they closed the casket. He leaned over as if to look into poor Warren's face, but surreptitiously looked down at the man's belt that held up his dress Western slacks. Ah, he was wearing the belt to the grave.

This belt was the stuff of family legends. For the last five years, Warren had worn a belt that had the name "Bradley" tooled into the leather. Actually, you had to turn your head to read it, recalled Luke, because he wore it upside down. Once when someone had the courage to ask why Warren wore this belt, Maddie slapped her thighs in mirth.

"Why honey, you know he can't read! So it don't matter anyways, right?"

And now that Luke thought about it, he couldn't say that there was any good reason for him not to wear a perfectly good and well-tooled belt. Even to the grave.

Luke turned to the widows to make his farewells.

"Gotta get back to work," he said tenderly. "You all let me know if I can help you."

"Oh, honey," Maddie spoke up. "You're too sweet, though, offering like that. I got Elbert to help me. He drives me everywhere now." She motioned to their only son, a slack-shouldered middle-aged man wearing an eye patch on his right eye. He spread his hands out apologetically.

Apparently Maddie must have made the connection between Luke's police uniform and his potential mental image of a one-eyed man driving through traffic. Maddie put her mouth close to Luke's ear.

"We got it all worked out, all the routes to the doctor and to the store and such," she whispered conspiratorially, patting Luke on the shoulder. "Elbert only makes left turns."

As Luke drove away from the funeral home, he felt a kind of admiration for the people he'd just left. They, like Helaman's grandmother, had adapted to life's troubles by doing whatever it takes. It is the Mormon way.

Whatever it takes, he thought, as Warren had; simultaneously supporting three wives and (Luke had forgotten exactly how many) children; dodging the law every hour of his now-truncated life.

Whatever it takes to bring order into your life. Using what you have, like a one-eyed driver. He created a mental picture of Maddie and her son leaning over their kitchen table peering at the street map in the phone book, plotting round-trip routes of only left-hand turns, marking them carefully with a red marker.

Using what you have, like a beautifully tooled leather belt with some irrelevant symbols on the back. Doing whatever it takes.

Symbols that had to be seen from a certain viewpoint. Luke settled back into his seat, driving with locked elbows. The hour-long drive back north to Salt Lake City from the funeral in Payson would give him some time to think about things. His troublesome epaulette radio was in the shop and he felt a little naked without it, even though it had been a crotchety companion lately, with as many misses as hits on conversations. One way of looking at it, having a radio transmitter that cut in and out when people were talking certainly developed both patience and insight as you guessed at the missing parts of sentences. Meanwhile, he thought ruefully, there was always a cell phone, technological reliability personified.

Symbols. He looked over at the pile of photocopies next to him on the car seat. Each was a reproduction of one of the "proof" notes left at crimes. He tried to give some order to his thoughts about these crimes. First of all, there were things that they all had in common. All but the one left with

190

Bernadette Rodriguez made a point about the LDS Church or its doctrines of the past. And of course, he admitted to himself, the Book of Mormon at her crime scene more than tied the LDS Church to her as well.

The overt connection of all the crimes to Mormonism was enough to engage his mind for a trip of thousands of miles. He had always thought, always been taught, that his Church's doctrines flowed forward—expanding and explaining, but never backtracking or contradicting. Those troublesome matters, like polygamy, that had become obsolete had been done away with—to everyone's relief. But what was beginning to tickle at his thinking was the notion—could it be?—that not just practices had changed but actual beliefs. He wondered if that might be what the person or persons responsible for these crimes was trying to highlight; for each crime pointed to doctrines of the LDS Church of the past or the present.

His head hurt. His back hurt. His stomach hurt. Better to go on to something less abstract. He would deal with theological issues later. He held up the sheet of what was called "the second proof." With the help of Donnell, Luke had translated the code in all of the notes. First was the one found on Bernadette Rodriguez who'd been laid out like the Virgin of Guadalupe; then the one on Heber J. Bruce whose body was suspended in a hammock; the one next to Alma and Mary Ann Angell Woodruff, the temple workers; and finally the note left next to Clarissa Clarissa Nightwalker.

Once you had the Deseret Alphabet key, all of the messages were easily read. There was something, though, about the one found on Bernadette Rodriguez that troubled him, like a background noise that was out of place. First of all, despite the marked section in the Book of Mormon at the scene, he could still see no clear connection to Mormon doctrine in the note. Saturday certainly had no special importance in LDS doctrine that he knew of; and he'd even done an Internet search of the murky unknowns of the Mormon past to verify that.

But there was something else about the message, a nagging, elusive detail that was driving him crazy. He couldn't figure out what was different about the message itself, even though it was written in the same Deseret Alphabet code and apparently even in the same handwriting and style. Whatever it was, this detail was important.

He took the crook of his will and dragged those thoughts off the stage of his attention. One thing at a time, he thought to himself. What about poor Kirsten Young. Helaman had met with a shame-faced Terrance Jensen who had reluctantly turned over the note he'd secreted in his fanny pack and finally decided to turn over to the police. Though the professor had been cleared of any suspicion of the murder itself because of an irrefutable alibi at Kirsten's time of abduction, nobody in law enforcement—even the most faithful Mormons—had much sympathy for his explanation that he thought the note would make the Church look bad. That boat sailed a long time ago, Luke thought to himself, and seemed to be calling an entire armada out after it.

For the twentieth time since he'd gotten Kirsten's note, Luke read aloud to himself the translation of what had been labeled the second proof.

Shall I tell you the law of God in regard to the African race? If the white man who belongs to the chosen seed mixes his blood with the seed of Cain, the penalty under the law of God, is death on the spot. This will always be so.
—Brigham Young

Luke winced. He had looked this quote up in the *Journal of Discourses*, a record of speeches given by early Mormon leaders. The "proof" note had quoted accurately, and what's more, Luke found numerous other examples of where Young had not only taught but apparently sanctioned—some even said commanded or facilitated—the killing of certain individuals. Troubled, Luke read numerous LDS apologists who asserted that only in a theocracy would Young's commandments be carried out regarding crimes that deserved capital punishment. In such a theocracy, certain crimes would require personal atonement by styles of capital punishment that would actually shed the blood of the criminal.

It was all just "revival rhetoric," these apologists said. Luke wondered why a church with God's voice like a Bluetooth headset in the ear of His prophet would need revival only twenty-five years after its founding.

A couple of nights before, Luke went back and read Young's comments in context, and wondered. He read about the Mountain Meadows Massacre. And John D. Lee, the man who'd served as fall guy when the Massacre's atrocities had come to light. Today, Luke was still wondering.

But his research had brought coherence to his thinking, at least about Heber J. Bruce's death. The note left with the man who'd been eviscerated and left hanging from a tree made a kind of twisted sense. He held up its translation, holding it between his thumbs at the top of his steering wheel and pondered it for a while. It, too, he recalled, had been an accurate quote, again from Brigham Young, again in the early records of speeches by that prophet who had succeeded Joseph Smith after his death.

His cell phone rang.

"Luke, hope you're done with the funeral." Helaman's voice on the phone was tentative.

"Oh yeah, Chief. I'm in the car, on my way back. What's up?"

"You're coming from Payson, right? I wonder if you could check something out for me. It sounds crazy."

"Oh man, tell me there's not another 'Alphabet Code'

crime!" Luke used the term that his officers had begun to whisper under their breath.

Helaman sounded impatient. "This is garbage. Irrelevance. And you'll be fighting with reporters at the scene, because somebody called this one in to the newspapers before they called it in to us."

A long silence occupied the phone line. Luke began to wonder—this was so unlike Helaman to just stop in the middle of orders. Luke coughed politely.

Helaman seemed to rustle back into the conversation. "Don't spend too much time on it," he said. "Just bring me back a report from the officers who are on the scene."

"Okay, Chief. But where is the crime scene?"

"Sorry. Guess I left that part out." Another pause. "It's there in Provo Canyon, right up the canyon from where Kirsten Young's body was found. I thought you'd be going past there—or have you gone past the exit?"

"Just coming up on it, Chief. I'll check it out and be back to the office in about an hour."

Luke turned on his flasher and was at the scene in fifteen long minutes. In the canyon, an ambulance was pulling away and the driver waved at him with what seemed to Luke to be inappropriate levity. Ahead, two civilian automobiles hung at crazy angles off the road into ditches. Two police units parked directly in the road, blocking it. Luke parked behind them and walked down a short path to an area marked off by yellow tape.

He brushed past the gangly red-headed man he'd seen with Selonnah outside Helaman's office—Lugosi? And—ah, there was Selonnah too. She flashed him a tense smile. "Hey, can you get us back in there?" she asked. "We got here a few minutes before them, but when they came they made us move over here."

Luke stopped for a minute. Press relations, press relations, he told himself. "Let me check it out, and I'll get you in there as soon as I can, I promise." He gave her a smile. "You know, crime scene integrity."

She rolled her eyes. "I've got a degree in criminology, did I tell you that?" Meanwhile, Lugosi furiously snapped pictures of the two of them.

Two officers, Sgt. Frank Ulibarri and Sgt. Sandy Tanner, turned as Luke approached. "Just look at this," said Tanner. She stood with her arms folded.

On the ground, a simple white sheet was spread in a rectangle. Well, it probably started out white, Luke thought to himself, but it was soaked through in places with dried blood. At one corner of the sheet were two small jars with labels in Spanish, and a music CD. At another corner was a small book with a blue cover, and a statue of Buddha. Between the third and fourth corners of the sheet lay the victim. A piece of paper in a plastic bag peeked from beneath the body.

Luke stood staring for a moment, then turned and motioned Selonnah and Lugosi over. "Take all the pictures you want," he said. "But you know the drill—don't touch anything."

"We already got our pictures," Selonnah said. "I told you, we were here before these guys got here." She motioned to the two other officers. "Now, what the heck is this all about? The guy who called this in to the newspaper office said he was responsible for all the crimes in Salt Lake City too. So what's the connection?"

Sgt. Ulibarri was kneeling down to look at the two jars. He snorted softly as he put the jars and CD into evidence bags. He motioned Luke to join him as he opened the pages of the small blue book. Its cover read *The Watchtower Society.*

Ulibarri put it in a bag. "Okay, so we're supposed to think this is associated with the Jehovah's Witnesses? And all those violent Buddhists around the world? And look at these jars of coconut oil and palm oil. And this CD—this is all Santeria stuff."

"Santeria? Buddha, I know, JWs I know about, but what's Santeria?" asked Luke.

Ulibarri pointed to the victim. "It's an occult, well, religion I guess. I had an aunt from Cuba who was into all this stuff. You know, spells and candles, and of course, animal sacrifice." He pointed to the sheet, where the body—a pitiful gutted goat—lay collecting flies. Luke looked closer. Its severed ears lay between its forefeet.

"Okay." Luke was impatient. "So why am I here? To investigate a goat? What does the note say? Is it in code?"

Sgt. Tanner opened the plastic bag gingerly. "We can't make heads or tails of it." She stopped herself. "No, um, pun intended. There's no code at all, just words typewritten in plain English. It says, 'East. February 30. Ten.'"

"What does that mean? Because I've translated the other messages and they don't sound anything like that," said Selonnah.

Luke noticed that when Selonnah said this, Lugosi's head spun toward her. He was staring at her. Something like a shiver seemed to shake his shoulders.

Nobody said anything. The only sound in the small clearing was Lugosi's camera and flies buzzing. Luke racked his brain to try to figure out what this message could mean. Maybe it was a mathematical code. And Selonnah was right —it wasn't anything like any of the other code messages.

"Wait a minute," said Selonnah. "There is no February thirtieth. It only has twenty-eight days. Or twenty-nine, in a Leap Year."

Lugosi's shutter snapped, snapped.

"So," she said, "February thirtieth would be—March first. If you leaped."

Each of the three officers laughed at the same time, the tension broken.

"Okay," said Luke. He didn't know how far to go in revealing the cool gush of relief in his relaxing gut as he looked at the scene. "This just feels silly to me. It feels wrong. Bag it all up and let's take it in. Helaman's not going to want to spend a lot of time on this."

The two officers heaved the goat into a body bag and began collecting the other objects around the scene. Luke turned to Selonnah. "I know you have to cover this, but I just don't have a statement for you."

"You said it felt silly, wrong . . ." she began.

"Look, that's not a statement," he said. He made sure that she looked him directly in the eye. This, he knew, was a woman of character. "You and I both know that when the wire services pick this story up it will probably get more national press than anything that's gone on in Salt Lake," he said. "People go ballistic over any animal torture stories. You know yourself that a lot of people were more upset about Heber J. Bruce's hunting dog and the bears that were shot than they were about the human being up in the tree."

Selonnah nodded, and seemed to make an effort to soften both her eyes and her voice. "Well, I'll try not to make it too sensationalistic. Or make you sound uncaring. And off the record, I think it feels, well, *wrong* too. Thrown together. Jumbled."

Luke gave her a grateful pat on the shoulder. A friend's gesture.

But as Luke walked away from the scene, he turned for a moment to look over his shoulder. It looked as if Selonnah were pacing across the clearing.

Lugosi wasn't taking pictures anymore.

CHAPTER 22

THE SAME NIGHT the goat was killed, the man final-
ized what he had hoped would be the final proof. He used the
rohypnol for what he also hoped would be the final time.

Later, when Orrin Porter Richardson, third-generation
owner of the Zion's Happy Camp RV Park, was interviewed
Wednesday afternoon about what happened, he was as astonished as anyone.

"You bet. I'd be happy to tell you what I know. You bet.
About a month ago, well, let's see, it was exactly four weeks
ago today from my records, see here, this man comes in dragging this twenty-four-footer rig—what? Yes, a twenty-four-
foot trailer, no slide-outs, nothing to look at on the outside,
that's for sure. Truck was on its last leg, too, I'd say.

"Said he was a writer, 'author,' he said, la dee dah.
Needed a place to get away, he said. Peace and quiet was
what he wanted, that's what he said. We pride ourselves on
that, you know. Man paid up front, cash for two months.

Course we get all kinds here, but golly fetch, he was no looker either. Long stringy hair, feed store cap pulled down over his eyes, those wraparound sunglasses 'cause he said he'd just been to the eye doctor. Just for ugly, you know?

"You bet. I think I could help with a sketch artist. Maybe. I don't want to be a pain in the seaterend, but most of what I saw was just hair and cap and shades. You bet. Happy to see the artist. Whatever.

"No, I didn't think anything of it. Some folks who come to RV parks don't want to answer many questions. A lot come in late at night and use our self-check-in and then they're gone before dawn. But some stay a couple days. You know, they can be real social and go around and meet everybody. For friendly. But some just want to be left alone. And you better leave such types alone or they can act real ignert, I've seen it happen. Flip, man, you wouldn't believe it. And I don't want trouble. We run a clean place here. Look us up—no trouble here, look us up in your records.

"You bet. Back to the man. So he comes several times after he checks in. But when he shows, he comes in the evenings, on a motorcycle. Don't know. Don't know about the truck. Always wearing the glasses, same clothes as far as I could tell, same hat for sure. But he doesn't stay, leaves in the night, walking that motorcycle out 'cause it's quiet hour, you know? We're real strict on that 'cause it's a family place, and folks need their sleep. You don't want to be wrangling one of those big rigs towing an SUV and get sleepy on the road. . . .

"You bet. When he comes, sometimes I watch him. I mean, I got to watch the pool and the washhouse always needs paper towels or some doodah has left the door open and the little potguts have got inside. You know, potguts, prairie dogs—you wouldn't believe the trouble those little pests can cause—

"You bet. Back to the man. So I figure he's either a quick writer or he's busy and couldn't stay. He comes at night, you know? Did I say that already? Um. Doesn't stay long. Maybe he's brown baggin'. I knew a bishop once who kept a rig here just for that purpose. A snort and then he'd sleep it off. Not mentioning a name, you understand, we keep such things confidential here. We pride ourselves on that kind of thing. Not condoning it, you understand, it's their business. If it's not illegal, of course. . . .

"You bet. The man comes, but he keeps the blinds pulled all the time. Except once. That time he comes and goes and the next morning I see one of the blind slats is hitched up a little bit. So I look inside, just making sure everything's okay, you know? Just being neighborly. And oh my, it looks like a padded cell in there. You saw it—no stove or icebox, just carpet run up the walls. Only thing in there is the dinette seats and the bed, up front. It's a fiberglass rig, you can see, so those are kind of built in the frame and you can't take them out. . . .

"You bet. So the one place in this whole park you don't expect to hear anything is this guy's rig, right? But this morning I get up and, fetch, his air conditioner's running. No sir, hadn't been, before that. Hadn't really been too hot before, so I'm not too surprised. I think, guess he's come and gone again. People do that, come and go here, I'm just glad I could notice details, make it my business to notice 'cause most park owners just shuttle them in and out like. . . .

"Well, for rude, Officer. I was getting to that. Scrud. Okay, so I call you this morning, you know that. Then your people tell me to check it out and I go up to the trailer and I hear this sound, you know? Sounds like some animals, snarling at one another. But then I realize it's people, like old people, coughing. I dunno, gagging maybe. Then there's moaning. And somebody is crying.

"And this note is taped to the front door. No, I didn't touch it. I told you. Fudge, man! Is it the code? I think to myself. You know, the Deseret Code—Alphabet Code—or whatever it's called? Like you read about in the papers. And then, Judas Priest, I get worried about those guys in the trailer. They're not right, you can tell. They don't answer, just making all those noises. But you said not to jimmy the door till you get here.

"And I think, there'll be H-E-double hockey sticks to pay. And now, here you are."

From: [mailto:adam1830@hivenet.net]
Sent: Thursday, June 6
To: liahona@hivenet.net
Subject: [none]

Like a dog who's attacked chickens, I have gotten a taste for fresh blood. I don't know how to go back.

I have nothing left for you. Just one last proof. And poems.

Poems I wrote you about fullness, when I feel cavernous emptiness. About light when I feel only darkness. Could I ever have felt this way?

CHAPTER 23

SELONNAH COULDN'T WAIT to get out of Lugosi's car. Their ride back to Salt Lake City was one of stony silence, with not one word exchanged between them after the shouting argument they had back at the goat crime scene.

Listen to yourself, she thought. Selonnah, *for mercy sakes alive*, you're thinking about a *goat crime scene.* She thought of her pretentious, pompadoured high school English teacher who emphasized important points by making every word a sentence. He would say: A. *Goat.* Crime. Scene.

She'd heard phrases from her mother all her life, describing people like Lugosi.

Dirt poor sorry. That's what Mary would say when somebody was not only stupid, they were worthless. *No-account.*

Lugosi was no-account. Dirt. Poor. Sorry.

Well, she had a few more for him. *When I get through with you, there won't be nothing left but a little greasy spot.*

She tried to retrace her steps, figure out how exactly she'd even ended up riding in his car on Wednesday to Provo Canyon to a goat crime scene. After last night's tense staff meeting in which everyone at the newspaper was told about—and tried to mentally process—what had happened to the Woodruff couple, Selonnah was mentally spent. People glued together was sure a step above disembowelments, she thought wryly, but still just weird.

She went to the house, made small talk—much to Roger's obvious relief—and went upstairs to tackle email and Internet research. When she came in early to the office the next morning, the whole staff was talking about the discovery of a pitiful homeless woman with her hands bleached. Then an electrifying call came in—there was a new crime scene, and this time the newspaper knew about it before the police. She was, as Mary would say, *ripsnortin' rarin' to go*. Perhaps she could use some of that forensics education she'd paid for so dearly.

She couldn't remember what turn of events got her into Lugosi's car. He'd followed her everywhere like a strip of toilet paper stuck on her shoe, and when he offered to drive since she didn't know the area . . . well, it just happened.

After trying fruitlessly to get Lugosi to give her some insight into what Mormonism might have to do with the Woodruff and Clarissa Clarissa cases they'd learned of at the previous night's staff meeting, she felt so drowsy in the car that she thought she might fall asleep. She found herself murmuring amiable responses to whatever he said. Before she knew it, Lugosi was asking her on a date.

She felt ambushed. Kind of, she now reflected, like walking through your garden at night and stumbling over a corpse. Even if you weren't responsible for the crime, you never will see your garden the same way again.

On the trip, Lugosi was unusually animated, even for

him. Even manic, she thought to herself. That's why it was so odd for him to become so silent at the crime scene once they arrived. She thought at first it was her half-conscious rebuff. She had wished at the time that she could have been more diplomatic. Now she wished she had razed the city of his feelings to the ground.

And that crime scene felt fishy from the first. Poor Luke Taylor, dragged from a funeral out to that sideshow. He was right—the whole thing was screwy. Thank goodness he hadn't been there when she imploded—it had not been a pretty sight.

Her anger with Lugosi was mounting when she started eking out the currency of that stupid note. She could just hear the way it had been composed: "East, *heh heh heh*; February 30, *giggle*; Ten."

How ridiculous she felt, first turning east, actually taking a leap forward!!!—and then walking ten paces. She turned to Lugosi, there at the last moment. He was literally clasping his hands together in delight. Her stomach churned. And then she found it—the can of sardines in catsup sauce, hidden beneath a log.

Nobody but Lugosi could be that contrived, that corny. Nobody but Lugosi was so arrogant that he would not only concoct a crime scene and call it in to his own newspaper, but manipulate it so that only someone as smart as he thought himself to be could discover that the whole thing was literally—literally, mind you—a red herring.

He didn't deny anything. Perhaps he was mowed under by her wrath. More likely he feared for his safety as Selonnah grabbed him by the camera strap and held his face at her level while she screamed at him. His breathing became labored bursts, rasping and hoarse.

"It's not fair to the Church—all these horrible crimes," he wailed, wheezing and gagging, even though she hadn't constricted his throat at all. "I just thought if I could deflect some of the attention elsewhere . . ."

She didn't let him finish, scythed his words off.

"You can't be a newspaper person and fabricate the news. You can't . . ." Her fury stifled her words. She felt she would choke. "But I guarantee you this. You will never work for a newspaper again."

Too bad you couldn't do with people what you did with words in a document. She'd do a global "search and replace" of him. Even blank space would be better. The syntax couldn't be more tangled than it was with him there.

And yet, when security guards walked Lugosi out of the newspaper office with his arms wrapped around a borrowed crate full of his belongings, she felt no satisfaction, no sense of justice satisfied, no peace. She was no nearer to understanding the Mormon mind-set than she had been when she arrived in Salt Lake City last week. And even with the trouble she took to decipher all the Deseret Alphabet crime scene letters that the police department had made available to the newspaper, she still was no closer to understanding the crimes, either.

Meanwhile, Roberta Carlson, who suddenly wanted to become her new best friend, called her in for a private meeting.

"Selonnah, you've got a good relationship with that Sgt. Taylor," she said. "Any chance you could go to his office and get this goat business smoothed over? I mean, Lugosi bought the goat from the farmer for slaughter, and he says he hit the goat in the head before he killed it—'one clean blow,' he assures me—and he cut off the ears after the goat was dead. So our legal counsel says there was no cruelty-to-animals stuff."

Selonnah's vegetarian mind tried to process the mental image of a hammer to the head. No, don't engage on that subject, she decided.

"Make sure the police know that," Roberta droned on. "No need for charges."

Selonnah considered how a police radio code would describe Lugosi. Maybe they'd borrow some computer language. Like: 404—Page not found. Broken link.

"I'll see what I can do." Selonnah was still smarting from Roberta's previous questioning of her own loyalties. "I'm pretty sure they're not going to forget this stunt. Even though we fired Lugosi. At the minimum they'll fine him for filing a false police report. I think they're going to want some sort of formal apology from the paper too—if not for wasting their time and resources, then just for plain old-fashioned aggravation. And I may not be cute enough to talk them out of it."

Selonnah sincerely regretted saying that last part. But she regretted even more meaning it. She felt a fondness for Luke Taylor. She cared about what he thought of her, from his vantage point of clean linens and fresh-mowed lawns and all the other clichés that describe someone so genuinely likeable.

And then there was the inexplicable physical reaction she had each time she saw Helaman Petersen.

Like a puff of air across the exposed nerve of need. She would have to watch that. But she couldn't explain the concurrent sensation that he was somehow perilous, unsafe. Perhaps it was because he was married, and yet seemed so lonely.

She made the appointment with Luke for Thursday noon. When she arrived, he smiled quizzically at her over the shoulder of a dreadful-smelling man and motioned for her to follow him. He stood with his left hand on the door frame as a woman handed him a folder. Selonnah noticed for the first time that he seemed to be missing the tip of his left index finger. How could she have missed it before? It was obviously an old, old injury. He saw her looking at it, and she tried to pretend she wasn't.

"Looking at my poor old finger, I see."

She reddened.

"Don't think anything about it." He motioned for her to sit down. "Everybody notices it, eventually. I'll tell you what happened to it, if you promise not to ask any questions."

"Okay." Selonnah was flustered.

He leaned over his desk as if passing on a confidence. "It was bit off."

"How—?"

"Uh-uh. You promised." He grinned mischievously, eyebrows up. "When you called earlier, I thought I'd have time to take you on another ride-along. But I think something is about to break in this—" he seemed to struggle for words, "—in these Alphabet Code cases."

Selonnah liked the phrase. But she had first a mission to fulfill: to deliver the newspaper's deepest regrets over what would become known as the Lugosi Fiasco.

Luke fielded an interrupting phone call with an apologetic wave, and Selonnah was left to her thoughts. She knew that the LDS-owned newspaper in town would be faced with a dilemma: Expose the schemes of a rival newspaper whose employee had attempted to manipulate the news, or bury the story because of what would be revealed about a man so desperate to defend his Church that he would sink to such a level. Scylla and Charybdis, she thought. Rough waters to navigate—she was glad she wasn't on their boat.

Luke's part of his phone conversation consisted at first of grunts and "um-hms." At one point he walked outside his office into a nearby conference room. While he was gone, Selonnah surveyed his office. Ansel Adams framed prints in plain black frames; solid, sensible stone bookends holding up nondescript volumes on forensics; a desk with perpendicular stacks of papers. In this hueless landscape was the sun of a wildly colored woven wall hanging (South American? Selonnah guessed) and the glint of gold from a line of marksman's trophies. She had picked one up when she heard him end his call.

"I shoot a little too," she offered, a bit embarrassed by having touched it without his permission. He seemed distracted, but rallied to answer her.

"You any good, little sister?" His voice was kind.

"I'm okay," she admitted. Actually, her last few visits to a shooting range had been quite a revelation. The Quonset-hut structure reeked of testosterone—even, it seemed, from the women. She hoped she wasn't like them. But she found to her surprise that gunpowder cleared her head, helped her think more clearly—a phenomenon with which she was not completely comfortable. She decided impulsively to share the secret of her own shooting accuracy with him.

"Actually, I'm pretty good," she clarified. "I wouldn't win any trophies—" she gestured around—"but because I know my failings and how to compensate for them, I usually hit well. When I fire, I pull up and to the right."

She put her hands up, aiming outside the window at an imaginary target, swinging her aim up with a fishhook motion. She continued to smile, but dropped her gaze.

"So—I aim low, and if I miss, I get the heart."

Luke winced. The bark-burst of his laughter was from the innermost reaches of his stomach.

"Remind me not to mess with you if you're carrying!" he said when he caught his breath.

It was in that relaxed atmosphere that she was able to deliver the message about Lugosi. Luke didn't seem surprised.

"Helaman has a sense about these things," he answered. "Usually, anyhow. He said it sounded hokey from the first.

My impression is that he will just want to forget about the whole thing. So—you owe us."

Selonnah felt a rush of gratitude, and a need to make a statement to this man.

"You need to know that I'm not making any excuses for any of this. Maybe I'm old-fashioned, but I believe that integrity is a precious commodity. I would never participate in cheapening it."

Luke looked at her with what she knew was a type of regard. But, unwilling to put him in the position of doing any more than nodding in agreement, she changed the tone quickly.

"Even though my tribe is now in your debt," she said as she bowed with a sweeping *salaam salaam* motion, "I still have some questions for you, about what you're calling the Alphabet Code crimes."

"You mean the latest one?"

Selonnah turned her head and looked at him from the bare edge of her left eye. Luke conceded.

He considered her face, her eyes for a moment. "Guess there's no harm in answering that specific question," he answered.

Selonnah noted the peculiar emphasis in his words, but was too anxious to get the information to call him on it.

"We have something that's just as bizarre as what happened to the Woodruffs and to the Nightwalker lady." It seemed incongruous to Selonnah that he would call a "lady" the person who'd been described to her as a "hobbling homeless woman."

"This time there were three vics, but only one of them died, and that one from what is apparently natural causes." As he spoke Selonnah recognized that he was using language that acknowledged her criminal-justice background. She felt a rush of warmth in her stomach, gratitude.

"We got a call from a nursing home up in Nephi—a town north of here," he added for her benefit. "Seems that a man came to the facility just at shift change time, when all the nurses were busy. Several people remember him—longish hair pulled back, hat, glasses, neatly trimmed moustache, dressed nice, seemed to know his way around. He escorted three of the male dementia patients out into the patio, one at a time. That's the last anybody saw of them. Some of the kitchen staff saw a white van parked around back that was gone by dark. But there's no proof that was the perp's van."

"Why are you calling this man a perp?"

"Because he called an RV park in north Salt Lake and said that he'd left them there."

"Just dumped them off?"

"No, he'd been planning this for a long time. He had an old trailer there that he'd taken everything out of except just padded surfaces. It looks like that sometime last night he put these elderly men into the trailer and locked them in."

"Hey, I've known some dementia patients, and some of them do not go gently into that good night," quipped Selonnah. "Just because their minds don't work right doesn't mean they can't be strong as oxen."

Luke was rubbing his cowlick with the palm of his hand. "No, my guess is that he used some drug to subdue them. After all, they'd be used to accepting pills from people. About the time that he called the RV park, they started regaining consciousness. While the men were being transported by ambulance, though, one of the men apparently suffered an asthma attack."

"I'm sorry about that. The kidnapper left a note, I suppose?"

Luke pushed a photocopy of the message written in the

Deseret Alphabet toward her. "You'll get this soon enough, but here it is."

"Do you know what it says?"

Luke squirmed a bit. "It's a quote from a book of scripture."

Funny he should hedge, Selonnah thought. No matter— she would translate it herself, and track down its source.

"But that's not the big news, Selonnah. We're going to have a press conference at eight in the morning. That's when you'll really get the information you want."

"Look, don't do that to me! I can't wait that long! You gotta give me something," Selonnah pleaded.

Luke dropped his head for a moment, thinking. "Okay. You're print media. We're preparing a press release about the press conference. But it's too late for your afternoon paper. The television news guys will be here this evening, so I'll give you a heads-up. Nothing on the paper's Web site, and no leaking to the television guys, okay? And you have to promise not to ask another question of me today."

She leaned across his desk and nodded. She thought she could still smell the sharp-scented evergreens from Provo Canyon. He looked at his watch.

"We have someone in custody, well, as of ten minutes ago, who has confessed to all of those Alphabet Code crimes."

It took a moment for his words to sink in to Selonnah's consciousness. She did not know what to say.

"I uh—boy, I bet Chief Petersen is happy to bring an end to all this, right?"

A look flickered across Luke's face. He held up his short finger. Without another word, he escorted her out his door.

CHAPTER 24

ROBERTA CARLSON, Selonnah's Salt Lake City editor, received voraciously the news that a suspect was in custody. Even as Selonnah sat in Carlson's office, the editor began dialing numbers to call in all her markers with other law enforcement officials to try to get some additional details.

Each time Selonnah rose to leave, Carlson flapped an impatient hand at her, bidding her to stay. But after half an hour of phone calls of pleadings and threats, the best Carlson could do was post night-beat reporters outside the SLC police department with instructions to photograph everybody who entered the doors for the next twelve hours.

"Even though you're the new girl on the block, you're getting some good stuff," Carlson admitted as she finally dismissed her.

Selonnah's articles that appeared in Tennessee papers had also made her somewhat of a celebrity there, according to her brother's grudging admission in a phone call she took as she drove to Anne's house.

"You're showing them how it's done," he said. "Mama's pleased as punch with the newspapers I bring her—shows your articles all over tarnation at the nursing home."

"How's she looking?"

"Hospital hair and beginning to shuffle when she walks. She fell again in the hallway and scared the dickens out of one of the nurses, but she wasn't hurt none."

"I don't think I'm going to be able to come back very soon."

"Don't give it no nevermind."

"Can I do anything? Send her anything?"

"Put your John Henry on a couple of articles you wrote and send them to her. She'd love that. And don't worry—not much you could do here anyways. She's not as nutty as half the people here. One woman sits on the couch and whinnies like a horse all day long." He laughed in spite of himself. "But Mama's mind is going, sure enough. Yesterday I went to see her and today she couldn't remember a bit of it."

Selonnah's guilt eased. An absence of absence was presence. She could see how having the articles in her hands would help her mother, even if she couldn't keep straight when she saw Selonnah last. She'd send a picture of herself too, even if it were just a publicity headshot. She'd mail it first thing in the morning, no matter what.

God help me never to lose my mind, she thought. You spend your whole life exercising self-control, taming and harnessing and corralling all your passions, and then you are undone, just undone, by a disease that opens all the gates and lets everything you've feared and checked and restrained and dominated come rampaging out. And you don't even know it.

She rounded the last corner on her way to Anne's house.

The young woman had sounded almost reluctant when Selonnah called her begging for more of her time and insight, but had relented graciously. Selonnah stopped at a grocery store and picked up some organic fruit and several bottles of pricey tea, hoping that Anne would see how much she appreciated the concession.

A block away, Selonnah squinted at what looked like a Realtor's metal sign in the front yard. Sure enough, Anne's little shy lady of a house was for sale. The hedges and trees looked recently trimmed.

Just beyond the sign, a man sat on the curb. His knees were spread far apart and his elbows rested on them, and his head hung nearly to his chest. Selonnah had suffered runner's cramps before, and wondered if the young man were ill. She turned to enter the driveway and rolled down her window.

"You all right?"

The man seemed startled, as if he hadn't heard the car at all. He had close-cut rough-textured brown hair and was dressed in khaki pants and deck shoes. His white shirt rumpled in the way that only heavily starched and ironed fabric can, in peaks and creases. When he looked up at Selonnah, his eyes were lifeless, like a perch on a platter, she thought. A split second later something animated behind those grey-green eyes and he seemed to focus on her.

"You're here to see her? You know her?" His voice was thick, as if unused.

Selonnah's brain played a warning note. She drew back from the window, but the man never rose to his feet, just spoke to her with his neck twisted upward and back in what must have been a painful position. He seemed to expect her silence and slowly turned again toward the street. She decided to roll the window up anyway and drive up closer to the house and think what to do.

She sat in the car for a while, hoping that Anne would come to the door and give her some guidance. On the curb, the man had turned his torso toward her again and was shouting to her.

"Can you get her to talk to me? I have to talk to her. I have to make amends."

Selonnah dialed Anne's number.

"For pity's sake, Selonnah, I'm sorry. I didn't know you were here. Just come on in. He won't hurt you."

"You'll explain, I guess, when I get inside?"

By that time Anne was opening the front door and glaring past her at the man. He walked across the street, sat down on the opposite curb, and held his hands out toward them, beseeching, as Selonnah entered the house and they shut the door.

"What is that all about?"

"You saw the Realtor's sign?"

"Yes—does that man have anything to do with you moving?"

Anne took the bag of groceries, smiled wanly at Selonnah by way of thanks, and put them on the kitchen table. Then she sighed and sat down on the couch, facing away from the street, absently rubbing the scratches on her forearms. So she had done the pruning, Selonnah thought. Her baby, K.C., slept serenely in an infant seat beside her.

"The new mother's equivalent of window-shopping," she said, as she apologetically tossed aside a catalog and a *TV Guide*. "Ah, the man outside."

"Who is he?"

"Remember I told you how my husband, Ryan, was killed?"

Selonnah remembered Roger's caution, implying that Anne hadn't been honest with her about the circumstances.

Or, Selonnah thought at she looked at the broad, honest face of a woman she was beginning to regard as a friend, perhaps Selonnah had misunderstood. Time to clarify it.

"Tell me, how and when did your husband's death take place?"

Anne seemed only momentarily surprised at what must have seemed to be an irrelevant question. She blinked and then answered.

"Out in a training field in the desert west of here, in an exercise. Ryan was in the Army Reserve, good at what he did, an instructor in fact. One of his feet was injured when he fell rappelling about two years ago, and it affected his balance. Sometimes he walked with a cane. Said it was a badge of honor, meant that he could face the dragon. He didn't really always need the cane and only used it when he was off duty; but he said that in Utah, it kept people from thinking that you're drunk." She smiled and was silent for a minute, lost in memories.

"But he was always an outsider in his reserve unit because he wasn't LDS. I always suspected that was one of the reasons his foot was injured—because he felt he had something to prove, maybe took risks that some of the other guys wouldn't. But he would just laugh it off and tell me not to worry. And the injury affected his hearing too, but I don't think anyone ever knew that. He learned to read lips and was good at that too.

"You know how he explained hearing loss? He told me that once his hearing started to fade, he had to pay strict attention to people's voices. He said that when someone talked, it was like a bunch of phonemes and syllables were tossed into the air. It would take him a moment or two, he said, to wait for them to arrange themselves. He trained himself to look very alertly into the eyes of the person who spoke to him, and to

219

answer slowly, so as to minimize the time he'd waited for all the syllables to take shape as words he recognized."

Selonnah saw that this must be talked out. She held her peace as Anne continued.

"That man out there was in his unit. His name is Noel Dean. He was with Ryan when he, when he . . ." She fell silent, then looked up at Selonnah.

"He wasn't just with Ryan when he was killed. He was actually a part of why he was killed."

Selonnah raised her eyebrows.

"What I mean," continued Anne, "is that he and some of the other guys in the company let him be killed." She waited a moment for this to sink in.

"There's a story in the Bible about a king who wanted one of his soldiers dead, but didn't want to kill him himself. As commander of the army, the king commanded one of his captains to take his troop out to the heat of the battle. The king told the captain to order all the men to fall back and let the enemy kill the soldier. The king thought he'd get what he wanted without getting his own hands dirty, if you know what I mean."

"That's what happened with your husband?"

"I'm not sure that anyone just set out to kill him. But he was always the odd man out, the only Christian. All the guys were super friendly to him until he made it plain that he wasn't going to become a Mormon."

"Surely Ryan wasn't the only non-Mormon in the company. Is this the way all of them were treated?"

"You're not from around here, are you," Anne said with a dry laugh. "If you resist pressure to become a Mormon, you find out why they get a reputation for being clannish. Those people who are atheists and just blow them off, Mormons leave them alone. But there's something about a vocal Christian who won't buckle. . . ." Her voice trailed off. "You don't get the jobs, you don't get the raises, you don't get the assignments. Especially in the smaller towns, somebody who's LDS is always in line in front of you even if you got there first. It's the good-buddy system at a whole new level.

"It raises the stakes when the job situation involves live ammo and hand grenades." She paused and took a shaky breath. "October 8, late afternoon. Ryan and his company were in a bunker—more of a rocky cave, really—during some war games, and some of the chemicals that were stored at the back became unstable. Everybody knew that they couldn't check it out and all get out in time. Ryan didn't get out in time."

"This was deliberate?"

"No, I don't think it was even conscious. Certainly not deliberate or preplanned. When the situation looked dangerous, Ryan told three guys to grab gas masks and follow him to investigate. But they didn't—in the end, he went in alone. Everyone there was LDS except him. At first the story they all told was that Ryan told them to all get out and he'd go investigate, and everybody believed that, because it's something Ryan would have taken on himself. And that's how it stood until about three months ago. The guy you see outside, Noel Dean, came to me and told me the truth. Said the lie was eating him up inside, and he couldn't stand it. And said that the oaths the men took, oaths of secrecy about what really happened, it shook his faith in Mormonism to the core."

Selonnah walked to the window. Noel Dean sat unmoving on the curb, his back now rigid, knees together and head up like an old gentleman waiting for a bus.

"These aren't bad people. Mormons teach and try to practice things like compassion and fairness. And loyalty. What he and his buddies did must have seemed natural to him. You stick together with people who are like you. When Noel

Dean first came to me and told me what really happened, I was beside myself, full of fury and blame. You're a reporter, you understand—I wanted to expose them all. But I began to understand that anger was going to erode me, one layer at a time, from the inside out, like a vat of acid.

"It took a long time, but I began to forgive him. Truly, I've put it behind me—at least most days—in spite of the fact that he went to a television reporter, came clean, made it all public anyway. He got reprimanded, and so did the others, kicked out of the reserves. I tell him that I've forgiven him but there's something else he needs. It's the whole LDS thing— it's all built on a culture of atonement."

"What do you mean?"

Anne sighed. "You said you don't really have a Christian background, so I'm not sure if I can get this across. Look. I make mistakes all the time. In fact, to tell it straight, with any precision of language, I sin. Big-time. I've done so many things I'm ashamed of in my life. I couldn't begin to make reparations for most of it—people move away, opportunities just evaporate. If you can't make it up, you're left with guilt and helplessness."

Selonnah knew all about guilt. And feeling bereft of ability.

"As a Christian, I have a confidence. There's always a ladder back up out of any pit I have climbed into. I do all I can to make amends but at the end of the day I am forgiven by God, who has the power to set things right, who can make it up to people in ways I never could. Power I don't have."

"This Noel Dean would feel the same way, wouldn't he? Don't Mormons believe they can get this, this . . ." Selonnah struggled with the words, "forgiveness or atonement or whatever you're calling it?"

"Not exactly the same. I take the Bible seriously, and it says everything I do wrong, and I'm truly sorry for, is washed away, by a onetime sacrifice two thousand years ago. The cross."

Could it be? Could such a thing be? Is there a cosmic Red Flag Hill redemption? One that covers all the bases, makes up for all the lapses and crimes against her own humanity and that of others? Selonnah felt something bare, yearning in her chest. Anne continued on, oblivious.

"But in Mormon doctrine, some things can't be washed away by what Jesus did," Anne said. "You, the perpetrator, have to do something extra."

"Extra?"

"Well, there are certain sins, LDS doctrine teaches, that are outside the pale of anything Jesus did. Certain sins that have to be paid for with the blood of the person who committed the sins."

"Like what sins?"

"Well, any murder of an innocent person. If you kill somebody, you have to be killed—and not just any kind of death will do, your blood has to be *shed*. Not by gas chamber, not by lethal injection. That's why Utah for many years gave convicted murderers the option to be shot by firing squad. I mean, the blood has to literally drip."

Selonnah must have looked skeptical. Anne was in journalist mode. "So we have a bit of a credibility problem? Just read Norman Mailer's book *The Executioner's Song* about Gary Gilmore. Spells the whole thing out. Or Jon Krakauer's *Under the Banner of Heaven.*

"This is all part of Utah politics—but even more, part of its history and culture. You can look through the speeches of early LDS prophets and other leaders at the time before Utah was a state and whatever the Mormon Church said was law, was law.

"You should google 'Mountain Meadows Massacre.'

Historians—even the honest LDS ones—admit that in 1857 Brigham Young knew about the order to kill over a hundred innocent 'gentile' immigrants to Utah. Men, women, even some children. Young had a band of henchmen he called the Danites, and one of the men who carried out the orders at Mountain Meadows was named John D. Lee. He ended up being the scapegoat of the situation, and he was executed by firing squad.

"From the beginnings of Brigham Young's time, if you committed certain specific crimes, you would have to shed your blood. Not just murder, but theft, adultery, breaking a covenant, whoredom, marrying a Negro, apostasy."

"What's that last term, apostasy?" Selonnah asked.

"Leaving the Mormon Church."

"Okay. So what has this got to do with your husband's death?" Selonnah felt as if she were in a tunnel full of papers, all flying around her, and only one had instructions for getting out. "Are you saying that his Mormon buddies were making Ryan atone for something?"

"Not at all! Mormons of our generation don't believe that theft or marrying an African American should necessarily mean blood atonement, but many would certainly say that breaking a covenant like you make in the temple or killing somebody would qualify for—that is, necessitate—blood atonement. Ryan's death was an accident, but a preventable accident. Those guys made a bad collective decision; they all drew back and let him go in alone. In the mind of a Mormon, it's something that needs personal atonement. Ryan didn't need to atone—his buddies did. They believed they participated in his death.

"What I'm saying is that you see, right there on my front lawn, a picture of someone who up until a few weeks ago believed he would be damned for all eternity if he didn't shed his own blood to set things right. He told me he doesn't believe Mormonism anymore, but he still feels a need to somehow personally atone.

"And all his buddies would be wondering if the death of my Ryan, an innocent person even though he was a Gentile, required an act of atonement. In Mormon doctrine, your blood can atone for one person that you kill."

"One? What if you kill more than one?"

"Potluck, I suppose." Anne was leaning toward the baby. "I guess you take your chances at judgment day." She shook her head regretfully as she looked back up. "I guess that was pretty flippant. I told you that my sister became a Mormon, right? She lives down in southern Utah in a little town. Some folks down there tend to think the old ways were better, that Danite avengers should be reinstituted and blood atonement is an act of mercy."

Selonnah wanted to ask how it was merciful, but Anne forged on before she could articulate the question. "My sister's husband's brother killed two people in a drunk driving accident. Yeah, he was a 'jack Mormon'—sort of the LDS equivalent of a lapsed Catholic—because of the drinking, but he still believed a lot of the doctrine. Or was afraid of the doctrine, I guess. My sister was just beyond grief because she believes her brother-in-law could die to atone for *one* person's death, but not more than one. I don't know if that's Mormon doctrine or just her take on it, but every single Mormon I knew felt the same way."

Selonnah thought for a moment. "So what you're saying is that Mormons would say those kinds of sins can be corrected, remediated, as far as the effect on the community as a whole." She was thinking back to sociology classes, trying to make sense of this foreign country with its own English

225

language right in the middle of twenty-first-century America. "So it's statistical, in a sense."

"Never thought of it that way," Anne said. "And I bet they don't either. But the problem is what we call victimless crime—where the society as a whole suffers a loss, but no one person can measure—you know, tally up—how just exactly it affects him or her. And what about our whole screwed-up lives? Who can make that right, ever?"

Selonnah felt out of her league and flustered. She felt again the internal tugging of a desire for what could happen on a Red Flag Hill. But her linguistic inventory, she realized with regret, was understocked for conversation about it. She felt the immediate familiar comfort of procrastination and deflection. She reached into her satchel and drew out a list she'd been working on all day.

In her mind, she called it the "What's the deal" list—because every question, if she could just ask it, would begin with "What is the deal with . . . ?"

"Look, I don't want to impose on your time. I've got to get back to the office and finish up another story. I've made a list of things I wanted to ask you about. This blood atonement thing, that's good, I'll take your advice and google it and maybe get some more good background."

Anne dipped her head, *you're welcome.*

"And what you told me about some of those temple vows, and now putting that together with what you said about blood atonement—so you think that's why that Heber J. Bruce was killed?"

"Well, nobody in the media has said anything about his Church membership," said Anne. "I mean, even the *Deseret Morning News* wouldn't call him an ex-Mormon, but I've heard rumors that he was once a 'temple Mormon'—been through a temple and taken vows. Then he left Mormonism and he didn't do it quietly. He had pamphlets about Mormonism's past printed up and he distributed them by the reams. That got somebody's attention: Best I can figure from what I've heard, the cuts that were on his body were just like the old penalties for breaking temple vows of silence—tongue cut out, disemboweled, et cetera."

"Ah. That would explain the note left with him." She produced a copy of the hand-lettered note in code.

Anne's eyebrows lifted. "So you can read this?"

Selonnah laughed. "Well, let's just say I figured it out with Internet help. See, here's what it says."

They both looked at the paper, with Selonnah's typewritten translation below.

"'I say, rather than apostates flourish here, I will unsheathe my bowie knife and conquer or die. Brigham Young, Journal of Discourses, Volume 1 p. 83.'"

"Whoa," said Anne.

"You think whoever killed Heber J. Bruce was maybe trying to reinstate the original way things were done in

Mormonism, the old laws and penalties?" asked Selonnah.

"Wouldn't be surprised. That makes sense. And there's another aspect of this you need to know. If someone believes in blood atonement, they would *want* to have their blood shed. They would see it as the only way to get out from under a crime nobody else can pay for. Blood for blood. And whoever expedites it would be doing the criminal a favor," Anne said. "If you're right about what ties those three murders together, boy, wait till all of this hits the headlines."

"That's my job. I just want to make sure that I understand what's going on here," Selonnah said. "So where could I do some more reading on the specific crimes that were punishable by blood in Brigham Young's time?"

"The Internet's your best friend there. And there are a lot of online organizations run by very vocal ex-Mormons who will give you some help—and some good quotes for articles. I doubt your cousin Roger is going to give you much for a sidebar article."

The thought stabbed Selonnah. Roger, what about Roger? She continued down her list. "In fact, I tried to talk to Roger about the death of that prostitute, Bernadette Rodriguez. I found plenty of information showing it's been generally believed that the Book of Mormon identifies the Catholic Church as the 'great whore.'"

It was Anne's turn to look skeptical. Selonnah sighed and thumbed through printouts to show her the same documents she showed Roger.

"I'll be darned," Anne said. "Now that I think of it, I do remember some kids in grade school talking about this little Catholic kid who moved to town. Seemed to me even at the time that there was more there than him just being a non-Mormon—I knew all about that. They made a particular point of making fun of his scapulars, tugging on them and leading him around by the straps. The family didn't last long in my hometown of Tooele."

"It's sounding more and more to me like whoever is behind these murders is not only somebody who knows about Mormonism but has some sort of personal stake in bringing public attention to it." Selonnah looked out the window, where Noel Dean's shirtsleeves flapped in the wind of each passing car. "How long ago did that guy come to you with the confession about what happened to your husband?"

"Just a few weeks ago. I guess it's died down, so to speak, with all the bomb threats to the Masonic temples and now with these recent murders," Anne said. "But before that we were the talk of the town, just before K.C. was born."

"Tell me what Dean told you."

"Well, he was a bishop in a local ward here. Great reputation, owned his own Web design company, successful. Nice family, seven or eight kids. When he and the other guys in the company first got together and cooked up their story about how Ryan died, they all decided it would come to light that Ryan wasn't LDS and people would know what happened."

"Why did they think that? In a military investigation, you mean?"

"Gotta understand the depth of loyalty these guys have to the Mormon Church. They thought first to protect it, and then to protect themselves. That's why they swore an oath to each other not to tell. It was only later when Dean's conscience got the better of him that he began to feel real pain for his part in my husband's death. But before that, his top priority was the Church. Now he's torn between his lifelong belief that he could atone for the sin of murder, and the realization that Mormonism itself is just as hopeless."

"Doesn't it look like the same thing was going on with these crimes, these murders?" Selonnah was standing now

229

at the window, looking at the epitome of abject penitence, a broken man sitting on a curb. "Could it be that whoever did this wanted to go back to the way Mormonism used to be? Maybe—take care of problems, give people the chance to atone for sins that would send them to hell without the shedding of their own blood. It would have looked like justice. And in a twisted kind of way, it would have looked like mercy."

Anne stood, too, at the window beside Selonnah, looking at the man. "Noel Dean was a true believer, that kind of man."

"I wonder . . ." Selonnah started. Could a man like that have killed others? "On the other hand, some guy, who says he has details and can prove he did it, has confessed to all those crimes. They're bringing him to Salt Lake tonight, and there will be a press conference tomorrow."

"What about the other Alphabet Code crimes?"

"Oh, you must still have moles inside the newspaper office," Selonnah said.

"Yes. There's been a rash of bizarre crimes done by someone—or someones—who also left notes in the Deseret Alphabet at the scene."

"Let's see, one was the elderly couple. They were glued together, is that what I heard? But no real damage?"

Anne nodded. "Just cosmetic damage, so to speak. And then there was poor old Clarissa Clarissa."

"You sound like you know her."

"She's kind of a downtown fixture. Homeless and apparently harmless." Anne's own hands seemed anxious to discuss this: go on, go on.

"Something about her hands, you already knew that too, I see. But the privacy laws make it so hard to find out anything about a medical condition, and there is something about her hands that I can't get to the bottom of."

"I heard they were bleached white," said Anne. "And that makes sense—if someone was trying to show that being even a fourth-generation Mormon won't get a Native American lighter skin, as the Book of Mormon promised them."

Selonnah raised her eyebrows, but Anne went on to her next question.

"And what about the old men, from the nursing home?"

"The three men from Nephi, well . . ."

"Stop!" Anne jumped to her feet.

"What? What?"

"You just solved part of it, girl!"

"How? You know what their note said? I have it here but it didn't make any sense to me."

"I bet it's something about the Three Nephites!"

Selonnah opened the note but Anne was too excited to look.

- 3 Nephi 28:25

"Nephites. Ancient Jewish Americans. Light-skinned ones. The Book of Mormon contains a promise that some of them would still be alive, after two thousand years."

Anne was laughing aloud, something Selonnah had not seen her do. For a moment the man outside on her curb did not exist. Anne was a little girl, giggling and clasping her hands in front of her.

"This is too delicious. It's a joke, an inside joke. See, every Mormon family has stories about the Three Nephites. The Book of Mormon said that Jesus came to the Americas—"

"Wait a minute." Selonnah was having a hard time digesting all this. "You're saying Mormons believe that Jesus came here? Like, to the United States?"

"Yep. Well, to somewhere in the Americas. Between the time He was resurrected and when He went back to heaven."

"Okay . . ." Selonnah wished she knew more about such things. "Okay . . ."

"So Mormons say Jesus promised three of these Nephites that they would never die."

"So they're still alive? Here, like around here?"

"Every Mormon family has a story about mysterious strangers who gave Cousin Al a ride when his car broke down, or who told Aunt Jenny not to go down a road that she later learned had a bridge out, or who stood in front of a soldier so that he wasn't wounded or pointed the way to a good investment or . . . you name it. Every Mormon knows Three Nephites stories. They're a folklore genre all to themselves."

"Ah." Selonnah's thoughts rattled into order. "So whoever kidnapped these three men would have chosen them specifically, not because of who they were, but because they were from a place upstate called Nephi and thus they were Nephites."

"Yes, that's what I think too." Anne settled down enough

to look over Selonnah's shoulder at the cipher. Selonnah's transcription was scrawled beneath each letter.

Behold, I was about to write the names of those who were never to taste of death, but the Lord forbade, therefore I write them not, for they are hid from the world. —3 Nephi 28:25

"Okay, so this verse is about what you're calling the Three Nephites. Okay. But these new crimes—the homeless lady, the old couple, and now these old men. What do they have in common?" Selonnah searched for more order.

"They are all vulnerable. And I understand that rohypnol was used in each case," said Anne.

"And nobody was hurt, not really."

"You must not have heard. One of the older men died, apparently from some preexisting condition. He wasn't deliberately harmed, it just happened."

"But all three situations had notes in the Deseret Alphabet?"

Anne sat down on the couch. "I'm thinking maybe a copycat. I mean, look at the difference between killing and mutilating people—and these other three situations that happened later. I know they all had code notes, but anybody could have written them."

"There is a difference. I can feel it," agreed Selonnah.

They looked again out at Noel Dean.

"Who is it? Who would do such horrible things to Kirsten Young and to Heber J. Bruce and to that Rodriguez woman? And what was the point? He was trying to make a point," Anne said.

"When you build a nation of zealots, they do zealous things," Selonnah said. "And I don't put any stock in confessions. Just because someone has come forward and seems credible, that means nothing. Crimes like this bring out all the loonies, the professional confessors. Do you think someone *like* Noel Dean—maybe even Dean himself—could have

233

committed those crimes? When I leave here, I'm going to call Lt. Luke Taylor and tell him what we've talked about. Have you had occasion to interview him, or talk to him, one-on-one?"

Anne shook her head, and Selonnah continued. "Luke's a Mormon—but he's a good man, I know it. I feel it. And besides that, maybe you need some protection."

Anne's voice was almost tender. "I don't think I need protection, just distance. I forgave Noel Dean, Selonnah. Or at least I'm in the process. But I can't take away his sin. There's a place where everything will someday be set right, all the debts paid, everything atoned for. But Noel Dean can't forgive himself. He's desperate. His mind could snap any minute. The police know about him and that's why he sits just on the other side of my driveway. When I call, and a patrol car comes, he will park across the way there." She motioned across the street to an elementary school's playground, with a street beyond it.

"That's why I'm moving—it's not that I'm afraid of him, it's just that I cannot bear his grief any longer."

CHAPTER 25

LUKE GREW UP in a colonia in northern Mexico, the son of Hyrum Ridgon Taylor, a vigorous colossus of a man whose hair was the color of the plumber's putty that clung to his wedding ring and shoestrings; a man who seemed to speak healing to a John Deere and could restring the crooked legs of baby dolls through their yawning torsos.

Luke's mother and her two sister-wives—Luke called them "aunties"—worshiped and competed for the attention of Papa Taylor as they called him, while all his twenty children and multitudinous grandchildren lived in awe of him, believed him to be invincible and immortal. Luke was the last of his offspring, born to Papa Taylor when he was nearly sixty years old. Not until Papa suffered his last heart attack, received his last valve replacement, and got the bad news at a checkup the next year that he only had a couple of months to live because no more surgeries could be done, did anyone ever consider his mortality. And even then, no one could really believe it.

Papa was strong enough to pitch hay and hoist pig feed sacks on his shoulders up until the day he suddenly died, just as the doctors had said he would. But for the last two months, he had a daily routine: Before breakfast, he would walk out beyond the farthest corral to the rocky hill that dominated the community. There, in the *campo santo*, the hallowed graveyard of their Zion del Sur, he cleared the stones and carefully measured, and then filled the air of the *madrugada* —daybreak—with the whining, scraping sounds of his shovel biting pebbles and slate.

The afternoon that he fell down and didn't get up, his last movement was the straining of his neck and eyes toward that hill, wondering, perhaps, if the coyotes or the night wind would push any dirt back into the precision of the square corners of his waiting grave before he got there.

Luke learned two great lessons from his father's death. One was that we are all clay, separated from the earth for a while, but clay nonetheless and irresistibly drawn to the aggregate that reaches patiently and persistently for our ankles each step we take. One day that airy insubstantial grip will suddenly materialize and gain a purchase and the person we thought so solid, so irreplaceable, is suddenly and irretrievably absent.

As he drove across Salt Lake City's tangled traffic, Luke pondered the image of a living earth that had been part of his thinking since the first time he read the speeches of Heber C. Kimball, apostle to LDS founder Joseph Smith. Kimball taught that the earth came from parent earths and was itself, as a living entity, able to conceive. And if it could conceive, Luke thought, it could covet.

We all dig our graves, thought Luke, all of us making

some preparation whether we know it or not, whether we like it or not, whether we intend it or not. Each day we arrange some feature of our final repose in the bosom of the earth.

And then there is the sense of urgency that escorts all such inevitabilities. Luke knew that, as an eligible young man with no prospects of marriage, he worried all his kinfolk both in the States and below. They saw it as a sort of unwarranted willfulness, a stubborn refusal to settle down with a wife (those in the States said) or with several (as the Mexican contingent and some stateside would have it) and produce bodies for all the spirits waiting up in heaven to come to earth. As a faithful Saint, it was his responsibility to propagate as lavishly as his resources and the durability of his wife (wives) would permit, so none of those anxious intelligences would be doomed to be sent to earth to live with gentile families.

Most polygamous relatives gave up on him years ago, though, when he decided to go on a mission for the LDS Church. All Mormon polygamists who trace their heritage and authority to Joseph Smith and Brigham Young believe that the Salt Lake City LDS Church went apostate when in 1890 one of its prophets made illegal what Joseph Smith had once proclaimed "the new and everlasting covenant" of plural marriage.

Thus it was incomprehensible to Luke's hundreds of kin that he would want to unite himself to the group that had so betrayed its roots—so they said—just so that Utah could be accepted into the United States. But Luke had moved to Provo, attended BYU for two years, and been approved by his local LDS bishopric to go on a mission. His motivations were twofold: First, he hoped that his language skills would probably expedite his "calling" to a South American country where he would undoubtedly shine and thereby attain, as a

"RM" or returned missionary, the credibility he'd need to survive in what he hoped would be a high-profile law enforcement career in Utah.

Second, he prided himself on being an exceedingly pragmatic young man, one who recognized that the winds of American favor were beginning to blow fair upon the once-beleaguered ship of Mormondom.

The Church's rosy days began, Luke knew, in the early 1970s in the era of the toothy-smiled Osmonds and full-page ads in *Reader's Digest*, as the LDS Church began to distance itself from its clannish image and embarrassing nineteenth-century past. Mormon politicians, athletes, financiers, and other public figures showed a scrubbed-clean family solidarity. Hundreds of Mitt Romney types entered politics. Brigham Young University built its law school with the express purpose of training LDS legal experts who, Brigham Young had vociferously prophesied, would be the only ones who would be able to save the United States Constitution from utter ruin in some certain and not-too-distant scenario of social chaos. A day was coming, Luke was confident, when Mormonism would be not only the dominant culture of the United States, but it would be the go-to resource for people outside the Church too.

In the more foreseeable future, Luke believed, as did many people, that polygamy would eventually be legalized. Even today in Great Britain, any immigrant who came from a country where polygamy was legal could bring all his wives and even receive extra British government benefits. Here in the United States, it was true that many television shows and other media regarded plural marriage as salacious fodder for the voracious maw of programming; but Luke noted with satisfaction that other shows were beginning to sympathetically portray polygamous unions. Combine that with the fact that the borders of what constitutes a marriage were beginning to erode with the acceptance of same-sex marriages, and Luke believed that the legalizing of polygamous unions between consenting adults was not far behind. In fact, some people were beginning to characterize polygamy as "the next civil rights battle."

Like many people, Luke's heart was torn when he saw children ripped from their mothers' arms in raids, and when he saw polygamous fathers hauled off in shackles, unable to support their families. Just the impact on the state's welfare system would be catastrophic if all plural wives and their thousands of children suddenly became Utah's dependents. Luke knew of seven brothers who claimed more than six hundred children between them. Perhaps the day of legal polygamy was coming soon, he thought.

He couldn't say he didn't occasionally enjoy the transparent attempts by friends and coworkers to set him up with cousins, widows, misunderstood divorcees, and sister missionaries just back from places ranging from the wilds of Papua New Guinea to the Gaelic air of the Isle of Man. Behind each friendly persuasion was an unspoken fear. Even the most devout single Mormon, though promised eventual residence in the highest level of heaven, would be doomed to eternal servitude to the married ones. And it wasn't that Luke was unwilling to serve others. . . .

However, his own wedding day always seemed illusive. He prayed all the time to a Heavenly Father who understood marriage, since he himself had gone through the process of choosing wives—many of them—during his sojourn as a human on some distant planet far beyond the strongest telescopes here on earth. Such a God would understand the prayers of a lonely man in search of an eternal mate.

Meanwhile Luke knew what it was to wait and ask. He'd

exhausted in prayer every word in English that begged: adjure, implore, ask, request, insist, require, solicit, appeal, pray, inquire, invite, beg, supplicate, beseech, entreat, plead, petition for, demand, sue, prithee, seek, importune, crave. Then he went on with Spanish: *Te pido, Te mendigo, Te ruego, Te suplico, Te imploro*; to Quechua's *mañapakuy* . . . He found that the first words he wanted to know in any language were petition words, any linguistic tool to prize the ears of a God who seemed, he thought without a trace of bitterness, to have developed a tone deafness to the sound of his voice.

What had he done with his life? He knew he was affable and well-liked, but what had he done with his life? He'd baptized a few Uruguayans, saved them, that is, if they'd just remember to come to church and live the Word of Wisdom and stay out of other people's beds.

The honking of a horn as he drove along brought back the only other memory he had of saving anyone. He remembered a time when his mother had left him and some younger cousins in a car in the shade while she picked vegetables from a communal farm. The car had begun to roll down the hill and Luke had vaulted over the backseat and placed both of his six-year-old feet on the brake.

Everyone was saved. It was the last time in his life he would be able to say that.

His epaulette radio crackled at his ear. Though the technician had assured him a few minutes ago when he picked it up at the repair shop that the problem was just some loose wiring that he had securely soldered, Luke no longer had confidence in the device. True to his distrust, the sounds that came from it sounded like angry shrunken heads.

"Call me on my cell," Luke shouted into his shoulder. "Call on my CELL."

Helaman's voice on the phone sounded strained. "You

heard about the confession," he more stated than asked. "The police department in Price sent me a video clip of this guy. I want you to watch it with me. They're flying him up here on their little prop jet plane, one of those four-seaters. It'll take them awhile. Meet me in my office."

Luke was glad for the face time with the chief. He mentally listed the elements of Selonnah's last brief telephone call to him. Should he share Selonnah's thoughts with the chief? He believed that her suspicions about Noel Dean were credible and wanted to discuss them with Helaman, but somewhere in his brain a caution light blinked. He had listened attentively to Selonnah's waltz around the LDS issues and tried to see, as she described, a man who could have done such things. Noel Dean was a man, she said, who had been a "true believer" but felt himself betrayed by too much obedience to the Church and its doctrines. Such a man would certainly be capable of trying to draw attention to the Church, to make public its flaws.

He turned off the caution light. Luke needed Helaman's insights.

But the chief wasn't in his office when Luke arrived, and he found himself once again staring at the family photos ensconced behind Helaman's desk chair, and thinking of the secrets they represented.

Salt Lake City is a large urban metropolis, but within it reigns the sovereign oligarchy and culture of the Mormon Church, a web of people and relations as fine and as strong as tatted steel. Thus it was that few secrets about families could stay secrets. For instance, Luke had known for months that Helaman was living alone even though the chief never came out and said anything about his wife, Janine, and daughter, Gracie—in fact, hadn't mentioned their names in months.

241

When Janine and Gracie first went to visit friends in southern Utah, Helaman had made jokes about having to do without his "Gracie fixes" while they would be gone for two weeks. But the actual physical toll of the absence on Helaman was like an etching away of all his softnesses too; and when the time stretched to a month, then two, now going on three—Helaman seemed lately to be made only of tendons and nerves.

Luke looked again more closely at the photo of Janine—peering through the peculiar powdery smears on the glass—to see if the hooded eyes of Helaman's wife, who looked directly, haughtily, and unapologetically into the camera, would tell him.

Luke wondered if Janine's long absence had anything to do with the area she and Gracie were visiting. Everyone knew that region of southern Utah was riddled with polygamous settlements; and Brace Crossing where they'd been for these months was among the most notorious. Even though Luke had polygamous roots, he regarded these people as on the edge of a fanatic fringe. It wasn't their appearance, he was used to that—long-haired unadorned women all in long dresses and clean-shaven men in lumberjack shirts and denims. But Brace Crossing was almost a caricature of Utah's polygamous towns with their ubiquitous old houses with multiple chimneys that showed the separate living quarters for plural wives who could range in age from middle-aged down to early teens.

The blank-faced unpainted homes behind chain-link fences in Brace Crossing breathed an almost-palpable air of hostile defensiveness and haphazard construction. The "No Trespassing" signs kept the curious away from the cobbled-together houses that spread like dividing cells as new wives—and children—agglomerated. In back of the houses were storage sheds containing emergency supplies and weapons. Some of those guns were hunting rifles, Luke thought. Some.

The women of polygamy, whom everyone outside seemed to want to rescue, were the most secretive of all, the least likely to talk to any strangers. Luke believed that polygamy could "work," under the kind of circumstances like his childhood. Was it the generations of constant hiding that caused all the pain behind those partitions in Brace Crossing? Luke wondered idly. Or was it the jealousies that simmered to rich broth over lifetimes?

Each such town had one (or more) buildings that proclaimed on signs that they were the only "TRUE AND LIVING CHURCH" or "APOSTOLIC SAINTS" or "FAITHFUL TRUE" or "LATTER-DAY FAITHFUL." Such verbiage indicated common roots intertwined with the Mormon Church, but contained, for those who knew, an insistent public corrective to the apostasy they saw in the Salt Lake City ecclesiastical leadership. Each splinter accused the plank.

Luke remembered hearing Janine comment acerbically on the "soft belly" of a church that would, in her words, "change its own scriptures just to get the ACLU off its back." The last time Luke saw her, it was just before she left for Brace Crossing. She was uncharacteristically talkative that night at a chamber of commerce dinner at which she sat next to Luke.

That night months ago, Helaman had just returned from a special assignment in upper New York State. He used precious vacation time for the off-duty trip, a matter on which Janine commented bitterly and freely. Luke remembered how unsettled it made him feel to hear Janine's steel-cut innermost thoughts so publicly (though not loudly) revealed.

The LDS Church had called on Helaman's bomb disposal expertise to electronically sweep the nonpublic areas of the

Hill Cumorah Pageant, an annual depiction of events chronicled in the Book of Mormon, as well as dramas about Joseph Smith's receiving the gold plates from which the LDS scripture was translated. The trip had been hush-hush, and Helaman's little-known past as a CIA operative certainly was no public knowledge. Luke, Helaman, and many other returned LDS missionaries were courted by the CIA because they had successfully been embedded in foreign countries and knew intimate details that would allow them to pass as natives, if need be. And need often was.

Luke declined his government's invitation, but Helaman accepted. The trade-off for those early years of covert service was for Helaman the specialized and secretive training in bomb disposal he received. Even now, he read voraciously about bombs and had the kind of cutting-edge knowledge that both the police department and the LDS Church called upon. In this case, Helaman's clandestine public-service trip had lasted longer than it should have, cutting into Janine's last hours at home with him before her trip.

"Wonder why the *prophet*"—here Janine pursed her lips, popping consonants as if they were chewed-stiff bubble gum—"why he can't use his gift of *prophecy* to know when somebody *plans* to attack his *people*. Surely he would know, if he were really a *prophet*, how to *protect* the site where the gold *plates* are, *for Pete's sake*."

Sure didn't sound very supportive of Salt Lake's Church leadership. Luke wondered at the time about the juxtaposition of her comments with the fact that she was leaving for Brace Crossing the next day. As far as Luke knew, she had no relatives there, and had no hobbies except oil painting of barren landscapes. And of course Brace Crossing had plenty of those.

"Is she going down to paint?" Luke asked Helaman, who

seemed happy to say that she was. As her absence wore on, Luke would have gladly shipped her art supplies had she been his wife, but the toll on Helaman seemed exponential.

Luke was startled out of his thoughts by Donnell, who put his head into Helaman's office to announce that the chief was on his way. By way of thanks, Luke rose and extended his hand to shake Donnell's and it was the handshake that solved one of the mysteries of the day. Donnell snapped off a latex examination glove and threw it into a wastebasket before he extended his own hand.

It was only as Luke rubbed the talc-smooth powder transferred to his hands from Donnell's did he understand why the glass over the photograph of Janine was so clouded. Someone, a glove-wearer someone who had this same kind of dust on his fingers, had pointed at her face, stabbing something at her, over and over and over and over.

Helaman's sudden appearance in his office startled Luke again. The chief tapped a few keys on his computer, then without a word pulled his monitor around to face Luke. Rustling sounds and the jiggling motions of the camera preceded the focus on a rangy man with equine teeth and lips who sat alone at a table and looked into the camera with unabashed curiosity and self-consciousness. When a uniformed officer took his place opposite the odd-looking man, he arched his back and leaned forward on the metal table, his forearms forming a triangle into the center of which he seemed to want to drop his head. But he kept jerking his head up with small motions to glance sidelong toward the camera.

"You have waived the right to an attorney, Mr. Benson?" the policeman asked. His voice seemed to wobble and fade in and out, Luke thought. Just as bad as his own epaulette radio.

The man nodded.

"State your full name."

"I'm LeBaron James Benson, and yes I did waive a right to an attorney." The man's voice sounded like a fat man's snore, toneless and abrupt. "I don't need one, I just need to confess. . . ."

"Hold on," said the officer. "I'll ask some questions and you just answer them, okay, Mr. Benson? Do you understand that we are videotaping this, and . . . ?"

Benson stood up and faced the camera. "I have the right to remain silent, and if I give up that right, anything I do say can be used against me in a court of law. I know that I have a right to an attorney, and I don't want one or need one, especially one of the stupid so-called free court-appointed flunkies that you assign to people who can't afford real lawyers." He straightened up, pleased with his recitation. "And furthermore, all this Miranda garbage is useless—did you know that Ernesto Miranda, the Miranda rights guy, was killed by a guy who got off the hook by staying silent? So who did that help?"

He sat down with a clatter of the metal chair.

"That guy has been through the system before," said Luke.

The veins on Helaman's temples were distended, and throbbed in tiny ropelike convulsions. He didn't say a word, just stared at the monitor and clenched his teeth.

Luke tore his attention from the chief to look at the monitor. Perhaps it was just poor picture quality, thought Luke, but the prisoner looked yellowish—his skin, his eyes, even those enormous horse teeth. His grey-streaked black hair was as disorderly as only a bad prison haircut could make it. Benson turned toward the camera with the confidentiality of a Shakespearean aside.

"I want to confess to the killings of Heber J. Bruce, Bernadette Rodriguez, and Kirsten Young."

Luke wondered if he alphabetized the victims intentionally. Watching the man count off the names on his bony fingers, Luke rather thought he did. Benson drew himself up and took a deep, hoarse introductory breath, but Luke didn't hear his first words.

Helaman struck the desk with the flat of his hand. "This guy's got a record a mile long. He's a con. This is his long con, his ticket to fame." In the background Luke could hear Benson reciting his address and date of birth.

Luke inclined toward Helaman as if to listen, but kept his eyes on the monitor. Emerging from the short sleeves of his polo shirt, Benson's arms looked like twisted jerky as he folded them in front of them.

Helaman's voice was strained. He drummed his fingers on the desk. "This guy is an idiot. He couldn't have done it. He's only been out of prison for a few weeks. Hardship parole. He's got terminal cancer. His parole officer said so."

"I killed Kirsten Young because she's all that's left of that crooked governor's breed," said Benson. "It was a business deal. I invested in some of the Young family enterprises and they shafted me. So I shafted her, right through her clothes, right on the marks." Benson again looked precociously at the camera as if to say, *and we all have heard about the marks.*

"Preposterous! He's a con, not a killer," Helaman grunted, but the officer on the video was already asking about Heber J. Bruce.

The man tipped his head back as if remembering, then looked at the camera. "He saw me killing Kirsten Young."

"Where? When did this happen?" the officer asked.

"I'll give you the details later." Benson seemed offended by the interruption. "I left you a note on Bruce, didn't I? In the code?"

Which anyone who read the newspapers in Salt Lake City

knew by now, thought Luke. Funny that he didn't mention the note that Terrance Jensen found beside Kirsten's body. At the request of the police department, the media hadn't released those details.

"And Ms. Rodriguez, well . . ." He licked his lips in a motion that was more pitiful than salacious, "well, that was just an accident of love. And then I just couldn't help myself, arranging her, that is."

Luke was alarmed when he looked at Helaman. The chief's shirt had come untucked, and it looked like he'd forgotten his belt. He was rubbing his hands vertically through his hair, and it stood up in patches like a weedy garden. He stared at the computer screen.

"That's all I have to say," Benson said, smoothing the back of his neck with his flat palm. "I sent a statement to the TV stations. Videotaped it myself." He looked pleased. "Nobody needs to know my reasons. Just that I did it. Right to remain silent, you know. So I'm remaining silent." He sat down and folded his arms, shaking his head as if regretful that he must stop talking.

The interviewing officer looked at the camera and shrugged. Benson continued shaking his head and peeking up at the camera. The screen went blank.

Helaman began pacing. "What a mess. This Benson guy surfaced in Price," he said, naming a medium-sized town in central Utah. "Their local PD is flying this nut here for more questioning. They're using a private plane so as to avoid the media. They don't believe he's any risk. Worst thing on his rap sheet is an old conviction for manslaughter—he and a girlfriend were doing drugs, passed out, and her two-year-old daughter fell out of a second-story window with no screen on it."

Helaman shoved a folder at Luke. "Here's some of the

paperwork. This Benson will be here in about an hour and I don't trust myself not to strangle him, so I'm sending you to meet the plane at the municipal airport in West Jordan," he said.

"It should only take me about half an hour to drive there, and I'll take one of the beat cops with me," responded Luke after a moment of silence. "That way, I'll be keeping it low profile so that we can get him here before any film crews arrive. Now, we've got a few minutes before I have to leave, so that gives us some time to talk about a few things. I think I've figured out the brown scapular on the Rodriguez woman."

Helaman stopped his pacing and sat down.

"Chief, it's not just the code, the alphabet that ties this one to Mormonism. It's what the note says too."

"Yeah, last time you were here you figured out it was written in Spanish. Something about Saturday, if I remember."

"Right. It said, 'She's not coming back for you on Saturday,'" Luke said.

"I wondered if the color of the scapular meant anything, so I did some research online." Luke pulled a few printouts from a folder. "And turns out the color does mean something. It's brown because it's like the robe worn by the Carmelites. The man who founded that particular Catholic order was named Simon Stock—because he lived in a hollow tree, or 'stock.'"

"Like the stock of a gun, I guess," said Helaman. Luke nodded, and continued. He could see Helaman beginning to relax a bit.

"Well, anyway, if you wear this scapular, you get a special blessing. Catholics believe that if you die wearing this color scapular, and you end up in purgatory, the Virgin Mary will rescue you."

"What's the Saturday part?"

"Forgot that. The promise is that she will come on the first Saturday after your death."

"So, okay. But what sense does that make?"

Luke drew a deep breath. "Well, you have to put a lot of things together. Bernadette's body was staged to look like the Virgin of Guadalupe, but the note says that the Virgin won't come for her on Saturday in spite of the fact that she's wearing the brown scapular. So it's making a statement, that maybe the brown scapular won't help her. Add that to the Book of Mormon scripture passage that equates the Catholic Church with a great whore . . ."

"Okay. So what does that mean?"

"I was stumped. Until I remembered something from one time when I booked Bernadette Rodriguez. I felt so sorry for her. I tried to suggest that maybe I could get her some help or some counseling, and she said she didn't want it if it had anything to do with the Mormon Church. Don't you remember? You were there. We picked up a bunch of ladies that night, and helped book them. We had done one of those late-night patrols downtown—you remember, really it was for the benefit of the news media."

Helaman nodded yes.

"So Bernadette said she'd had enough of Mormonism. Remember, she wasn't hardened like so many of the ladies are, but she had a hard life. Maybe you weren't in the room when I was talking to her, I don't remember. Anyway, her parents became LDS down in Mexico before she was born and immigrated here. Like many parents, they tried to cram it down her throat, is the way she put it; and when the parents fell on hard times and the Church's welfare system dropped the ball and they nearly starved to death, Bernadette left the Church and became a Catholic."

Helaman seemed weary. "But why kill her?"

"It was her pimp who killed her, remember? She was in the hospital for several days but he had beaten her too badly, she just couldn't come out of it. But she died—I'm sure of this—a good three or four weeks before her body was found."

"What are you thinking?"

"I think somebody kept her body—maybe even froze it, the autopsy report's not in yet—and then staged her body to make a statement."

"What kind of statement? The note didn't tell us much."

Luke swallowed hard. "I think it was a statement about what happens to people if they leave the LDS Church. It's saying that Catholicism is the whore of all the earth, like it says in the Book of Mormon. And that it can't save anybody." He fumbled with his papers. "Seems like there was something else I wanted to discuss with you. . . ."

"So why would someone want to make those particular points?" Helaman seemed much calmer. Maybe just the mental exercise was taking his mind off other things, Luke thought.

"Why would someone want to kill poor old Heber J. Bruce?" Luke countered. "And what about that Kirsten Young? But somebody did, and the crimes are, well, seem to be, all tied together by the notes. Same Deseret Alphabet, and looks like even the same paper and handwriting. Not to mention that Woodruff couple, and that homeless lady, and those poor old senile men. They all had notes, in the code. Same paper, same writing.

"And of course those old men, that's not just a kidnapping case anymore, it's a homicide. Did I tell you that one of them died?" Luke wondered if the chief were listening to him.

"Who died?" Helaman looked at him with surprised eyes.

"One of the old men. Must have been an asthmatic attack

or panic attack or something. It wasn't from the drugs used to sedate him, apparently."

Helaman stared blankly at him. A great canyon of silence separated him from Luke, so Luke decided to bridge it in the few moments left.

"When we get back, though, and get this guy processed, let's talk about Kirsten Young's autopsy."

Helaman seemed to stir out of some private mental miasma. "What about it?"

Luke was gathering, buttoning, snapping. "The autopsy. The baby."

Helaman was shaking his head and staring down at the top-heavy stack of papers on his desk as if he could by intensity of his gaze see through the layers to the forgotten autopsy report.

"Ah, come on, Chief, don't tell me you never got around to reading it? Kirsten Young was three months pregnant."

"Oh no." Helaman's voice was husky. He put his head in his hands.

Luke's epaulette radio stuttered to life and he turned quickly out the door so Helaman wouldn't know that it was not working right again. He regretted his childish bolting, started to go back in. He heard sounds from behind the door, strange, hurting sounds, but none of them was calling his name and he completed his escape. He heard in his head the chant from playing with his dozens of cousins. *Olly, olly oxen free.*

He ducked into a windowless interrogation room and returned the radio call confirming his pickup of Benson. Then Luke paused in the stuffy, silent space that seemed to buzz with the beating of his own heart and steady breath. He stared at his cell phone. He thought about the second great lesson that he learned from Papa Taylor, his legendary grandfather.

One day Luke had asked his grandfather what was the secret to the harmony in his plural marriages. Papa looked long across the purple and magenta sierra before he answered.

"I know I should quote a scripture or one of the prophets," he said finally. "But I can't think of anything like that. But I do know this. 'Hell hath no fury like a woman scorned.'"

Or a man scorned, Luke thought. He saw powdery fingerprints, pointing, accusing.

Or hell hath no fury like a man who learns to scorn those things he once treasured, like Noel Dean learned to scorn his Mormon religion. It's one thing to be betrayed by a woman. It's quite another to feel betrayed by your own faith.

What to do with the increasing discomfort Luke felt, the inner storm? There was no proof, only a feeling about what these crimes all meant. Whom to call? He needed somebody who was outside the situation to talk to about what a desperate man would do, a man who would feel himself driven to desperate acts.

Luke knew he might someday regret it, but he dialed the number anyway. It belonged to the only person he knew who might give him some insight, could be trusted and know what to do with the information. He sighed and spoke softly of suspicions and fears.

He had entrusted himself to a Gentile. Papa Taylor certainly would have had something to say about that.

Later, Officer Shoemaker rode with Luke to the little airport southwest of Salt Lake City proper. What Officer Shoemaker would file in the official report was that the ride was uneventful, the arrival of the small airplane onto the tarmac was unremarkable. The two officers who flew in with Benson also reported a quiet ride without incident and that everything seemed just fine until the one officer from Price went to the can and Lt. Luke Taylor announced that he would walk around the front of the airplane to talk to the pilot who'd said he wanted to check the landing gear.

What kind of bait was he using these days to catch those big ol' kokanee salmon at Porcupine Reservoir? Luke wondered, and went to find the pilot to ask.

It was at that point that the other two officers in the plane were faced with a dilemma: The narrow door and steep-stepped exit stairs required that they detach the prisoner's leg shackles so he could deplane.

As soon as one of the officers bent down to reattach the shackles, Benson whipped his hands over the officer's head and began choking him with the handcuffs until he passed out. Then Benson kicked Shoemaker in the groin. Shoemaker regained his breath only in time to see Benson escaping across the runway, his leg shackles still detached, screaming, "I'll kill more, I'll kill more."

Officer Shoemaker radioed to Lt. Taylor to stay back, stay down, because he was going to fire on the suspect; but Lt. Taylor ran from behind the plane anyway just as the shots were fired.

Ten-One, Ten-One, can't copy.

Ten-Double-Zero, Ten-Double-Zero. Officer down.

For his part, in the following moments Luke had several thoughts that were, in his mind, quite logically connected, assignable, lovely in their symmetry.

He remembered a poem that Helaman once quoted to him at a crime scene, but only one line. Was it about the buzzing of a fly?

He remembered a trip to Alaska that he took last summer, a secret vacation, one of those foolish singles cruises that made him crave solitude. It was there, on the narrow-gauge train from Skagway, that he experienced the most complete, the most satisfying keepsake experience of his life: one of such sparkling clarity and insight that at that very moment he knew he would remember it always, to his dying day.

He looked straight up into the profound steel-grey crevasses where even in May the snow still sagged. He peered into the mists for the genesis of this whiteness, its origins unseen and unknowable.

Perhaps, he'd thought, it was the shining blood of angels, slain for kings in glory, in time immemorial, on the mountains' unapproachable heights.

Then he remembered, felt the heritage of his fathers, as he wondered about the squareness of dirt corners—

Then he remembered:

Then, he could not see to see.

From: [mailto:adam1830@hivenet.net]
Sent: Friday, June 7
To: liahona@hivenet.net
Subject: [none]

You have cost me far more than I was willing to pay. But I must thank you—through gritted teeth, I thank you—for opening my eyes. Remember when I used to write you love poetry? Here is a villanelle. It is the truest thing I ever wrote.

ECCLESIASTES
As a child, I understood differently than in the end
The stories they told me, which I believed,
Of the clarity of high-pitched bells in the wind.

I never truly lived. I blessed and sinned;
And strangely, was not disheartened when deceived.
As a child, I understood differently than in the end.

What ideals I had! I even tried to mend
Old rents and forgotten cracks in fear, unrelieved
By the clarity of high-pitched bells in the wind.

I erred in loving. I make no attempt to defend
My foolishness. What I termed success was achieved
As a child. I understood differently than in the end.

Ripened by exposure, I find I must suspend
Judgment on the world. I am wearied, not grieved
By the clarity of high-pitched bells in the wind.

I have been aged and hardened by refusing to pretend:
In spite of all, I remain still undeceived.
As a child, I understood differently. In the end,
There is no clarity, no bells, only wind.

CHAPTER 26

HIGH ABOVE THE CITY of Provo are trails tramped over the years by thousands of meandering students and serious hikers. One trail in particular is the ultimate hike: a shimmering alpine lake with its own glacier, long-limbed waterfalls, hills-are-alive meadows with boisterously colored wildflowers that clamor in late summer. Many hikers on that trail sleep the first night in a sixty-year-old musty stone shelter with a concrete floor after their climb to Emerald Lake, home of dreadlocked mountain goats and air so clean-edged it feels antiseptic.

On the second day of the hike, the trail to Mount Timpanogos leads near the site of a 1950s airplane crash. Both engines of the WWII B-25 are still extant, as well as parts of the wings and tail and landing gear.

Despite the violence of impact, the plane did not catch fire. To this day there is a faint odor of old fuel around the wreckage.

How life can change in an instant, Dr. Terrance Jensen thought to himself as he stared out his office window at the distant Mount Timpanogos. And for how many years, decades, generations afterward, reality is warped. You can take away the evidence, cart off all the wreckage, and still an aroma lingers. You can't uncrash a crash. You can't unpublish a book. You can't undo revelation. Either it came from God or it didn't. You can deny it happened, change your scriptures, swear people lied. But there's always the ghost essence of what once was.

He stared around the room where he had created an archipelago of small tables onto which his work spilled. He had commandeered an end table from his protesting wife's study, two folding card tables, and numerous dining chairs held Hebrew grammar books, Egyptian dictionaries, and study aids. Yet none of them would say what he wanted them to say. Not even the legendary six degrees of separation could connect Joseph Smith's writings to Egyptology. Not a single reputable non-LDS scholar would vet "The Book of Abraham," the Mormon scripture supposedly translated from some papyrus scrolls by the first Mormon prophet. Such scholars would without exception note that the word-for-word translation of the text on the scrolls didn't mention a single biblical—or Mormon, for that matter—concept.

Jensen sat behind a little antique oak desk containing only his laptop, and smoothed the wood's rippled, brown-grained surface with his hands that loved it, blessed it. His great-great-grandfather had pulled a cart carrying this desk, the yoke marking permanently his own shoulders, when his family had eaten the last of his oxen that died in the trek to the Salt Lake Valley; pulled it because his wife miscarried three times after they left Nauvoo in 1847; pulled it because she said she had nothing left, nothing to live for if the desk were left behind at the Great Platte River Road.

Jensen looked out at the mountain, the place where airplane fuel soaked into ancient stone. Where would his help come from? Where could he go?

He wondered if finding the note that was left beside the body of Kirsten Young was the apex of his life, if that one small moment of inadvertent discovery, the decision to take the note and hide it, if that were the one thing for which he would be remembered. He laid his head back onto the headrest of his chair and envisioned a gravestone: Dr. Terrance Jensen. Found the first Deseret Alphabet Code Note. Hid the Note. Turned in the Note. Never the Same.

Nobody trusted him now. Not the police, who kept him sequestered for hours and hours questioning him about exactly where he found the note, who speculated over and over at the damning coincidence that one of the few men in the world who could read the code would find a note written in that selfsame code. *Sorta funny, don'cha think? You said yourself that you read it and knew it was playing with fire. You kept it how many days? Protecting the Church, huh—or covering your own trail? You knew what it was, sure you didn't write it? Need a little boost for your career? That wife of yours happy?*

Nor did his bishop or anyone further up the LDS food chain appreciate the fact that he'd kept the note for quite a different, quite altruistic reason: so that no one else who could read it would connect the Church to the crimes. The Church, his priesthood quorum leader told him indignantly, wasn't in the hit-man business. Whatever gave him the impression it was?

Just history, he wanted to say, just the records of the last 175 years that you won't ever bother to read.

There was no way that Jensen could have known at the

time about all the markings on Kirsten Young's body, the same markings on his own temple garments he had worn every day of his life since he was eighteen years old. Even if he'd known about the mutilations, he would still be thinking that some nutcase had killed the poor girl.

Was the nutcase LeBaron James Benson? Terrance Jensen and his wife, Linda, had watched the ten o'clock news last night, and tried to process the information as it came in contradictory waves from an anchorman with a grating, anxious voice, and an anchorwoman who intoned each sentence as if it were fraught with history-altering power. Good news: Someone had confessed to the ghastly murders and was in custody. Bad news: Gunfire, policeman shot, prisoner shot.

Jensen wondered with all the rest of the uneasy city of Salt Lake if perhaps all this nightmare were coming to an end. Perhaps the murders that had brought such unwelcome attention to the city and its history were finally over. Perhaps the weirdness of bleached hands and glued couples and wailing old men would be reassigned to Boulder or San Francisco or Santa Fe where all such strangeness was at home.

So the man who confessed was dead. Was the policeman who shot and killed Benson a hero? Is the killer of a killer a hero? Or a crowbar in the gears of civilized justice?

Jensen rotated his neck to his wife as husbands making obligatory conversation do, his eyes still on the television. "What do you think?"

"I grew up with that guy LeBaron Benson. Did you know that? Always the class clown, not a lick of sense. I heard he's dying of cancer, and that's why they let him out of prison. That man's a performer. He's no killer. Maybe he thought getting himself shot would pay for letting that little kid die all those years ago. They wouldn't have given him the death penalty, no matter how many ways he tried to get them to do that. This way he was able to atone."

Jensen now turned his whole body in the chair to look at this woman he had lived with all his adult life. She had never had an original insight in twenty-three years. And yet as her crochet hook dipped like a frantic, starving duck into the tangled lake of thread in her lap, she made order out of it all.

Blood atonement explained it all.

This morning's news had more details about the West Jordan airport incident. There were the same camera shots of tarps on the runway, the same bewildered Officer Somebody blinking at the lights and trying not to sound responsible. A news reporter quoted from a terse statement from Chief Helaman M. Petersen who announced he was taking a leave of absence for a few days as the FBI took over the investigation. "Family responsibilities." That worked better in Salt Lake than any city in the country. And it was a good thing, Jensen thought. The chief had looked strained last time he saw him, verging on something that looked to Jensen like a combination of rudeness and despair. That was a man who needed some time off.

The ping of Jensen's laptop computer alerted him to incoming emails. He read them with his delete finger on the trigger. The last one had an ominous subject line: New Alphabet Code Message.

When he opened the email, the familiar scrawls of letters in the Deseret Alphabet began to emerge like clarity on a fogged glass shower door, squeegeed into sight one line at a time.

Why him? Why was someone involving him? He wanted to forget he'd ever learned this code. Yet he could not tear his eyes away from the screen.

For the prophet and the General Authorities:

You must stop the baptisms for the dead

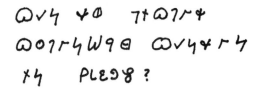

Can you picture Cottonwood Canyon in flames?

Let the dead sleep with their fathers.

Terrance Jensen knew the significance of Cottonwood Canyon. This time, this note, he would not keep.

PART THREE

CHAPTER 27

ONCE WHEN ROGER was covering a story on a fugitive criminal for the television news show he anchored, he researched the concept of triangulation: the way that a cell phone's moment-to-moment location could be charted by computing its signals as they bounced off different cell towers. That same day, he saw Eliza for the first time.

He remarked to himself, even as the event of meeting her was unfolding, that he was quite sure that there would be no need to triangulate subsequent experiences with her, that what he perceived of her would not need revision. He acknowledged in that moment the inexplicable and unshakeable belief that while he would delight in filling in the gaps of his understanding, yet the ontology of this exotic, musky woman—her being—would remain fixed.

She saw herself—even stated it this way—as a woman from the bargain bin of life, who reasoned that those who pursued her saw her as inherently downgraded or deficient in some way. At first, she saw Roger as one of many people on a hunt for that which could be gotten for cheap.

Her early childhood still bore the eraser crumbs, ghostly rubbed-out writing of her birth in a six-sided hogan on the Navajo reservation. Her life supposedly began with her subsequent adoption by a white Mormon couple through the LDS Church's Indian Placement Program. This couple wanted to rescue her and show her the nobility of her dark Lamanite heritage while making her as Nephitish as they possibly could.

What did she remember about growing up, he asked her once, when did she realize that she was going to be beautiful? She shook her head slowly and gave Roger one of the few concrete stories of her childhood.

"I remember looking in a mirror when I was a little girl, about seven I think," Eliza said, her voice dropping in timbre to remember. "I squeezed my eyes together until the light could barely come through my lashes. I tipped my head back and peered through them until I could see the feather-edged blur of myself in the green light of that bathroom. It was that moment that I first knew how to pray."

Roger knew not to interrupt with a question.

"I prayed to know if there was enough mercy in that form of blindness to make me beautiful."

It hurt him even now to think that she still believed that she was only beautiful to those who couldn't see her clearly. And yet he admitted that he himself could never see her clearly—not on the inside, at least. He consciously, deliberately chose to marry Eliza in spite of the inexplicable lacunae of her past; chose her over the blandness of piecrust Molly Mormons who were only characterized by what was placed into them.

Roger had lived all of Eliza's years, and daily breathed

her air, too, but he realized he would never know Eliza. It was beyond exclusion. And now he had the same now-familiar feeling about Mormonism, the sense that he'd missed the first day of class and now everyone would always know things he couldn't ever learn. By beginning earlier, he wondered, could he have learned Mormonism as effortlessly as children acquire language, as babies who still remember womb-water learn to swim?

"Cancel the trip to Cumorah, Eliza." His voice echoed in the kitchen as if it were empty. She sat across the table from him, her stacked luggage framing her profile like background architecture in a portrait. Her arm lay straight out from the elbow before her on the table, palm up. The skin on her cupped hand was so dry that the tiny parallel lines on her fingers stood out in contrast like the scratched-out day count on a prisoner's wall.

Roger was mesmerized. *I have seen this before*, he thought, and then he knew where: in the sand that settled inside the carvings on his parents' rose granite tombstone, buff on pink. He shook his head to dislodge the imposition of death and endings, and Eliza stirred from her silence in response. Her voice was threadbare.

"I can't. I promised Maria. We promised Maria. And there's no reason to not go."

Roger considered the implications of the fact that she'd cancelled their reservations to fly to Cumorah (oh, beloved Hill of treasures and revelations, he thought) with the BYU tour group. Instead, she booked tickets for herself and Maria on a different flight. He'd thought he overheard her booking a car too. Yet, she was still going. He felt a brightening hope. "Maybe it will build your faith, to be in those places, those places of our history. . . ."

"What history?" Was it sadness or desperation he saw

before him now? Her eyes drooped so much at the outer corners that the insides of her lower lids showed pink against her paling cheeks. She continued. "All the early Mormon prophets said Cumorah was the place where the final battle took place. Where the gold plates were hidden. Where the angel retrieved them to give them to Joseph Smith so he could translate them into the Book of Mormon."

He held his breath. These things he knew. . . .

"Where the angel put them back?" She seemed to be asking for verification. He had none, nobody did. "And now they're saying it might not be . . . be . . ." She faltered for words. "Be so."

She had avoided using the word "true." They both saw the parry. Even she did not have the heart for the thrust.

"Look, Roger. I stuffed my doubts for years. There was a time, once, when I wanted to face them, but then I met you. . . ." She didn't meet Roger's surprised eyes. "Now they've risen up inside me again and this time I have to deal with them. I can't run from them anymore. Look." She stretched out those lined hands to him, appealing, listing with imperceptible jerks of the fingers. "It's not just that Book of Mormon archaeology doesn't exist. It's not just about who has the authority to start a church. It's not just about prophecies that didn't come true. It's not just about the things I told you Monday night."

Roger found he was holding his breath and cleared his throat noisily to allow the air to escape. Eliza had not addressed anything about Mormonism directly since that awful evening, and now it was Friday. Roger had spent those days in agonizing episodes of life-chunks and incidents. He presided with increasingly frightened eyes (he'd seen the clips, he saw himself as if watching an edgy, skittish stranger on the television) over two more press conferences, feeling himself in defense grow a stiffening shell around himself that he now pushed up against his wife, his Eliza.

"Now, all these things are explainable." He hoped his voice carried authority.

"No, they can be explained *away*, that's your job." Roger felt the foible edge of her sword-words in his heart. "But they can't be explained, really. For the past few days I've watched you memorizing 'dodges' for press conferences, practicing spins, looking for anything to try to justify the Church. Did it ever occur to you that anything God was truly behind wouldn't need constant human finessing?"

Eliza's cell phone rang. She opened it, then looked perplexed as it went silent.

"Dropped calls," she murmured as it rang again. With a sigh, she responded to questions about who would be covering her Relief Society class.

Roger pondered what she said about finessing. He'd always thought it was a good word, a useful one, for a good practice.

"Let's consider my leave of absence open-ended," she told the caller. "I've got some additional responsibilities that have come up."

Her side of the conversation sounded to Roger like the way shale flaked off to reveal only more shale. Roger felt cold, rubbed his hands together.

He tallied, as he had over the last three days, the reasons why he must stay in the Church, the emotional bankruptcy that leaving it would mean to him. He was quite certain that he would never again, or elsewhere, find the saturation of happiness he'd known within Mormonism. He saw it quite clearly: either a universe peopled with comfort and peace, or a sterile featureless sandscape. But he didn't want to live in either without Eliza.

"We have a few minutes before Maria gets here and we have to leave for the airport," he said, harvesting time, thinking to reason with her. "Before you leave, you must tell me what you're thinking. Give me something to research while you're gone. I want to help."

She looked at him again with that day's-end look. "You won't find the answers in the library, Roger," she said, her speaking tender. "I'll leave you with a few questions to think about. Unless you come up with some really good answers before I come back, I'll . . . I'll . . ." Her voice trailed off. Roger could see her gathering herself as if she'd scattered towels around on the table between them.

"Do you know who Hosteen Klah was?"

He shook his head, marveling as he always did when Navajo terms emerged in her speech, that this glottal-stopped name jutted up from the flow of English phonemes from her lips. Like a rock in a stream.

"Who is that?" he asked.

"Was. Hosteen Klah died about sixty years ago. He was a very famous Navajo weaver—as you might know, unusual in itself because almost all weavers have always been women. But he was a hermaphrodite, a condition greatly revered among *Dine*, The People, because they—we—believe such a person is unusually wise, and can understand things more completely."

Roger's expression must have asked her where this was going. What in the world would a dead physiological oddity have to do with Mormon theology? Or worse—was she retreating from the Church, into some animistic vestige of the culture of her childhood?

"I always wanted to believe what the Church has said about Heavenly Father—that he used to be a human," said Eliza. "So he could understand us, see both sides of things, sort of like Hosteen Klah was supposed to be able to—but not from seeing both sexes but seeing life and eternity at the same time. On top of that, I treasured the thought of a Mother in heaven too—someone who had gone through the process of living and dying and could help me out as I go through the same process. But with all these doubts and questions I've been having—I can't pray anymore."

"Why not?"

"Because if our God, our Heavenly Father . . . had a Heavenly Father . . . who had a Heavenly Father . . ." Her voice snagged on the repetition and caught in a sore-lunged sob. "I want to know the head Guy, you know? Not just someone who's on the road of eternal progression with me. I want to know where the real power, the real authority is. Where the great cosmic buck stops. A God Almighty."

Roger mined for an answer that would satisfy—or at least comfort—her. "Don't throw the baby out with the bathwater," he pleaded. "Couldn't you just pray and assume it's going to . . . to the top, so to speak?" He noted with short-lived peace that she seemed to accept that notion. But her silence was just more of the gathering-motion he'd seen before. He wondered, with pain, if it were his words that had the capacity to scatter her so.

"I think I have a way of explaining some of these things to you," she said slowly, as if she were coming to a discovery, finding a method for sorting and folding what was between them, the invisibles on the table.

"It's one thing to change practices and policies in a church," she began. "Like hemlines, for instance—when I was a teenager they were specified for Mormon girls. Those things can change—should change—and no harm is done to eternal truth.

"But how do you change history? How can someone tell

you to believe that something happened at a certain place on a certain calendar date—and then turn around and say it never happened? Do you suddenly say that eternal principles just don't apply anymore? *Eternal*, Roger. How can that be? I understand that representations of facts often change. But how can the facts themselves change? How can you ask people to believe something with all their hearts and then tell them that it never existed?

"But it's more basic than even that, for me. For me to worship—to obey—a God, I have to know Him. Or at least have a way to get to know Him. In other words, He has to be a fact, a representable fact. And that fact-ness of Him has to be solid and stable. I can be mistaken in the way I represent Him, or others can be mistaken or even lie about it—but He has to be. *Be*. Not change. Not learn as He goes along. If I'm going to entrust myself to a divine Being—ask Him to help me, or ask Him to save me, ask Him to do something I can't do myself, make a universe, create an afterlife for me—there has to be something beyond advanced humanness."

Roger nodded mutely.

"I want the great I AM who spoke to Moses out of the burning bush. Not the Getting There Ahead of You on the Road. Maybe I want to believe in a swashbuckling God." The frozen tension across her eyebrows melted for the first time in days with the thought. "I want a Rescuer who's always been a Rescuer. A God who's always been a God. I don't want to depend on a fabrication of a johnny-come-lately wannabe. I don't want the human in a fantasy witness protection program who has an invented history—a representation, if you will—that happens to intersect at a few places across the Bible with that fierce-eyebrowed, no-nonsense, Love Incarnate God. The One who's always been around. Like *eternally around.*"

272

Roger felt himself blinking and blinking yet found he was not seeing the scene before him.

Eliza sighed, a deep-ridged release of air and voice from within.

"Look, Roger. I know this is hard on you. I'd hoped to use the time on the trip with Maria to be able to sort a lot of things out. Maybe I still can, and you can too. We both need some mental space. Since I'm not leaving with the tour group and we'll have our own rental car, Maria and I will just have a pajama party at the hotel, and just leisurely meet up with the group at the Cumorah Pageant. But I'll have my phone off, so I can think."

For reasons he could not fathom, a phrase entered Roger's roiling mind. *Son of perdition.* That was the name in Mormon doctrine for someone who loved, then rejected, the Church—an image of complete and irretrievable loss. He wondered with an almost-academic curiosity if there could be such a thing as a daughter of perdition.

"But you'll call me to let me know you arrived safely?" He didn't mean to whisper, but he did.

She nodded slowly.

The silence that hung in the room had an animal-chemical quality to it, like the smell of a boot repair shop. Eliza's eyes were staring beyond him, but he could not stop looking at her. He felt an emptiness that was like the hollow feeling just before breaking a long fast; a hunger that was not only itself—its mindless craving—but its scheming, yearning for a satiety for which there were no resources to assure.

Eliza's words, her reasonings, roamed in his head as concepts and logic but found no harbor there. He looked down at his hands and discovered that each was atop the table, cupped palms up as if he were weighing two things against each other.

The Church or her.

He remembered a time when he'd visited a rehabilitation clinic and saw two amputees in the waiting room evaluating their prostheses as if comparing consolation prizes.

The silence in the knotty-pine kitchen persisted and he was incapable of breaking it, lost in the image his hands evoked, an image of ancient balance scales and the warning—"weighed and found wanting."

Outside were sudden, sweet sounds—Maria on the porch, shouting, telling the school bus driver good-bye, that she wouldn't be back for a week, that she was going on a really truly field trip to Cumorah with her mom.

Eliza stood up. She turned wearily with her purse over one arm, manhandling a suitcase toward the door, finality in her eyes.

"A religion, to be a religion, a faith, has to be divine," she said softly. "Not human. Not some beloved, sweet fiction embroidered onto the fabric of fact. I just have to believe that. The missionaries always ask a prospect to listen to some King-Jamesish section of the Book of Mormon"—here she wrestled an arm loose to make a grand sweeping motion to an invisible audience in the living room—"and they ask, 'Could any man have written this?'"

The doorknob turned. Eliza looked Roger straight in the eye. "And the answer is, well, yes." Her mouth showed an uncharacteristic bitterness as she spoke her final words to him as she went out the door.

"And today it occurs to me that a woman would have done a better job."

PART FOUR

CHAPTER 28

EVEN TO SOMEONE who had once believed with all his heart, the mystery was great. Helaman M. Petersen came to characterize the Hill Cumorah in his own mind as the Hill Conundrum.

Everybody agreed on certain facts about the innocuous little drumlin—a whale-shaped hill that is the scraped-together vestige of glacial action eons ago in the earth's geological history. Upon this unassuming little topological prominence in upper New York State, the first prophet of the Mormon Church, Joseph Smith, conferred the immortality of repute early in the nineteenth century.

When Joseph Smith was only about fifteen, he said that his adolescent questionings about which church to join had been settled in a nearby grove by the appearance to him of two unearthly beings—God the Father and Jesus Christ—who he said pronounced all churches on earth corrupt and put the mantle of cosmic religious reformation upon the teenager's shoulders.

Three years went by. Then, on September 21, 1823, Smith said a resurrected personage—the Angel Moroni, an ancient, long-dead inhabitant of the Americas—came to him at night and over the course of that night and day gave him information that, like returning to the same chapter on a DVD, he repeated four times with only minor variations.

Young Joseph Smith was led to the neighborhood prominence, the hill the Angel Moroni called Cumorah, where Smith saw a great stone box that was buried on the hillside. Every year on that date, September 22, Joseph said he returned. In 1827 his training in patience was rewarded.

Salt Lake City Chief of Police Helaman M. Petersen remembered the coloring books of his childhood, the flannelboard stories, the Sunday school lessons that imprinted on his mind what every Mormon child knew.

There at the Hill Cumorah, on that fall day, Smith said he pried open the remarkable dome-lidded box made of stones and cement that peeped from its frame of dirt on the slope. Within the box were two ancient objects of what people of that time would have characterized as being "of curious workmanship." The first object in the box was a book written in curlicued script upon paper-thin plates of gold. The other object in the box was what Helaman, with twenty-first-century acumen, had come to think of as a primitive mechanical Babel Fish: a translation device in the form of a breastplate with two silver bows and two precious stones attached to the bows.

Joseph Smith reported that he took the two ancient objects to his home and began the translation of what would become the Book of Mormon, a project fraught with frustrations, threats, robberies, and unreliable scribes.

The priceless plates were kept hidden, and on a tight, albeit temporally lengthy, rein. The Angel Moroni on May 2, 1838, came calling again to take his plates back. According to the ancient American's own words, he had waited over a millennium and a half to assure that the plates, some of which he'd written himself, had been properly translated. With a spiritual dusting off of his resurrected hands, Moroni's soteriological job was done. The plates were returned to their resting place within the Hill.

But the history of the Hill Cumorah—and Joseph Smith's visits to it—were far from concluded with the disappearance of the Angel Moroni.

As late in the ill-fated young life of Joseph Smith as 1842, this first Mormon leader spoke rapturously of "Glad tidings from Cumorah!" No Mormon of his time doubted that Cumorah was the site spoken of in the Book of Mormon, the place of the last blood-drenched battle in A.D. 421, the slaughter of all the good Jewish Nephites by their evil dark-skinned cousins the Lamanites. The victors' descendants would languish in bare-teethed savagery and obscurity until being discovered centuries later by the European explorers who mistakenly called them Indians. The Nephite records, inscribed on the golden plates, would sleep in Cumorah until the Angel Moroni, their compiler, would awaken from death in order to awaken young Smith from sleep to tell him of the plates' existence.

But even after the plates were finally taken back to Cumorah, the Hill's story had another chapter, Helaman recalled. Scant years after the death of Joseph Smith, by 1877 in fact, enough controversy and rumors had circulated about the Hill Cumorah that the second "prophet, seer, and revelator" of the Mormon Church, the iron ruler Brigham Young, took it upon himself to set the record straight. He was afraid there was a part of the young lore that would be forgotten or lost. Others for years had whispered of the fabulous riches still hidden in the Hill, and Brigham wanted to canonize those stories.

Ah, the ever-present Mormon penchant for Record-Keeping and Setting of Things Straight, thought Helaman. And fantastic stories they were that Brigham told, of secret rooms and buried treasures within the Hill Cumorah. No less than ten different extant accounts cached the legends.

Once three men walked with Joseph Smith up to the Hill, one document said. A door inexplicably yawned in the soil before them, leading into a room some sixteen feet square. Oh, the wonders they said were there. An angel! A trunk! Gold plates and swords and breastplates!

Another account told of labyrinthine cells bored into the entrails of the Hill, with more records amassed in stacks there than ten strapping men could heft—"records upon records piled upon tables."

The men went back again and again, Brigham said. They saw all that they'd seen before, along with a massive stone table and an unsheathed sword of fearful portent within the recesses of Cumorah.

And then, as Helaman thought about the stories, he considered all the accounts of the inexplicable light source that lit it all—not, Brigham said, from the sun or any artificial light, yet bright as day. And the treasure wasn't just the brilliant gold that was everywhere—wagonloads of it—but the wealth of documents that chronicled the people who hid them there.

Such a precious history, filled with secrecy and awe. All given as physical evidence of the veracity of the document, the Book of Mormon, that Joseph Smith said he translated with his wondrous devices: with the box's silver-bowed breastplate and its linguistically optic gemstones; with a chocolate-colored egglike seer stone; with his hat held tight to his face as persistent English words danced across the blackness of its claustrophobic screen.

All this Helaman had believed. All this he had pledged and affirmed, and staked his life on. He had invested, with purity and fervor, in what these witnesses said.

That there was an everlasting gospel that rose ghostlike from the dust of that Hill, armed with a sword of truth and angelic armies, to clear away the corruption and deficiencies of all other faiths.

That the American Indian was the descendant of the Lamanites who were themselves Jews exiled to the New World.

That the book Joseph wrote was what it claimed: a "fullness." It was complete, corrective, canonical.

That, in fact, fair Cumorah was the mineral-veined womb of all truth.

And so had millions of others believed. Immigrants from all over northern Europe had crossed oceans and plains because of its message. It explained the lost tribes and lost truths. The Hill's story became part of heritages and bequests beyond blood.

Then beginning in 1935, reverential actors and musicians and composers and workers—from directors down to volunteer stagehands—began to pilgrimage to their holy Hill to enact scenes from the book Joseph Smith said he translated from the golden plates, the ones he reinterred into the Hill Cumorah. They believed, reverentially, that they stood where their grandfathers saw the plates and roamed through the hidden passageways and testified of ancient inhabitants revivified —all to validate the message from the dust of Cumorah.

Helaman himself had been one of the faithful. Even up to

the time, months before, when he'd first been summoned to Cumorah, he had believed. And now, coming back to that hill, as he drove his car past the last rippling fields of grain before he reached the turgidity that is Rochester, he recounted to himself how his fate had become so inextricably tied to the innocuous grassy knoll.

It began months ago. He remembered every detail of the last time he saw Janine, just hours after his return from his first trip to New York State and Cumorah.

A relentless two-day wind had suspended dirt particles in the air above Salt Lake City until the diffused daylight seemed to come from everywhere and nowhere at once. The weak-tea April sun tinged caramel every unyielding wave of his wife's hair. With alerted posture, she sat across a table from him in the solarium of a restaurant on the southern outskirts of the city and pierced him through with her give-no-quarter gaze.

His daughter, Gracie, was draped across him, one arm caught between the nape of his neck and the high padded chair back, the other tucked under his armpit. Exhausted by crying, she had fallen asleep on his chest, still making small shuddering noises. His shirt front was wet. He thought of Elizabeth Barrett Browning:

Thank God for grace,
Ye who weep only! If, as some have done,
Ye grope tear-blinded in a desert place. . . .

Helaman looked down at his daughter and completed the line: *And touch but tombs.* Then his gaze rose to meet the unflinching eyes of the death of his dreams. Janine had not moved a poised muscle for several minutes as she waited for his response. He thought of Browning again and inclined to inhale the moist air of his daughter's whorled hair.

He chose his words carefully, like an awakened dreamer

who must account for the tangled state of the bedclothes.

"The fact that we're here, and you're leaving against my will, means I can't and won't stop you." Out of the corner of his eye he thought he saw the tendons of Janine's right forearm, resting on the table, soften. He looked beyond her, out the window to where her car, the backseat a fortress of suitcases, was parked.

"I don't know where, exactly, I failed you. I don't know why you have come to believe that my faith is less than yours, or that I'm any less . . ." he searched for a word, "any less distressed than you by what's going on in the Church."

Her every molecule stiffened again. She looked like an offended god who glared at him through a translucent bronze ceiling.

"I know what to do about it." Her voice clipped off each consonant like cuticles.

For the first time, he felt himself falter. His voice caught. "And I can too. You don't have to leave. We could work on this together. We could . . . there are fundamentalist groups all over the valley."

Janine blinked rapid-fire in scorn. "And Police Chief Helaman M. Petersen could hide out as a polygamist, here? The very fact that those groups are here in the valley means they're trying to fit in. They're compromisers." She spat the word out. "You're talking about reforming a church that's too far gone. Like trying to heal a corpse."

Helaman considered that image. Janine, he was certain, knew nothing about corpses.

"The Church has lost its nerve. There's no reforming it. There's only returning to the way it once was, someplace away from here," said Janine. Helaman felt the heat of her eyes cool and realized that she had looked away and was reaching below the table for her purse. The distraction was only temporary. Her next words made his sternum ache.

"And you've lost whatever little nerve you ever had."

He hugged Gracie toward him but Janine was standing, reaching toward the sleeping child's elbow. Helaman grasped Janine's wrist. There was something amiss with her hand, but he could not take the time to identify and address the issue. For the last time, he looked her directly in the eye, and when he spoke, his voice was low and firm.

"I will prove to you that I believe in the purity of the restored gospel. What Joseph and Brigham lived and died for." He noted with satisfaction that her eyes widened. "I will prove to you that I can live the covenants just as we promised each other and Heavenly Father in the St. George Temple, on June 22, 1985. I will prove to you that I not only believe but will enforce those covenants."

He wondered why the brittleness of her face seemed to tighten. Then he understood her fear. But he never meant he would enforce them on her. He only meant that he would enforce the covenants' penalties on those who broke them.

And so had he done, wholeheartedly and deliberately.

The first time was hard, yet the mutilation of the body of Bernadette Rodriguez was a serendipity, really. Helaman sighed with the irony of it all, because certainly Bernadette had never been anyone else's good fortune. The poor wretch lay alone and unclaimed in the morgue of the county hospital as forgotten in death as she had been forgettable in life. The pity Helaman felt for her abandoned body was soon swamped by an epiphany: a surge of understanding that he could use her—it—to manifest at least one eternal truth. This woman was an apostate, had deliberately turned her back on the security and safety of the Mormon Church and gone into the idolatrous morass of Catholicism, *that great and abominable church, which is the mother of abominations, whose founder is the devil.*

284

It was so easy to pose her, a whore, as the Virgin of Guadalupe.

The final sarcasm of the scapular was self-indulgent, he knew. But he knew the promise of a brown scapular, and knew that nobody was coming for Bernadette's soul, just as nobody had come for her body. She was herself a cipher, a nothing. Helaman alone was able to make her useless, meaningless life useful and meaningful.

Of course he couldn't tell Janine about what he'd done and what he planned. In the first days she was gone, she had been flintlike in response to his daily email reports that he had immersed himself in the *Journal of Discourses* that recorded the speeches of Joseph Smith, Brigham Young, and others. She had been unmoved by the action plans he drafted to show her (what else could he do? what else would she listen to?) that he understood the implications of living as those early prophets did: the communal living conditions of the United Order, the implications of "eternal" marriage, which meant plural marriage. In a great paroxysm of devotion, he declared he would take another wife if that's what she wanted.

She was icy in her replies. How would that great sacrifice prove anything?

Janine was right. He would have to make a statement so overt that his loyalties would be, at least to her, beyond question. So it was that even when he had spirited the body of Bernadette Rodriguez to his home (astonishing even himself that so little security existed at the county morgue) and stored her black-bagged body atop the slick white paper packets of venison in his chest freezer, he knew that poor Bernadette, even eventually bedecked iconically as the patron saint of Mexico, had not the star power to attract the national attention that would impress Janine.

Ah, but Kirsten Young—that was another matter. Here

was a woman who was local royalty, sainted, pedigreed, paparazzi-worthy. She joyously broke all the rules. Some said she researched obscure rules to break. She hadn't just rejected Mormonism, she had chosen every symbol she could to represent her disconnect with her former faith. The scanty clothing she wore showed that she tossed the temple garments she once wore as blithely as she tossed her temple marriage and the vows she made there. Supporting abortion rights groups and gambling franchises for Indian reservations, writing left-wing letters to editors about legalizing marijuana as a "recreational drug"—these actions and more hit Salt Lake City's conservative belly below the belt of its ecclesiastical and cultural dress slacks.

Then she quite publicly took up residence with an African-American man. Funny, Helaman never could remember his name. But Helaman, like all other Mormons over the age of thirty-five, remembered vividly what he was taught as a child, what his parents and grandparents and great-grandparents were told in Sunday school about African Americans and anyone who was even part black. For the first century and a half of Mormon history, men of color could join the Church but were excluded from any priesthood—read, leadership—role of any sort.

Helaman remembered memorizing the definitive statements by the Church's apostle Bruce R. McConkie, who literally "wrote the book" on Mormon doctrine in the mid-1960s. He said that blacks were inherently "less valiant" than whites and the black skin was a sign of the curse of God who was punishing them for a moral flaw—fence-sitting in the preexistence, before their births on earth. All premortal whites had signed on for freedom and allegiance to the Christ, but blacks had dragged their as-yet-unbodied feet. They were born with a mark of their cowardice.

And Brigham Young, as Helaman's note in the Deseret Alphabet quoted, said that intermarriage with a black was a mortal sin, one that could only be atoned for with blood.

Many adults in the know in Salt Lake City were not surprised in 1978 when the LDS Church bowed to considerable social and legal pressure and announced a "revelation" that overnight gave black LDS men priesthood privileges. But Helaman was surprised, even disoriented by the proclamation. He did not know how to understand that something was true one minute and not true the next. He watched McConkie's backpedaling, his pleas to "forget everything" he'd ever said about the matter. But as Helaman thought about it, he became tremendously relieved—as were most of his LDS friends. They would leave the theological niceties to the Church leadership. Some things, he and his young friends decided, were just beyond the understanding of regular people.

His grandmother said it was all a smokescreen, that the Church only was pretending to give priesthood to blacks but God wouldn't recognize it. His mother's father muttered about it when Helaman was around. But once he heard a group of the older men talking in terms that reminded him of a movie about the Ku Klux Klan. Helaman felt shocked and hurt. From that day on, he never forgot that for older people and fundamentalists, the questions never went away. Did the new revelation mean that the last of the "unvaliant" ones from the preexistence had finished earth-life and died? And now the ones living at present were no longer cursed, just dark?

Most LDS families of several generations, like Helaman's, played it safe with ancestral prejudices intact. Janine had often said that Kirsten Young was an example of why blood atonement should be reinstituted. There were brownnosing new police officers with stars in their eyes, fundamentalists in their family trees—and their temple garments in a bunch,

Helaman thought sourly—who jumped at the chance to surveil, if only for a night or two, such a woman as Kirsten Young.

Thus Helaman had records of her comings and goings for weeks. It made it easy for him to await Kirsten Young's late-night return to her apartment after her weekly massage and pedicure. In the parking structure, she did not question Helaman's respectful request that she get in his car with him (perhaps the death of her parents made her resigned to—and apt to want to procrastinate hearing—any news delivered by a uniformed man). She did not seem alarmed until he threw her cell phone out the window with a latex-gloved hand.

She went to strangled unconsciousness with an air of fulfilled resignation, as if she'd been expecting someone to enact blood atonement. Helaman had been more shocked by the hate letters found later in her apartment than he had been shocked by his own act of cutting her throat and her final, clear-eyed gaze at him before he closed her eyes.

After staging the bodies of wild girl Kirsten Young and frosty lady of the night Bernadette Rodriguez, another serendipity occurred. When, as administrator of his grandparents' ranch at Chalk Creek in northern Utah, he received a hunting permit request from Heber J. Bruce, the high-profile apostate and distributor of inflammatory pamphlets, well—the cake could be frosted, could it not?

But it had been worth it. Helaman heard in Janine's voice the first sign of admiration in years.

"You're willing, I see," she said slowly over the phone, mincing the sentence into syllables, "not only to enforce blood atonement but to let everyone know the rationale from the Church's early history. Well."

Well? He read in this word a conjunction with another statement that never came. He believed in an implicit promise that she would come back, that she would bring his precious Gracie, that things could be repaired and restored between them. He was even willing to quit his job and find work—as a ranch hand, if need be. He would move with them to a fundamentalist settlement, even a *colonia* if she wanted. He had begun to dream of the new life that his dangerous efforts had surely earned.

Thinking of that now as he drove to Cumorah, he gave a savage punch to the steering wheel of his car with the rage that had become his conscience.

Helaman had believed his work was finished, that justice had been administered, that only the wicked had been punished, the unmistakably plain statements charred into Utah's consciousness. He was willing to let Janine begin to detach herself from Brace Crossing.

After murdering Bruce, there was an unbearable period of silence from Janine. For his part, he was overswept by a sea change in his own thinking as he began to read early Mormon history in his long, lonely nights alone. When Helaman researched the stories of Cumorah and the early days of his beloved Church, the world turned over like an upended tree. It was never again the same. He had always thought that apostasy—the losing of faith—was a gradual, erosive process. But to his great surprise, it turned on a single day. Once the final footing was dislodged, he found that it was more an avalanche.

Scarcely daring to believe he had wasted his whole life in pursuing the fables of a Smith boy and the foibles of a Young man, he turned from the bloody deeds that would validate their teachings. But now that he had the attention of the Mormon Church and the national news media, he thought wryly, *ya que la casa se quema, calentémonos: Since the house is burning down, we might as well get warm.* He began to turn attention to Mormonism itself and its old magicks, its unkept promises, its blind-alley oddities. With a kind of coolly desperate sarcasm, he enacted hidden divine embraces, bleached Lamanite skin that would never turn white on Book of Mormon promises, revealed the Three Nephites.

In his mind, in his heart, in his conscience, he had meant only rescue in providing atonement for those who would not have sought it, for Kirsten and Heber. And tipsy Alma and his wife, poor Clarissa Clarissa, those pitiful old men—they were just private jokes made public, the exposing of Mormonism's lies and legends.

The blood on his hands had been that of a priest, washing away into propitiation until—

Until he unwittingly killed two innocent people: the old man from the nursing home, and Kirsten Young's unborn child. He had thus put himself beyond the pale of the blood atonement he had administered to others: two murders, and he had only one lifeblood to offer.

Helaman now turned the car into the parking lot of the small, dingy motel in Rochester, New York, and checked in with his forged identification. The clerk, a blowzy dark-rooted woman who reminded him of an overripe game-show personality, swatted a gnat on her forearm with a rolled-up copy of *Self* magazine, and leaned over the counter to half-heartedly attempt small talk with him about the weather. She marked "paid in cash" in a painstaking, loop-lettered printing on the registration card. A distant television set's canned laughter seemed to catch her darting eyes, but she craned her corrugated neck to look at his left hand.

It was then that he realized why his wife, Janine's, hand had looked so odd to him the last time he saw her. It was the white band of skin on her ring finger, just like his now.

It was beginning to rain. Outside, he paused briefly to cover over with a tarp the extra license plates in the trunk of the stolen car he took from the evidence lot in Salt Lake City.

The plastic explosives were secure and ready. He ran down the mental list as if browsing grocery store aisles: blasting caps, detonation cord (reels and reels of it), cardboard, electrical tape, and glue. And the large blue canvas bag he carried last time he came to the Hill, the one emblazoned with the yellow letters: SALT LAKE CITY POLICE DEPARTMENT. EXPLOSIVE ORDNANCE PATROL.

Two lines from Tennyson kept running through his mind. He appropriated the first line for today, and would keep the second line for tomorrow. He recited them aloud.

. . . *Time, a maniac scattering dust,*
And Life, a Fury slinging flame.

The email he sent to Dr. Terrance Jensen would have Salt Lake City in a stir as people raced to protect the millions of genealogical records stored in great vaults in Cottonwood Canyon.

Only Janine would know the real target.

Tomorrow, Helaman M. Petersen would keep his date with Cumorah.

CHAPTER 29

SELONNAH CALLED ANNE and left a message that she'd like to see her. Needed to see her. Needed to hear her quiet reasoning.

Selonnah felt a groan from below her sternum, the protest of her unwilling body against the secret she carried, the one she couldn't tell. She knew that part of what she felt was mourning for the genuineness that Luke Taylor had, the straightforward goodness of his personality, the irretrievability of the death of this man she knew to be her friend.

Before he died, he called her and entrusted her with the gravest of information: representations she could not yet verify with facts.

Luke's voice had been soft on the phone, as if he were afraid of being overheard. More than that, it seemed that he had the crisp edge of tears on his words.

"Selonnah, I may be crazy for calling you. In fact, maybe I've made a mistake. I only have a few minutes before I have to get on a plane, but I have to talk to you."

Selonnah wondered at first if he were working up the courage to ask her, gentile forbidden fruit, for a date. She began to try to set him at ease but he pushed on.

"I know you're not a Mormon. And it's for that reason I'm calling you. I need to tell somebody."

She waited while he struggled for words. His throat sounded thick.

"I remember what you said about integrity the day you came to apologize for what that nut Lugosi did with that goat. I have a suspicion about the other crimes, but I can't share it with anyone I know. I can't . . ." He couldn't find the right words, so he started a new sentence. "They're good people, loyal. To the Church. Do you hear what I'm saying?"

Selonnah could only murmur assent. She had no idea where this was going.

"I believe in your integrity, in your loyalty to truth—even more than loyalty to your newspaper," Luke said.

She remained silent.

"Is that—is that the case?" he asked.

"Yes. That is true, that is the way it is with me. You've read me correctly."

She could hear his exhalation of relief, followed by the catch of air behind his next words.

"I have suspicions. No proof yet. But very strong suspicions. And reputations are at risk—I can't afford to be wrong."

"Suspicions of whom?"

Luke was silent so long she took her cell phone away from her ear to see if the call had been dropped.

"Give me your word that you will keep this to yourself until there's proof."

"Wouldn't want it any other way," she responded cautiously. "I can't write rumors. That's for the tabloids."

"What I mean—I want your promise that you will wait to write anything. Or tell anyone who's . . . what I mean is any Mormon. That includes your cousin. And anybody at the newspaper. Or anyone with media connections. Until there's rock-solid proof. In exchange, you'll have the head start on the story."

A sweetheart deal, Selonnah thought. All for listening. But she was not prepared for his next words.

"It's Helaman, Selonnah. I'm sure of it. All the . . . all the murders. The Deseret Alphabet crimes. I trust your judgment. I guess I want you to talk me out of this, to tell me why it couldn't possibly be true."

She felt the same electrostatic sensation at Helaman's name as she'd felt the first time she saw him. She could hear little swallowing noises.

"Helaman—the chief?" Selonnah waited.

"Yes."

She felt the catch in her own breath she'd heard in his. But her training kicked in.

"Okay. Okay. Let's see, the first thing we'd have to know is if he had opportunity. Case by case. Let's leave intangibles like motive for later."

Luke seemed to relax as he responded, calmed and comforted by the solidity of procedurals. "Okay. First. Helaman knew Bernadette Rodriguez—the prostitute. In fact, we both were there when she was arrested one time. And of course he had access to the morgue and could have taken her body somewhere and kept it frozen until he was ready. And the autopsy showed that it had been frozen."

"Okay."

"Second. Helaman's wife, Janine, hated Kirsten Young, and . . ."

"You think Janine was involved too?"

"No, she just . . ."

When Luke didn't continue, Selonnah filled the silence.

"Let's just talk about opportunity now. Would Helaman have had opportunity to kill the Young woman?"

"I'm not sure, but I think so. I remember that he took a long weekend off the end of May, and that's when she was killed. I guess we all assumed Helaman went to Brace Crossing, down in the southern part of the state, to visit his wife and his little girl. But if he were here, I'm pretty sure he could have killed Heber J. Bruce during that time too."

"What makes you think that?"

"Nobody at headquarters made this connection, but I did. Bruce was killed on land that was near—or maybe actually on—Helaman's grandparents' ranch near Chalk Creek, up in the northeast corner of the state."

Selonnah remembered Helaman's speech at the Alzheimer's meeting. Ruby Lee's ranch. The chicken coop they lived in. The root cellar where the wolves were. *Someone who would always do whatever it took to get a job done.*

"But why?" Selonnah had no doubts about whether Ruby Lee's grandson would do whatever it took, as well. She was furiously writing notes as she listened.

"Let's keep to your plan of just looking at opportunity and leave motive for later. I think Helaman kidnapped those old men, and bleached the Nightwalker woman's hands, and wrapped up that old couple too."

"Wait a minute." Selonnah's mind was reeling. "You're talking about a serial killer here with the two women and Bruce. And serial killers don't start out with violent crimes and then do things that look like pranks. I don't buy that, Luke."

"Okay. I'll show you. Let's start with the old couple, the Woodruffs. I know Helaman knew them. I guess you could say that he and I protected them."

"What do you mean?"

"Well, they were veil workers—" Luke stopped himself and searched for a gentile description. "They officiated at the Mormon temple, downtown."

"So how did you protect them?"

"Helaman and I both had stopped the old gentleman more than once for drunk driving. Never arrested him, though—it would have ruined their reputations and they'd never have been able to work at the temple again."

"What about the homeless lady, Nightwalker?"

"Clarissa Clarissa." Luke sounded tired. "This is a slender connection, but I know that Helaman's favorite restaurant was where she lived. In the parking lot, I mean. And since Janine has been gone, he eats out all the time. Besides, everybody who works downtown knows her."

"And those old men? The Three Nephites?"

Luke laughed in spite of the grimness of the conversation. "Three Nephites?"

Selonnah was embarrassed to have caught him so off guard. "I mean, there were three of them and they were from Nephi, right, and . . ."

"Well, I'll be. You're right. No wonder . . ." Luke was talking more to himself than her, but returned to the conversation. "I don't know. I'll try to see if he was gone during that time, but since it happened after hours, I don't think I can check on that. But a disguise could have made him fit the description of the kidnapper."

"But why would he do such things? Kidnapping is a federal crime, not to mention murder! Let's talk motivation now. Why would this respected chief of police do such things?"

Luke sounded weary, far away. "I think it has to do with proving something to his wife, Janine. She left him a few months ago, took their little girl. They're staying with a group of people who . . . who . . ." He searched for words again. "People who believe in 'the principle.' That is, plural marriage. But more important, they believe in some of the old ways of administering justice."

"Are you talking about blood atonement?"

Luke cleared his throat. "I think Helaman wanted to demonstrate something, that he believed and could live the old ways. And yes, that means blood atonement. He was willing to be part of that system, at least at first. But I don't think it swayed his wife—at least, I don't think she was willing to come back, and I think he just lost heart. So then he backed off from wanting to be part of that kind of fundamentalist Mormonism, to something else, maybe. Sort of sour grapes. More like poking fun at Mormon doctrine with the less violent crimes." He was silent for a moment.

"I just told him that Kirsten Young was pregnant when she died. He was horrified, aghast, beside himself. Selonnah, you should have seen him. I'm wondering . . . if he might lose his . . . his . . . faith altogether."

On the phone, Selonnah heard the sound of a door opening and another voice. Luke's tone became businesslike. "I have to go. I'm still on duty, and I have to meet a plane. Think about what I've said and let me know if I'm crazy to think that this is even possible. I'll call you tomorrow. Remember your promise."

And so it was that twenty-four hours later Selonnah sat on the dusk-shrouded back porch of her cousin Roger's echoing house with a newspaper in her lap and her head in her hands, mourning the profound weight of secrets, and a promise she made to a dead friend.

CHAPTER 30

IT WAS THE NEWSPAPER that made the decision for Selonnah.

She walked back into the house and spread it out on the kitchen table and had the same feeling she always got when she went into a bookstore. Why would anybody ever want to write another book? She felt overwhelmed not only by the words on the newsprint before her but by the glut of information she herself harbored. She was a writer. What should she edit from her consciousness? What was important, for right now?

A teacher once asked Selonnah's Memphis colleague and columnist Al Brant to address a sophomore writing class at his former high school. He would be treated as an alumnus dignitary, the teacher promised. He could regale them with stories about writing. They'd have cookies. He could autograph copies of his articles they would have printed.

Despite Al's protests to the teacher that his writing methods were unorthodox and that she wouldn't really want him teaching her class, the teacher cajoled, threatened, and (as he later related to Selonnah) finally guilted him into coming.

"How to write." Al began his presentation to a group of lounging bodies strung like drying seaweed across the desks.

"I start typing in whatever I think. Then I go get a drink. Then I come back."

Eyelids opened a bit.

"I type some more. Then I do my editing with the colors, then I'm done."

The teacher waved an arm from the back of the class. "Edit with the colors? That sounds interesting, right, class?"

Al could hear the soft snore of a teenager whose face was buried in his arms atop a desk.

"Yeah. With the colors. You know, when you use a word processing program, all the misspelled words have red lines under them. I fix those first."

"But what about the structure? Topic sentence and supports?" Heads turned toward the teacher who took this revival as signs of interest. "We learned about topic sentences, right, class? And grammar?"

She looked again at Al. "Do you use an outline?"

"Nope."

The class became small undulations across the room.

"You don't use an outline?" The teacher's voice had a crease of irritation in it.

"Nope."

"Okay, go on about the colors."

"Well, anything that's not grammatically correct shows up with a green line under it. I just keep typing in stuff or taking out stuff until the green lines go away."

"Cookies anyone?"

The class loved Al, the teacher hated Al, and Selonnah

thought the whole idea wasn't half bad. If only there were a mental program that would allow her to keep punching in information until all the green lines of irrelevant information—and feelings—went away and she was left with just what would work.

She heard a tune sounding like tacks on the felt of a piano hammer and picked up her cell phone from the vibrating metal top of the toaster oven in Eliza's dark, lonely kitchen.

"Anne, I'm so glad you called back. Is K.C. down for the evening? Can I come over? Do you have a life I'm interrupting all the time?"

Anne's voice was reassuring and inviting. Within five minutes Selonnah was in her car, a legal pad on the passenger seat on which she scribbled questions as she drove. She hardly noticed the road, barely remembered stopping for the bag of crisp Fuji apples she now presented to Anne.

A denim bag and empty paper grocery sacks sagged on the pink countertop. Anne must have just come home, because the house still had a closed-up smell, like old yellowed library books. The door to the baby's room stood ajar.

"I can't thank you enough for letting me come. I'm confused. I need help in sorting out some things." Selonnah hoped sheer pity would grease the path to answers. Anne smiled, real welcome on her face, and patted the end of the couch on which she stretched out, biting into an apple whose juice ran down her chin.

If only I could know what you know, Selonnah thought. She looked at the young woman dabbing her mouth with her sleeve as if Anne were the document containing all her answers.

"I made a list," Selonnah began. "If I can just ask you some questions. I'm just going to start at the beginning, from the time I arrived in Utah."

301

Anne nodded. The apple made satisfying snapping sounds when she bit.

"So. When I got here, the National Guard was everywhere. All the Masonic buildings were guarded. What do you think that was all about?"

Anne shrugged. "Mormons are pretty sensitive about Masons anyhow."

"Why is that?"

"Well, most of the last century—up until the mid-1980s as I recall, Mormons were forbidden to join a Masonic lodge."

"Why?"

"Because, I guess, Mormon leadership didn't want their members to see how similar their own temple ceremonies were to Masonic rituals. Even some of the regalia, like aprons and hats and such, are the same. Oh, and the handshakes and penalties, all that. Practically carbon copies in some cases. The Grand Lodge of Utah had retorted by saying they didn't want any Mormons as members anyhow. The Masons lifted the Mormon ban about the time the Mormons let their members be Masons. Tit for tat."

"Do you think the threats against the Masonic buildings were connected with the Deseret Alphabet crimes?"

Anne studied the slender core of her apple and glanced over at the sack of apples on the table. Selonnah smiled and retrieved another one—and a paper towel—for her.

"Well, if you think about it, nothing ever came of that. In fact, I'm wondering if the threats against Masonic lodges were made with a very different purpose," Anne said.

"What?"

With one hand, Anne folded the paper towel on her thigh neatly into fourths. "I've been wondering if they were just to divert attention away from the actual killings of Kirsten Young and that Bruce man, and the staging of the prostitute's body."

They both were silent as Selonnah considered the fact that having the National Guard around could have freed up a lot of Helaman's time. Anytime you bring in national muscle—the Guard, the FBI, CIA—the local law enforcement is made to understand that they're outgunned, outmanned. And outclassed and unwelcome. She really wanted to run that past Anne, but the promise . . .

"Okay. Item two, chronologically speaking," said Selonnah, consulting the legal pad. "I was told when I came here that polygamy was not Mormon doctrine. But I hear things all the time here. At the paper, we run stories about the FBI's most wanted list and at the top of it is a picture of a fugitive polygamist clutching a Book of Mormon."

"Polygamy is Mormon doctrine, yes. Practiced today by the Salt Lake City LDS Church—no. Everyone in Utah dances around that. Because everyone here knows a polygamist, or at least someone who's the child of a polygamist union. It could be your dentist or the kid checking your groceries or the librarian." Anne was wrapping the two apple cores in the paper towel as she spoke. "So the only way the government can handle the legal part of it is to pursue the one angle all Gentiles understand. Most of the LDS splinter groups, say in southern Utah and Arizona, who live polygamy—as a doctrine and a lifestyle—often have old guys marrying underage girls. Of course such marriages aren't legal. So they go after the men for statutory rape, child endangerment, et cetera. The only legal action is to take the young girls and children into protective custody because the men usually run for the hills. You know, like the raid on the Yearning for Zion compound in Texas in 2008. That way the government can take action and still avoid the doctrinal stuff."

Selonnah wondered suddenly about something Luke said about Helaman's wife and little girl. And the southern part of the state. She saw Anne yawn surreptitiously and went on with her list.

"Item three. I noticed some weirdness—I mean, beyond the ordinary weirdness—in how the Salt Lake City police department spoke about the prostitute who was found. I don't know if I told you, but I was there, on a ride-along, when the body was discovered. It was garish, sure—but even beyond that, I got the impression there were things that people there knew, and I didn't."

"That one's easy too. Remember I told you that for years the LDS Church portrayed the Catholic Church as the great whore of the book of Revelation. But what you may not know, something I just learned, Bernadette Rodriguez was an ex-Mormon too—turned Catholic."

Selonnah had to process this information with nods and gulps.

"Well, to be complete, I should add something else," said Anne, an impish light in her eyes. She seemed to be enjoying Selonnah's unbalance. "Joseph Smith taught unequivocally that all churches were corrupt but his. Talk about going on the offensive. . . ."

"Okay. Item four." Selonnah would deal with Church squabbles later. Much later. "Let's make an assumption that what happened to Kirsten Young, to Bernadette Rodriguez, to Heber J. Bruce, to the old couple the Woodruffs, to the homeless lady with the double name, and to the three men from Nephi—let's assume the same person or persons could possibly be responsible for all those crimes."

"Noted. And possibly agreed."

"The last time we talked, we said that the notes in code were something they had in common. And you told me about the marks on Kirsten Young and Heber J. Bruce, that those were temple garment marks—or temple oath penalties, right?

And we figured out the 'Three Nephites' business together. But why the taping and gluing on that old couple, the Woodruffs?"

"I asked somebody at the paper who interviewed the couple," said Anne. "There were some crime scene pictures taken that showed them lying on the concrete in a kind of sideways embrace when they were first discovered. No doubt about it, it's one of the ritual postures that people used to assume in the LDS temple." She blotted at her lips with a corner of the paper towel. "Well, standing up, that is; making vows and giving secret passwords. Embracing God through a veil."

"So somebody was making a statement about these secret ceremonies, then. Like, exposing them."

"Perhaps," Anne agreed. "And as for the homeless lady, she was a Native American, third or fourth generation Mormon. Here's what I think the person who bleached her hands was trying to bring attention to. Up until they changed the wording in the Book of Mormon awhile back, all Native American Mormons believed they were promised that they were going to turn white. Somebody bleaching that homeless woman's hands was pointing out, I think, the fact that this prophesied skin change never happened."

"Huh." Selonnah grunted, writing furiously on her legal pad, speechless. She looked up after a while to see Anne studying her gravely.

"But wait a minute. The police had a suspect. With a confession. I want to know what you think about why that Benson character confessed to all those crimes," Selonnah said.

"You don't think he committed those crimes?" Anne was grinning at her.

"Nobody thinks he did it. But it seems like he wanted to get killed."

"Bingo."

"Why?"

"It's the blood atonement thing. I remember Benson from way back in his hippie days, when his girlfriend's baby fell out of a window and died. He served his time for child abuse and negligence; and while he was in prison he became reconnected, so to speak, to his Mormon heritage. Since the courts said he was responsible for the shedding of innocent blood, he would have concluded that Mormonism would require that his blood be shed to pay for it. I guess it might have been a disappointment to him that he didn't qualify for capital punishment."

"What are you saying?"

"Prison officials have said off the record that he was always trying to figure out a way to get himself killed before he died of the cancer that was eating him up."

"Suicide by police. That's what he did." Selonnah sat back in her chair, her hands at her sides.

Anne nodded. "Any more questions?"

"Just two more." Selonnah waited, staring at her list with its remaining items. *Helaman.* She had to ask this question just right.

"I've had almost all my dealings with the Salt Lake Police Department via Luke Taylor," she said. "If now, I have to deal directly with the chief, Helaman Petersen, I wondered if you could help me get a handle on . . ."

Anne laughed. "So he has the same effect on you."

Selonnah stared. "I mean, but . . ."

"No, there are men like that. Let's face it—that's the way women who escape from polygamous LDS compounds describe the way that their leaders and husbands could affect them. In fact, Joseph Smith, the founder of Mormonism himself, apparently had some mesmerizing effect on women. I've read firsthand accounts about how he could walk into a room and every woman in it would be ready to marry him after an hour."

Selonnah nodded. "And dozens of them did—marry Joseph Smith, that is. Even some who were already married to his friends, from what I've read."

"Yes. I don't know if it's chemistry, something inexplicable and powerful, or what with Chief Petersen. Even Roberta Carlson brought it up in an editorial meeting one time at the paper. You just have to factor it in, and go forward professionally."

That sounded easy enough in theory. Ah, the unfathomable mysteries of aphrodisiac personalities would have to wait till later. She flipped pages back to the last item on her list.

"Why would anyone want to bomb Cottonwood Canyon?"

Anne looked at the newspaper folded under Selonnah's legal pad. "Well, you've already read about how it's where the Church stores all its genealogical records. Really, a state-of-the-art facility. Millions of man-hours of research and documentation, birth and death records. Some not available anywhere else in digital and retrievable form."

"You think it's going to be a blackmail situation? Somebody is trying to extort money out of the Mormon Church to protect the records?"

"No, I don't think so. It has to do with the reasons why Mormons are so adamant about genealogical work." Anne sighed. "How to explain this briefly. Hmm. Well, Mormons believe that anyone who doesn't become a Mormon while they're alive—and that would include anyone born before Mormonism was started in the 1800s, as well as any non-Mormon who lived and died since then—all those people's souls are walking around on this earth, invisible. And each one is waiting for someone to do a Mormon baptism in his or her name. A proxy baptism. That's one of the ceremonies that Mormons perform in temples. A Mormon will climb up into a big baptismal vat that's on top of the statues of twelve oxen—for the twelve tribes of Israel, and—"

Selonnah waved her arms: *stop, stop.*

"I saw pictures of those, fonts I think they called them, when I did my research on Mormon temples. But I didn't know they were for dead people."

"Not dead people. For Mormons who act as proxies for dead people. My sister—the one who lives down in southern Utah—was baptized in the Manti, Utah, LDS Temple fifteen times in a row in the names of fifteen women she'd never heard of; and in the Provo Temple thirty times for thirty other women. Only that time, some of the names were of distant relatives she'd done research on."

"Why?"

"Girlfriend, there are thousands of these proxy baptisms done every day in over a hundred LDS temples worldwide. Because Mormons believe everyone has to be baptized a Mormon to spend eternity in the celestial kingdom."

"Celestial kingdom? You talking about heaven?"

"Well, the highest level of heaven." Anne smiled. "They believe there are three levels. And you don't want to miss out on the top one."

"Okay. I get the proxy baptism thing. But why would someone want to bomb the place where they keep all this genealogical data? Why not threaten to bomb, say, a temple?"

"I have a theory on that. Two theories, in fact," said Anne. "One. If you had been here in Salt Lake City over the last four or five years, you would know that there are a whole lot of Jewish people who are furious about some of the proxy baptisms that have been done in LDS temples."

"Why?"

"Because the Mormon Church has performed proxy baptisms in the names of prominent Jews. And Holocaust victims

—in some cases, right off concentration camp rolls. The point of view of many Jews is that this is the ultimate humiliation, to have a ceremony done that purports to change the eternal status of Jews who died for being Jews, into Christians."

"Well, they are dead," said Selonnah wryly. "What does it matter?"

"Well, it could be a good thing. On the one hand I've always thought if Mormons are in temples doing these baptisms for the dead, they're not out trying to convert some of us live ones."

Selonnah rolled her eyes, and Anne continued. "Okay. I see that wouldn't matter to you. But to a Jew, the issue is reputation. About what you spend your life building to leave to people in general and your children in particular. Think of it this way: Can you bear the thought that after you're dead people would say that you're a racist? A killer? A child molester?"

"No."

"That's what Jews are saying too. Some researchers say they have proof that Mormons are doing proxy baptisms for Jews even today. They say that the Church promised to stop doing proxy baptisms for Holocaust victims, but the zealous keep doing it and it's being swept under the rug."

"I can see how that would anger some people," Selonnah said.

"But the Church denies it and tries to divert attention elsewhere. It's all smoke and mirrors. For instance, the LDS Church routinely presents public officials with giant bound books that show that their relatives have been researched and documented. The recipients think, hey, free genealogy."

Selonnah stared at Anne, who began, inexplicably, to laugh.

"Did you hear the story about the man who paid a professional genealogist five thousand dollars to research his family tree—and then paid him ten thousand to not tell what he found out?"

Selonnah laughed too. The break in tension felt good.

"Don't laugh too hard. Probably already did the same with all your relatives, girl," said Anne. "Roger's a member, right?

"Mormons did all of Jimmy Carter's genealogical research awhile back, gave him the big 'book of remembrance,'" said Anne. "And I bet he would have blown a Baptist gasket if he knew that book represented the fact that every one of his relatives had a proxy baptism done in his or her name to consider them as Mormons."

Selonnah shook her head. "Okay. You said you had a second theory about why someone mailed Terrance Jensen that threat about Cottonwood Canyon?"

Anne looked off into the distance. "Well, bombing the vaults would be impersonal. Like the threats against the Masonic temples were impersonal. No bloodshed, no person targeted, just a place. And I'm thinking now that since the Masonic threats were just a diversion, maybe the Cottonwood Canyon threats are just a diversion too."

"From what? You think there'll be more crimes?" Selonnah asked.

"I don't know."

They both sat quietly.

Selonnah didn't want to leave. A wintry feeling had seeped through Roger's house since the first of the week, almost as if there were a giant hose sucking all the warmth out of the house. Her schedule had only intersected with Roger's a few times and with Eliza's more often, but the time or two she saw the couple together, they passed each other with exaggerated politeness and nothing else. She realized that she did not see them occupy the same room at all this week.

Something was wrong, and now Eliza and Maria had left on their trip to Cumorah.

Perhaps it's me, thought Selonnah. Not every household is set up emotionally for relatives that stay past the three-day-fish-stink period. She considered checking in to one of the hotels she passed on the way to the newspaper office every day; was thinking so intently of the mental map of the route that Anne's next words startled her.

"So, how is all of this settling in, on you personally, I mean?"

Selonnah ducked her head almost unconsciously, looked away, did not want to engage. She was afraid she'd betray Luke's confidence; but even more, she did not want to hurt Anne's feelings by saying what she really thought. But when she looked into Anne's searching eyes, she knew that honesty—to the degree that she could offer it—was best.

"I tell you, Anne, it seems crazy to me, that people would fight over Church doctrines. I mean, does it really matter what ceremonies you spend your time performing, or which book of legends you happen to believe and which you don't?"

Anne sat quietly, looking down at her hands for what seemed like hours.

"It only matters if the concept of truth is important to you. If you think it's relative, that everyone can have his or her version of reality and must accept everyone else's, then it wouldn't matter so much, I guess."

Selonnah knew she was taking a personal risk in asking for more information.

"So why does it matter to you?"

"We'll leave that for another time." Anne rose from the couch.

"No. I know it's late. Just give me a sentence or two, something I can understand without any doctrinal stuff. You

311

obviously have reasons. I don't think you're motivated by revenge, and I don't see any mean-spiritedness in you. But this really matters to you, and I'd like to know why."

Anne sighed.

"Imagine, if you will, wrap your mind around a concept of an ultimate Creator Being so vast, so powerful, and so intelligent that He would leak out the cracks in infinity. Imagine that this Being cares very much about the lives of human beings that He crafted and made individually. He knows every detail of their every thought. And He, for reasons I'll never understand, yearns to *be known*, just as He knows. He wants to be understood. Hence, a need for a reliable communication, an inviolate Scripture."

Selonnah felt the whisper of something inside her lungs, something Anne couldn't hear as she continued speaking.

"A religion is exemplified by its people. But it is defined by its God."

Selonnah folded her hands to listen.

"Selonnah, I love this non-Mormon God because He's the only God. That's the bottom line for me. The concept of a Savior who came to earth as God—always and ever God— means everything to me."

Give me umption in my gumption, let me function function function. Selonnah heard her mother's voice singing, describing the kind of young widow who would carry on to make a life with an infant, wrestle with forgiving her husband's killers, sit patiently at midnight with a hardheaded reporter she hardly knew. Selonnah owed such a woman the courtesy of an explanation.

"Let me give you four word pictures." Anne waited for Selonnah's assent. "You don't have to know any theology. Just images. I want you to *see* that I have reasons for hope.

"One. I want you to think of a book that is invulnerable,

312

that survives the timeline of events and global geography in the rough hands of regular people; and yet it stays itself, keeps its identity, is more alive and evergreen than sequoias four millennia old. That's the Bible, and unlike the Book of Mormon or the Qur'an or any other writings the world has produced, it has the ability not only to endure but has authority to represent reality as God Himself sees it."

Selonnah was not willing to affirm, but she was willing to listen. She motioned for Anne to continue.

"Two. I want you to think of all of human history—the fates of billions of people living, dead, and yet unborn—resting across the shoulders of a defenseless, knobby-kneed little lamb. That's Jesus—a Savior who saves through His own vulnerability, His own willingness to die."

Selonnah nodded.

"Three. I want you to think of a baby, who leaps with inexpressible joy inside his mother's womb, because he knows the voice of hope. That's you and me."

The whisper within Selonnah became a murmur.

"Four. I want you to think of a place and time that is not a place, and beyond time, when everything in your life and my life can be set right. Every lapse, every fault, every mistake wiped off a cosmic tally board. A gentle hand that wipes away each tear as it forms in your eye. And neither of us will have to do anything to create—or earn—that place."

Selonnah no more remembered the drive back to Roger's house than she could recall the drive to Anne's. She climbed up the stairs in the silent house and fell into bed fully clothed and was asleep immediately.

The ringing of her cell phone awakened her and she heard Anne's frantic voice.

"Selonnah. I'm sorry—it's late—but I have to tell you. My sister called, the Mormon, who lives in a small town near a

313

place called Brace Crossing. It's where Helaman Petersen's wife and daughter are staying, have been for several months. My sister called to tell me that there was a federal raid on Brace Crossing tonight, like that one in Eldorado, Texas. Some of the men of the compound of course have escaped into Mexico apparently, but they've got the women and children in custody. But they can't find Helaman's wife and preteen daughter. In fact, they've issued an Amber alert. I just verified it on the Internet. Nobody knows where those two are."

"Why? Protective custody? What does Helaman's daughter need protecting from?"

"The leader of the fundamentalist Mormon group there—when I say, fundamentalist, I'm talking some really strange offshoots of Mormonism that not only believe in polygamy but are semimilitant as well—anyway, that guy, Val Anthony, has been arrested for his marriage to a girl not much older than Helaman's daughter."

"Thanks. I'll check it out in the morning—"

"I'm not calling you because you're a reporter who would like a scoop, Selonnah." Anne's voice sounded a little testy. "I'm calling you because apparently somebody—from that group? I don't know. It wasn't clear. Somebody is threatening to blow up the Hill Cumorah, up in Palmyra, New York. Apparently soon."

"But that's where Eliza and Maria—"

"I know. Tell your cousin Roger. You have to get word to them. You have to warn them not to go."

PART FIVE

CHAPTER 31

ELIZA AWAKENED with a profound sigh and a shudder that showed her body's attempt to shake off the dream she'd had of her early adult life, the recollection she spent years to both claim and demerit, appraise and evict. The images of a snowbound canyon and the cries of children lingered around her like a stubborn vapor no matter how she blinked and tried to concentrate. She knew that such things do not readily abandon their territory.

But by the time the seats were returned to their full upright and locked position, her seat belt was fastened, and all items were securely stowed below her seat, she began haltingly to rejoin the present. Her call to Roger a few minutes later to tell him that she and Maria had completed the four-and-a-half-hour plane trip was, in contrast to her dream, as trite as a television commercial.

First of all, her cell phone kept dropping the call. And then there was the trade-off between talking loudly enough to be understood in the metallic hallways of the airport, and feeling the studious averted eyes of fellow travelers: like her, numb-footed, herded beyond fatigue, and unwilling to hear any more conversations. But at the end of it all, Roger did understand one thing. She was turning the cell phone off so that she and Maria could sleep in tomorrow. Tonight's call to him, they both understood, was marital courtesy.

Marital. Eliza wondered at the fact that this word was only reversed letters away from martial.

Beside her, Maria tugged at her own little wheeled suitcase and sagged beneath her lumpy purple backpack. The stuffed dog Selonnah had given her peeked backward from under one flap of the pack, one arm out as if escaping, its ears swaying to and fro.

On the plane Maria had eaten and drunk with a pretentious little finger crooked in the air and watched the silly movie with an earphone headset that kept falling forward over her eyes when she giggled. Now, pigeon-toed stumbling over her own feet, she pulled her hand away from Eliza's each time they stopped, rubbing her eyes to wake herself up.

The rental car company had long since closed for all but those with the open sesame of credit cards and reservations. A yawning slot spat out an envelope with a key, rental paperwork, and maps. When they reached it, the green sedan smelled like melted crayons. Eliza wondered wearily if they kept records on people with children, like the computers remembered people who sneaked a smoke in their cars.

Maria seemed to revive with the thought that she was needed as navigator and sat erect and strained against the seat belt, searching anxiously for hotel signs until Eliza assured her that their reservations were at a small inn, the Haven of Rest, at least an hour away. That's what you get for trying to book something at the last minute, Eliza thought to herself, four-star quaintness and extortionary prices in a town she'd never heard of and could hardly see on the map. She squinted toward highway signs.

"Let's talk, Mom." Maria's voice was authoritative, adult-serious. Eliza hid her smile.

"Yes, sweetheart."

"Why didn't you want to talk to Daddy?"

"I did—it was just that the phone kept losing its signal."

"I think you're mad at each other."

"Oh, sweetheart, we are just trying to work some things out."

"You're not very good at this, are you?" Maria's tone was grave and gentle. The little girl turned her body around in the seat to place her face closer to her mother.

"It's Church stuff, isn't it? That's what you are both mad about. Does that mean I won't get to go to the Hill Cumorah Pageant?"

Eliza felt her eyes widen in surprise.

"No, of course we're going. I promised you, remember? We're just not doing it with the group." She reached to hold her daughter's slight hand. "We're going to be our own tour guides. Tomorrow morning we'll sleep as late as we want," she coaxed, "and then we'll eat eggs Benedict and drink chocolate milk and then prowl around the Smith Farm and Sacred Grove on our own."

"But you'll tell me everything about them? All the good stories?"

"Got the self-guided tour book right here." Eliza slapped the side of her purse near Maria's feet on the floor of the car. "We'll take our time and not have to be rushed to get back on a bus with all those people with walkers and funny sunglasses." She affected a tour-guide voice. "And here, ladies and gentlemen, on the right we have the monument to the sister missionaries, the untold thousands who died unmarried but who kept their 'sweet spirits and shining testimonies' to the end."

Maria giggled with the LDS inside-joke description of an unattractive woman, and began, Eliza thought, to relax. She was wrong about that.

"So why are you and Daddy fighting about Church stuff?"

"Your daddy and I love you, and we love each other, and we love Heavenly Father. We're just trying to figure out the best way to love each other." Eliza felt Maria's searching eyes and turned for a moment to meet them. "That's the truth, sweetheart."

Within moments Maria's braided hair was resting on the seat console next to her as the child's exhaustion gained a toehold, then surmounted her slack body.

Her job as a travel agent took her away from Salt Lake City often, so it was not the unfamiliarity of the car nor the ghostly lit road, Eliza thought, that gave her the sense of uneasiness she had, the feeling of being off balance and foreign. This trip had great import. It was her last-ditch effort to believe in the faith of her youth, the Church of her marriage.

Though she'd never before attended the Hill Cumorah Pageant, at BYU she had known several students who had played roles in the annual production. She knew almost every Lamanite maiden in the cast—girls like herself who were Native Americans, members of the campus club called Tribe of Many Feathers. Not only that, she had dated one of the Nephis and an "Alma the Younger," and one semester sat next to a "Joseph Smith" in geology class.

Her stomach clutched with the sudden apprehension that all those roles—with the exception of Joseph Smith—might be only fictional characters.

This jarring feeling was familiar. As a teenager, she had

weathered her own internal mental storm years ago when she investigated—and found to be true—the shocking admission by the Church's foremost archaeologist that there was "no such thing as Book of Mormon archaeology." But that was before her catastrophic first marriage in which she focused on personal survival, and then when she met Roger —she stuffed her doubts, trading them for Roger's delight in the structure and culture of Mormonism. She became a travel agent, visiting the River Jordan and Golgotha and Corinth and other places chronicled in the Bible, and pushed to the back of her nagging conscience the fact that there was not a single verifiable Nephite site in the entire Western Hemisphere. In spite of the book's supposed thousands of years of history and occupation.

Then again the doubts arose at the spectacle of the backpedaling of Mormon scholars who began to seek a Central or South American site for the Hill Cumorah described in the Book of Mormon, saying that the New York site just had the same name, sort of an honorary title for its function as a repository for the golden plates. Convenient, now that hundreds of years of archaeology had not uncovered a single vestige of the catastrophic wars chronicled by Joseph Smith's rendering of markings on golden plates that nobody actually ever saw, she thought. Unless the old dodge of "seeing with your spirit eyes" counted. And for her, today, it didn't count.

How do you document an absence of evidence? There were no antebellum piled-up swords or other metal armaments, nothing to show the postapocalyptic demise of an entire nation on Cumorah's battlefield around Palmyra, New York. Generations of Mormons had lived and died without the fulfillment of what had been her dream too—a bullet-proof archaeological evidence of the stories on the elusive golden plates.

So, as the ever-pragmatic Mormon Church decided, just

relocate the "other Cumorah" somewhere else. And hope its new site of ancient soils may yield something.

Now Eliza suspected that the characters Joseph Smith wrote of never lived in the United States. She could not bear the thought, but could not shake it, that they never lived at all. With all her young-girl heart, she had loved them as people, ancestors, guides, and friends, and lived by their stories as if they were her own personal history. She felt as if she were called to commemorate a mass funeral.

Eliza turned, with yeoman-weary arms dragging the stiff steering wheel of the car, into a brightly lit parking lot where she consulted a not-so-helpful map and her watch. She dialed the number for the hotel but no one answered.

She wanted to call Roger. She closed her eyes for a moment and breathed in memories of him. When she awakened an hour later, she was dreaming of the way the hair at the back of his neck whorled when he cut it too short; dreaming of pentagram messages and scenarios of fury and despair in snowy canyons; dreaming of stop-action scenes that sampled her life, washing over themselves again and again until the colors faded from definition.

This man had taken her just as she was, and never tried to open the vigilantly guarded cache of her past. He knew nothing of the desperation of what seemed a former life altogether, as if it had transpired in someone else's body-space and time. And yet she could not abandon what had made her who she was.

A Yei rug hung in the hallway of their home and she knew Roger had seen her stop to trace an outline with her finger but he held his peace, gave it to her by so doing. An old cigar box in her closet contained an empty perfume bottle, a tiny hank of silken multicolored hair tied with a piece of yarn, and a branch of alligator juniper. At first she kept it hidden, until she understood that Roger's response was his gift to her: the bequest of a purposeful and utter lack of curiosity.

He knew she had been married before, but did not once require of her so much as a comparison. From the beginning she knew Roger was aware that he delighted her, could see it in the swagger of his walking away from her and knowing that she was watching.

Their lives together had been a knitting of souls, a fact she early recognized when she heard herself repeat one of his Tennessee phrases or found herself standing with her hand circling the back of her neck, thumb down the spine, fingertips touching the jugular, as he did when he was weary. She loved him with a purity she never imagined possible; in intimacy that made all that was earthly about them melt off until they were cleansed of everything that had to do with flesh, and all that was left was purest personality in union.

Now the great gulf was fixed between them. They battled over nothing less than the prime reality that underlay all that was theirs. He dared not even touch her doubts, she could see that; his fear of contamination was too great. But his very breath was integrity, and she was certain that the ongoing battles he was fighting inside himself were etching his soul.

Now hurtling down two-lane roads with a sighing, sleeping child beside her, Eliza Greathouse Zee turned her thoughts to consider eternity.

She reflected that she had staked all her shy dreams on her own future status as a goddess—in humility, in hunger, in hope. Yet now something inside her rebelled against the logic of such a thing: the never-before-challenged assumption that God is simply us, only more so.

With mingled loss and barely dared relief, she considered that perfection should not—cannot—come out of the mold of meat and bones.

If her soul told her that she herself could not seize divinity in the future, then what did that imply for the past of the god of Mormonism? She had memorized, canonized, internalized the motto, the words of the prophet Lorenzo Snow: *As man is, God once was. As God is, man may become.*

What was this deity she'd enthroned? A glorified former human, flesh and bones and miraculous liquid beyond blood, someone she'd always imagined—reasoning backward—as a good man at his greatest potential? As her temple vows, kneeling across an altar, would lead her to extrapolate—as a perfected Roger?

Eliza stretched her neck from side to side, rubbed her weary eyes one at a time.

She thought of Easter season the month before, when they watched the old movie *The Ten Commandments* together.

"Why do you think Moses was so mad at the people when they had a party while he was on the mountain, Mommy?" Maria had asked.

"I don't think it was just the party," Eliza had answered, sensing that her daughter was preparing a childish snare, ever cautious of parrying with this precocious young human with whom she lived. "Parties aren't wrong, are they? We have them all the time. So, when you watched the movie, what did you see happening that would make somebody become that angry?"

"It was the lie," Maria had said, soberly and without hesitation.

"What lie?"

"The lie about the golden statue, the calf, remember?" Maria prodded her mother's memory, and Eliza congratulated herself for meeting this challenge, staying alert. She realized that she was about to learn something valuable, even from a mind that often concerned itself for days with the relative virtues of different flavors of lip balm.

"The people said it was the statue that had done all the good things for them," continued Maria. "But it was God. And He doesn't want people to think about Him as a cow."

What wisdom, Eliza thought. A prolific and ingenious God doesn't want people to give a cow credit for parting the Red Sea, or inventing the Matterhorn and Jupiter and DNA and the human brain.

Nor can someone appropriate wholesale the history of the Creator of the universe, and say that an animal—or even a super-enhanced human—did it all, and get away with it.

Maria knew that, and now Eliza did too.

Eliza was glad that Maria was asleep and could not see the hot tears she wiped away with the heel of her hand. With the fellowship of millions of wives throughout human history, Eliza had known long ago what it was to be betrayed by the man to whom she had entrusted herself in marriage.

She knew that Roger wasn't capable of such treachery. Thus, she had come to believe she was finally safe. How bitter it was, she thought, to realize that she had invested even more of herself—her time, her energy, her dreams, her most selfless focus, her best efforts, her best self—in a god who never existed, a character in a nineteenth-century melodrama.

The map now lay beyond her reach on the floor of the car. The stretch of road along which her little car sped had no lights, no billboards. Eliza, the car, the sleeping child—all passed through the gauntlet of an infinity of sword-sharp fences that disappeared alongside the road in the distance ahead, where her assignation with the Hill Cumorah and its secrets lay.

She began to admit the possibility she was lost, when up ahead the flickering sign of the hotel beckoned her to safety and sleep.

CHAPTER 32

THOUGH HELAMAN TRIED to lie quietly on the cheap hotel bed, he was too alert to sleep. He could smell old colognes on the snag-thread bedspread. He scanned the six channels on the television and set the alarm on a bolted-down clock radio on the bedside table, so he could test the bomb's timer.

He thought of Janine.

When was it that he realized their marriage was never going to work? From the beginning, she was boulevard, he was ranch. They spoke of celebrating differences, of creating union out of disparity, but impassable chasms separated them. She had a grandfather who was an ambassador to Liechtenstein; he had an otherwise-charming old aunt who could not help barking like a dog when she was nervous.

He had craved Janine—mindlessly, he later came to realize—and refused to be denied, winning her from competing suitors with sheer force of will and what she described variously and vaguely as an irresistible magnetism to which she succumbed.

Thus it was that neither of them, upon later reflection, was able to agree on how they found themselves kneeling across a block altar in the St. George, Utah, LDS Temple; each of them looking past the other's shoulder to the opposing mirrors that showed Helaman/Janine/Helaman/Janine in an infinity of ironically prophetic, diminishing reflections.

He came to regret whatever it was in himself that made women he didn't know incline their ears as if listening even when he wasn't speaking, that made their nostrils dilate in his proximity.

A wedding ring—which he thought, foolishly, would serve as a social prophylactic—made some women more bold in pursuing him in what he realized with shame was a replication of his own ancient pursuit of Janine.

Ignoring such women made them go through what he'd come to recognize as a cycle of challenge, distress, and then distance. Once—only once—he tried to soften that sequence for a truly sweet and fragile young woman in the police department's secretarial pool by taking her to a restaurant to talk to her as father or uncle, to call her to higher things and more eligible men.

Janine had entered the restaurant, caught his desperate eyes with her furious ones, and left.

That incident became the collateral Janine had long sought for new negotiations on his failings. He wasn't bishop material, she was still at the height of womanhood and fertility despite what she interpreted as his misgivings, public servants never become rich, policemen walked in blood.

It was then that her visits to Brace Crossing began and she described upon each return her growing ambivalent fascination with the clannish town-compound where her second cousin Ruth lived. Timid Ruth had become the third wife of its wealthy and charismatic leader, Val Anthony. His piercing grey eyes could see into people's souls, Janine told Helaman at first. His voice, she said, was that of a true prophet.

After one of her trips Helaman found a sheaf of watercolors Janine had painted. Though she was a landscape artist, among the paintings was one of a man's hands. The greys and russets—just barely staining the paper in places—depicted only the wrists, palms, and graceful fingers. Helaman noted the length of the fingers, the lightness with which she painted the fingertips, the seeking, reaching posture.

But about that time, Janine seemed to run out of adjectives for the wavy-haired man who commanded an allegiance of community. They never spoke of Val Anthony directly again.

Anthony, a multitalented man in his own right, saw himself as a collector not only of prophetic doctrines and adherents but of art that depicted the rugged landscapes of southern Utah; and he showcased with pride his new plural wife Ruth's mosaic murals of the windswept vistas. He was articulate, even eloquent in speech, well-read, charming, renaissance in his abilities. He courted Janine—for her paintings, he told her at first, for the gallery he was building—but soon Helaman realized she was equally wooed by the prestige of Anthony's attention and the raw power of his convictions about what he described as the insipidity of the traditional LDS Church. Never before, Helaman noted, had he heard awe in the voice of his wife—not for him, not for their newborn child, not for God Himself.

Her trips to the south corroded their marriage and there was absolutely nothing Helaman could do about it. A public man serves at the pleasure of the people, she reminded him, and she could create an emasculating scandal that would evaporate that pleasure if he did not allow her to go when she felt a calling to do so.

At first he spent the times in his house wandering from room to room, and falling over in exhausted sleep as he kept vigil on his Gracie's little trundle bed. He found companionship in Keats and Wordsworth and their friends whose words he memorized. Many nights he read his patriarchal blessing —a kind of written personal prophecy given to young Mormons by a local official—until the words seemed burned into his retinas and he ceased to wonder at the promises of being a leader in the Church and a father of many, as infinite as the reflections in the St. George mirror.

Now, in the cheap hotel room, he was less alone than in his own home. He looked at his watch. He should test the bomb timer. In a while.

In charting his resentment, he found he could only think of Janine now in analogies.

He thought of her soul as fissured, with a deep uncharted canyon in the flat plain of her disdain for him.

The marrow of her bones was duplicity. Her tendons were guile.

She was unrealized infection, lurking at the mouth of a wound.

And yet he loved her more than he loved his own soul and knew, told her, he would do anything to regain her.

She told him he must read what she told him to read. He had a calling. He must be made to see how things once were in the Church, in the days of Joseph and Brigham. Helaman thought of his own maternal grandfather, who like Alma Woodruff had been a veil worker in the Salt Lake City Temple. In his youth, this man had spoken the words of the oaths, promising to have his tongue cut out and his entrails scattered if he revealed the secrets. Then those words were replaced with slashing pantomimes that themselves were eliminated over a decade ago. The temple and its god of threats had been defanged. No wonder Val Anthony railed that purity of purpose and energy must be restored.

What, Helaman now wondered, had Janine hoped to accomplish by asking him to read the old documents? What did she expect him to conclude about an entity, a church, whose native tongue from infancy was victimization, which lapsed into self-protection and illusions? How can one crawl around in the intestine history of Mormonism and keep faith?

And here at Cumorah, physical proximity demanded that he contemplate the gold plates. Like the best of urban legends, which, once traced to accounts of actual sight and touch, the records were always just one degree of relationship away from actual experience.

At first in the readings he marveled at the images of the men of early Mormonism drunk on power and prophecy who spoke of vegetable spirits and the marriages of Jesus to Mary and Martha and inhabitants of the moon and ancient tribes transported into the arctic wastelands. How could anyone unravel all those tangled personalities gone amok, how could one knit them back together as scores of them followed Joseph's example and formed new churches, of which they were supreme leaders—each ordained to correct all other corrupt churches on earth? Including that of Joseph? And Brigham?

Helaman had heard that one must never ask to see how sausages and laws are made. From his reading, he concluded that the same was true of Old West churches. And this one's leaders taught that gold and silver grow in the ground like hair on the head; that buried treasures can move themselves around underground, and that the wearing of folk-magic talismans and the use of divining rods and seerstones were compatible with Christian living.

Thus for a while he smothered his own doubts. On the corpses of three people, he carved the proof that he could sustain his loyalties in spite of all such things, could "magnify his calling." But with each act, he marveled at what he had often seen in his work as a policeman: how quickly—in a moment, in a breath—a living human being goes from cunning to carcass.

Like Sampson Avard, a nineteenth-century Danite who persuaded a group of followers to become a "covert renegade band" to avenge wrongs done against the Mormon Church, Helaman acted decisively.

It was his calling.

He of all believers was most true.

It was not enough.

It was not enough for Janine, and it was not enough for him. Mormonism in all its incarnations was rotten to its roots. What he had learned was not the stuff of salvation—it was what he must save Janine and Gracie *from*. This thought stopped his world.

He held his throbbing head in his hands and felt every supporting ligament within him sag. He remembered the infamous feminist Mormon of the sixties, Sonia Johnson, who called the LDS leaders "prigs and toadies." You can excuse the excesses of mere men, he thought. But those who claimed direct access to God were a different case. He rather thought Johnson had been too kind.

He lay in the near silence of the hotel room on his back. Helaman remembered the very first time he rode a train, the unobstructed views of skies and clouds for hundreds of miles, the sensation that he was being hurtled effortlessly and without external propulsion through space. This feeling embodied all he came to know about the passage of time: that it pushed him along without his permission nor even, sometimes, his consciousness; and thus it held the promise of the surprise of hope.

But once he came to doubt the Church of his fathers, he began to see the passage of time quite differently. He perceived it to be as uniform as a corrugated tin roof over which he was soundlessly pulled—across the increasingly hotter humps of days, gliding into the cooling rifts of oblivious sleep at night. He felt himself held mute, arms tied to his sides, drawn up and down rhythmic, meaningless slopes that slid frictionless under him. Finally only one thing gave him meaning, stood him up on that tin roof and loosed his bands.

Wrath alone rescued him. Boundless anger, the friend of his bosom. How odd it is, he thought, looking at his watch, that when you are not angry, anger seems the most unreasonable and costly of emotions. Anyone could see how counterproductive it is. But when anger is your own treasured possession, it becomes a refuge, comprehensive and precise in its own internal and unchallenged logic.

Nothing can motivate and focus the mind like a sense of injustice, the awareness of one's own offended state. Though he had been distraught beyond devastation by the knowledge that he had killed the unborn child of Kirsten Young, that was in his former life, during a time when he believed that he could still atone, shed his own blood, to pay for the death of that innocent little one. But later when he learned that one of the homeless men had died, he lost all hope that he had enough propitiatory platelets within him to pay for both crimes.

The coup de grace came when he learned that Janine's cousin Ruth had a thirteen-year-old daughter, who had become Val Anthony's newest wife; and with that Helaman entered wholesale and with banners into the waiting, welcoming arms of rage.

He knew that Janine was lost to him when she coolly rejected his own offer to join Anthony's community. Perhaps she at that very moment was already married to Anthony as a plural wife, he no longer cared. But he saw with sudden clarity that his golden Gracie could join Janine as sister, as *plural wife*, to share a bed with the wavy locks and long, sensitive fingers of Val Anthony. He could not bear that thought.

He reflected that the raid on the Brace Crossing last night took the priceless child out of harm's way. A phone call to a fellow Mormon CIA official sent a covert team into the community and the child and Janine were spirited away in the night before the FBI raid that made all the headlines. Best to let everyone believe that Janine and Gracie were missing instead of held in a safe house where Janine had raged and pled and threatened—and remained. Everyone but the CIA assumed since Helaman was unaccounted for, that he had taken his visiting family out of harm's way with some sort of professional courtesy advance notice.

That's good, he thought, because no one would be looking for Helaman M. Petersen at Cumorah. He would gut the Hill. He would expose the barren womb of Mormonism, to show that no golden treasure lay enfolded in its depths. To show that nothing ever had.

The damage of a bomb on its back side would be to the Pageant structures and perhaps to some of the workmen, but collateral damage can't be helped, as he had learned in the CIA. This was about exposing the lies of Mormonism, not killing any more of its people than necessary to make the point about the emptiness of the Hill.

The genial old year-round resident caretakers, the MacPhersons, who had fed him fried chicken and rhubarb pie on his last official visit, would be glad to see him early tomorrow morning. He would charm them with a believable lie. His visit was a follow-up to his last year's professional services. Tonight, he was bringing his own family, he would tell them.

He could not shake a sudden chilling thought, that he was watching all this, a novelist recording his life. Yet the thought brought him comfort, helped him calm as he narrated.

He looks down at his short-range transmitter.

He had mounted it into a cell phone so that he could type in instructions to the explosives. Though he had tested the timer before in the privacy of his home, changes of altitude and humidity did strange things to electronics.

The blasting caps and other paraphernalia lay on a coffee table and three chairs at the four corners of the room like compass points that cannot, must not be allowed to, intersect before their time.

He sits on the edge of the bed and points the transmitter to the small timer on the peeling dresser. It blinks a yearning appeal to be connected to something, for union, to have purpose for its existence.

He types in 4:00 and notes with satisfaction that the timer mirrors each numeral. It is a holy hour. He and Janine were married at that hour; Gracie was born at that hour. He toggles the timer off and on, off and on.

Tomorrow the world will drink the wine of astonishment, he thinks.

He catches a glimpse of his reflection in the dresser mirror above the timer. The yellow lamp in the corner seems swamped by the pewter light of the hotel sign outside his window, making what he sees look like an old daguerreotype.

His eyes are maroon-lidded with fatigue and tension and tears. A ropy vein at the end of his left eyebrow buries itself in his stiff, disheveled hair. His teeth are bared, his lips cracked. Even in the poor light he can see the muscles tensing themselves on his unshaved jaws.

"This, then," he says aloud in the neon-washed room, "this is the gnashing of teeth."

From: [mailto:adam1830@hivenet.net]
Sent: Friday, June 7
To: liahona@hivenet.net
Subject: [none]

I will show you, my Sarah. Can you not see that if the root of the tree is rotten, it cannot bear good fruit? If the womb is barren, it cannot give birth to life?

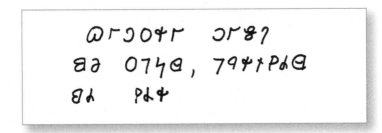

Cumorah must be opened, purified by fire.

The cup stands before me, brimming.
I must drink from
The sullen unrelieved crucifixion
Of my only dream

Adam, your first man

CHAPTER 33

SELONNAH LOOKED at Anne, who dozed in the airline seat opposite her, the tiny arm of her baby reaching upward from the nursing sling. Ahead of her on the plane, men were arguing loudly with Roger, who was waving a blue folder at them and shouting back.

When Selonnah burst into Roger's house a few hours ago, after her phone call from Anne about the threat to bomb the Hill Cumorah, she was frantic with apprehension. She stumbled through the darkened hallways to the master bedroom and began knocking on the closed door with both fists, trembling with dread. She jumped when a terrified Roger touched her on the shoulder.

"What! What!! What's wrong?" He grasped her upper arms and turned her around to clinch her wild arms in a boxer's embrace, but she fought him off like an enemy with one hand and appealed with the other to the closed door for an explanation.

"I fell asleep on the couch." His voice was still groggy but alarmed. "What's wrong?"

"It's Eliza and Maria . . ." she began. She saw him begin to sag and step backward, so she grasped his forearms. "No—no! They're all right," she began to reassure him and then realized that she could not. "Aren't they? When did you talk to them?"

"A few hours ago. When they got to the airport—"

"You have to call them right now! Tell them to get as far from that Hill Cumorah as possible!"

"Why? What's wrong? What happened?" Roger was already fumbling in his breast pocket for his cell phone, speed-dialing the number that Selonnah could hear went straight to voice mail. "Eliza Zee here, and Eliza's All-World Travel Services. We can't come to the phone right now. . . ."

Selonnah searched Roger's crestfallen, desperate face. "Surely she just couldn't get to the phone, right? She'll call you back, right?"

His eyes were shamed. "You have to tell me what's wrong."

"Someone says there's a bomb threat at Cumorah. It's on the news."

His eyes opened wide. "When? When are they saying they are going to bomb it?"

He was already opening the bedroom door and striding with long legs over to the television on the dresser, patting it and the clothing-strewn bed for the remote, turning it on, finding the news station with the crawler information at the bottom of the screen. They both sat on the edge of the bed, leaning forward like racers before the gun.

"Look," said Selonnah. "There it is. About the raid on Brace Crossing. . . ."

"But you said Cumorah. That's thousands of miles away. . . ."

They both stopped talking to watch the reporter who looked like she, too, had just awakened. She held her vertical, blowing hair with one hand and a microphone in the other and turned toward a background of SWAT and FBI vehicles and rattletrap old buildings.

Roger stabbed his thumb into the remote control and the woman's tiny voice grew.

". . . and although the raid seems to be finished, the sect's leader and self-proclaimed prophet, Val Anthony, is not in custody. There are still many unanswered questions. The arrests of men accused of marrying underage girls continues, though." The woman's hair seemed to spiral upward. She turned toward a small commotion and moved aside so that the camera could zoom in on two heavily uniformed men with helmets pushed back on their foreheads. They were urging forward by the elbows a handcuffed, angry-looking middle-aged man whose paunch showed through his misbuttoned shirt. Behind him was a bus, its windows framing dozens of young faces.

Over the protests of the reporter, she too was pushed to one side. The television cut to a commercial and Roger turned his face—though not his eyes—to Selonnah as he flitted through channels that made blip-blip sounds.

"You said a bomb, you said Cumorah."

"Anne called me. She saw it on the news. They said that a witness at Brace Crossing turned in a laptop computer that had an open email on it, with what looked like a threat to blow up the Hill Cumorah. But no time frame."

Roger's bedside telephone rang and he rolled over the corner of the bed, falling to his knees, scrambling for the phone. Selonnah stood in respectful silence but soon could tell from the conversation that it was not Eliza calling. Roger's voice was hoarse.

"News conference? You have to be kidding. My wife and daughter went to Cumorah today. Do you hear me? They're *at* Cumorah. I'm not staying here to do any news conference, I have to get to them, warn them. I can't locate them, and my wife, my wife . . . her phone must not be working." He began pacing, one arm across his stomach as if he were ill, listening. He stopped suddenly, his torso frozen in a forward lurch.

"You do? When can we leave?"

He nodded at Selonnah, his eyes wide. "And my cousin—she can come?"

The phone clattered into its charger base.

"The LDS Church has several private planes. They have all kinds of resources. I'm one of their resources, and they need me." Selonnah must have looked a question at him. "I'm the 'face' of Mormonism right now, at least in front of cameras. So they are going to help us find Eliza and Maria before this thing gets any more public." Roger's face was twisted as he pawed mindlessly through the slacks and shirts on the bed. "They will have an airplane fueled and ready at the airport. It's a fifteen-passenger—plenty of room—please help me pack an overnight, Selonnah." He sat back down on the side of the bed, his forearm full of clothing, and began to cry as he searched for the remote control again.

Selonnah's phone rang and she cradled it against her shoulder as she folded into a duffel bag the clothing that Roger tossed to her. Anne's voice on the phone was concerned.

"What did you find out? What can I do to help?"

Selonnah remembered Anne's words from days ago. "Don't ever underestimate the will, nor the ability, nor the financial resources that the LDS Church has, and will expend, in defending itself."

She looked at Roger. "Roger, you said it was a big plane.

I need some moral support and you do too. What if Annabel MacAlister came along?"

Roger swatted the idea in the air. Selonnah wasn't certain he heard her. He was muttering to himself before he met her eyes. He straightened up and spoke clearly for the first time since Anne's phone call. "You bring anybody you want with you. We need all the help we can get, and they better not say a word to me."

Selonnah tried to contain her surprise at the coarseness of his voice.

Roger had the presence of mind to bring along a photo album with pictures of Eliza and Maria. They were at the airport quickly and police cars inexplicably moved aside for them. Anne arrived at the night-shrouded, droning plane before they did, a bastion of hope and sanity, standing in the darkness on the tarmac, swaying and soothing her baby.

The three suited men who waited inside the suitelike little airplane were grim.

"NO. I don't know which airport she flew into," Roger said, his voice raising. "Look at this map. You see? Rochester is twenty-five miles away from Palmyra. Buffalo is ninety-five. Syracuse is seventy."

Two of the men leaned over the map.

"And she made her reservations at the last minute. And no, she didn't tell me which one."

"So let's track her through her rental car." The man who said this had a sneer in his voice. Did he think that someone was crying wolf again? How many times had he been summoned in the middle of the night when someone threatened the LDS Church? And yet nothing had happened, and so he sauntered. He seemed oil-jointed, like the languid checker players at Selonnah's hometown café. *Slack-jawed layabouts,* Mary called them.

Roger was visibly trying to control himself but he paced anyway in the short aisle, holding his left hip, unconsciously pledging allegiance to his sciatic. "Well, if I don't know which airport, and don't know the name of the rental car company, which by the way wouldn't be open right now, and I don't know the name of the hotel . . ."

"There can't be that many hotels in that area, right?"

"The Cumorah visitors Web site lists fifty of them." Another of the men consulted a laptop. He pulled a cell phone from his pocket, checked it for a signal, and dialed a number. "The Cumorah visitors site. List of hotels. Start calling them. I know it's the middle of the night, keep calling the ones who don't answer until they do answer."

So much for cell phones interfering with the plane's navigational system, Selonnah thought. She patted her own cell phone in her vest. Over and over Roger pressed a speed dial on his like a morphine drip.

The chairs in the back of the plane where Selonnah and Anne sat were arranged conference-style, two and two, with a table between them. Dawn's red light began to pour through the windows. Selonnah calculated that they were halfway there. The airplane roared again in ascent, and she tired of straining to hear what the men were saying. Selonnah had seen Oklahoma City. She had seen the Twin Towers. She knew the up-front fee a rescuer agreed to.

She leaned back in her chair and stretched out her arms. Fatigue sent tendrils of dream images into her thoughts and she drifted in and out of consciousness like a drowsing driver, back and forth over the centerline of wakefulness. Could she be a savior? Must it involve one's own death to save others? Her father had slipped away in death, her mother's mind eroded each day. She saw the knobby-kneed lamb that Anne had described, carrying all the weight of billions of people across its shoulders. She could not bear such a weight; was staggering under just her own parents' decline—and the very thought of Eliza and Maria dying.

She submerged fully into a pithy, fitful sleep in which she dreamt of a Red Flag Hill that towered beyond Cumorah, a rocky place higher than she, a place where she was released from rescuing anybody. Where she could be rescued . . .

Both Selonnah and Anne roused from sleep when Roger collapsed, as if he were boneless, into the chair next to Selonnah. He groaned and grimaced as he stretched out his left leg. The folder he'd been waving around at the front of the plane slapped the table and broadcasted its contents. Selonnah could see what looked like printouts of emails.

"Well, they didn't want to show me, but here are the emails off the laptop from Brace Crossing. And you'll never guess whose laptop it is," Roger said.

Anne and Selonnah lifted their eyebrows in tandem.

"Janine Petersen, the wife of Police Chief Helaman Petersen."

"They're polygamists?" Selonnah asked.

"No, she just visits down there. A lot." Anne's voice was authoritative, and both Roger and Selonnah turned to stare at her.

"I know because my cousin lives down there and she has told me that the Petersen woman is an artist and goes down there to paint. She has become, shall we say, heavily involved in the community." Anne seemed to be sorting through a basket of words, choosing only the ones that would best serve her purpose. Selonnah suddenly realized the reason for her caution. Roger was LDS. These polygamists were like cousins.

"So why would someone tell her about this bomb threat that's supposed to take place somewhere clear across the country from Utah?" Selonnah asked.

The three heads bent over the table, tense fingers culling the most telling messages, passing them to the left like polite diners. Each one blinked as they read, when they came to words bitter as wormwood, the deliberateness of the words that could sting even strangers. Selonnah spoke first.

"I can certainly see why the LDS Church would see these as a threat," Selonnah said.

Her mind was reeling. She heard Luke's voice in her memory, "It's Helaman, Selonnah." She cleared her throat to buy some time. "Whoever wrote this is not just angry but heartsick."

" 'Cumorah must be opened, purified by fire,' " Anne read. "Does that necessarily mean a bomb? Everyone is saying this is a bomb threat."

Roger looked over his shoulder at the three men who huddled around the cockpit door, talking, animated. One man turned stiffly aside and picked up a portable cooler and lumbered down the center of the plane. He opened it without a word, showing Roger, Selonnah, and Anne the bottles of water and juice, and placed a stack of paper napkins on the table beside the email printouts before he walked back to the companions to whom, it was now obvious, he had lost a bet.

Knuckleheads, Selonnah thought.

Roger spoke quietly. "In view of the other bomb threats in Salt Lake City, especially the one concerning Cottonwood Canyon, nobody is taking any risks."

"So, if these were on the Petersen woman's laptop, we're going to start by assuming they were her emails? Not accessed off, say, a mail server," Selonnah suggested. She ached to tell them about Helaman, but was bound by her promise to Luke until she had proof. The other two were nodding.

"And therefore Janine Petersen must be Liahona." She struggled with the pronunciation of the word and was surprised when Roger supplied it immediately. "Think that's a middle name?" she asked.

"Could be," responded Roger. "But it's the name of a compass in the Book of Mormon."

"But the compass wasn't invented until centuries later," Selonnah began. Anne shot her a warning look and Selonnah apologized to Roger. "Oh, sorry. Okay, a compass."

"For the time being, let's assume Liahona is just a screen name, one that we know at least refers to Mormonism. But if the letters are addressed to Janine Petersen, who is this Sarah?" asked Selonnah.

Anne looked pointedly at Roger. "Roger, can you think of why a Mormon man would call a woman a name like that?"

Roger fidgeted. "That's a name used, ah, in the temple sometimes," he finally said reluctantly. "In weddings."

Selonnah looked at Roger, seeking more information. Yet she felt already mired in facts that disoriented her, as if she were wading around in a muck of information that pulled at her mental shoes. For some reason she was reminded of the brain condition that Alzheimer's produced, tangles of knotted nerves, the cellular debris of plaque that clogged the synapses.

"But there must be thousands of women who get married in temples," she coaxed. "And it's supposed to be secret. How would you know that Sarah would be Janine's name?"

"There are only a limited number of names that women are, um, given." Roger held his head in his hands.

Anne spoke softly, a voice-over tour guide of this documentary. "Women in the temple are each given a 'new name' when they get married, one that only their husband is supposed to know." She looked for confirmation to Roger, who nodded imperceptibly. Anne continued. "The special name her husband has to call to raise her from the dead, at the end of time."

Roger remained silent.

"But what most Mormons don't know is that there are only a few names used, for all the women." Anne's voice was cautious as she continued. She didn't take her eyes off Roger. "Bible names, mostly. Sarah is one of them—but it would also be the name for lots and lots of women."

Selonnah paused and swallowed. "Okay. So we're going to assume that Liahona is a screen name and Sarah would be a kind of, say, pet name, secret code name, both for Janine Petersen." She looked down at the papers again.

"But who do you guys think is this Adam who is writing her? Do the men get Bible names in the temple too?"

Roger stared straight ahead.

"It's somebody who knows her, that's for sure. He calls her 'Sarah, my Sarah'—see, here?" Selonnah pointed.

Anne's baby began to whimper and she sat back in her chair, putting the baby to her breast as invisibly as she did the first time they met.

"He's calling her a wife's name. But I don't know why Helaman Petersen would take on the name Adam." Roger rubbed his eyes.

"Anybody know if Adam is Helaman's middle name?" murmured Anne.

"No, his middle initial is M, I remember," said Selonnah. "Helaman M. Petersen's middle name is Michael. It stuck in my mind when I heard it because of cousin Michael Bob, remember?" Selonnah and Roger exchanged familial smiles.

"That's LDS doctrine. The archangel Michael is Adam. Michael is Adam in old Mormon writings. And some new ones." Anne was murmuring again. "Same thing."

Roger nodded. A dark look came over his face. "Of course, Brigham Young said that God Himself was Adam. Talk about identity crises. So take your pick."

Selonnah struggled to understand. "So, a lot of other Mormon women have the secret name of 'Sarah,' but since the emails are on Janine's computer, we are assuming she is Sarah." She waited for the other two to nod, Roger more slowly than Anne. "And since Helaman Petersen's middle name is Michael, which equates to Adam, we can assume these are his emails to his wife, Janine." Again the nods. Selonnah stood the papers on end and tapped them on the table.

"I guess that's enough proof for me," she said. "I made a promise to keep some things to myself until I had proof."

Anne and Roger looked intently at her.

"Helaman Petersen's second-in-command, Lt. Luke Taylor, and I became friends as I covered the case of the prostitute. Not really close, but for reasons I guess I'll never know, he confided in me just hours before he died. He made me promise not to say anything until there was proof." She swallowed hard. "He believed Helaman Petersen was responsible for all the Deseret Alphabet crimes."

She heard the intake of two sets of lungs, even over the ambient airplane roar. Roger looked over his shoulder to the men who had returned to their seats, still out of earshot.

He sighed. "Well, I guess I can see that. One of these emails had an attached graphic that they didn't print out. It was written in the Deseret Alphabet. If Helaman Petersen wrote these emails to his wife, I guess that sews it all up in one neat, bloody package."

"Wow." Anne shook her head.

"I always suspected that those first crimes were committed by a superfaithful, even fanatic member of the Church," said Roger slowly. "It looked at first like someone wanted to reestablish blood atonement, and the old ways."

"Like they talk about in the fundamentalist LDS churches,"

said Anne. "Like polygamy and communal living . . ."

Roger looked across the seat at Selonnah, one finger in the air. "If you take what Joseph Smith and Brigham Young and all the early Mormon prophets taught and commanded," Roger stretched out one hand, "and how you would practice their Mormonism today, you get someone like Helaman Michael Petersen, enforcing blood atonement." He stretched out the other hand, then rose from his seat and slammed the table.

Inside the sling, the baby began to cry. It was eight o'clock, past anybody's breakfast time.

"I'll tell those guys about Petersen," he said, looking ahead at the sprawled, dozing men. "They have a network of influence you wouldn't believe." His voice sounded bitter. "They'll get the wheels turning before we even land. They aren't willing to evacuate Cumorah since the other bomb threats in the past never materialized. If they can find Helaman Petersen without involving the federal government at another Mormon site, it won't bring any more negative attention to the Church." He stood up, stretching in his rumpled clothing, and gave a low, sere laugh. "As if I cared anymore about its image."

Selonnah and Anne turned surprised eyes toward him.

"Look, Selonnah. Maybe Anne has some answers for us, I don't know. I'm at a loss. And you and I, Selonnah—don't we deserve a God who doesn't lead us on? You know what I mean? I want a God who doesn't give spiritual red herrings to those who are searching for Him."

I'd like that too, Selonnah thought. She nodded.

"I can't get in touch with Eliza right now," said Roger, not meeting their eyes. "She's turned off her phone. She has some of these same doubts. She's taking this time to think them over."

His disheveled shirt was unbuttoned and he nodded as he pulled at and stretched the neckline of his temple garment away from his skin as if it were made of horsehair.

"We'll deal with that later. A lot of mental bridges are on fire right under my feet. But my focus is on Eliza and Maria." His voice broke. "I may not know where they are right now but I'll find them."

Roger looked at his watch and calculated the thirty minutes left until they would land in Rochester. It would be nine o'clock.

His eyes were torches of grief and hope. "And if he is at Cumorah, we will find Helaman Petersen too."

CHAPTER 34

WHEN ELIZA awakened in the dream-disoriented state where frequent travelers spend their first moments of most days, her eyes could not focus at first. But then she saw Maria, fully dressed, coloring a picture at the hotel room's small French provincial desk, her legs crossed at the ankles and swinging rhythmically.

"What's up, sweetheart?" Eliza tried to make her voice work.

"Good morning merry sunshine, why did you wake so soon," sang Maria, *"you scared away the little stars and shined away the moon."* Roger taught Maria that song from his own Tennessee childhood. Roger—

"Mom, I've been awake *forever*. I have everything ready. Let's go."

Eliza craned her neck to where Maria pointed to four precisely spaced juice boxes, two apples, and some granola bars on the dresser. Her purple backpack leaned against the door.

"I would need to get dressed of course." Eliza stretched and yawned as she turned to see the clock. Seven thirty.

"Better take an umbrella. The sun is up but it's still kinda dark out there." Maria held the drapes open.

"What about the eggs Benedict? And chocolate milk?"

"I made a picnic breakfast, see? And we can fill our thermoses with ice from the machine."

Eliza stood for a moment and looked at her cell phone. For all her love for Roger, she had to face Cumorah without his input. She would call him tomorrow, after she had made the decision to either continue with the tour group, or come home. When Maria turned away, she put the phone into the dresser drawer.

She and Maria put on what they had dubbed their "touring outfits": hiking boots, khakis, lightweight jackets, and purple floppy-brimmed hats, the kind that could be rolled up and stashed. Eliza nimbly rebraided Maria's crimped hair and her own and pinned the braids in loops along the back of each of their necks. With sunglasses, backpacks, and the hats, the two giggling tourists were practically in disguise as they drove to their first stop, munching the granola bars.

"The Grove doesn't have guided tours," said Eliza, "so here are the books I promised I would bring."

"Sacred Grove, you mean," Maria said.

"Yes, Sacred Grove." Eliza looked up from her consultation of the walking map, squinting in the blurry, diffused light of the morning. Maria was several paces in front of her on the sidewalk, her stout arms and legs pumping like pistons. The visitors center loomed ghostlike through the fog.

A man and woman—husband and wife, Eliza supposed—sat on the benches outside the visitors center, watching a teenage girl walking her German shepherd. When the dog began to limp, the girl sat on the curb and examined his paw, then stroked his rough fur to comfort him. Eliza suppressed a laugh when she saw that the man on the bench had begun to idly scratch his wife's knee in perfect sync with the motions of the girl with the dog.

Within minutes, laughter seemed to Eliza like an incomprehensible foreign language, one to which she had no access, as she and Maria walked across the long field to the stand of trees. The sign read "The Sacred Grove."

Eliza drew a deep breath before entering, gathering herself together. Maria, too, was subdued, her hat drooping with the moisture, her face hidden.

The fog seemed deeper inside the grove, as if the leggy, dense trees and shrubs had snagged and captured the mist not only of that morning but of the two centuries since Joseph Smith walked through it. Through the wisps of vapor, she could see other people coming and going on the grove's twelve serpentine paths, but the trees seemed to inter their hushed voices as it had the fog.

Eliza shivered. Maria moved close to her.

"This doesn't look like the pictures, Mommy."

It was true, all the guidebook pictures showed dancing leaves and preternaturally bright light filtering down in swordlike, emphatic shafts.

"Show me where it happened, Mommy. Where he saw Heavenly Father and Jesus."

"I don't know. The books don't say," she answered, thumbing helplessly through a damp guidebook. She had spoken truly. The books also didn't say what she had learned, these past painful months: that Joseph Smith's story of what happened in that grove in 1820 had metastasized in the telling. Though he never wrote or spoke of anything happening in the grove until over a decade after the supposed event, the accounts morphed from meeting an angel named

Nephi in the grove, to meeting an angel named Moroni in the grove, to meeting two heavenly beings who hovered in the air and announced themselves to be God and Jesus.

Maria looked around the path. "Maybe it was here," she said. She sat on a bench and gazed upward to where the treetops disappeared into the haze. "Bet Joseph was surprised."

As was the rest of the Christian world, to hear that God the Father had been pulling their legs for all these thousands of years insisting He was spirit and not flesh and bones, Eliza wearily thought, and then showing up all tangible and everything. *Surprise.*

"So read me something out of the guidebook, Mom."

Eliza stumbled through dates and historical background while Maria listened respectfully.

"Do you want to hear more?"

Maria shook her head slowly.

"You're really not good at this either, are you?" She gently took the book from her mother's hands. Her slender wrists could barely sustain the weight of the open volume. She sat down and put it in her lap and found a color photo. Then she held it up at quivering arm's length to make her own comparisons as she pivoted in front of the bench. "Are you sure this is the Sacred Grove?"

"Saw the sign, sweetheart, back where the path began." Eliza felt the press of lost sleep, and lost marriage, and now lost god. She felt as if something were being extracted from dry sockets in her chest. She did not know if she could bear all these losses.

It was so organized, so precise, so comfortable and manageable for a Mormon to believe that God was one supreme being, and Jesus another, and the Holy Ghost yet another, though disembodied, god.

And Heavenly Father being a former man made praying

so simple. You could talk to someone else who had once slammed his finger in a door, and hurt somebody's feelings with juicy gossip, and overate at a buffet table, and felt envious and sarcastic and petty.

And yet such beings didn't exist. These two compartmentalized, skin-bound, divinity-awarded beings never were. Their holy spirit compatriot with his inexplicably unearned godhood, never was. Prayers to any and all went up into the mists of Mormonism's grove, she thought, and stayed there, trapped like the mists by the trees.

She poured water from the thermos into two cups for her and Maria.

The cool liquid, the ice, the fog. That was the way a book she read explained God—the God everybody else worshiped. Like water in its states of being, could a single God have states of being as well? All sharing the same substance and yet individual—personalized? For the first time in her life, the God of the Bible seemed perhaps knowable without being Mormon-packaged.

Eliza felt a great sigh escape her.

Then, to Maria's obvious amazement, Eliza tipped her head back and filled her mouth, letting the liquid pour down her jaws and onto her neck and into her ears. She gasped at its refreshing taste, the brittleness of the cold on her skin. She was more grateful for water than she had ever been in her life.

"Isn't water wonderful?" Eliza laughed, wiping her face with her sleeve. Maria giggled with delight. Eliza wondered if she could teach Maria about water, so she would someday no longer feel that sense of dearth, of doubt.

The two walked slowly back across the field, holding hands. Maria was uncharacteristically sober and wordless as Eliza began to rehearse in her mind the phone call she would make to her beloved Roger tonight after she'd assembled the right words.

We will work it out together, she thought. *I will show Roger what I've found—as friend, not adversary. I can explain to him about the wonder of water. Surely there is enough of an almighty God to be shared among the three of us, my Roger, my Maria, and I. Nothing will tear us apart. Roger will listen. And he will care. And it will be all right.*

The sun began to breach the fog and here and there, fingers of steam rose languidly from the concrete as if beckoning the sky.

A hot dog stand's sign summoned them, and the piquancy of the mustard and relish, the rubbing off the yellow drips from their forearms, the comfort of normal, familiar things made Eliza believe they could travel away from the grove and its tangled mists.

She could endure the rest of the day with the thought of sharing all this with Roger. Meanwhile, she was grateful she did not have to explain anything she and Maria saw at their next stop, the log cabin where Joseph Smith once lived. She tried to balance what the LDS Church had always told her about the sterling character of Joseph Smith and Brigham Young against their true histories: braggarts, bullies, blasphemers. If only all her LDS history books—what the Church called "faithful history"—had been more honest about the peculiarities of these men, thought Eliza, the truth would never have shocked her so much when she finally stumbled across it.

The tour guides, earnest-voiced missionaries with large Adam's apples who tag-teamed the growing groups of tourists, fielded questions that Maria, suddenly bashful, and Eliza, suddenly brash, dared not ask. By the time the two finished with the visitors center and collected brochures and bought a hand-carved wooden pen for Roger, the road in front of them was clogged with buses and cars. Some—actually many, she remarked to herself—uniformed men on motorcycles, bicycles, and horses wove in and out of the traffic.

"I want to walk up the Hill Cumorah, Mommy. Before the Pageant starts, please let me walk up the Hill."

They would walk up the Hill, Eliza promised. It might have to be the back side, but if they had to jump a fence, bribe a guard, create a diversion, they would walk up the Hill.

It was three o'clock. Roger's two girls pulled their purple hats down over their eyes to block the undecided sun's erratic glare off the cars all along the road, and made their way with hundreds of other pilgrims into the entrance of Cumorah.

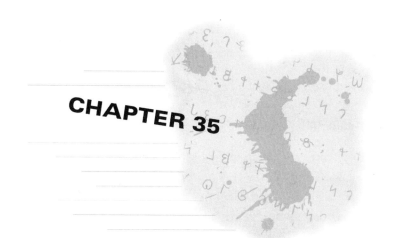

CHAPTER 35

THE MAN OF PURPOSE—the killer of Kirsten Young, her unborn child, Heber J. Bruce, and a nameless old man; mutilator of Bernadette Rodriguez; kidnapper and production designer of the fraught and pitiful tableaus of the Woodruffs and three old men and a homeless lady; now triumphantly surveys his territory, brings to perfected fruition his plan, his four o'clock plan.

He thinks, *This is how I would begin my final code note*

This is the way the world ends

He had been his clean-shaven, top-of-the-morning self before dawn when he greeted the caretaker MacPhersons, jolly, and jolly well should be, he thought, remembering the morning. They fed him those crusty yellow-edged biscuits with sorghum molasses that he stirred together with butter, and scrambled eggs and tough, salty bacon just on the blue edge of rancidity.

Now the man puts away lesser things and sees himself from a distance as he walks. He opens up the vast eternity inside himself to serve a greater purpose. He is T. S. Eliot's hollow man, and savors Eliot's words:

The eyes are not here

How wise-eyed, these long-departed planners of this ever-increasing Cumorah extravaganza, to create a site so thoroughly furnished for a bombing, he thinks. For days workers have been bringing out from winter storage and assembling the ten-tiered stage on which over six hundred actors will stand. A marvel of engineering, part of it is rigged as an ancient building that collapses nightly before the astonished eyes of eight thousand people. Ships burn, fountains erupt, even the jewelry in the women's ears resound with the vibrations of the music.

But his bomb will destroy the Hill first.

The workmen with sunburned necks and roughened knuckles arrive at seven thirty, their hammers swaying rhythmically from leather tool belts. But the man has already spent his workday in the hour since the thirsty breakfast. The man rubs his palms where blisters have erupted from the shovel's friction on his flesh when he interred the bomb in a slot-tomb in the wind-sighing, wooded side of the Hill.

He thinks of resurrections. He remembers that Joseph Smith said he would call priesthood holders, like himself, from the grave. But the man knows that this afternoon he will open the womb of the Hill. He will excise lies. He will instigate the resurrection of truth.

There are no eyes here

The workers grunt with the hefting and hoisting and pay no attention to the man who walks around the stage until he gets in their way with his annoying questions about the pyrotechnics of the ship facade that will seem to burst into flames during the performance. They will remember that, he notes with a sated heart.

Behind a splinter-covered timber, he unpacks more of his bag: the grey wig of a Nephite man, his head-covering cloth and his flowing robe of silk; sandals with toes pointing together in awkward shame. He turns the nearly empty bag inside out to black anonymity. How clever of it. It snaps itself together to a politely smaller day pack that just holds the Nephite costume. He puts the sandals on and drops his shoes into a construction trash can.

The fog is almost all burnt off now. The man stands on one of the tiers to view what will not exist tomorrow.

In this valley of dying stars

Before the massive stage, thousands upon thousands of folding chairs pierce the grassy earth with their metal legs. Hundreds upon hundreds of people carry more of them to the chalk lines that sift through the blades of grass.

He sees the police cars, clustered like grapes. Could they know . . . ?

In this hollow valley

In a restroom he punks his hair up in uneven clumps with wax and puts on a fry cook's paper hat. The little moustache that he glues on matches because it is his own hoarded hair. In the mirror, he hardly knows himself, a stranger with the aviator's eyeglasses that darken in the sun and the gold earring. He thinks of lounge lizards with French fries, and as he walks out, his gait changes to that of the loser-man.

This broken jaw of our lost kingdoms

Adrift in a swirling lake of people, the concession stands seem mired in undercurrents no one knows what to do about. On this first day of Pageant, they are still working out the logistical kinks inside this cooking structure. Outside, children jerk on the arms of their mothers, who bite their lips and peer at the menu on the wall and calculate hours against dollars against endurance.

The man lifts an already-brimming garbage bag from a can and ties it up neatly and takes it over his shoulder. Someone points to the Dumpster and yells at him to clean a table.

In this last of meeting places

No one looks in his eyes because they have not come to Cumorah to talk to the hourly-wage man past his prime, not even the manager of the concession stand who tries to wipe his forehead with his wrist before the drops fall into a plate. He tells the man to wash his hands, over here, quick, use soap, and lay out hamburger buns. The manager doesn't even notice the sandals.

We grope together

He takes no breaks. He keeps his head down. It is two thirty.

And avoid speech

The chairs nearest the stage are filling with women who sit sprawl-legged and fiddle with their umbrellas, their purses, the brochures, their drooping hair. The men stand with arms folded like Arnold Friberg sentinels and kick at the grass and get cold drinks for the women and children who have spread their rain ponchos across rows and rows of the thousands of chairs.

Gathered on this beach of the tumid river

On a large crazy-quilt knoll, people are spreading out blankets, weighing down the corners with the binoculars and the cameras and the picnic baskets and the coolers. The chil-

362

dren run and howl and roll down the hill, again and again and again.

Sightless, unless
The eyes reappear

The man knows, now. He can see men in uniforms, their sight arcing and sweeping from side to side as they walk. They have come for Helaman M. Petersen. They linger at the groups of workmen. They talk into their own shoulders like preening birds and soon all of them are looking up at the mountainous stage.

The voice in their ears tells them, like the seagulls of Mormon lore, to gather from the perimeters of the sea of grass in search of the single locust that can undo them all.

The man stretches his neck to see, but a waddling woman with her arms full of greasy sacks is angry because the tables are all dirty.

And it is only three o'clock.

He hears the babel of other languages and smiles at what the Latinos say about him. They are pitying him because such a faceless man of his age ought to be in the chairs, fanning himself and wondering about why the children's voices are so loud. He should not have a cleaning rag hanging from his pocket.

A man speaks French to his child. The man with the cleaning rag remembers that his mother studied French for years, and yet could only recite a single phrase: *Je suis fatigué.* I am tired.

He would teach the world in every language: I mourn.

As the perpetual star
Multifoliate rose
Of death's twilight kingdom

Then he sees Selonnah Zee in the distance.

She seems to be walking in entourage, in a clutch of others who have no brochures, no guidebooks, no umbrellas. There is a man beside Selonnah—the man of the press conferences. It is bright-toothed Roger Zee. And a woman who carries a baby in a sling. They all look at the stage with desperate, panning eyes.

Aha, aha. One of the construction workers must have reported that a man, yes clean-cut, could have been Petersen, was very interested in the pyrotechnics part of the show. They have been searching it for hours, dismantling and reassembling. But they are far away from the back of the Hill, where the bomb is buried.

The three heavies who walk in front of Roger and the women peel off like formation jets on dark, secret missions.

The man turns as if summoned. He sees that something living is on the Hill of dead hopes. He sees purple hats, near the clump of trees where he buried the bomb.

Then, snarled in a catastrophic rush of insight, the man finds he cannot walk, freezes in midstep, feels one foot poised an inch above the earth as he considers the incongruity of these people, here, now, in his place. The mists are gone now, and the sun dazzles the moisture that drops from leaves and the underside of sodden branches. High on the wooded hillside of Cumorah, two figures move among the trees.

He cannot stop looking at his watch.

The timer. The toggle. The timer. The toggle.

The hope only

It is eight minutes to four.

Of empty men

High up on the wooded back side of Cumorah, the bomb aches for consummation of its parts, the electronic fulfillment of its purpose, like a bride behind the doors, counting the minutes.

This is the way the world ends

Someone pulls at his arm. Is he all right? Are you all right, mister?

The two purple hats are in a little clearing now. It is a woman with a little girl. They have stopped to talk about something. They drink long, slow draughts from their thermoses. Then they take off their matching jackets and tie them around their waists. They hold oblivious hands as they continue up the Hill.

He groans from deep beneath his gut. The people sitting at a table catch his elbow as his knees start to buckle. But he is able to stand, able to walk, just fine, just fine, need some air, must walk.

Must get his bag in the back room of the concession stand, get the bag, get the bag, find the cell phone transmitter.

He thinks of the shedding of innocent blood. He thinks of collateral damage become personal, of Luke, faithful friend Luke.

The man walks quickstep into the concession building. Someone hands him a box of drinking straws to take outside, and they slide out of his hands onto the floor because he cannot get his hands to grip and does not recognize the function of the objects now on the floor. He steps aside, hands in the air.

One minute until four.

His hands are slippery with sweat. They slide, glide, lose their purchase, find it again on the door handle to the storage room where his pack sits on a shelf among the worker women's purses and the men's keys and water bottles.

This is the way the world ends

He walks outside trembling.

He did not want the taste of blood in his mouth, but has gnawed the insides of his cheeks. He holds the cell phone in trembling hands trying to disable the bomb.

Fifteen seconds.

He fumbles with the code to unlock it, to activate the toggle. His fingers have never seemed so thick, so clumsy.

Four seconds. Still fumbling.

Three.

Two.

One.

Silence.

Perhaps nothing, he thinks, is past all redemption, even him.

No one notices him because they are buying cotton candy or kicking grass or rolling down hills or telling missionary stories or picking up straws from the floor.

And lo! the costumed actors who will take part in the evening's performance have begun to arrive. They walk, resplendent in their robes and plumage, among the chairs and mingle with the crowd, pretentious and pleased with themselves.

This is the way the world ends

Dry heaves. The man sags in elastic-kneed anguish against the back of the concession stand Dumpster.

From the corner of his eye, he sees motion, not of a running child but a man. It is Roger Zee. Roger breaks away from Selonnah and the other woman. He begins to run, one leg stiff-hip halting, toward the two purple hats, far away there up on the Hill.

The man collects himself, wipes his mouth with the rag from his pocket, and looks at Selonnah. She is jumping and writhing like an adolescent at a revival meeting, her entire being a hallelujah of relief.

The man throws the rag and the paper concession stand hat and apron away. He smoothes his hair down as he walks into the restroom with his bag.

When he emerges, he is an old, wise, bearded Nephite with his trousers rolled up out of sight under the robe. He moves majestically through the adoring people. They cannot know he has spared them all, that it is not yet the fullness of times. There will be a second coming. There will be more signs to this unbelieving generation. There are many more lies to be exposed, of old scrolls and other codes.

Perhaps more will have to die, but not today.

He does not see the uniformed men behind him, but they see him.

This is the way the world ends

A little girl tugs on his robe. It is a Gracie-like child and he wants to weep because he loves her, he has saved her.

She asks him about the Gadianton robbers.

He points off in the distance to them, the costumed brigands of Book of Mormon stories, as they swagger menacingly through the crowds. The little girl's eyes are frightened.

"Don't worry. They're just pretend." She looks away and he slips into the moving stream of people who part like the Red Sea for him, then out on the other side. The men have not caught up with him, but the little girl has. She holds his hand.

Not with a bang

"I can bear my testimony," she says, searching his eyes. "Do you bear yours?"
He feels the limitless void of annulled faith.
Yes, my child, yes, he says.
I bear
I bear
I bear my testimony

This is the way the world ends
This is the way the world ends
This is the way the world ends

Not with a bang

but

a whimper

AUTHOR'S NOTE

MORMONISM IS ALWAYS in the news, it seems. But the mainstream Mormonism of today barely resembles the "eternal gospel" that Joseph Smith said he restored in the 1800s.

I wondered what would happen if the Mormon doctrines of that time were lived out today—blood atonement, polygamy, and communal living. What if someone decided to be a "pure" Mormon today?

The answer is that you would probably have a fundamentalist Mormon, like the ones who are most often in the news and depicted in movies and popular television shows. What many people don't realize is that these groups aren't evangelistic. But they are growing—because of accelerated birth rates, that is true—but also because converts to the Mormon fundamentalist movement come from the mainstream Mormon Church. They are people who believe that the present leadership of the thirteen million–member Salt Lake

City Church of Jesus Christ of Latter-day Saints is apostate. Fundamentalist Mormons believe in living "the principle"— polygamy and communal living, absolute patriarchal authority, and the presence of living prophets who can dictate even the most minute details of an individual's daily life.

At its core, this book is about representations and facts— the way that both mainstream Mormonism and its offshoots convey information and portray reality. It is significant, I think, that Brigham Young attempted to formulate and popularize an alphabet just for Mormons. That peculiar use of language is the "cipher" of this book.

I also wanted to depict a character who mirrors the apparent effect that Joseph Smith, founder of all groups that go by the name Mormon or Latter-day Saint, had upon women. If any descriptions of this attraction seem over the top, I urge the reader to research the life of Joseph Smith, who charmed parents and even husbands out of any woman he wanted.

My years as a faithful Mormon who deeply loved that church, and my subsequent studies of what is called representational research, formed the foundation of this book. Millions of people who were baptized Mormons no longer consider themselves part of that church. Though myriads of Web sites and books deal with their reasonings, I am not aware of a work of fiction that attempts, as I have done, to look compassionately at the process of making such a decision.

ACKNOWLEDGMENTS

TO DAN, who first suggested this book; to Upton Sinclair, whose example *The Jungle* inspired me in high school; to my four children who encouraged me; to Paula Paul who taught me in my first novel class; to Janet Grant, my agent who took me on; and to Andy McGuire and Diane Eble, my editors, I give most profound thanks for inspiring and believing in me.

I also begged many friends to read this and comment on it as it was being written. They include: my enthusiastic family; J. Michael, Susan Scott, Sharon Sofia, Paula Paul, Larry Fiese, May Marchese, Judith Couchman, Beth Robinson, John Blackwelder, Susan Blassingame, Kathy Jo Hargrove, Joyce Frashier, Amber and Taylor Weems, Brandt Butler, Ryan and Collen Sundlie, Stephen Parks; and undoubtedly others whose names I have neglected to list because of numerous email crashes during the process. Find forgiveness in your heart if I did not list your name.

FURTHER INFORMATION ON THE DOCTRINE OF BLOOD ATONEMENT

UNDER OLD TESTAMENT law, a person's life was often required as punishment for grievous sins. But that was the Old Covenant approach to sin, before the blood of Jesus paid all prices. For instance, the Old Testament prophet Elijah ordered the execution of all the priests of the false god Baal (1 Kings 18:40). But when Jesus' disciples came to him with Elijah's example as justification for their own planned violence, Jesus "turned, and rebuked them, and said, 'Ye know not what manner of spirit ye are of. For the Son of Man is not come to destroy men's lives, but to save them'" (Luke 10:55–56).

LDS doctrine *and practice* in the Mormon Church's early days reinstituted what Jesus terminated: the concept that one's own death can atone for sin. Brigham Young and many other LDS leaders incited this doctrine and behavior repeatedly in official declarations. Here are some citations that can be accessed online at http://journalofdiscourses.org—vol. 3, 243–49 and vol. 4, 51–57, 215–221.

Such sermons were also published in the Church-run *Deseret News.* Mormons say these sermons were just "theoretical" and an example of "revival rhetoric." These "theories" became reality. *That murder and blood atonement were openly practiced at the behest of early LDS Church leaders is beyond any doubt.* An unbiased source of information, links, books and videos about this is The Mountain Meadows Association, online at http://www.mtn-meadows-assoc.com. Many quotes are also available by searching for "blood atonement" at UTLM, www.utlm.org. Furthermore, some Latter-day Saint fundamentalist groups of today who trace their heritage to Joseph Smith and Brigham Young also teach and have practiced murder and blood atonement. A good example documenting this is the secular bestselling book *Under the Banner of Heaven* (Jon Krakauer, Doubleday, 2003).

GROUP READING GUIDE
QUESTIONS *for* DISCUSSION

Latter-Day Cipher
by Latayne C. Scott

1. What was your response to the novel's title? Did you understand it? Did it compel you to want to know more?

2. When Terrence Jensen decides to keep the murderer's note to himself, what does he try to hide? What does this act reveal about Jensen and his community? (chapter 2)

3. When you first meet Selonnah and her mother, what does the interaction reveal about their relationship? About each of their personal pains and issues? (chapter 3)

4. How do Roger Zee's personality and actions reflect the attitudes and problems in the Mormon Church? (chapters 4, 9)

5. At the crime scenes, what do the symbols represent and mean? Think about the symbols on the victim's bodies and in their surroundings. (chapters 1, 6, 10, 13, 14, 30)

6. What are Roger and Eliza Zee's misgivings about the Mormon Church? How do their questions contribute to the novel's action and message? (chapter 17)

7. How might the murders relate to the Mormon belief in atonement? How does this concept of atonement differ from the Christian belief in forgiveness? (chapter 24)

8. Any good mystery has clues that the detective follows but also that the readers must follow. Discuss some of these clues. Which of them became essential in finding the murderer?

9. What are some elements of the Mormon Church that you didn't know or didn't understand? Do readers have to understand Mormonism to fully appreciate the story?

10. Do we fully understand the villain's motivation? What about the motivation of the reporter and her cousin? What about the motivation of the Mormon Church in disseminating information and/or disinformation? How do these motivations play in the story?

11. Selonnah is an excellent reporter/researcher, able to intuitively piece together the facts. At the same time, she seems uneasy in her personal life, especially about being single. Do you feel confident in some areas of life and insecure in others? Do you think most people feel this way? Why, or why not?

12. The murderer used complex symbolism to communicate his message at the crime scenes. Why would he use this symbolism? What does it reveal about him? How did you respond to the symbolism? Why?

13. A few people in this novel felt desperate about their circumstances and took action to changes their lives. Who were they? Some say, "Desperate times call for desperate measures." Do you think this is true? Explain.

14. Do you think this novel's purpose was entertainment or communicating a message? Or both? Explain.

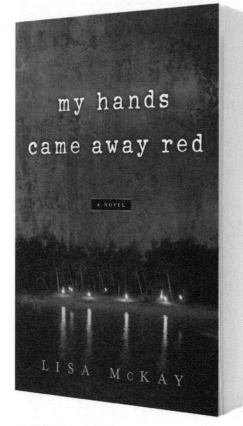

ISBN: 978-0-8024-8982-1

Cori signs up to take a mission trip to Indonesia during the summer after her senior year of high school. Inspired by happy visions of building churches and seeing beautiful beaches, she gladly escapes her complicated love life back home. Five weeks after their arrival, a sectarian and religious conflict that has been simmering for years flames to life with deadly results on the nearby island of Ambon. Within days, six terrified teenagers are stranded in the mountainous jungle with only the pastor's teenage son to guide them to safety. Ultimately, Cori's emotional quest to rediscover hope proves just as arduous as the physical journey home.

by Lisa McKay
Find it now at your favorite local or online bookstore.